THE N
SHOP

BY
CHRISTINE MELVILLE
KENWORTHY

To Helen

Christine Kenworthy

Dedicated to the two men in my life:
my Dad
James Anderson Melville
and
my husband
Peter Kenworthy.

Thanks to friends and family who read the first draft of The Nut Shop and were so supportive and encouraging: Heather Burton (thanks for the loan of your famous mushroom jokes), Janet Douglass, Sally Jackson, Irene Kenworthy, Joan Kenworthy, Peter Kenworthy, Susan Kenworthy, Tricia McDougal, Ian Melville, Joe Melville, Lorraine Melville, Rachel Melville, Emma Miller, Emma Reed, Vanessa Ryland, Margaret Valentine.
Cover design by Marie Walker, many thanks Marie.
An extra big thank you to Lorraine, Peter, Janine and Joan for living the Nut Shop story with me.
And thank you to Rose, Anna and Joe for bringing so much joy into my life.

CHAPTER ONE

I had always dreamed of owning a little antique shop but was just beginning to realise that the reality was not living up to the dream.

For six years I had been selling old furniture and bric-a-brac that I hunted down, cleaned up and displayed in my overflowing shop on a side street near the beach. Each Sunday my partner Peter and I packed the car with baskets of china, books, pictures and small pieces of furniture and set off to our local antiques market for a day of buying and selling.

Initially I loved the challenge of hunting for a constant supply of stock to fill the shop and spent many contented hours rummaging through boxes of junk at sales and standing in dusty auction houses waiting with anticipation and excitement as I bid for lots. I also loved the days spent in the shop, happily sorting through the pickings as I chatted to customers while they browsed. Some were collectors who came looking for pieces for a prized collection, some were dealers, others holiday makers stopping to browse on their way from the beach.

After a while, however, the constant hunt for stock became a bit of a strain and I found myself envying those types of shops where stock could easily be ordered from a wholesaler's brochure to be delivered at a convenient time to the door. The novelty of rising at four on Sunday mornings was also wearing thin. At antique markets the main business of the day, that is the buying and selling amongst dealers, is over before six o'clock in the morning. Rising before dawn was necessary to enable us to drive to the shop, pack the car, drive to the market and unload and set up the stall by at least five o'clock. On dark winter mornings this was not much fun, especially if we had been out on the town on Saturday night.

Also, the fashion for antiques was changing. During the eighties, antique collecting had enjoyed something of a revival. DIY magazines and television programmes were full of advice on how to achieve Victorian and Edwardian style schemes and we were all encouraged to go out and scour our local antique shops in search of authentic accessories.

However, this was 1991 and trends were beginning to change. Britain had just been hit by a large Swedish chain store specialising in inexpensive modernistic furnishings. Other retailers quickly took up the trend and fashion followers were moving away from the cluttered retro look towards much more contemporary ideas. Although business was still brisk it was not as frantic as it had been and it was obvious that the boom was over.

I was beginning to feel increasingly bored with the business and began to neglect it.

Our wedding day was planned for September and I found that I preferred to spend my weekends searching for shoes and underwear rather than stock.

'How's business?' my sister Lorraine asked during one of our wedding shopping trips. We'd stopped for coffee after spending the morning tracking down sugared almonds in the right shade of lilac. 'You haven't mentioned the shop today, it used to be your favourite topic of conversation.'

'I'm getting a bit bored with it, to tell the truth,' I told her. 'My heart doesn't seem to be in it any more.'

'Perhaps it's just with the wedding coming up,' she said. 'It's a busy time. Once you're married and life settles down you'll probably be raring to go again.'

'Possibly,' I said. Although I doubted it. Once I lose interest in something there tends to be no going back. 'How about you?' I asked. 'How's work?'

'Same as ever,' she said. 'Late nights, drunken customers, the Ferret on my back all the time. At least you're your own boss. You're not at someone's beck and call like I am.'

Lorraine worked for a wine-store chain and managed one of their busiest branches situated in town, where she rented the flat above the shop. The Ferret was Ryan Ferris, an arrogant power-crazed little man whose constant nit picking and pettiness in his capacity as area-manager made Lorraine's life at work a misery.

'Do you know,' she said, 'I've told him loads of times that the lock on the metal shutter is broken leaving the shop an easy target for thieves and he's done nothing about it. Yet if he finds a speck of dust on one of the shelves he threatens me with a written warning.'

'Silly little man,' I said. We took a few minutes to totally assassinate his character then when we were done Lorraine tidied our cups and said, 'Right what's next?' I consulted my collection of lists.

'Stockings, white,' I said. 'Napkins - lilac, calligraphy pen and gold ink, Boots 17 eye shadow shade - champagne…'
'Ok, ok, that'll do for now. Back to the battle,' Lorraine said and we picked up our bags of shopping and headed back into the throng of shoppers.

The summer passed by in a haze of preparations. Slowly but surely I ticked the boxes on my lists as the weeks passed. I attended dress fittings and Peter worked on his speech. We chose rings and wedding stationery, ordered flowers and booked a honeymoon. The cake was made, cars hired, and our cases lay ready and waiting, packed with swimwear and suntan lotion.

At last our wedding day dawned and I was woken by rays of sunlight pushing through the blinds and promising a beautiful day.

The promise was upheld. The sun gave a kiss of golden light to a day that could have easily belonged to early summer except for the presence of a slightly sharp breeze; a gentle reminder that autumn was waiting nearby.

We married in our local church and I emerged, holding Peter's arm, to the sound of pealing bells, greeted by a fragrant breeze as the last flowers of summer released their scent into the air. We walked beneath showers of snowy confetti to our waiting car, the sun glittering through red and yellow leaves as they swayed gently above us.

The day presented everything I hoped it would; happiness, romance, fun and the joy of sharing it with the people we loved. As it drew to a close, family and friends waved us off with much hugging and joking, and a few tears, and we flew off to the sun.

After three carefree, sun-drenched weeks honeymooning in Florida we came home to resume normal life.

Peter went back to work and I returned to the shop with a distinct lack of enthusiasm.

'It's just post-holiday blues,' I told myself as I approached the shop. 'I can't be on honeymoon forever. Once I get into the swing again, everything will be fine.'

I unlocked the door and glancing in the window, saw the old familiar things. A floral tea set, a Victorian jug and bowl, a set of carved ebony bookends and a hand stitched quilt, all dust covered and sprinkled with dead flies. My heart sank as I stepped inside. The air held a damp mustiness and I shivered. Dropping my bag onto the desk I pulled my coat about me and looked around. The window plinths that had once displayed carefully arranged pieces now exhibited a haphazard hotchpotch of clutter. China and glassware no longer sparkled, a tarnished bloom had crept over the silverware and the beeswax-and-lavender furniture polish lay forgotten beneath the desk.

For the next few months I kept the shop running and it continued to pay me a living, but my heart was no longer in it.

Christmas came and went, and at New Year I resolved to find a new challenge. Something new to get my teeth into. Something that would light my fire. I toyed with a few ideas but it wasn't until a freezing February night that the spark was finally lit.

I had arranged to meet Lorraine for a glass of wine in the pub near her flat. Glad to get out of the biting wind, we made our way to the bar to order drinks. The pub was unusually empty. On such a dark wintry night as this most people would have been glad to hurry home through the icy wind and sleet to the warmth and comfort of their own homes. It was too early in the evening for those who came to have a few drinks with friends and try their luck at the weekly pub quiz. A couple were seated next to the fire, still huddled in thick coats and a group of workmen sat at the bar, complaining about the weather.

We carried our drinks to a table in a cosy nook near the fire. Settling ourselves at the table we set about our usual topic of conversation, work. Or more precisely, complaining about work.

'I've had a right pig of a day,' Lorraine said. 'You wouldn't believe the number of complaints I've had today. I think it must have been National Awkward Customer Day and nobody bothered to tell me that my shop had been designated as headquarters.' She took a drink from her glass and sighed. 'I've had complaints about prices being too high and people getting annoyed because we don't stock what they're looking for. Then I had a religious nutcase quoting the bible at me. She told me I needed to repent and then she lodged herself in the doorway spouting off about the evils of drink and stopping people from coming in. I thought at one point I was going to have to call the police to have her forcibly removed.' I couldn't help laughing as she related her day. Talking to Lorraine always cheered me up. She could always make me laugh with tales of her misadventures.

'Then later on I did have to call the police because I caught a shoplifter with three bottles of cider down his trousers. I grabbed hold of him but he wriggled free and legged it up the bank with the bottles clanking down his pants.' I laughed at the mental picture that this scenario presented.

'I've had kids in and out all afternoon trying to buy cigarettes and getting abusive when I refused them and to top it all I had an unexpected branch visit from The Ferret.'

'Did he come in to see about having the shutter lock mended?' I asked.

'No,' she answered. 'I did remind him about it again but he was more concerned about the shoplifter getting away with three bottles of cider. He went off it. Told me I have to pay for them out of my wages. Apparently it was my responsibility to retrieve them. I told him I'd already put myself at risk by grabbing the bloke without fishing down his trousers. Then he reprimanded me for giving away too many free carrier bags, oh and apparently I don't write heavily enough on the carbon paper in the stock book so he can't read my figures on the copies.'

'Sounds like a pretty crap day,' I admitted. 'But at least it's been eventful. All I do at the moment is to sit amongst a load of old tat, dusting it and trying to sell it.'

'Had any more thoughts about what you'd like to do?' Lorraine asked.

'No not really. I need a change but I don't know what to do. I thought perhaps of opening a little tearoom near the beach, or maybe a gift shop, but nothing really grabs me.' I took a sip of my wine.

'What about the health food shop across the road from my shop?' Lorraine laughed.

'What about it?'

'Well the guy who owns it is selling up. You could buy it,' she said.

'Is he really selling?' I choked on a mouthful of wine 'When? Why? How much does he want? A health food shop! I could do that, we could do it together, you and me, run it as partners...'

'Whoa, slow down,' said Lorraine, recognising the danger signs. Once I have an idea in my head I plunge headfirst into it, rational thinking goes straight out of the window. I was off in one of my fantasies, lost in a vision of myself surrounded by pots of fresh herbs and loaves of brown bread as I ladled lentils into recycled paper bags.

'I wasn't serious,' she said, interrupting the picture. 'I said it as a joke.'

'But why not?' I said. 'We could do organic vegetables, and home-made stuff. We both love cooking. We could sell goat's milk...cheeses... Just

8

think of the lovely window displays; baskets of free-range eggs, jars of herbs and spices…' I could see it all so clearly.

'Chris, listen to me,' Lorraine said, leaning over the table toward me. 'The guy who owns it has practically run it into the ground. When it first opened it was a brilliant little shop but over the months it's deteriorated.'

'A health food shop, you know, I never once thought of that!' I said ignoring her.

'It was well stocked and beautifully set out originally,' Lorraine said. 'But now there's hardly anything on the shelves and when you ask for something it's always supposedly on order and he's waiting for a delivery.' She took a drink then continued. 'I think he's in financial trouble and can't afford to buy new stock and pay the bills and things. He knows it's going down and he wants to get out before it goes down any further.'

'We'd be a great team,' I said enthusiastically. 'You're good at organisation and dealing with staff, and I'm the creative one, thinking up new ideas, doing all the arty-farty stuff.'

'Chris, there's not much of a business left to take over. He's lost interest in it. He often closes early and disappears for the afternoon, especially if it's a sunny day and you know as well as I do that you just can't do that when you run a shop, you have to be consistent and reliable. There's too much competition around. If you don't provide a good service there's always another business that will. I reckon he's already lost loads of custom judging by the amount of people I used to see going in and out of the place compared with lately. There used to be a constant stream of customers and at lunch times the queue of people waiting to order sandwiches extended from the shop into the street.' She paused for breath and took a sip from her glass. 'Did you hear what I said?'

'Yes,' I said dreamily. 'A constant stream of customers and queues extending into the street.' Lorraine looked exasperated.

'He's run it down; it's on its last legs. It would be madness to take it on.'

'We could bring it back. Build it up again.'

'You're not listening,' said Lorraine. 'I said it would be madness to take it on.'

'It would be madness not to.' Lorraine looked at me then closed her eyes in frustration.

'Let's at least just find out about it,' I said. 'Ask him for details. How much he wants and stuff.'

'Ok, ok,' said Lorraine. 'But, I'm sure you'll change your mind when you speak to him and have a good look at the premises.'

I was sure I wouldn't. I had found my next challenge.

CHAPTER TWO

I could hardly contain my excitement as we left Lorraine's flat. She pulled the door shut behind us and we crossed the road to the health food shop.

'I didn't sleep last night,' I told her. 'My head was buzzing with all the ideas and plans I have for our new venture.' She gave me one of her looks usually reserved for those she considers to be beyond help.

'We're just having a look, remember,' she said in the kind of voice people use to explain something simple to a very small child. 'We're not actually buying it. We're just curious, being nosy. We're going to have a look around then leave, so don't go committing us to anything.

The shop was on a corner site and had two huge glass windows, one facing the main road and one on the side street. The floor above the shop was being used as a gym, and at the back of the property was a shoe repair and key cutting business.

I noticed a 'closed' sign hanging in the window. As I pushed the door open an aromatic fragrance drifted out, a smell that was to become very familiar. A delicious mixture of fresh herbs and piquant spices, newly baked bread and heady essential oils all mixed up together. It is a smell that to this day, the slightest whiff caught passing a health shop transports my mind straight back to our days in the health food trade.

I stepped inside and had my first look at the interior. Dappled sunlight filtered through the blinds, filling the shop with the pale sunlight of a winter's day. A pinewood counter stretched across the rear, dividing the shop front from the kitchen area. Two long pinewood-shelving units stood in the centre of the floor, and matching shelving lined the walls.

The shop had obviously been closed for business for at least a couple of weeks. The shelves were very sparsely stocked; a few packages and bottles lay here and there, and a forgotten loaf of bread stood on a shelf behind the counter.

A tall, dishevelled man came from the back of the shop and made his way around the counter to greet us. Dressed in old jeans and a crumpled tee shirt, his dark hair was tousled and he was unshaven. He looked as though he had at one time been quite attractive but tiredness and neglect had taken over leaving him with a sallow, careworn look.

'Hi there!' he said. 'John Kirk. Pleased to meet you.' He leaned forward and shook my hand. 'So you're going to buy the business?' I opened my mouth to introduce myself but was nudged aside by Lorraine.

'Hello John,' she said 'This is my sister Christine and as I explained to you on the phone she would like to have a look around and maybe ask your advice about a business she's thinking of starting. It's very kind of you to…'

'Yes, yes,' I butted in, pushing her gently but firmly out of the way. 'So, the shop John. Tell us about it.'

John led the way around the building talking as he went. He explained that he was heartbroken to have to leave the place but it was the only option open to him due to family events that were out of his control.

'More like finances out of his control,' muttered Lorraine and I nudged her to silence her, afraid that he would hear.

I soon realised that the sales figures he was reeling off were obviously highly exaggerated and strangely enough he had always been 'too busy with customers to bother keeping proper accounts.' However, for all his unkempt appearance, with his roguish smile and charming manner it was difficult not to like him, even though I knew that he was inventing facts and figures as he went.

My heart sank as we were shown around the kitchen and I noticed the grimy shelves and cluttered work area. A box on the floor contained cooking utensils where someone had started dismantling the kitchen. My eyes scanned the cooking area taking in a pile of old cutlery, a broken tin opener, an unwashed chopping board and – horrors - near the hob, a saucer holding a mound of cigarette butts. Lorraine gave me a sideways glance and grimaced exaggeratedly and I stifled an urge to giggle.

John gave us a ridiculously magnified figure of how many sandwiches were supposedly prepared and sold daily. I was quite fascinated at the way he could make these embellished statements so sincerely without the least sign of embarrassment. He had such an appealing way that it was impossible to be offended, in fact it just seemed funny, and I deliberately avoided looking at Lorraine as I knew we would be unable not to laugh if we made eye contact. We managed to utter 'Really?' or murmur 'Mmm' in false agreement to his statements even though we were all aware that he was talking rubbish.

John led us through a door at the side of the kitchen that led into the office-cum-storeroom. This was almost worse than the kitchen. Piles of paperwork covered a makeshift desk that had been assembled from an old piece of wood with cardboard boxes for support. The weight of the mound on the surface had caused the boxes to collapse at one side and consequently the floor had been flooded in a torrent of paperwork. Stacks of crates and boxes filled every corner, along with discarded lengths of wood, a broken vacuum cleaner and a dismantled cot. We stood in an uncomfortably small space amongst the chaos and I could sense Lorraine's silent mirth as John said, 'Actually, this office is deceptively spacious.'

The three of us carefully squeezed out of the office and made our way around the wooden counter. The afternoon light was beginning to fade and an ambience of gloom now filled the shop. I realised that the lights were not switched on. As we passed the large freezer and fridge I ran my hand along the glass-fronted doors. They too were switched off and I guessed, correctly, that the electricity supply had been disconnected.

As John waffled on to Lorraine, I looked around, deep in thought. This place would take weeks of work to get it up and running again. Apart from the mammoth task of clearing out the junk and giving everything a good scrub, I noted that the kitchen needed to be refurbished and equipped, the building needed repainting inside and out and the shelving needed to be replaced or at least repaired. I started making mental lists. Advertising to organise, staffing to arrange, product knowledge to swot up on, suppliers to source... a thrill of excitement and enthusiasm rippled through me and I knew that I wanted to do it.

'...so in view of everything included, that is stock, equipment, fixtures and fittings, I think a figure of around fifteen thousand would be fair.' John's voice brought me back to earth with a bump.

'Fifteen thou...sorry, how much did you say?' I stammered.

'He said fifteen thousand' said Lorraine giving me a Let's Get The Hell Out Of Here look.

'Fifteen thousand,' repeated John confidently. 'I know it doesn't sound much for all this but there's no catch, honestly. I'll be happy with a fair price. I'm a fair man.' More like a mad man, I thought.

'I'm after a quick sale. This shop is a little goldmine. I don't want to leave it, but as I've explained I have no choice. I don't want to get tied up in red tape, just a quick deal and move on. I'm a free spirit you see, money means little to me.'

'Right,' said Lorraine, a bit rudely I thought. 'Well we must be off. Thanks for your time; we'll let you know. Come on Chris we'll go and er ...have a think about it?' She picked up her bag and walked towards the door.

'Just a minute,' I said. 'Fifteen thousand you say?' I turned my head as I slowly scanned the interior of the shop. 'Could you break that down for us?'

'Sorry?' John said. 'Not sure what you mean...' For the first time he seemed lost for words.

'You know, just run through how you calculated a figure of fifteen thousand. For example, what sum did you include for stock?'

'Oh right,' he said. 'Now then.' He ran a hand through his dirty hair. 'Let me see.' He regained his composure and said boldly, 'Three thousand pounds.'

'Three thousand,' I repeated. 'And for the fixtures and fittings?'

'Well, ahem, I don't know, let's say about four thousand.' I looked at Lorraine.

'And the lease?' she asked joining in. 'You haven't mentioned how long there is to run on it.'

'Don't have a lease,' said John. The confidence he had shown so blatantly earlier now seemed to be draining away from him. 'I've always had a verbal agreement with the landlord to pay month by month, much easier not to be tied to a contract. No hassle with solicitors fees and of course if you want to move on you can do without any fuss. Makes life much more simple.' He shrugged his shoulders and laughed.

'Oh I'm sure it does,' said Lorraine. 'Except of course that if the landlord decides to throw you out you haven't got a leg to stand on.' John stopped laughing.

'How is your relationship with the landlord?' I asked. 'I take it you're up to date with your rent payments?'

'Oh yes, yes,' said John, resuming the nervous laugh. 'Well almost up to date. I always pay a little in arrears anyway, so it's really not a problem.' Lorraine looked at me and raised her eyebrows.

'So,' I said. 'Three thousand for stock and four for fixtures and fittings, that's seven thousand. What would the other eight thousand be buying?'

'Well. You know. Good will, customer relations, that sort of thing.' The conversation was becoming more ridiculous. It was time to cut through the bluffing and talk sensibly about the business.

'Howay John,' I said. 'The shop's obviously been closed for weeks, there is no good will.'

'But I had loads of good customers...' John started to say.

'Yes John. You *had* loads of good customers but by now they'll have found somewhere else to shop.' I saw Lorraine pick up a couple of packets from a nearby shelf and begin to examine them.

'As for the stock,' I said, 'There's nowt left. Now that the electricity is off the stuff in the fridges and freezers will be unsellable, and there's not much left on the shelves, hardly three thousand pounds worth.'

'Actually this dried fruit is out of date.' Lorraine said and she threw two packets of apricots back on the shelf.

'So that just leaves fixtures and fittings, most of which seem to have seen better days,' I said. I walked over to the back wall where one of the shelves had a broken bracket and lay with its edge resting on the shelf below. A pile of packages had slid down the resulting slope into a heap, and as I lifted the broken shelf to illustrate the state of disrepair, one of them toppled off, hit the wooden floor and burst, spraying out grains of brown rice.

'Nothing that can't easily be put right,' said John. Beads of perspiration had appeared on his forehead, although it was cold enough in the building for me to be shivering in my thick jumper and winter coat. He lifted the shelf and tried to rearrange the bags of rice into a stack to support it. Another bag slid and joined the one on the floor. He stared at it for a moment and Lorraine and I waited for him to speak.

He turned to face us and thrust his hands into the pockets of his jeans. He looked at Lorraine and then at me and said, 'All right then, just make me an offer.' I took a deep breath wondering if I could keep my nerve. Just go for it I told myself. As my granny used to say 'shy bairns get nowt.' Just say it.

'Ok John,' I said and took another breath. 'I'll give you five hundred pounds.'

Lorraine and John looked at me and then at each other in amazement. Lorraine opened her mouth to say something but changed her mind and turned away in the pretence of examining a poster on the wall that showed illustrations of different varieties of beans with instructions on how to cook them. In the silence that followed I felt my whole body tense and I could feel the heat of my face burning red. I waited for John to laugh at me, or to get angry and shout at me or even throw me out. He gazed at me seemingly deep in thought and I fixed my eye on a black mark that I thought might be a fly, on the wall above his head as I found that I could not meet his staring eyes. The black mark began to move slowly up the wall towards the ceiling, and then flew off, out of sight. Finally, after what seemed like hours, he leaned back against the wall, and looking at the floor said quietly, 'A thousand.' I heard Lorraine gasp quietly and she turned to look at us. I shook my head.

'Five hundred,' I said, amazed at my own nerve.

'Eight hundred,' he said pleadingly. 'Or seven, I'll take seven.'

'Five,' I repeated. 'Sorry John. It's my only and final offer.' He hesitated then sighed heavily.

'I'll take it,' he muttered, and then added in a pained voice 'but it must be cash. And I need it soon.'

Back at Lorraine's flat I collapsed onto the sofa. Lorraine dropped her handbag onto the floor and threw her keys onto the coffee table.

'Well!' she exclaimed, flopping into an armchair. 'I don't know whether to open a bottle to celebrate or to have you certified!'

'Break open a bottle,' I said. 'We're definitely celebrating.' I hoped I sounded a lot more confident than I felt. Now that the initial euphoria was wearing off, like always in these situations where I rushed in impulsively, I was beginning to wonder just what I'd taken on. How would I be able to organise all the work needed and how on earth would I finance it? And what had made me think that I could make a success of it if John Kirk hadn't been able to? Although I'd been self-employed for six years and had been able to support myself financially in that time, I was not particularly business-minded. I tended to muddle my way along following hunches rather than logic and I always let my heart rule my head. I groaned inwardly. What have I done? I thought. What on earth will Peter say?

Lorraine came out of the kitchen with a bottle, two glasses and a corkscrew that she set down on the table in front of me. She proceeded to open the bottle and gave a laugh.

'I can't believe what's just happened,' she said. 'I must admit that when we first entered the shop and I saw the state of everything I thought no chance but the more I saw, the more I felt it had potential. It will be an amazing challenge to take it on and get it up and going.' She handed me a glass of red wine. We both took a sip then she laughed, saying, 'When John said he wanted fifteen thousand I thought he must be off his head and I was expecting you to drop the idea like a hot potato. But when you offered him five hundred pounds, well! I nearly died!'

'So did I!' I spluttered. 'I don't know how I had the nerve really, I was terrified!' We both laughed and Lorraine said, 'But he accepted! He asked for fifteen thousand and accepted five hundred! I couldn't believe it.'

'I know,' I said. 'Neither could I.' Lorraine slumped back in her chair helpless with laughter.

'I thought he was going to throw me out,' I said, wiping my eyes. 'I felt a bit sorry for him in the end. He tried so hard to bluff his way through. Fifteen thousand huh!' I took another sip of my wine and hiccuped. I leaned my head against the soft cushions of the sofa and thought about how desperate John must

14

have been to accept my pitiful offer. It was obvious that he hadn't paid the electricity bill and who knew how many other suppliers would be chasing debts.

'Oh my God!' I said, suddenly sobered. 'Am I mad? Do you think there's any chance I can make this work? Where on earth do I start?'

'Of course you'll make it work,' Lorraine said loyally. 'You'll have it kicked into shape in no time. And yes you are mad.'

'Do you really think I can do it?' I asked feeling a little more heartened.

'Why aye,' she said. 'Anyway, there's time to change your mind if you want to. You haven't signed any legal documents or anything, you can always back out.'

I thought for a moment. At present, all I had to lose was five hundred pounds. I still had the antique shop full of stock, which when sold would be a good start towards financing the health shop. But more importantly than that I needed something to get my teeth into, a new start. My optimism began to return.

'No.' I said. 'No turning back now. I'm going to do it.'

CHAPTER THREE

After the freezing months of winter, March arrived with an unexpected spell of mild weather. Spring seemed to appear with the changing of the calendar and the previously stark trees now wore a spattering of green that had seemingly emerged overnight. Clusters of crocus sprouted everywhere and daffodil buds were ready to burst into flower at any moment.

Things were progressing well, if a little slowly. After viewing the shop with Lorraine I telephoned the landlord of the health store premises, Mr Stoker and explained that I wished to take over tenancy of the shop. He was very reluctant to allow it initially, believing me to be an acquaintance of John Kirk, and probably fearing that I would be an unreliable tenant. However, after I supplied references from my previous landlord, he agreed, and he was happy to leave me to make arrangements to collect the keys from John.

I rang John and arranged to meet him at the shop on the following Friday. I planned to use the coming week to start clearing the antique shop and spent a couple of hours on Sunday evening making a huge 'Closing Down Sale' banner with an old piece of canvas and a tin of red paint.

Early on Monday morning Peter and I hoisted the home made sign above the shop window and secured it by tying the sides to two drainpipes.

'Good luck,' Peter said as he left to go to work. 'Hope you sell everything,' and he kissed me and set off for work.

'Bye. Expect to see an empty shop when you return!' As he drove off I switched on the radio and set about changing price labels and reducing prices.

It was a beautiful morning; still a little chilly but bright and cloudless. The sun streamed through the window illuminating the front of the shop with radiant light and casting long shadows into the rear. As I propped open the door I breathed the salty sea air and a delicious warm breeze loaded with the promise of spring brushed over me. Singing along to the radio, I dragged some pieces of furniture outside and piled them up in front of the shop including a chaise longue that was in desperate need of new upholstery.

By twelve-thirty I had re-labelled everything and had already sold quite a lot of stock. I made a cup of tea and flopped on the chaise longue to sit in the sun and enjoy a well-earned break. I had just taken a first sip of tea when the telephone began to ring and I cursed and got up to answer it.

'It's me,' said Lorraine's voice. 'You'll never guess what's happened. The wine-store was burgled last night.'

'No!' I said. 'What have they taken?'

'Everything,' she said. 'The place has been cleared out. They couldn't get into the safe but they cleared the shelves and the cellar of all the wines and spirits. All the lagers and ciders have gone too, and the Sherries and ports. They've even taken boxes of chocolates and crisps. All that's left are a few odd bottles of mixers and soft drinks.'

'Bloody hell!' I said. 'How did they get in?'

'Walked in through the front door. Remember the broken shutter lock? All they had to do was push open the shutter, jemmy the door and cut the alarm wire.'

'The Ferret will be in big trouble,' I said. 'He's known about that lock for ages and never bothered to have it fixed.'

'Yeah, well that's the trouble,' said Lorraine 'He's been here this morning talking to the police. He said he knew nothing about a problem with the shutter lock and he's throwing the blame onto me, saying that I left the property unsecured.'

'You're joking!' I said. 'You've reported that broken shutter to him loads of times, the lying little creep. He can't blame you for this.'

'He can and he is,' she said. 'The Regional Manager is on his way here from Head Office now to interrogate me about it. You see, the insurance company won't pay out if the correct security measures weren't in place.'

'You can't let him get away with that!'

'Look, I'd better go. I've just sneaked out to the phone box in my lunch break so I'd better get back and face the music.'

'What time do you finish tonight?' I asked.

'Six o'clock.'

'Right,' I said. 'I'll meet you at the flat at about six-fifteen. I'll bring a takeaway and you can give me an update then. We'll see if we can come up with something to sort this out.'

By five thirty I had cashed up, tidied and locked the shop and was standing outside, huddled in my coat as Peter pulled up in the car to collect me.

'In a hurry to get home?' he asked. Usually he made us coffee and we chatted while I leisurely cashed up and tidied the displays.

'Yes,' I said. 'I'll explain on the way.'

Peter was as furious as I was.

'I knew he was a snivelling little git but I didn't think he'd be so cowardly as to blame something like this on to one of his staff,' he said.

'She needs to prove that he knew about the broken shutter lock,' I said.

'It'll be difficult,' said Peter. 'He's the kind of man who will do anything to save his own skin.'

We arrived at Lorraine's flat at ten past six with boxes of pizza and a tub of coleslaw. Lorraine was just leaving the shop as we pulled up, and she locked the door behind her and pulled down the shutter.

'Hi,' she said. She looked pale and tired and close to tears. She bent down to lock the shutter. 'New lock. Amazing how quickly he managed to have it repaired after the event.'

'Come on,' I said hugging her. 'Let's go up.'

Upstairs in the flat Lorraine picked at her pizza.

'Today has been awful,' she said putting down her fork. 'I got a hell of a shock this morning when I went down and found the place ransacked. The burglars had pulled down the shutter behind them, I suppose to avoid arousing suspicion. As soon as I pushed it up I saw the broken door and the empty shelves. To think that I was asleep upstairs and never heard a thing.'

'What did you do?' I asked.

'I phoned the police first and then Ryan Ferris. Two Police Officers arrived fairly quickly and I gave a statement. I told them the truth, that the lock had been broken for a while.'

'When did the Ferret arrive?' I asked.

'At about nine thirty. He spoke to the police but denied that he knew anything about the broken lock. I got really annoyed and called him a liar and it all got a bit heated. Julie, one of the sales assistants arrived to start her shift in the middle of the argument and she joined in. She told him she'd overheard me telling him about it on the phone but he just accused us of putting a story together to cover our backs.'

'Scumbag,' I said.

'Police Officers kept arriving and leaving all day asking questions and looking around, so Julie spent most of the day making cups of tea. She hadn't much else to do; we couldn't open for business without stock to sell. The Regional Manager arrived after lunch. He believed everything that Ryan Ferris said. He told me that I'd let the company down and gave me a written warning. Julie got a verbal warning. I was really angry at the injustice of it all but I just feel dejected and deflated now.' She pushed her plate of pizza away and sank back into her chair.

'Is there no way you can prove that Ferris knew about that lock?' asked Peter.

'I don't think so,' Lorraine said shaking her head.

'Did you ever inform him in writing?' I asked.

'Yes I did,' Lorraine said thoughtfully and she sat up suddenly. 'Every Friday I fill in the weekly stock figures form in the stock book and send the top copy to him. I remember about three weeks ago, I added a note to the bottom of the form saying that I was concerned that the lock had still not been mended and asking him to arrange to have it fixed. The copy should still be in the book.'

'Where's the book?' Peter and I asked in unison.

'Under the counter downstairs,' said Lorraine and we all jumped up and ran down the stairs, Lorraine grabbing her keys on the way.

Minutes later we were back in the sitting room with the stock book. I flicked through the pages.

'Well there's one thing that the Ferret is right about,' I said looking up. 'What's that?'

'You don't write heavily enough on the carbon paper. There's nothing here, just a few blue marks.'

'Let me see,' Lorraine said. I pushed the book forward so she and Peter could see it. She took the book from me and turned the pages, counting backwards through the previous weeks.

'Thirteenth of March, sixth of March, twenty-eighth of February, this is the page,' she said. 'Look, you can just make out a couple of words at the bottom.' We all peered at the page.

'I can see the word *remind* here,' said Peter pointing at the faint marks scarcely visible on the form. 'And that says *have* and there's an *s* and a *t* here, but that's all I can make out.'

'Well that's the end of that,' sighed Lorraine.

'No it isn't,' said Peter, settling down at the table with the book in front of him. 'Pass me a piece of carbon paper and a pencil. We'll soon fix this.'

Tuesday morning. After an early shower the sun came out causing the wet pavements to sparkle in front of me as I left the Metro Station. The air was fresh and I felt invigorated as I strolled towards the shop.

I arrived to find two women waiting impatiently in the doorway after spotting something they liked the look of in the window display. They bustled in behind me, and a few minutes later bustled out again carrying a small wine table, an umbrella stand and a box filled with various pieces of china.

News of my closing down sale had spread and throughout the morning an endless procession of bargain hunters paraded through the shop. It was hugely satisfying to see the shelves emptying and even more so to see the increasing stack of banknotes and cheques in my cash tin. The telephone rang several times during the morning but each time I was occupied with customers and although I twice managed to race to the telephone and snatch up the receiver it was only to hear the dialling tone as the caller hung up.

By one o'clock I was ravenously hungry and decided that as soon as I got the chance, I would nip to the local deli for a sandwich. After helping an elderly lady carry a basket chair to her car, I returned to the shop and quickly turned the sign to 'closed'. I collected my keys and bag and was just about to leave when the telephone rang again. It was Lorraine.

'Hi,' she said sounding very cheerful. 'Caught you at last. Have you been closed this morning?'

'No, just very busy,' I said. 'You sound chirpy. How are things?'

'Pretty good,' she answered. 'Had your lunch?'

'Not yet. I was just about to go out for a sandwich.'

'Well if you can wait a bit longer perhaps I could come over and join you? I've some news for you and an idea to run past you.'

'Mmm! Sounds interesting,' I said. 'You could meet me at Wild Oats Deli in the café upstairs?'

'Right. About half an hour?'

'Ok. See you then.'

The smell of fresh coffee greeted me as I walked upstairs to the Wild Oats café. I walked between the small lace covered tables, with their pretty little vases of narcissi, and sat at my favourite table in the bay window. Here I was able look down onto the main street, busy with traffic and people. After a moment I spied Lorraine striding along the pavement past the shops. She walked with a spring in her step, hair blowing in the breeze, looking a lot more carefree than she had yesterday.

Presently I heard footsteps tip-tapping up the polished wooden stairs and knowing that it was Lorraine, turned around to greet her.

'Hi,' she said as she breezed in and took a seat next to me. 'Have you ordered yet?' She picked up a menu.

'No I was waiting for you. But never mind that, what's your news? How are things at the shop?'

'Food first,' she said studying the menu. 'Let's get our priorities right.' I was bursting with curiosity but I knew I'd get nothing out of her until she was ready to tell me, so I too picked up a menu.

We ordered home made mushroom soup and wholemeal rolls filled with cheese and chutney that were served with a huge side salad and mounds of coleslaw and potato salad.

'Blimey,' I said when I saw them. 'I'll never eat all that!'

'I'm sure you'll manage,' Lorraine said.

'Right,' I said, picking up my spoon and tucking in to the delicious creamy soup. 'You can spill the beans now.'

As we ate she told me how she'd verbally backed Ryan Ferris into a corner and had produced the book with the copy of her note as evidence.

'You should have seen the look on his face,' she said. 'I told him I'd sent a copy to the Regional Manager.'

'That'll have him squirming,' I said. 'When did you send it?'

'I didn't send it,' she said. 'And I'm not going to.'

'Why not?' I asked, surprised. 'It's your chance to prove him wrong and to have the written warning retracted.'

'Because I'm not bothered any more,' she said. 'I'm tired of the whole company and of being bullied and intimidated. I'm going to resign.'

'Resign!' I said. 'But what will you do?'

'Well it's like this, you see. I've got this sister who's opening a health shop. Thought she might need a business partner?' she said with a grin.

'Oh brilliant!' I said overjoyed. 'I'd love us to be business partners.'

'Are you sure?' she said. 'I don't want to rush you into a decision.'

'Of course I'm sure,' I said. 'I've said all along that we'd be a great team. Although I don't know what makes you think you won't be bullied and intimidated!'

Lorraine laughed. 'Great. I'll write my resignation tonight.'

'Are you sure you're not making a rushed decision?' I asked. 'I don't want to change your mind but have you thought carefully about what you're giving up?'

'All I'm giving up is a load of stress.'

'Yeah, and planning to take on a new load.'

'That's different. This time we'll be in control,' she said. 'Anyway, I know it's the right thing to do. I've felt great since I made my decision.'

'Right then,' I said. 'It's a deal.'

'This calls for a celebration,' Lorraine said and spoke to the waitress who had arrived to remove our plates. 'Could we have two large cream cakes and another pot of tea please?' I groaned aware of my already straining waistband.

'I've already eaten too much,' I said as the waitress returned with two enormous choux buns bursting with whipped cream and strawberries and smothered in chocolate sauce.

'Stop moaning and enjoy it while we can,' Lorraine said. 'We're going into health foods soon.'

CHAPTER FOUR

The weather began to change on Tuesday afternoon. An easterly wind began to stir; bringing from the sea heavy grey clouds that accumulated to a dark mass and obscured the last patches of blue. Storms raged through the night and on Wednesday morning I arrived at the shop wet and bedraggled after fighting my way along from the station. After hanging up my wet things I switched on the radio and made a hot drink, expecting to have a quiet day.

Surprisingly, despite the bad weather and the fact that I was unable to display any goods outside, the shop was busy all day. The remaining stock diminished steadily and between serving customers I occupied myself by clearing out the desk and getting the last accounts up to date.

The rain and wind continued, and on Thursday morning the shop felt cold and dismal due to a combination of the gloominess outside and the starkness inside. All the elements that had colluded to give the shop its warm cosy atmosphere had gone; the table lamps with their soft yellow light, the pictures that had covered the walls, even the old faded rug with its worn patches had been sold.

Business was slow and I pottered around trying to find tasks to fill my time. A few people did come to browse but there was little left now. A pile of books stood on the floor and pieces of glass and china were scattered around the otherwise bare shelves. The walls looked bleak dotted with empty picture hooks; the only picture left was a 1960s print of a flower seller with huge eyes and a distortedly rounded figure. A monstrous 1940s wardrobe that even priced at ten pounds had not sold stood in the corner against the wall along side a three-foot high plaster Buddha.

I prowled around the shop, moving things and rearranging the few pieces in the window. There was nothing left of any great value. I looked at my watch. Ten to two. Three hours at least until Peter would arrive to take me home. I made a sudden decision, and pulling on my still damp coat, stuffed the takings into my bag, closed the shop and headed towards the Metro Station.

I arrived home soaked and weary. After removing my wet things and phoning Peter to let him know I was home, I had a hot bath and spent the remainder of the afternoon lounging on the sofa browsing through a pile of health food books I'd picked up from the library.

Friday arrived at last. I awoke with a feeling of anticipation, remembering that today I would collect the keys to the new premises.

'What time are you meeting John Kirk?' Peter asked as we were eating breakfast.

'Eleven o'clock,' I said, buttering a piece of toast.

'Will you still be there at twelve?'

'I should think so,' I said. 'Why?'

'I was thinking of coming over in my lunch hour so you could show me around.'

'That would be great,' I said. 'We could buy sandwiches on the bank and have our first ever lunch in our new shop.' I poured myself another cup of tea. 'More tea?'

'No thanks,' Peter said and he finished off the cup he had. 'I'd better get off to work.' He stood up and pulled on his coat. 'See you at lunch time.'

I arrived at the wine store at half past ten. Lorraine was busy with a queue of customers.

'Hi,' I said to Lorraine when the shop had emptied. 'On your own?'

'Yes. Julie's not in until twelve today which means I can't have a break until then and I'm dying for a cup of tea.'

'Any sign of John Kirk across there?' I asked.

'No, not yet,' she said. 'I've been keeping an eye out for him. The place looks a bit abandoned actually.' She turned to greet a customer who'd just entered.

I stood at the window and looked across the road to the health food shop. It looked grim. The shutter that pulled down over the door was daubed with graffiti. The grimy windows were dotted with faded and torn posters. Grubby venetian blinds hung drunkenly behind them with broken and unevenly spaced slats one of which was partially detached from the ceiling.

The customer left with two bottles of sherry and Lorraine came to join me at the window. We stared at our new business premises.

'What a state,' I said. 'It looks like a right dump.'

'Well the worse it looks now, the better the transformation will be when we're finished with it,' Lorraine said optimistically.

'I wish he'd hurry up,' I said. 'I can't wait to get in there and have a good look around.'

'Me too,' said Lorraine. 'I'll be over as soon as Julie arrives.'

'There he is,' I said, suddenly spotting John Kirk making his way down the other side of the street. He walked with great strides, his old army overcoat unfastened and billowing out behind him as he paced along. He glanced in the direction of the wine store and saw me watching him from the window. He waved and began to stride across the road and by the time I'd opened the shop door he greeted me on the pavement.

'Hi. How are you?' he asked, without waiting for an answer. 'Keys,' he said, handing me two keys tied together with a piece of string. 'Got me money?'

'Er, yes,' I said, a little taken aback. I had expected to have this conversation inside the new shop. 'Aren't we going to go inside?' I looked up and down the road. 'I don't really want to hand over a bundle of cash out here in the street.'

'Ok,' he said and he thrust open the wine store door and swiftly stepped inside. I caught hold of the door as it swung shut behind him and followed him inside. Lorraine looked up as we entered, surprised to see us.

'Hello,' she said.

'Hello! Great to see you,' John said to Lorraine as if she were his greatest friend.

'When I said inside, I meant inside the health shop.' I said

John ignored this and gave a nervous laugh. 'Right, you've got the keys so…?' He held out his hand for the money. I fumbled in my bag for the envelope containing five hundred pounds.

'I thought we'd go into the shop so that you could show me where everything is,' I said.

'But I've already done that,' he said, taking the envelope from my hand and giving me one of his charming smiles. 'You had a good look around last time didn't you?'

'Well yes I suppose so,' I said. 'It's just…'

'Good, good. I'll be off then. Thanks for this,' he said holding up the envelope. 'I'm sure I don't have to count it. You've got an honest face!' He opened the door. 'Good luck and all that. I'm sure everything will be just great.'

'But what about things like…' I thought frantically as he began to leave. 'Aren't there things you need to tell me?' I called desperately after him.

'Don't worry,' he said over his shoulder 'You'll be fine.' The door swung shut behind him and he passed by the window, lifting his hand in a wave and winking as he made off down the street.

'Well!' I said to Lorraine. 'What do you make of that? He was in a bit of a hurry wasn't he?'

'Oh never mind him,' she said. 'Come on, let's get across there and take a look.' She moved around from behind the counter and grabbed her jacket and keys from the storeroom.

'Can you do this?' I asked as she locked the shop door.

'No,' she said. 'But they can only sack me, can't they?'

We hurried across the road and I used the two keys on their piece of string to unlock the shutter and after pushing it up, unlock the front door.

'Item one on list: windows cleaned,' I said noticing the filthy glass panel in the door.

'Item two, a second set of keys cut for me,' added Lorraine. 'Did he just give you the one set?'

'Yes,' I said. 'But I think we should have the locks changed anyway, we've no way of knowing who could have spare keys.' I pushed open the door and we stepped inside. It was dark and dirty inside and there was a stale musty smell.

'Is it only three weeks since we were here?' Lorraine asked with disbelief in her voice. 'I thought it was bad then but it's horrendous now!'

'It's the smell. It stinks in here now. It's lost that lovely spicy smell it had,' I said and then fell over something lying on the floor. 'Ow!' I yelled.

'Just a minute, I'll open the blinds,' Lorraine said and I heard her clambering into the window. As she opened each blind, light filtered into the shop and I looked around in shock. The floor was strewn with all kinds of rubbish, discarded paperwork, junk mail, old carrier bags, broken pieces of wood and cardboard boxes.

'What a state!' I said.

'I don't believe this!' said Lorraine. 'Look over there.' I looked to where she was pointing, to a large empty space at the rear of the shop and it took a few seconds for my mind to register that this was where the display fridges and freezers had stood.

'They've gone!' I said, stating the obvious.

'No wonder he didn't want us to come inside, the robbing sod,' said Lorraine angrily.

'They've gone!' I said again, staring at the wall as if they would reappear if I stared long enough. Lorraine marched over to the telephone that was standing on the counter.

'Give me his number,' she said 'I'm going to have this out with him, we've paid for those fridges.' She lifted the receiver then clicked the cut off button a couple of times. She looked at me and said, 'The phone's dead. It's been cut off. Can you believe it?'

'Yes I can actually,' I said. 'After seeing the state of this place I could believe anything.' I picked some of the rubbish up from the floor and threw it into a pile. 'I think it might be better if we go to see him face to face anyway rather than speak on the phone. I have his address, it's not far, we could walk it in five minutes.'

'Yes,' said Lorraine. 'I think you're right. I can only stay a few more minutes. I'll come over when Julie arrives and we'll go straight around there.' I continued to pick up rubbish from the floor and Lorraine went into the kitchen area.

'My God,' she said. 'Environmental Health will close us down before we even open if anyone sees this.' She began pulling out rubbish that was stashed beneath the work surfaces her nose wrinkling in disgust.

'This is shocking,' she said throwing old carrier bags and dirty tea towels onto the growing mound of rubbish near the door. She hauled out a huge plastic bucket with a lid.

'What do you think is in here?' she asked. She turned the pot around.

'Pritchett's Real Mayonnaise' we said together, reading the words on the side.

'I can't get the lid off,' she said straining as she tried to lever it off. 'Give me a hand with it.' We bent down and each taking a side tugged and strained at the lid as hard as we could. It loosened suddenly, releasing a foul smell that sent the two of us reeling backwards from our crouched positions on to the floor.

'Oh my God!' Lorraine said, covering her nose and face with her hand. I leaned forward and peered into the bucket. It was mayonnaise – very old mayonnaise. So old it had grown a furry covering of luminous yellow mould.

'Aw, the dirty buggers!' I said, slamming on the lid, and we moved out of the kitchen area, coughing and wafting hands in front of faces to disperse the smell. I moved towards the door intending to open it and let in some fresh air, but before I could do so it burst open and Peter appeared.

'Hello. I managed to get away a bit earlier…' he started to say then his face contorted and he said, 'Bloody hell, what's that stink?'

The Saffron Café, situated a few yards down the bank was, in contrast, clean, warm and filled with a delicious smell of roast peppers and hot garlicky bread.

'There's no way I could have eaten lunch in there,' said Peter as we tucked into bowls of steaming pasta. 'It's absolutely minging.'

'I know,' I said. 'It's such a mess I don't know where to start.' There was so much to do. 'I need to make a list,' I said thoughtfully, at which Peter laughed.

I am a compulsive list writer, I write shopping lists, things-I-must-do lists, Christmas lists, lists of weekly menus, lists of household chores, lists of anything and everything. I love the satisfied feeling I get when I cross out a completed task from a list, and yes, I admit I do sometimes add already done tasks to a list to be able to immediately cross them off.

'There's definitely scope for list-making over there,' said Peter. 'You could write a whole series of lists. Then you could write a list of your lists.' He leaned forward. 'Could be your greatest collection of lists yet.'

'Ha ha,' I said finishing off my pasta. 'I really need to go and clear out the old shop first before I start on the new one.'

'We could do that tonight,' said Peter. 'It shouldn't take long, there's not much left is there?'

'No, just odds and ends. I thought we could pack them up and take them to the charity shop.'

'Good idea. We'll do it later,' said Peter. 'Put it on the list.'

Just then Lorraine appeared round the door signalling to us that she was ready to go. We hurriedly paid the bill and bundled out.

'Get in the car and I'll drive you there on my way back to work,' Peter said.

'Got the address?' Lorraine asked.

'Yes,' I said, '51 Wallinger Terrace. Past the double roundabout at the bottom of the bank, then second left and left again.'

Wallinger Terrace was a cheerless shadowy street lined with rows of tall, oppressive looking Victorian houses, standing shoulder to shoulder as if to deliberately block out the weak rays of the afternoon sun. As we slowly drove along the street, I looked up at the neglected Victorian fascias and it was apparent that in their day these had been grand, majestic houses. I imagined that the tall windows were sorrowful eyes looking down in despair through their peeling, rotting window frames, aware of the hard times fallen upon, giving out a silent plea for a little loving restoration.

'You know, these houses could be really beautiful if someone took the time to restore them,' I said. 'You can tell they were once grand and dignified, they just need a little love. They look so sad and abandoned.'

'There it is,' said Peter and Lorraine at the same time, completely ignoring my fanciful observation, and the car pulled up at number 51.

'You wait here,' I said to Peter.

'No, I'll come too,' he said. 'He may get aggressive.'

'He won't,' I said. 'He's not the type.'

'Then I'll watch from here,' he said. 'I'm here if you need me.' Lorraine and I climbed out of the car and walked towards the house.

'There he is!' I said, as Lorraine pushed the gate, which promptly fell flat on the ground in front of us. I saw, momentarily, the shadowy figure of John Kirk peering from behind a curtain but as Lorraine turned to look the curtain was swiftly whipped back into place. Lorraine stepped over the gate, walked to the door and taking hold of the doorknocker rapped loudly. We waited. Lorraine rapped again.

'I know he's in there. I saw him at the window,' I said. We rapped for a third time, but to no avail. I took hold of Lorraine's arm.

'Come back to the car,' I said, leading her back down the path and over the gate.

'No way,' she said. 'He's in there hiding from us. I'm not giving up so easily.'

'Neither am I,' I said. We got back into the car.

'Pull up around the corner, Peter,' I said. He did and we got out of the car again.

'Follow me,' I told Lorraine and I moved stealthily down the edge of the block of houses. Lorraine followed, tip-tapping on her high heels.

'What exactly are we doing?' she asked.

'Shhh!' I said, 'Just follow me,' and we edged along the wall to the side of the end house. I spied around the corner and saw the front door of number 51 slowly open. John peered out cautiously. He stepped out onto the path and looked up and down the street.

'Now!' I yelled and we ran up the street to his gate.

'Hello John!' Lorraine said. 'We'd like a word with you.'

'Oh hello there!' said John, feigning surprise. 'I've just come in and I'm on my way out. I'm a bit busy at the moment,' he gabbled.

'This won't take a moment,' I said. 'We just want to know where the fridges and freezers are that we paid for.'

'Oh,' he said. 'Yes. The fridges and freezers.' Behind him, a little face appeared round the door. It was very grubby, but smiling and very appealing.

'Where are they?' Lorraine said. 'We want them back, we've paid for them.'

'Hello!' said the little face.

'Hello,' I said to the child. I nudged Lorraine and nodded towards the little boy in case she wasn't aware of him. It would not be good to have a full-blown argument with his father in the street in front of him.

'Where are they John?' she asked, this time in a calmer voice. John shrugged his shoulders and smiled weakly.

'Sorry girls,' he said. 'Desperate times call for desperate measures.'

'What?' said Lorraine.

'What do you mean?' I said.

'That's my Dad,' said Kirk Junior.

'Is it really?' I said sweetly with a forced smile then turned to John and said: 'Can't you answer a straightforward question?'

'I've got wellies,' said Kirk Junior.

'Look,' John said. 'I was skint. I sold them. I needed the money.'

'I can go in puddles,' the little boy said proudly.

'But you'd already sold them to us!' yelled Lorraine.

'You…you…' I started, and then remembering that Junior was present, racked my brains for a suitable non-swearing insult. 'You…dirty double crosser!' I yelled, vaguely remembering an old black and white film I'd watched the previous evening. It was the best I could come up with on the spur of the moment. Lorraine looked at me with disgust as though I'd just uttered an obscene oath and Junior giggled.

'Dirty double crosser,' he said. 'Dirty double crosser.'

'I'm sorry,' John said. 'But I was desperate. And after all you only paid me five hundred quid. You still got a good bargain.'

'A bargain?' I ranted. 'Have you seen the state of the place? It'll cost another five hundred pounds in bleach to get the place cleaned up!'

'Come on girls. What do you expect for five hundred quid?'

'That's not the point,' said Lorraine. 'It's the principle. You went back on your word; you've ripped us off. It's fraud, it's stealing.' John shrugged his shoulders.

'Like I say, sorry and all that, but it's done now. I was in a tight corner and I needed the money. I had to do it. I can't get them back and it's no good asking me for money because I've got nowt.' He folded his arms and leaned against the doorframe.

'Oh come on Lorraine,' I said. 'We're wasting our time here, he couldn't care less.' Lorraine reluctantly started to follow me back down the path.

'No hard feelings girls?' called John and Lorraine turned and gave him one of her best snooty looks then tripped over the prostrate gate.

'Bye bye,' called Junior, waving from the door.

'Bye sweetheart,' I called.

'Bye bye,' he yelled again. 'Bye bye dirty double crosser.'

CHAPTER FIVE

April the first. April Fools Day. Peter dropped me at the shop door with my two bags of cleaning equipment and went to find a parking space. I lugged the bags into the shop and looked around, discouraged at the sight before me.

My day had started full of optimism and determination. I rose early and drank a hurried cup of tea as I dressed in old jeans and sweatshirt. I gathered together bottles of bleach and cleaning agents and hunted out old towels and cleaning rags. I had set off in the car with Peter, intent on spending the day performing a miraculous transformation. The electricity supply had been re-connected and family and friends had offered to come and help with the grand clean-up operation.

I could see the finished product in my mind. A sparkling clean shop, neat and orderly, with scrubbed pine shelves, polished parquet floor and immaculate fresh white walls reflecting light into the airy and spacious interior. My mind moved to the kitchen area, complete with spotless cooker and oven, sterile work surfaces and immaculate systematic storage area, hygienic and sanitary, ready for use.

Now, standing amongst piles of rubbish in the dark and squalid shop, my spirits sank, the vision crumbled and enthusiasm evaporated leaving a residue of lethargy.

The door opened and Peter entered. 'Took ages to find a space. I hope parking's not going to be a problem for customers.' We didn't know it at the time but lack of parking spaces was going to be a huge problem for customers. 'Haven't you started yet?' he asked, looking around at the mess.

'No I haven't,' I said. 'Just look at it! I don't know what to do first. I feel like giving up before I even begin.' I can't give up already, I thought. I have to get myself motivated. 'I just need a good kick up the arse to get me going,' I said.

'Well I can give you one of those,' Peter said and playfully aimed a kick at my behind. I caught his foot and he hopped after me laughing and grabbing at the shelves to maintain his balance. The door opened and Lorraine arrived carrying a mop and bucket, just in time to see Peter trip and fall and me tumble on top of him, the two of us laughing hysterically.

'Oh for goodness sake!' she said. 'Can't you leave him alone? The honeymoon period ended ages ago.' She disappeared outside to collect some pots of paint and brushes she'd brought and Peter and I started to clear the floor of rubbish, still laughing and throwing things at each other.

Lorraine returned and joined in and soon my parents arrived, closely followed by Peter's parents, Joan and Roy. Everyone was given a job on arrival. Joan and my Mam began scouring the kitchen while my Dad cleaned and polished the parquet floor. Peter and Roy made several trips to the local tip to get rid of the seemingly never-ending pile of rubbish. Peter's sisters, Susan and Irene arrived and set to work clearing out the office and storeroom. Soon the place was a hive of activity with everyone labouring diligently. Peter had brought a cassette player and we listened to music as we worked, all of us singing and laughing and bantering with each other.

Lorraine produced a kettle and a jar of coffee and made hot drinks and handed out chocolate biscuits. Friends who kept arriving and leaving all day cleaned windows, washed paintwork and helped to carry out rubbish. My cousin Anth arrived to remove the lettering from the window with a liquid solution he'd brought specially for the purpose. He offered to replace it with our new name in plastic letters he would cut for us at his studio but we hadn't yet decided on a suitable name.

Lorraine and I took the grimiest jobs ourselves. She disappeared up the small flight of stairs at the back of the shop, armed with rubber gloves and bleach to tackle the toilet and washroom. I too pulled on rubber gloves and picking up an old knife began scraping thick layers of congealed grease from the rubber blades of the extractor fan. I worked as quickly as I could; it was a disgusting job and I wanted to get it finished as soon as possible. Once the grease was scraped off and collected up into newspaper to be thrown away, I scrubbed the blades with hot soapy water and was delighted to see the clean cream coloured surface appear beneath the grime.

'Morning!' said a voice suddenly and I turned to see a postman holding out a pile of letters that I took from him.

'Thanks' I said.

'You're welcome, flower,' he said then turned and looked around the shop. 'Holy mackerel, you've got your work cut out here! I'm Nige, by the way, your friendly postman,' he said and he introduced himself to each of us individually, shaking hands and joking about how hard we were all working.

'Is that coffee I can smell?' he asked. It wasn't, but we were soon to learn that it was Nige's way of hinting for a cup of coffee.

'Ta very much,' he said as he was handed a mug of hot coffee and a chocolate biscuit. 'I may as well stay and help for a while, I like to be useful and help people. Pillar of the community, me.'

His idea of helping was to sit with his feet propped on a box and drink two refills of coffee whilst filling us in on the local gossip and occasionally throwing in comments such as 'You need a bit more elbow grease there darlin'' and 'You've missed a bit there, flower.'

At one o'clock we stopped for a break. Peter and Roy walked up the bank to the chippy to buy lunch. Nige left at the same time to walk up the bank with them (and presumably finish his delivery round.)

More tea and coffee was made and we each found a place to sit, either on upturned boxes or perched along the counter and window shelf, and tucked into steaming hot vinegar-drenched chips, eaten straight from the paper.

'We really need to make a decision on the new name,' said Lorraine, at which suggestions were thrown at us from all directions.

'Healthy Times!' 'Healthy Way!' 'What about Help Yourself to Health?' 'What about Health R Us?'

'No,' Lorraine said. 'I don't like names with Health or Healthy in them. It sounds too preachy. It might put people off.'

'We need something wholesome, like All Good Things,' I said. 'Or Nature's Pantry.' The barrage of suggestions started again.

'Good and Wholesome!' 'Country Store!' 'Cornucopia!' 'Down to Earth!'

'What about something with a bit of humour?' suggested Peter. 'Like Has Beans?'

'Or Beanies?' called a voice and the suggestions again came thick and fast, becoming more bizarre. 'The Bean Pot!' 'Trade Winds!' 'Wind and Wuthering!' 'Have Beans will Travel!' 'Gone With the Wind!' 'Blow your own Trumpet!'

'Now you're just being silly,' I said. 'I think we should have Wholefoods in the title, like…'

'Just Wholefoods!' 'Wholesome Wholefoods!' 'Station Road Wholefoods!'

'Something like…' I continued 'Honey Pot Wholefoods.'

'Aw, that sounds naff!' Lorraine said. 'I prefer Harvest Wholefoods.'

'Well that's even more naff!' I said, peevishly. We didn't seem to be getting any closer to making a decision. I suddenly had one of my amazing brainwaves.

'I've got it!' I said. 'There's a dictionary in the office. You flick through it and I'll shout stop and the word you're pointing to will be the name with Wholefoods after it.' There was a chorus of 'Good idea!' and Lorraine went to fetch the dictionary.

'Ready?' she asked, holding out the book in an exaggerated way. Someone played a drum roll on the counter. Lorraine flicked the pages dramatically.

'Stop!' I called and she stabbed a finger at the page. There was a moment of hushed anticipation.

'Well?' I said. She coloured slightly.

'It's not really an appropriate word,' she said.
'What is it?' I asked, 'Let me see.'

We all agreed that Testicle Wholefoods would not be a suitable name for our business and amongst much hilarity Lorraine went back into the office to fetch a cookery book that we'd discovered when clearing out a box of old paperwork.

'Right,' she said. 'Let's try again. The Big Book of Wholefood Cookery. There'll be loads of suitable words in here. Here we go.' Again the drum roll, the flick of pages.

'Stop!' Lorraine looked at the page.

'Spoon,' she announced. 'Spoon Wholefoods.'

'Best of three?' I suggested. 'Stuffed' was the next result. I was beginning to think that this was not such a good idea. The process was repeated for a third time.

'Nutmeg!' Lorraine called out, looking around. 'Nutmeg Wholefoods!'

A cheer went up. We had our new name. It was concise and befitting and I was pleased with it. Little did I know that I was unwittingly setting the mould for our future nickname of 'Nutty Meg's' which we endured with waning good humour over the years. Lorraine held up her coffee mug and toasted the shop.

'To Nutmeg!' she said.

'To Nutmeg!' came the echo.

'And to all who sail in her!' added Peter, and with a clink of coffee mugs, Nutmeg Wholefoods was born.

CHAPTER SIX

The next few days passed in a whirl of activity. On acceptance of her resignation Lorraine relinquished her flat above the wine store. She moved into a flat with Cheryl, a friend of hers who worked as a psychiatric nurse. We packed her belongings and furniture into as many cars as we could gather together and drove them in convoy to the large Victorian flat, working into the night to get the two rooms she now rented into some semblance of order.

We spent long days in the shop, arriving early in the morning and often staying until midnight. Our workload seemed to be never ending. My clipboard of lists was growing rapidly; for every task completed and crossed off, several more were realised and added.

Family and friends continued to drop in and help. Anth returned with the adhesive vinyl letters spelling 'Nutmeg Wholefoods' that he'd machine cut for us. He and Peter went out in the pouring rain to bond them to the window by a slow and tedious process of immersing the letters in water and meticulously sliding them into position on the glass.

Meanwhile, inside Lorraine and I put the last coat of varnish onto the freshly sanded pine shelves. The rain lashed against the windows and the door rattled intermittently with each sporadic gust of wind.

I looked through the window to where Peter and Anth were working outside in the pouring rain. Anth was perched precariously at the top of a ladder smoothing the letter 'M' onto the window. His dark hair was plastered to his head as water ran over it and down his face. Peter was using one hand to cling to the bottom of the ladder preventing it from lurching in the wind and with the other was grappling with the vinyl letters that flapped madly as the wind threatened to tear them from his grip.

'Do you think they're all right?' I asked Lorraine, feeling guilty that we were inside and dry and enjoying the warmth of the calor gas heater.

'Mmm?' Lorraine looked up as she finished varnishing the edge of the last shelf. 'Oh yes. They'll be fine. Vinyl is quite strong and the rain won't damage it.'

'I meant those two, not the letters!' I said. Lorraine collected the used brushes together and put them into a pot of white spirit then pulled up a box to sit near the heater.

'Don't worry about them,' she said. 'It's self-inflicted. I mean, why are they still out there? If it were you and me we'd have been back inside at the first spot of rain.'

'That's true,' I said. 'After all there's no deadline to say that they have to do it today is there?'

'Exactly!' said Lorraine and we watched, amused at Anth's startled expression as he suddenly lost his balance and almost fell, sending Peter into a panic, then lunged at the ladder and regained his poise. I hummed a couple of lines of the Laurel and Hardy theme tune and Lorraine laughed and joined in.

'Look at them!' Lorraine said. 'They're like two drowned rats struggling on, why don't they come in and leave it until tomorrow?'

'Because they're men,' I said. 'It's a man-thing isn't it? Finding the most difficult way to do something.' We absorbed ourselves for the next fifteen minutes or so in an engrossing conversation about the absurdity of male logic until interrupted by the two drowned rats entering the shop. The door opened with a great spurt of rain like a bucket of water flung in from the wings of a nautical themed Morecambe and Wise play, and Peter and Anth were thrown in with it. Peter wiped the water from his face with the back of his hand.

'Bloody awful weather out there,' he said as they stood dripping onto the parquet floor. 'It's pelting down, we're soaked through.'

'Yes,' I said. 'That's what we were just saying, weren't we?'

'Yeah,' said Lorraine. 'We were talking about what a great job you've done and how you didn't let the weather put you off.' Peter and Anth looked pleased.

'There's some clean towels upstairs in the loo,' I said. 'Go and dry off and I'll make you a hot drink.'

Actually they had done a great job. The lettering was bright and eye catching and looked very professional, and more importantly had not cost us a penny. Purchasing replacement fridges and freezers had hammered our budget and we had become proficient in tracking down bargains. We bought, very cheaply, a second-hand till from a haberdashery shop holding a closing down sale, and pricing guns and a safe were found at an auction house in Newcastle specialising in the disposal of equipment and stock from liquidated businesses.

Peter had performed a miracle renovating the kitchen using off-cuts of worktops, lengths of wood and several leftover tins of white paint gathered from various garages, sheds and understair cupboards. The kitchen had also been equipped, if a little domestically, mostly thanks to Joan who provided a box of cooking implements and my Mam who bought us a microwave. Lorraine donated her spare electric kettle and a set of cooking knives and I brought from home cutlery, pans and an ancient sandwich toaster. We begged, borrowed and scrounged, spending as little as we could aware that what was left of our dwindling budget was needed to stock the shop.

The following morning I approached the shop with pleasure at seeing the new sign in daylight and with excitement at the prospect of spending the day ordering stock. The telephone was due to be connected at nine-thirty and I had a pile of price lists and catalogues and was raring to go. I looked up at the sign proudly, the dark red letters stood out impressively against the spotless glass of the windows gleaming in the sunlight, and as I looked I saw the reflected image of Lorraine pulling up in her car.

'Morning,' I called. 'Looks good doesn't it?'

'It certainly does,' she said, locking the car and following me inside. We looked around at the polished wooden flooring and shelves and white-painted walls.

'It's like a different place,' Lorraine said.

'We should have taken before and after photographs,' I said and I climbed onto the window shelf to pull the blinds up.

'Wow!' exclaimed Lorraine as sunlight filled the building reflecting off the white walls and giving the wooden surfaces a warm golden glow. 'It's gorgeous. I can't wait to see the shelves filled up with lovely things.'

'And the fridges,' I said, running my hand along the stainless steel top of the long counter fridge. 'Just imagine this filled with huge cheeses and dishes of olives... and pates and salads... and baskets of organic vegetables over here...' I wafted around the shop waving my hands about. 'And free-range eggs here... and jars of spices here...'

'And lots of money in the till here!' said Lorraine dancing around the counter and mockingly flinging her arms around. I was used to being teased about my over-active imagination and my frequent delves into my own little world. Planet Christine Lorraine called it.

'How can you think of money at a time like this?' I said in a pretentious voice, pressing the back of my hand to my forehead in a swooning gesture. 'I'm here simply for the artistic value. Of course everything will have to be absolutely scrutinised for colour and texture before being placed in the most suitable place on the shelves. Yes, I think red lentils next to green lentils will be most visibly pleasing, green and red being on opposite sides of the colour wheel.' I pranced around the floor. 'I will of course use my expertise as the company's Art Director to create a spectacular, sumptuous visual delight...'

'Don't you mean the company's Art Soul?' said Lorraine laughing at her own joke. It took me a couple of seconds to realise the play on words and when I did I grabbed a nearby tea towel flicked it at her bottom like we used to do as children with our swimming towels at the pool.

'Ouch,' she said, 'that stings!' A ringing sound suddenly halted our laughter. We clutched each other in fright.

'It's the phone!' we said together.

'Our first call,' said Lorraine. 'I wonder who it is?'

'It must be Peter,' I said. 'He's the only person I've given the number to.' I picked up the receiver.

'Hellooo!' I said in my best snooty voice. 'Nutmeg Wholefoods. Christine Kenworthy here, Company Arsehole, how may I help you?'

'Hello?' said a male voice that was not Peter's.

'Oh sorry, I was expecting a call from someone else,' I laughed into the phone, cringing with embarrassment. Not a great way to answer our first ever phone call.

'I need to speak to John Kirk,' the voice said abruptly.

'Who is it?' mouthed Lorraine. I shrugged.

'John Kirk isn't here,' I said. 'He doesn't own this business any more.'

'Then I need to speak to the new owner.'

'Um, that's me,' I said.

'Right,' said the voice. 'This is Oliver Nugent calling from Ollie's Organics. I'm calling about an outstanding debt of £672.18 for goods supplied during the period September to December last year, invoice numbers…'

'Excuse me,' I interrupted. 'John Kirk is no longer here. You'll need to take the matter up with him.'

'You are the new owner?'

'Yes.'

'Then you are legally responsible for the business debts. Your name is?'

'I've got nothing to do with John Kirk's business or his debts.' I said flustered.

'If you bought the business, then you bought the debts. Could I please have your name?' Oliver Nugent said.

'No you can't,' I said. 'And I didn't buy the business. Kirk moved out, I moved in. Different business, no connection.'

'Can you prove that?'

'I don't need to prove it.' My voice was getting louder as I became more stressed.

'Then can you give me John Kirk's forwarding address?' I hesitated for a moment.

'No I can't. I don't know it,' I lied.

'I thought not. Now give me your name and details and we can sort this out without going to court.'

'Going to court?' I repeated looking at Lorraine who was mouthing something that I couldn't understand.

'Nice try,' I said. 'But you're wasting your time. I do not owe you money and I shall not be paying you.'

'Unless this debt is paid off in full within forty-eight hours,' shouted Oliver Nugent, 'my solicitor will be contacting you…'

'Tell him to get stuffed,' hissed Lorraine.

'Get stuffed!' I yelled and hung up hearing a startled 'I beg your pardon?' before the cut off click.

Unfortunately that was the first of many; the telephone rang constantly during the following hour. We had settled down with price lists and catalogues to make lists of stock but were continually interrupted by the phone ringing.

'Do you think we should have the telephone number changed?' Lorraine suggested.

'We can't afford to,' I said gloomily. 'Anyway we can't change our address so they'd find the new number easily.'

'Well I think we should start giving out John Kirk's home address and telephone number and direct them over to him,' she said.

'I don't really want to do that to him,' I said.

'Neither do I,' said Lorraine. 'But why should we take all this aggro?'

'Let's leave it for now and see how it goes,' I said and then we both groaned as the telephone rang again.

We decided to unplug the telephone for a couple of hours while we compiled our orders. Before unplugging it I rang Peter to tell him that he wouldn't be able to contact us until after three and I told him about all the menacing phone calls.

'Just stay calm and polite when you deal with them,' he advised. 'Remember they could be people you may want to do business with at some point in the future. Stand your ground but be reasonable and don't get drawn into an argument.'

'Ok, I will,' I said, not mentioning the dozens of callers I'd already told to get stuffed.

We were sitting on stools at the counter surrounded by catalogues, calculators and coffee cups when Nige arrived. He was wearing a hand knitted green and pink striped scarf that must have measured at least nine feet long, wrapped round and round his neck over his regulation Post Office uniform.

'Morning girls,' he chirped handing me a large pile of mail.

'Morning,' I said, taking the wad from him. 'Are you sure this is all for us?'

I flicked through the envelopes.

'Oh man,' I said. 'Most of these are addressed to John Kirk and they look like bills.' Lorraine explained to Nige about the phone calls.

'Well that doesn't surprise me,' he said. 'John's a lovely bloke, quite cute actually, but I wouldn't trust him as far as I could throw him. Here, give them back to me and I'll pop them through his letterbox, but don't let on because I'm not really supposed to deliver mail to anywhere other than where it's addressed to.'

'Thanks Nige,' I said and handed the pile back to him.

'In future I'll vet them before I deliver,' he said. He looked at the coffee cups on the counter. 'Is that coffee I can smell?'

While he drank his coffee Nige entertained us with tales of his relationship with his partner, a would-be actor named Gus Jossland who Nige clearly adored but who was evidently an egotistical drama queen who treated Nige like a doormat.

Lorraine and I sat listening, spellbound, and for the present all thoughts of work disappeared.

'Go on,' I said fascinated. 'What happened next?'

'Well,' said Nige, apparently enjoying telling the tale as much as we were enjoying listening, 'When I found out that he'd spent the bill money again, this time on a designer shirt I did me nut! 'Where would we be if I spent all our money on fancy clothes too?' I asked him. And do you know what the bugger did then? Picked up one of my Capo-di-Monte roses and flung it at me. Just missed me head it did. Nearly had me nose off. It smashed into a hundred pieces on the floor.'

He paused to take a drink from his coffee cup. 'Anyway, when we calmed down he explained to me that he always has to look his best and be seen in the right places in the interest of his career. Well I tell you, I felt so guilty. I apologised of course and I paid the bills. I offered to take him out for a meal to make it up to him but he said if it was all the same to me he'd just have the money because he'd booked a facial and manicure for a party he's invited to at the weekend and it would pay for that.'

He stopped to drink the last of his coffee. 'I didn't even know he was going to a party actually,' he said and sighed. 'Sometimes it's difficult living with a celebrity.' Celebrity my arse. I'd never heard of Gus Jossland and I'm sure no one else had either.

'It's his artistic temperament you see,' said Nige. 'He's so talented and passionate about his career, sometimes I just have to make allowances.'

'I think he's taking you for a mug,' Lorraine told him. 'You should kick him into touch.' But Nige wouldn't have it.

'No, he's lovely, really. I don't deserve him.'

It was after two by the time Nige left and we got stuck into compiling our lists of orders.

'Here we go!' I said, plugging in the phone so I could make the first call. We were as excited as two kids putting in an order to Father Christmas. The first company I rang were Karma, an ethically run co-operative who had been trading successfully since the sixties and stocked a vast range of products. We were aware of their good reputation both as being fair and reliable people to trade with and also of the level of quality of their own branded goods. The woman I spoke to certainly lived up to this reputation, she was extremely helpful, giving advice about products and offering discounts and free samples. But when I gave our address her manner changed.

'I'm sorry,' she said abruptly. 'I'm unable to process your order.'

'But why?' I asked. My heart sank as I suspected I already knew what she was going to say. Karma were to be our main supplier; if they wouldn't deal with us it would make life very difficult. It would mean hunting out hundreds of individual producers and attempting to order direct from each of them.

'I've entered your details into our computer system and there's a substantial amount of money owed to us from that address. I'm afraid your account is on hold until the debt is paid off.'

'But I don't have an account, or a debt, that was the last owner. He's gone now and I have nothing to do with him. I really need you to supply us or we won't be able to open for business.'

It took twenty minutes of explaining, persuading and wheedling to convince the-powers-that-be at Karma that I was not an associate of John Kirk trying to obtain more stock for him and that I had a good credit history. Eventually, they agreed to supply me but only on a cash on delivery basis, which was a bit of a blow to our already limited buying potential. I had been hoping for a couple of month's credit to get us up and going. Still, it was that or nothing so I accepted gratefully and placed a vastly amended order.

It was the same procedure with every supplier we rang. It was such a disheartening process. We took it in turns, one of us anxiously gripping the phone pleading our case, while the other gave moral support sitting on the opposite side of the counter prompting and whispering suggestions.

At last all the contacts on our list had been called and I put down the telephone with a sigh.

'Thank God that's done,' I said. 'That was so gruelling, I feel exhausted.' I went through to the kitchen to switch on the kettle.

'I need more than a cup of tea,' Lorraine said. 'I need chocolate.' She delved into her handbag and found her purse. 'I'll just nip out and get us some,' she said. 'Won't be long.'

Alone in the shop I glanced through the lists of products we'd ordered. Some were very familiar; rice, pasta, cashews, apricots, peanut butter – things I used regularly myself at home. But of others I wasn't so sure. What on earth was quinoa? Miso? Dulse? – Wasn't that a type of seaweed? Terriaki? – An irritating little dog? I scanned the lists. Tahini. Tofu. Tempeh. Vine Leaves. Well at least I knew what vine leaves were although I couldn't for the life of me imagine what you would do with them. Stitch them together to make a bikini a la Adam and Eve? Or was that fig leaves? The telephone rang interrupting my musings and I absent-mindedly reached out to answer it, momentarily forgetting that I had intended to ignore it.

'Hello there,' said a very deep Scottish voice. 'Can ah speak tae the owner please?' Oh no. Here we go again. Why hadn't I just let it ring unanswered?

'That's me,' I said reluctantly.

'Oh aye,' said the voice. 'Ah'm ringing tae ask when am gonnae get paid for the stuff I sent ye?'

'That would have been delivered to the previous occupier, John Kirk,' I said. 'Not to me.'

'Och no! Ah definitely delivered the stuff tae a lassie, ah remember distinctly.'

'Well it wasn't me.'

'Hev ye sold it?' Because if ye havenae, ah'll come and tek it back.'

'I don't even know what it is you're talking about,' I said. 'You did not deliver anything to me.'

'Vegetarian prawns,' he said. Vegetarian prawns? What on earth were vegetarian prawns? I was beginning to think there was a lot more to being in the health food trade than I'd previously imagined. I'd never heard of vegetarian prawns.

'Aye,' he continued. 'Five hundred kilos of frozen vegetarian prawns.' For a moment I was speechless. What had John Kirk done with five hundred kilos of vegetarian prawns, whatever they were?

'As ah say, ah brought them ma'sel and it was a wee fat lassie who took delivery and ah think it was ye.'

'Well it wasn't!' I shouted.

'Well I think it was. Ye sound fat.' My temper suddenly snapped. I'd had enough. All the frustrations of the day let loose as I yelled at him.

'Don't be so ridiculous, you stupid man! How can anyone sound fat? How dare you! I've never heard of anything so ridiculous in my entire life!'

'Calm doon lassie!' came the reply. 'Dinna start greetin'!' and suddenly the penny dropped.

'You're not funny Peter!' I yelled down the phone and I heard him laughing hysterically and calling 'Och aye tha noo!' as I hung up.

CHAPTER SEVEN

The next couple of days passed slowly as we waited excitedly for our first deliveries. I designed some leaflets that we intended to post door to door around the local area to advertise our new business and some 'opening soon' posters. Sitting at the counter with my box of coloured drawing pens and sheets of card I sang along to the radio as I worked.

'You're like a pig in poop there aren't you?' Lorraine said.

'Oink, oink,' I said. She was right. I love doing creative things, even simple tasks like making posters. Before we had a computer in the shop, I spent hours making labels, signs and posters by hand.

Lorraine spent the morning in the office telephoning local newspapers and arranging to place ads.

I stopped for a break at eleven and went into the kitchen to switch on the kettle. I was standing at the sink rinsing the coffee mugs when Lorraine came bounding out of the office.

'Guess what?' she said. 'I've just been on the phone to the advertising features manager at the Daily Echo and she's running a special weekly feature on women in business. Her name is Julie Bradley and she's coming to interview us and take photos and because it's a feature rather than an ad it won't cost us anything!'

'That sounds good,' I said. 'It'll be great publicity. When is she coming?'

'She said about an hour.'

'What? Today?' I said. 'To take photos?'

'That's a point,' said Lorraine looking down at her faded teeshirt and baggy tracksuit bottoms. I wasn't much better, dressed in ripped jeans and one of Peter's old shirts.

'And look at the state of my hair!' I said running up to the washroom to peer in the mirror. I gazed at my reflection in despair. With no make-up to hide my pale wintertime skin and my hair in need of a cut I looked awful. I ran back downstairs and grabbed my bag and coat.

'I'm off to 'Cuts-R-Us', that hair salon up the bank,' I said. 'I need an emergency quick fix.' Lorraine was frantically getting into her coat too.

'I'll nip home and change my clothes and get my make-up bag,' she said and we almost got jammed together in the doorway in our panic to get out.

'Bring a clean top for me to wear,' I yelled over my shoulder as I ran up the bank towards the salon and she ran down it towards her car.

The salon didn't seem particularly busy, having only one elderly lady positioned under a huge domed hairdryer that covered nearly the whole of her face but the stylist seemed to be very put out that I hadn't made an appointment.

'I can't have people walking in off the streets when they feel like it,' she said huffily. I was hoping people would walk into our place off the streets whenever they felt like it and hoped that they would feel like it a lot.

'Take a seat,' she said. 'I'll see what I can do.' She flounced off and I looked at my watch. I was like a cat on hot bricks, worried that I would be late back and miss our big opportunity. I actually only had to wait about ten minutes but it seemed like forever, as it does when you are in a desperate hurry, and by the time I sat in the chair I was stressed.

'What do you want doing with it?' the stylist asked, picking up strands of hair and examining them.

'Just a quick tidy-up,' I said desperate to get it done quickly. 'Whatever you think. I'll leave it to you.' The stylist seemed to cheer up at being given carte blanche with my barnet and stood behind me alternatively fluffing up my hair then flattening it to my head as she considered the options. I wish she'd get on with it, I thought. I wondered what time it was and how long the whole operation would take. I could feel beads of perspiration on my forehead.

'A pageboy,' she said at last. 'Never really in fashion but never really out. A classic style that will take you anywhere.' But I want to look gorgeous, I protested in my head, but sat in silence while she did her stuff. By the time she'd finished, forty-five minutes later, I was close to nervous breakdown.

'There you go,' she said and held up a mirror behind my head. Bloody hell, I thought. Is this payback for not booking an appointment? My fringe had been cut to two inches above my eyebrows and the rest had been left so long it just skimmed my shoulders, giving me the appearance of a medieval simpleton. To make matters worse, my face was bright red from the heat of the dryer.

'Would you like hairspray?' she asked.

'No thanks,' I muttered. To add insult to injury I now had to go and pay for the privilege of being made to look as though I was wearing a very badly fitted wig.

'Thanks very much,' I said, flinging the protective cape from around my shoulders and hastily paying my bill. I didn't bother to leave a tip.

I raced back up the bank to find Lorraine, now dressed in a fawn trousersuit with a pale pink shirt, carefully applying make up. She looked up and her expression turned to one of horror when she saw my hair.

'Where did you go?' she said. 'Cuts-R-Us?'

'No,' I said grabbing a white shirt she was holding out to me. 'I went to 'Bad-Wigs-R-Us'. I ran into the office and quickly changed into Lorraine's shirt. Shame about my ripped jeans but there was no time to do anything about them. Hopefully the photographs would not include my lower half. I slapped on some of Lorraine's blusher and lipstick and stepped into the shop.

'How do I look?' I asked Lorraine, not really sure if I wanted to hear a truthful answer. She looked at me.

'Fine,' she said. 'That blouse suits you. You've always looked good in white.'

'And the hair?' I asked. She hesitated.

'The truth!' I said.

'Well, the fringe is a bit short, but it'll grow.'

'Not before the photograph is taken it won't,' I said picking up Lorraine's make-up mirror.

'Why don't you go back later and ask her to take a little more off the sides and back?' Lorraine suggested. 'The fringe looks shorter because she's left the sides so long. It looks out of proportion.'

'Yes, I think I might just do that,' I said. But there was no time to think about it further as Julie Bradley had arrived with her photographer, Michelle, in tow.

'Right,' she said, after the introductions had been taken care of. 'Michelle has to rush off to another job so if you don't mind we'll do the photos first and then the interviews.'

'Ok,' said Lorraine. 'Where do you want us?' Michelle looked around the shop.

'I think if you stand against the shelves at the back, that's where the best light is,' she said and she started to unpack camera, tripod and lenses. 'Could you just pull up the blinds as far as they will go to let in the maximum amount of light possible?' Lorraine climbed into the window and pulled up the blinds, letting in bright light, then came back to stand with me next to the shelves. I squinted in the direction of the camera. The sun was reflecting off the white surfaces of the shop and the glare from the lens shone straight into our eyes.

'It's bright isn't it?' I said to Lorraine, who also had her face screwed up. Before she had time to answer there was a click and a flash.

'This time turn to face each other,' directed Michelle and we both turned, bumping into each other as the camera clicked and flashed again.

'And looking at me...' said Michelle.

'I can't see!' I said, black spots floating in front of my eyes. I heard Lorraine say: 'My eyes are watering,' and then the click of the camera and I scrunched up my face in anticipation of the following blinding flash.

'That's it,' said Michelle. 'All done,' and began packing away her equipment. Lorraine and I looked at each other. Was that it?

'Would you like a coffee Julie?' Lorraine asked, still blinking rapidly.

'That would be lovely,' Julie replied. Lorraine went into the kitchen and Julie, looking around said, 'It's a lovely big airy shop isn't it?'

'It is,' I said. 'I'm looking forward to seeing it up and running.'

'Have either of you run a business before?' she asked.

'Yes I have,' I said. 'Although not a whole food business.'

'And I used to work for that grotty off-licence over the road,' Lorraine chipped in from the kitchen.

'I'll have to come back when you're open,' Julie said. 'Have a proper look around. You never know, I may become one of your best customers!' she joked.

'I hope so,' I said. 'We could do with a few of those!' Lorraine carried a tray of coffee cups over to the counter and we each took one.

43

'What's happening with the stock?' asked Julie. 'The place looks a bit bare at the moment.'

'Most of it's due to arrive in the next couple of days,' I said. 'We're looking forward to unpacking everything and getting it on the shelves.'

'Especially as we don't even know what half of it is,' joked Lorraine. Julie drank her coffee. I wondered when she was going to start interviewing us. I had loads of answers ready; information I wanted to make sure was included in the article.

'Wasn't this a health shop before?' Julie asked.

'Yes,' I answered, not wanting to go into detail. I gave Lorraine a sideways glance, which unfortunately Julie noticed.

'What happened? Did he run off with all the money or something?' she joked.

'Something like that,' muttered Lorraine.

'What would you like to know about us and our business?' I asked, partly to change the subject and also because I thought it was time we got on with it instead of drinking coffee and chatting.

'Oh I think I've got enough here,' she said.

'But you haven't written anything down,' I said.

'Don't you have one of those little tape recorders?' asked Lorraine.

'I don't think that's necessary today. As I say I've got the basics,' said Julie. 'I can easily pad it out.' She put her cup back on the tray.

'Thanks for the coffee,' she said. 'The article will be in tomorrow's edition. I'll send you a complimentary copy. Bye.' And she was gone.

CHAPTER EIGHT

'I just wondered,' I said timidly. 'Could you possibly take a little more off the sides and back?'

'You don't like it?' the stylist asked in amazement.

'Oh yes I do, I'd just like a little more taken off,' I gabbled. 'But not off the fringe,' I added hastily as she picked up her scissors. Why am I saying this? I thought. Why don't I just tell her she's made a mess of my hair and demand that she put it right? I sat and watched in the mirror as she sprayed my hair with water and combed it. She positioned her scissors just below my ear. That's too short, I thought. Surely she's not going to cut it there. But did I protest? Did I say 'Not that short please?' Did I yell, 'STOP' at the top of my voice? No I did not.

What is it about a hairdresser's chair and plastic cape that turns me into a helpless victim? I simply watched in the mirror as she snipped at my hair, this time leaving me not only with a forehead-revealing fringe but also with a bob cut to just below my ears. Of course as my hair dried, it pulled up making it look even shorter and I left the salon with an above-the-ear bob.

'Don't say anything!' I warned Lorraine as I stomped into the shop, and she didn't, although I could see her struggling not to laugh.

'I'll just make us a pot of tea,' she said hurrying into the kitchen, coughing and spluttering. If this was the reaction from Lorraine then I was not looking forward to the stick I'd get from Peter. From the moment he'd seen my hair last night, he'd been unable to speak to me without adding 'verily sire' to the end of each sentence, which greatly amused him. I'd finally taken the pip when he serenaded me by singing 'with a hey nonny nonny'.

'Oh come on, I'm only joking,' he'd said hugging me. 'You have to see the funny side.'

'Well I'm sure I would,' I'd said sulkily. 'If it were on your head and not mine.'

'There you go,' Lorraine said putting down a cup of tea in front of me. She looked at my hair, struggling to maintain a sympathetic expression. 'I think you should go somewhere else next time,' she said.

'Funnily enough, I'd already thought of that,' I said.

We drank our tea and worked on our sandwich menu. The big dilemma was whether to keep to vegetarian only fillings.

'I really don't want to handle or sell meat,' I said. I'd been vegetarian for a couple of years and felt it would be compromising my principles. Lorraine, who had recently become vegetarian after watching a disturbing documentary about the meat trade and the treatment of animals in abattoirs, agreed.

'I feel the same,' she said, 'but I'm not sure if selling vegetarian only fillings will be feasible. It will limit our market.'

45

'Yes,' I agreed thoughtfully. 'I suppose it would exclude a lot of potential customers, but do we go for profits or principles?' We pondered a while. 'After all,' I said. 'We're not strictly a vegetarian shop we're a health food shop so we could sell organic meats.'

'But do you want to do that?' asked Lorraine. 'I don't.'

'No, I don't.' I said. 'Let's start with a list of veggie fillings first, then we can make a decision.' I pulled over a piece of paper to begin (another) list.

'Right,' said Lorraine. 'Cheese. We can do loads with cheese. Cheese and onion, salad, chutney, coleslaw, tomato.' I scribbled frantically.

'Egg and cress,' I said 'Egg mayo, egg salad.'

'Cottage cheese with salad, pineapple, chives,' Lorraine added.

'What about hummous?' I suggested. 'We could make our own. It's lovely with grated carrot and cress.' Lorraine pulled a face but I wrote it down anyway.

'What about tuna?' she said suddenly. 'As a sort of compromise? We could do it with salad or sweetcorn and mayo. It's popular and it's healthy.'

'Yeah, I could cope with that!' I said and added it to our list.

'I think that's our basic menu,' said Lorraine. 'We can amend it later when we get up and running.'

'How about having a 'Daily Special'?' I suggested. 'Something a bit different, a bit more exciting.'

'Such as?'

'I don't know. What ever you think. Stilton and apricot chutney? Or kidney bean pate with salad. Or peanut butter and banana. Or...'

'Stilton and apricot chutney. That'll do to start with,' said Lorraine.

'Are we going to make to order, or have them ready made?'

'I think making to order would be best,' said Lorraine. 'We could have everything ready in tubs in the fridge and people could design their own sandwiches, and have them made fresh.'

'That's a good slogan, Design your own sandwich. I'll put it on the leaflet. We could have lots of different types of bread rolls, white, wholemeal, granary, and seeded ones and that would give even more combinations.'

'Let's cost them out and decide on pricing then we can get the details on the leaflet and get it to the printers,' said Lorraine.

We were doing this when Nige arrived with the morning post.

'Holy smoke!' he said looking at me. 'New hairdo?'

'Don't mention the hair!' hissed Lorraine, in an exaggerated aside whisper. I'd forgotten about it for a while and now immediately my hand moved involuntarily to my head.

'It's a sore subject,' I said.

'Yes,' he said, looking at my hair and rolling his eyes. 'I can see why darlin'. Never mind. It'll grow.' He handed over our post and searching through the pile I found the copy of the Daily Echo. I leafed through it to find the article.

'Oh my God!' I said, as when turning a page I was confronted with a quarter page photograph of Lorraine and myself. I spread the pages on the counter and Lorraine and Nige huddled around to take a look. For a moment

Lorraine and I could only stare in horror. Nige however, took one look and collapsed over the counter, shaking with hysterical laughter.

'Look at the state of us!' Lorraine said. The picture showed us standing in front of our empty shelves caught in the flashlight like two startled rabbits. Lorraine was wide-eyed; a look akin to mock surprise on her face, while I stood with hunched shoulders and face screwed up, eyes squinting. As for my hairstyle, the less said the better.

'We look like a right couple of divvies,' I said.

'Well I agree with that,' chortled Nige wiping tears from his eyes. 'It's made my day that, cheered me up. Eeeh, you should have it framed!' and again he collapsed into a helpless giggling heap. Lorraine suddenly clutched my arm.

'The photo's not the worst of it,' she said. 'Listen to this,' and she began to read from the page:

'Sisters Lorraine Melville (24) and Christine Kenworthy (49) have together created 'Nutmeg Wholefoods' an innovative new health food business situated on Station Road, Fordham.'

'Forty nine?' I said. 'They've got me down as forty nine?' Nige gave one of his high-pitched giggles.

'How old are you then?' he spluttered.

'Well not forty nine!' I said. 'I'm only twenty-nine. They've added on twenty years.'

'Well mind, you look forty-nine in that photo,' said Nige and he was off again, laughing uncontrollably at his own wit.

'Don't you have letters to deliver?' I yelled at him.

'Not until I've heard the rest of this,' he said.

'Sshh!' said Lorraine. 'Listen, it gets worse.

'The sisters admitted that although they have no experience of the health food trade, they are confident that their experience in selling wine and antiques will enable them to make a success of 'Nutmeg'. The girls are looking forward to their first delivery of stock arriving and Lorraine said 'We don't even know what half of it is.' Christine commented that they would need lots of customers. The business is sure to be a great improvement on the previous owner who is rumoured to have left under shady circumstances.'

Lorraine paused.

'I can't believe she's printed that,' I said, leaning over to have a look. 'Is that it?'

'It just goes on to give a brief outline of what we intend to stock and gives our proposed opening date,' Lorraine said and she threw the paper down in disgust.

'We didn't say those things did we?' I asked Lorraine.

'We said some of it,' said Lorraine. 'But she's been very selective in what she's included.'

'They're like that, reporters,' said Nige. 'Inaccurate facts, selective reporting. I should know after what poor Gus has had to put up with. He can't even go to the supermarket for the shopping, I have to go because he says he might get mobbed by reporters and photographers.'

'That was supposed to be good publicity for us,' I said miserably. 'It's just made us look a laughing stock.'

'If we'd paid for it I'd sue her,' said Lorraine.

'Oh come on girls,' said Nige, putting an arm around each of us. 'Let's keep things in perspective. Those ugly mugs will be wrapped around someone's fish and chips by tomorrow.'

At three, Peter telephoned to tell me that he'd just seen the article.

'Did you really say those things?' he asked.

'Sort of,' I answered.

'I can't believe how bad it is. And the photo! You look like an advert for a pantomime.' He obviously had the article in front of him as he kept going off into great guffaws of laughter.

'Something I'd like to warn you about,' I said. 'I've had my hair cut again and it's even worse than before.'

'No.' he said. 'Impossible!'

'I look like Friar Tuck,' I said ignoring his remark, 'without the bald patch.'

'It can't be that bad,' he laughed.

'Well it is. So I don't need any monk jokes thank you very much.'

'Ok,' he said. 'No jokes. I'm sure you still look gorgeous whatever your hair's like.'

Later, when he came to pick me up he looked at me and grinned in amusement. I held up my hand.

'No comments, thank you,' I reminded him.

'Ok,' he said, peering around the back of my head, but it was too difficult for him to resist.

'Didn't you get a bit suspicious when she put the pudding basin on your head?'

'No jokes, you promised,' I said huffily. 'Can't you see I'm upset. You should be trying to help me find a way to put it right instead of taking the mick.'

'I'm sorry,' he said seriously, then looked at me and said 'What about shaving off your eyebrows and painting some on further up?'

CHAPTER NINE

I awoke on Friday morning to the sound of rain pelting against the bedroom window. After a solid night's sleep I was still dog-tired, my body ached and I had to force myself to climb out of bed. Pulling back the curtain I sleepily peered outside. The sky was dark, overcast with heavy black rain clouds. Resisting the urge to climb back into my warm bed and snuggle into Peter who was still sleeping peacefully, I turned on the shower and stepped in.

I managed, with the help of a bottle of styling mousse, to blow dry my hair to a softer looking style and made even the fringe look a lot better by drying it to one side. I ran some gel through it with my fingers and ended up with a tousled, slightly messy look.

'Not bad,' I said to myself in the mirror and Peter even gave a grunt of approval across the breakfast table when he saw it.

It was still raining heavily when I arrived at the shop. I made a pot of tea, and Lorraine arrived just as I was pouring out two mugs.

'Morning,' I said, handing her one. I reached under the counter for my clipboard of lists.

'Friday. First delivery to arrive should be Karma at around nine-thirty, then Saffron Chilled and Frozen, then Wild Country herbal teas, then…'

'Yeah, yeah, I know,' said Lorraine. 'They're all arriving today. Just give me a chance to wake up, I'm exhausted.' She lugged a parcel onto the counter.

'We need to go out and deliver these sometime too,' she said. 'The leaflets. I called at the printers on the way in to collect them.' She tore open the packet and handed me a sheet.

'Hey these are good!' I said pleased. 'They look very professional. Very eye-catching.'

'They gave us quite a substantial discount too, as a good-will gesture to welcome us to the bank.'

'That was good of them,' I said.

'They're really lovely people,' Lorraine said, dipping a chocolate cookie into her mug of tea. 'Family business. They were so friendly and helpful. They're going to drop in and see us when we open.' I looked out of the window at the rain.

'We really need to get these delivered today or tomorrow if we're opening for business on Monday,' I said. We turned to watch sheets of water running down the glass. 'Let's hope it clears up by lunchtime,' I said. 'We should be finished sorting the stock by then.'

How wrong we were! The first delivery to arrive was the Karma order, which covered the whole shop floor with sacks, boxes and crates. We started to unpack and stack stock onto the shelves, which was a slow process, as everything had to be located and checked off on the delivery note, then priced and placed. Every so often we would unpack something that would not fit into its allocated space and would have to re-organise the whole shop to accommodate it. We spent hours having conversations such as: 'if we move the cereals to *there*, and the dried fruit to there, then beans and lentils would fit *here* and we can move the flour to over *there*…' only to start again ten minutes later.

Nige arrived with our post and climbed over the piles of boxes to hand it to me.

'Holy polony!' he exclaimed. 'Look at all this stuff!' He read some of the labels on the packages. 'Hazelnuts, brazils, peanuts, cashews, almonds… hey, is this a nut shop or what?'

'Feels like I'm in a nut shop sometimes,' I said. I looked around at the piles of boxes.

'Fancy staying to help?' I asked him.

'I'll put the kettle on and make you both a cuppa,' he said, clambering over a pile of sacks to get to the kitchen. 'You both look exhausted.'

'We are,' said Lorraine. 'We've loads to do before Monday.'

'Hey Nige,' I said. 'Do you think you could deliver some leaflets for us while you're on your round?'

'No chance,' he said. 'Sorry darlin'. I'd love to help but it's more than my job's worth. Not allowed, see. Not unless you pay the Post Office.'

'We're going to have to do it ourselves,' I said. 'But I don't know how we'll fit it in before Monday.'

'Take my advice,' Nige said. 'Pay someone to do it. It's not an easy job you know. Grappling with gates, fighting off vicious dogs, not to mention being out in all weathers,' he nodded towards the window at the rain.

'We can't afford it Nige,' said Lorraine. 'Honestly we're totally skint. It's taken everything we've got and more to get this place to this stage in the game.'

'A couple of students might be glad of a bit of beer money. You wouldn't have to pay much,' he said. 'There's plenty of students in the flats above these shops.'

'When I say skint, I mean *skint*,' Lorraine said. 'We're cleaned out. Nothing left.'

'We'll do it ourselves,' I said. 'It shouldn't take long.' I was sure Nige was exaggerating. It couldn't be that difficult to post a few leaflets.

As usual Nige drank coffee and watched us work then left to finish his delivery round under the impression that he'd been a great help.

'See you soon, have fun in the nut shop!' he said.

We were less than halfway through sorting the Karma consignment when the next load arrived in an enormous refrigerated lorry and so the Karma stock was temporarily abandoned while we hurried to fill the fridges and freezers.

It felt as though we were taking one step forwards and two back, as each time we cleared a bit of space, another vanload of goods arrived. The kitchen became littered with mountains of empty boxes and packaging and the counter was festooned with delivery notes, invoices and odd packets and jars that at present could not be found a home.

Peter arrived at lunchtime and went out to get us sandwiches. I boiled the kettle and made drinks while he was out.

'I can't see and end to this,' said Lorraine wearily piling packets of wheatgerm onto a shelf. 'This is just the pre-packed stuff, we've got those big sacks to tackle next.' We'd bought a lot of our staples, red lentils, oats, rice, museli and the likes in twenty-five kilo bags, which needed to be weighed and re-packaged into five hundred gram bags and then labelled with product details, weight and sell-by date.

'Do you think we'll get everything done by Monday?' I asked. I sat on a crate and looked at her. We were both weary, drained of energy and enthusiasm. Lorraine sat down heavily and sighed.

'I think we may have been a little over optimistic. We have two and a half days to sort this mess and deliver the leaflets.'

'And there's the window to dress and I need to write up all these invoices into the ledger,' I said.

'The accounts could wait until next week, couldn't they?' Lorraine asked.

'Yes I suppose they could, as long as we're careful not to lose any paperwork. I just want to keep on top of it. If it piles up too much I'll get into a muddle.'

Peter returned with the sandwiches and we ate and drank as we worked.

'I can't see you getting through all this today,' he said. 'Can't you change your opening day, give yourselves a couple more days?'

'We've just been discussing that,' I said. 'I don't think we could. All the posters and leaflets have been printed with Monday's date and we have fresh bread and quiches and stuff ordered for delivery on Monday morning.' I opened a box and pulled out some bottles.

'In that case,' he said, 'I'll ring around and see if we can get some help,' and he disappeared into the office.

'Aaagghh! How irritating!' I yelled as I realised that I would have to move everything on the shelves along by about four inches to fit in some bottles of sesame oil.

'Can't you just put them somewhere else?' snapped Lorraine as I picked up packets and roughly slapped them down further along the shelf, which meant that the stock that she had just arranged also had to be moved.

'No I can't just put them somewhere else, actually,' I barked back at her. 'If we're going to have any kind of logical layout in here, sesame oil needs to go beside olive oil, walnut oil and sunflower oil.'

'Well pardon me,' Lorraine said. 'I wouldn't want you to have a nervous breakdown at the sight of a bottle in the wrong place.' I felt my temper rush up from my toes and I yelled, 'Well what's the point of just hoying stuff on the shelves anywhere? We've spent every penny we've got on this and used

51

every last ounce of energy. I'm not going to spoil it over such a stupid little detail.' Lorraine turned around and kicked out at a nearby box.

'All right, keep your hair on!' she yelled 'If you didn't spend so much time fannying about we might have been finished by now.' I slammed the bottles down on the counter and put my hands on my hips.

'Yes well while I'm fannying about in here,' I screeched, 'you're out there puffing and blowing on your cigarettes so don't you dare stand there and accuse me of wasting time.'

'It's none of your business what I do,' yelled Lorraine. 'I don't complain about your irritating habits!' I looked at her in shock.

'That's because I don't have any,' I said.

'Ha!' she said. 'How about your obsession with lists to start off with? Lists of this, lists of that. I bet you've got one listing each time you fart.' I was cut to the quick. Surely I wasn't that bad. I decided that the best method of defence was attack.

'Great advert you are for a health shop, standing outside smoking like a trouper,' I fired.

'CHIMNEY!' Lorraine shouted into my face.

'WHAT?'

'CHIMNEY!' she yelled. 'I smoke like a CHIMNEY!'

'I know you do. And it's DISGUSTING!'

'I didn't mean that,' she started to say then changed her mind and flung a packet of bran at my head.

'BUGGER OFF!' she screamed and grabbing her bag stomped over a pile of boxes and out of the door slamming it behind her.

'What on earth…?' said Peter coming out of the office. 'I've been on the phone, I could hardly hear with you two screaming at each other like a couple of banshees.'

'Well she said I waste time just because I like to make everything perfect,' I said sulkily as I started opening another box.

'Yes I know, I heard,' he said. 'And you had a go at her for smoking.' I ignored him and pulled out some bottles of biodegradable washing-up liquid. Damn. We hadn't allocated space for non-food items.

'Look it's no good huffing with me or fighting with Lorraine,' he said.

'I'm not huffing,' I said. 'I'm just getting on.'

'Yeah, right.' said Peter. 'Look, you're both stressed and over-tired. You need to pull together, you're so close to finishing, don't let it go now.' He was right. As he annoyingly usually is. He opened the door and called to Lorraine who was sheltering from the rain in the bus stop, smoking a cigarette.

'Hey! Fag Ash Lil.' he yelled. 'Get back in here!' Lorraine dropped her half-smoked cigarette and trod on it then marched into the shop.

'What?' she asked aggressively.

'Never mind 'what'!' he said. 'If we're going to get this show on the road you two need to stop shouting at each other like a couple of tired toddlers and get on with it.' Lorraine and I looked at each other, both of us trying to maintain a menacing expression. Lorraine gave in first.

'Sorry,' she said reluctantly. 'I'm trying to give up smoking, but it's really hard.'

'I know,' I said. 'And this might surprise you but I don't actually keep a list of when I fart.'

'She keeps one of when I do though,' said Peter and the argument dissolved. He was used to our rare but explosive rows that erupted from nothing and subsided just as quickly.

'Now that's over and done with you'd better get on,' he said. 'There's a load to do. I'll get back as soon as I can. I've made some phone calls, your Dad's on his way over, and my Mam and Dad will be here in about an hour. Your Mam, Irene and Susan will be here as soon as they finish work. I couldn't get hold of Anth, Margy or Karen but I've left messages on their machines. Better go, see you later.' He kissed me and was gone and Lorraine and I continued with our never-ending task, dispute forgotten.

My Dad arrived first and set about taking the empty boxes and packaging to the tip. Each time he returned we had a new load waiting for him.

Joan and Roy arrived and set to work in the kitchen weighing dried goods from the huge sacks. Later when Susan and Irene arrived they joined in and a production line was set up with sacks, scales, bags and labels lined up along the kitchen worktops.

I unpacked a box containing recycled carrier bags and a sheaf of tissue paper for wrapping loaves of bread. I faffed about arranging them under the counter near the till along with pens, receipt books and spare till rolls, and was enjoying myself thoroughly until it suddenly dawned on me that this was probably the kind of thing that Lorraine meant so I hastily left them and edged around the counter to continue unpacking before I was spotted.

At four my Mam made coffee that we drank while we worked and at five-thirty we ordered pizzas from the local takeaway and stopped for a break. While we were sitting chatting I flicked through my lists of jobs taking great satisfaction in crossing out those completed. Near the bottom of one of the lists was written 'Katharine Stewart, seven-thirty Friday, eggs'. Its meaning suddenly dawned on me and I said, 'What time is it?' as I jumped up to look at the clock on the wall behind the counter. Six-forty.

'We need to be in Thornbury Newton at seven-thirty to see Katharine Stewart about free-range eggs,' I said.

'Oh bugger!' Lorraine said. 'I'd completely forgotten.'

'It'll take about an hour to get there,' said Peter. 'Why don't you ring her and put it off until later in the week?'

'Because we won't have time,' I said.

'And we need free-range eggs for opening day, for the shelves and for our sandwich fillings,' added Lorraine. I searched through the papers on my clipboard for the address.

'Why don't you go with Peter and I'll keep things going here?' Lorraine suggested. 'It's just a case of checking that the birds are truly free-range and if so buying enough eggs to last our first week.' 'Ok then,' I said. 'Let's go.' Peter grabbed his car keys and we rushed off.

CHAPTER TEN

'Got the address?' Peter asked as we climbed into the car.

'Yes,' I said. 'Head for Thornbury Newton and I'll look it up on the map as we go.'

Katharine Stewart's farm was in a remote vale a couple of miles past the village of Thornbury Newton and proved extremely difficult to locate.

'Down there!' I said, pointing to a dirt track on the right hand side of the road. Peter jumped on the brakes and the car swerved across the road and we shot into the narrow opening and along a bumpy earth track. After being bumped and shaken for twenty minutes, the road suddenly petered out into a field. Peter stopped the car and I studied the map.

'I think you took a wrong turning,' I said, following the road on the map with my finger.

'I took a wrong turning?' Peter said good-humouredly. 'You're the one with the map.'

'Well I could hardly read the map when my brain was being rattled about in my head could I?' I said. I showed him the map. 'Look, that's where we went wrong. We need to turn around and go back down the track we've just come along.' Peter turned the car around and we set off again back down the dirt track.

The rain had stopped and there was a break in the clouds allowing bright sunshine to stream through. Trees and hills threw long shadows across the landscape, and I watched lambs nestling into their mothers as we drove past. I glanced at Peter and noticed how attractive he looked in the rosy evening light as he concentrated on guiding the car around the potholes in the road. It's ages since we had a nice relaxing evening together, I thought as we bumped along. I realised how tired I was, how intense about the shop I'd become. It took up every waking moment - if I wasn't working in it I was thinking about it and making plans for it. I wished we were just out for an evening drive, looking for a country pub to visit. Sitting in a cosy room next to a roaring fire, or outside having a drink and perhaps a bar meal watching the sun go down. Chatting and telling each other about funny events that had occurred during our day. And then a leisurely drive home listening to music on the cassette player.

'Oh no,' said Peter, breaking into my thoughts. 'Look at that.' As we skirted a bend, the road ahead was obscured by a white bleating mass. As we slowed down, the sheep enveloped the car and we came to a standstill.

'Shouldn't there be a shepherd or something?' I asked.

'They've probably just wandered down from the hill,' Peter said. 'Get out and shift them.'

'What me?' I said. 'No chance.'

'Go on. Sheep are scared of anything. Just clap your hands or shout or something and they'll move.'

'Well if it's so easy you do it.'

'I need to manoeuvre the car.'

'Get lost, I'm not going out there.'

'We'll be late for the farm. Remember you need those eggs.'

'Oh all right!' I said. Reluctantly I opened the car door and gently pushed against the fleecy bodies trying to make room to squeeze out.

'Shift!' I said to them. 'Shoo! Move!' Cautiously I pushed my way through the jostling flock holding my hands up at shoulder height as I went. I'd never been this close to sheep before and I wasn't enjoying the experience.

'Shoo!' I said. 'Move, get off the road!' I could hear Peter laughing behind the driving wheel and I turned and frowned at him.

'Shoo! Go on! Off the road you stupid creatures!' Unfortunately my attempts to scare them off the road only served to agitate them and they became skittish and flustered. They huddled closer together, bahing and gurgling in their panic, crushing me amongst them. I too began to panic now.

'Help!' I called to Peter but he was helpless with laughter. I was wedged between two sheep's bottoms and I screamed in dismay as one of them cocked its stubby tail and peppered me with black pellets. Peter's laughter reached new heights.

'SHOO!' I was screeching now and I clapped my hands and waved them hysterically. 'SHOO!' One of the animals at the edge of the cluster impulsively broke from the crowd and sprinted up the craggy grass verge and with much bleating and pushing the troop followed, carrying me along with them. I staggered along with them upwards over scrubby grass and boulders, shrieking loudly, until I stumbled on a rock and the sheep dispersed leaving me face down in the grass. I heard Peter scramble out of the car.

'Are you all right?' he asked, helping me to my feet, and then realising that I was, began laughing again.

'Let's just go and get the bloody eggs,' I barked and I brushed myself down and marched back to the car. Peter started the car and we drove off. Giving me a sideways glance he laughed and took my hand and squeezed it, and of course, like always my anger dissolved and seeing the humour of the situation I laughed with him. I can never stay angry with him for very long; those deep brown eyes of his can melt me with a look.

Katharine Stewart turned out to be a widow with four young sons, who after the death of her husband had refused to listen to advice to sell up and move into the village, and also the offer of a job in the village shop. She had fought to keep her farm, determined to keep the business running for her boys until they were old enough to inherit. This had necessitated selling off the dairy herd and leasing out land to other farmers, whilst increasing the poultry stock from a handful of layers providing enough eggs for family use to several hundreds of birds kept in free range conditions. I admired her determination and courage and after a chat over a cup of tea and a quick look around the farm I arranged to ring her the following week to give her our next egg order. She took our address so that in future she could deliver the eggs to us and waved us off with two crates of her fresh free-range eggs on the back seat.

It was nearly twenty to ten when we got back to the shop, and although we could see an amazing difference from when we left, everyone was tired and downhearted at how much more there was still to do. However, after yet more coffee and a re-telling of the sheep incident along with actions and sound effects by Peter, our spirits soon lifted and we soldiered on.

As it got late, people started packing up and leaving, both Joan and my Mam telling us not to work too late and to make sure we had a good night's sleep. Peter, Lorraine and I worked on and on in virtual silence, our actions mechanical, until eventually Peter said, 'This is ridiculous, it's two-thirty we need to go home.' I looked at him.

'Two-thirty?' I repeated. 'In the morning?' We had gone beyond tiredness and were working on autopilot. I felt slow and dull minded. Lorraine was pale faced and wide-eyed and I suspected I looked the same.

'Let's tidy up and call it a day,' I said.

'No, let's forget tidying up and just go,' Lorraine said. 'I'm shattered.' So we left everything as it was, just picking up coats and bags and headed out into the cool quiet street. The damp pavements glistened in the yellow glow of the street lamps as we walked to the cars.

'Goodnight,' I said to Lorraine in a hushed voice. 'Drive carefully.'

'Goodnight,' she answered. 'See you back here at eight-thirty to deliver those leaflets.' I groaned. Eighty-thirty. That was less than six hours away and all I could think of was my bed.

CHAPTER ELEVEN

'Right, here we go,' Lorraine said and we stepped outside, each clutching a photocopied map of the area surrounding the shop, the streets we intended to deliver to highlighted in bright yellow marker pen. We each carried a stack of leaflets that were heavier than I'd anticipated, and I was already regretting refusing my Mam's offer of her shopping trolley before we'd reached our starting point.

We made our way along our planned route, alternatively striding in and out of pathways, overtaking each other as we posted our precious leaflets.

'I wish we'd thought of folding them before we came out!' I grumbled stopping in front of a door to fold the sheet of paper before posting it. At first I'd carefully folded each one into three before sliding it through the letterbox, but now I roughly scrunched them in half before stuffing them in.

'I'm tired already,' panted Lorraine as she marched past me to take the next house.

As Nige had warned, gates proved to be a pain. We encountered all sorts of perplexing devices designed to keep gates fastened. Bolts, latches, boulders, bent nails, iron bars, pieces of rope tied in intricate knots, all of which had to be unfastened and then secured again behind us. One gate was bound with a chain and padlock and I deliberated for a few seconds as to whether it would be worth vaulting it, but decided I did not have the energy or the inclination and so passed on to the next gate.

Letterboxes were also a conundrum. There were the ones placed about an inch from the foot of the door, which meant balancing a pile of leaflets on one arm whilst crouching down to extract a leaflet, folding it and posting it with one hand while holding the flap open with the other. Some letterboxes were placed so high you had to practically jump to reach them and there were a few that Lorraine had to give up on and leave for Peter. There were also the spring-loaded variety that trap your fingers as the flap is released, which after the fourth or fifth time you cease to be aware of due to the numbness at the end of the digits.

'I'm beginning to have a whole new respect for Nige,' I said to Lorraine who strode past me as I wrestled with a gate latch. I slid a leaflet out of my bundle in preparation as I walked along the path. Suddenly a huge hairy shape flew at me over a flowerbed, snarling and barking. I turned on my heels and fled, leaflets fluttering in my wake, and clanged the gate shut as the dog's glistening teeth snapped behind me. I leaned against the wall panting in shock as Lorraine, laughing loudly came to see if I was all right.

I subsequently scanned every property for signs of canine activity before entering, and passed by any gates behind which dogs lurked. I even left an inoffensive looking Yorkshire Terrier to sleep peacefully in his porch undisturbed. Once (nearly) bitten, twice shy.

After a couple of hours we were footsore and weary. I was limping slightly due to a painful blister on the back of my heel and Peter had a bleeding finger caused by an attack from an angry letterbox. Lorraine had suffered an unpleasant encounter with an objectionable man who had told her to get off his property and stick her leaflet up her backside. Lorraine and I were ready to call it a day but Peter was adamant we should not give up until every sheet was delivered.

'But it's starting to rain,' I whinged, longing to go home to a hot bath and a glass of red wine.

'No, he's right,' Lorraine said. 'Every leaflet could potentially bring a customer.'

We slogged on, uphill, downhill, around cul-de-sacs, up and down blocks of flats and in and out of ridiculously long drives, while the rain grew steadily heavier. It seeped through my jacket making my shoulders ache with the damp weight of it. My hair was soaked and dripping, my hands wet and smarting. Lorraine and I grumbled incessantly about being tired and cold and about the weather and gates and letterboxes, but Peter remained cheerful and marched ahead of us giving encouraging remarks so we grumbled about him too.

The intensity of the rain increased until it stung our faces and hands like tiny needles and ricocheted off the pavements.

'Can't we go back now?' I pleaded, shouting above the reverberating noise of the rain. I had stuffed my remaining leaflets down the front of my jacket in an attempt to keep them dry, but the simple act of extracting and folding one rendered it a useless soggy mess, and I found myself shoving handfuls of ink-smeared pulp through the last few letterboxes.

At last every sheet was delivered and we waddled back through torrential rain, three pitiful apparitions of weariness.

Inside the shop we looked at each other and laughed weakly, I think more from nervous exhaustion than from humour. I looked at the clock.

'Half past three!' I said. 'We've been out for seven hours. No wonder we're exhausted and starving! I think we should go home and have the rest of the day off.'

'Hear, hear!' said Lorraine, trying to dry her hair with a tea towel.

'There's still lots to do,' said Peter looking around.

'Well I couldn't work in these wet clothes anyway,' I said. 'These jeans are sticking to my bum.'

'And we need to have lunch,' said Lorraine. 'I'm starving.'

'We could go home and change and eat then meet back here at say, six?' suggested Peter. I looked at Lorraine and interpreted her expression.

'Sorry Peter,' I said. 'You've been out voted this time. We're going home and having a night off.'

'Hot bath here I come,' said Lorraine, and we trudged back out into the rain, leaving him to lock the door.

The next day was Sunday. One day to go to the grand opening. We started work as usual with a pot of tea. Lorraine worked on the shop floor, finishing off the last few tasks, putting up posters, tweaking displays, making sure everything had a price label and generally tidying up.

With much enthusiasm I climbed into the window area to arrange the display, taking with me as many colourful foods as I could find. Scoops of red, green and brown lentils. Black beans, creamy butter beans, maroon kidney beans, speckled pinto beans and spotted black-eyed beans. Pots of herbs, glass jars of earthy coloured spices; tumeric, ginger, garam masala, cumin, paprika, cloves, coriander seeds. Whole nutmegs, bundles of cinnamon sticks, vanilla pods and bouquet garni tied up in little muslin circles.

Over the last few weeks I had gathered a collection of containers, earthenware pots, baskets and glass jars and some offcuts of fabric to drape over the shelves.

I was engrossed in arranging some of Katharine's free-range eggs in a basket when something caught my eye. A man on the other side of the road was watching me. He was dressed in a suit and held a briefcase as he stood outside the wine store. He smiled across at me and I realised who he was. Ferris the Ferret.

'Lorraine,' I called. 'Does the Ferret know who I am?'

'Don't think so,' she said. 'Why?' The Ferret raised his hand and waved at me. I waved back.

'Does he know that you're involved with this shop?' I asked. 'No. Julie thought it best not to mention it to him just in case he decided to cause trouble for us in some way.' The Ferret winked and leered at me. I kept my smile fixed on my face.

'Why do you ask?' Lorraine asked again.

'Because the arrogant sod is leering at me from the other side of the road,' I said, still smiling coyly in his direction. I beckoned him over and he straightened his tie and sauntered across, oblivious to the traffic until a car blasted its horn at him. Lorraine peered through the shelves, making sure that she couldn't be seen.

He's coming over!' she said 'The slime-ball!' He reached the kerb and swaggered towards the window giving me a leering wink. I waited until he was standing close to the glass then I leaned forward and looked into his eyes. Smiling sweetly I made a very rude gesture and mouthed some choice expressions at him. His leer immediately dropped and his face reddened with anger as he quickly slunk off up the bank. I know it was very immature of me but it was just a little sweet revenge and Lorraine found it very amusing.

CHAPTER TWELVE

'That's it we're finished,' I said.

'At last!' said Lorraine. 'What do you think?' I looked around at our creation.

'I think it's perfect. It looks great.'

We wallowed in self-pride as we wandered around admiring our handiwork. Everything was clean and sparkling. The shelves were full and beautifully arranged and the displays artistically set out. The fridges were filled with great glass dishes of olives and capers, coleslaw, potato salad and hummous. There were trays of delicious savoury pastries; spinach and ricotta, mushroom and nut, curried vegetables, tomato with chickpea and basil, fetta and olive, and cheddar and broccoli. Next to them stood huge quiches and plates of onion bhajis, vegetable samosas and pakora. Spring rolls and filo parcels filled with mixed vegetables and cashew nuts, feta and spinach and spiced peppers were piled on stainless steel plates. The kitchen looked clean and fresh with utensils laid out neatly ready for the morning.

We collected our bags and coats, and after one last look to make sure we hadn't missed anything, opened the door to leave.

'Just a minute,' Lorraine said, and she delved into her handbag. Extracting a shiny new penny she walked across to the counter and dropped it into the till.

'To bring us luck!' she said.

'Hope it works,' I said and we walked back to the door unable to take our eyes away from the fruit of our labour. Suddenly my eye rested on the giant-sized tins of tuna stacked on the shelves at the back of the kitchen.

'Tin opener,' I said. 'We don't have one.'

'Oh man,' said Lorraine. 'Just when we thought we were finished.'

'We'll have to call at the supermarket on the way home,' I said. 'Come on, they close early on a Sunday,' and I pushed her, grumbling, out of the door.

'I didn't know they stocked all this,' I said as we walked down the 'Healthy' aisle at SuperSaver Supermarket that was filled with boxes of veggie-burger mix, cous cous and lentils.

'Same prices as ours though,' said Lorraine, 'and not such a good selection as we have.'

'We'll have to focus on the more unusual items that they can't sell in big enough quantities to warrant stocking,' I said, 'because there's no way we can compete with them directly.'

'Yeah, I think you're right,' said Lorraine. 'We need to keep one step ahead. I notice there's no organic produce here, we have a really good selection so we need to push lines like that.' A woman stopped next to us to fill her basket with packets and boxes.

'We should tell her we've got a much better selection,' said Lorraine.

'I've got some leaflets in the bottom of my bag,' I said. 'Let's give them out to likely looking customers.'

'We can't do that,' Lorraine said. 'We can't tout for business in someone else's shop. We'll get thrown out!'

'Only if we get caught,' I said. 'Go on, you do your sales pitch and I'll keep tooty.' I slunk up and down the aisle keeping watch for any of the sales assistants as Lorraine gave out leaflets and spread the word about Nutmeg's opening day.

'Hadn't we better get what we came for?' Lorraine asked when we'd run out of leaflets.

'What's that? Oh yes. Tin opener.' We found one fairly quickly and made our way through the checkout.

'Did you keep the receipt for our accounts?' I asked Lorraine as we walked past the cigarette kiosk toward the exit.

'Yes it's here,' she said, pulling it out of a carrier bag and reading it. 'Look at this, we've been over charged!'

'By how much?'

'Only a pound,' she said. 'We've been charged two ninety-nine instead of one ninety-nine.'

'Well that's another thing we have over supermarkets,' I said. 'Attentive customer service. That would never happen in our shop.'

'Come on, I'm going to Customer Services to get my money back,' Lorraine said. 'I know it's only a pound, but every little helps, and anyway, it's the principle.'

We stood at the un-staffed customer services desk for a few minutes waiting for an assistant.

'Here she comes now,' I said as a plump woman dressed in a lime green tabard with the large red double 'S' logo of SuperSavers on the front squeezed her ample rear end behind the desk.

'Hello,' began Lorraine. 'I wonder if you could help me...' The woman, oblivious to Lorraine's request, picked up a microphone that was hooked to the wall behind the desk and said into it '*Mr Thompson to the checkouts, Mr Thompson to the checkouts,*' her voice rising and falling in the singsong tone that all tannoy operators seem to be trained in. Her amplified voice echoed around the store as she repeated, '*Mr Thompson to the checkouts, Mr Thompson to the checkouts*,' then apparently satisfied, replaced the microphone and disappeared, leaving Lorraine and I alone with our over priced tin opener.

'Are you thinking what I'm thinking?' asked Lorraine, her green eyes gleaming. I looked at her blankly.

'I'm thinking that those tabards are not very stylish,' I said. 'I think a fitted style would look more shapely and...' Lorraine tutted.

'Hold that,' she said, thrusting the tin opener at me and I watched, perplexed as she moved behind the desk and picked up the microphone.

'You wouldn't dare!' I said, but she did.

'*Looking for something healthy and delicious? Then don't waste your time here, visit Nutmeg Wholefoods, opening tomorrow.*' I laughed in disbelief as her voice reverberated above me.

'*For all your health food requirements, herbal teas, cereals, pulses, nuts and dried fruits. Freshly made sandwiches daily at Nutmeg Wholefoods, Station Road...*'

'Quick!' I said. 'She's coming!' SuperSaver woman was tanking down the washing powder aisle like a woman with a mission, her face like thunder.

'*I repeat, Nutmeg Wholefoods, Station Road, opening tomorrow,*' piped Lorraine's voice and I grabbed our tin opener with one hand and Lorraine with the other and we scarpered.

CHAPTER THIRTEEN

After an interminable night of sporadic dozing and tossing and turning I finally fell asleep only to be immediately awakened by my alarm clock. Monday. It was here at last. Opening day. Today Nutmeg Wholefoods, the finished product of weeks of careful planning, inventive creativity and sheer hard work would be opened to the public to be viewed and appraised. Today we would be at the mercy of the local residents, whose approval, respect, disinterest or scorn would forge the direction of our future. Certainly today's trading would give us a huge indication of how our chances of success lay.

Unable to eat breakfast due to a mixture of excitement and nervous tension, I showered, blow-dried my hair and was raking through my wardrobe frantically pulling out clothes when Peter came in carrying a tray.

'Do these trousers make my bum look big?' I asked him.

'No. Your bum's just big, nothing to do with the trousers.' I ripped them off and threw them onto the pile of other rejected clothes.

'I was only joking,' Peter said. 'They look great,' he said. 'Put them back on.' But I'd moved on to skirts.

'I've made you tea and toast,' he said, putting the tray onto the bed next to a pile of discarded clothes. 'You should eat something.'

'Thanks,' I said inattentively as I held up two skirts and inspected them in the mirror. I decided on the plain black pencil skirt worn with a crisp white blouse. I wanted to look professional but not too formal, approachable but not too casual. I managed to eat a triangle of toast and I drank my cup of tea as I slapped on make-up.

'Do I look ok?' I asked Peter who had returned to retrieve the tray.

'Gorgeous,' he said, without looking. 'We need to leave in a couple of minutes, I'm going to get the car out.' I looked in the mirror, scrutinising my appearance, my nerves getting the better of me. I look as though I'm wearing a uniform, I thought, in a last minute panic. I look like a waitress. Scrambling through the racks at the foot of my wardrobe I quickly selected a pair of high-heeled black sling-backs from my mound of shoes and put on a gold necklace and earrings. I still wasn't really happy with my appearance but I heard Peter calling so I pulled a black jacket from the rail and hurried downstairs.

'Will you be comfortable in those shoes?' he asked as I staggered to the car. 'You'll be on your feet all day.' Peter can never grasp the fact that women's shoes and comfort are not connected.

'My feet are the least of my worries,' I said. The butterflies in my stomach had now evolved into monsters trying to fight their way out. All sorts of worries, some completely irrational were beginning to surface.

'What if we don't sell very much? What if we don't sell anything at all?' I said to Peter as we drove to the shop. 'Imagine if we sit there all day and no-one even comes in. Or if people complain about what we're selling? Or we get shoplifters? What if we have an armed robbery? We might get gangs of drug addicts wanting money or threatening us with a knife!'

'Chris, calm down,' Peter said calmly. 'The shop's in Fordham not the Bronx. Everything will be just fine. Stop worrying.'

Lorraine was pacing about in the shop when I arrived, obviously in the same state of anxiety as myself. She too had dithered about what to wear and had finally plumped for a pair of smart grey trousers with a pale blue striped blouse, black stilettos and a full face of make up.

'Do you think we've overdone it? We're done up like a pair of dog's doo-dahs,' I said looking at Lorraine's perfect complexion and styled hair. We teetered about leaving wafts of perfume in our wake.

'Nah,' said Lorraine. 'We're starting as we mean to go on. Setting a standard. We said from the start that we wanted to get away from the old fashioned sandals-and-lentils hippy look.' She finished putting coins into the till drawer and pushed it closed.

'Ready?' she asked. I peered through the blinds on the door.

'My God,' I exclaimed. 'There's a huge queue of people out there.'

'Really?'

'No, only joking,' I opened the door and peered into the street. 'Not a sausage.'

We were in the kitchen haphazardly gathering utensils and ingredients when the jangling of the bell above the door announced the arrival of our first visitor.

'Morning.'

'Morning, Joan,' I said surprised to see her. 'You're our first customer.'

'Not a customer, I'm here to help,' she said. She deposited her bag and coat in the office and emerged wearing an apron. 'Where do you want me to start?' she asked, rolling up her sleeves.

Joan was the grounding force we needed that day. Her down to earth, no-nonsense approach quelled our nerves and our focus cleared, enabling us to face our first day with enthusiasm and confidence restored.

I can still remember vividly the emotions of that first morning, the anticipation and churning anxiety that gradually dissolved as it was replaced with optimism and relief as customers came steadily to browse, to chat and to buy.

Joan insisted on taking on all the behind-the-scenes work, cleaning and chopping salad vegetables, preparing sandwich fillings and washing up, claiming that our time was better spent on the shop floor, getting to know our customers. She was an invaluable help during those first weeks, arriving early each morning to stand at the sink working tirelessly and refusing to be paid for her toil.

Our first customer was an elderly man who entered the shop with the aid of a walking stick, to buy a loaf of wholemeal bread. On hearing the bell, Lorraine and I raced to the counter both wanting to be the one to take the first sale. I got there before her greeting him with a beaming smile and snatching the loaf quickly from the shelf before Lorraine could reach for it. As I meticulously wrapped the loaf, making sure the corners were perfectly mitred, she managed to extract payment and rang it into the till, dropping the coins into the till drawer with a smile of smug satisfaction. She closed the till drawer and bustled ahead of him to open the door as I placed the loaf in his shopping basket. We guided him out of the door.

'Thank you my dears,' he murmured, obviously bemused and a little embarrassed at being fussed over so attentively.

'Goodbye,' we called after him down the street. 'Thank you so much. Please call again.'

It took a little while for the novelty of selling to wear off. Each time one of us sold something, we'd wait for the customer to leave then call out 'granary loaf, sixty-five pence!' or 'organic peanut butter, ninety-eight pence!' to the others.

Several customers requested items not stocked, so a new list was born noting names and telephone numbers so that customers could be informed when the required goods arrived. We also took many telephone queries, some from potential customers but also many asking for John Kirk or for money or both. The latter had to be dealt with discreetly if there were customers in earshot but otherwise we dealt with them swiftly, leaving the caller no doubt that John Kirk had moved on and his debts would not be settled by us.

At midday I went upstairs to the washroom and was washing my hands and checking my make-up in the mirror when I heard Lorraine frantically calling for me. I hurried downstairs to see a long line of customers meandering in front of the long counter fridge and out through the door into the street. A second line of people holding wire baskets filled with goods stretched from the till around the opposite side of the shop, blocking access to the upright fridges and freezers. Other shoppers were milling about filling baskets and causing disruption by asking those in the left hand queue to move aside so that the freezer doors could be opened.

Joan had abandoned her post at the sink and was now in the kitchen juggling bread rolls and dishes of fillings yelling, 'Did you want mayonnaise on that dear?' and 'White or brown for the tuna salad?' I quickly fastened an apron around my waist and called out, 'Who's next please?' in the direction of the queue and was bombarded with sandwich orders.

'Cheese-pickle-no-butter-on-white, tuna-salad-extra onions-poppyseed bun, egg-mayo-no-salad-brown,' I chanted to myself as I grabbed bread rolls from the shelf and joined Joan at the kitchen workbench.

'Could you take over here?' Joan asked as she stuffed two enormous filled rolls into paper bags. 'I need to make up some more tuna mayo and we're nearly out of grated cheese.'

'Yeah, no problem,' I said, passing her a tin of tuna and she hurried up the stairs back to the sink.

The three of us worked at top speed to make sure everyone was served. We knew that if the queue didn't clear fast enough customers would grow impatient and go elsewhere for their lunch. There was a huge choice available on the bank; Chinese and Indian takeaways, fish and chips and pizza, as well as two cafes and butchers and bakers shops that sold sandwiches.

We fell into a system for tackling the queues. Lorraine stayed at the till taking orders and calling them out to Joan and I who would quickly make and wrap them and pass them back to be handed out and paid for. Sometimes we had ten or twelve sandwiches being assembled at once and we worked in deep concentration passing dishes back and forth and constantly muttering to ourselves, 'cheese-salad-granary-no-butter, egg-mayo-tomato-poppyseed bun, tuna-onion-banana, tuna-onion-BANANA? Can you check that? Yes? No problem, tuna-onion-banana,' as we darted about filling the lines of open bread rolls.

Between sandwich orders we flew around the kitchen, clattering up the stairs to the sink, replenishing the bowls of salad and fillings, washing tomatoes, slicing cucumbers, grating cheese and shredding lettuce.

'My feet are blooding killing me,' I muttered to Lorraine as I handed her a batch of sandwiches and in return she gave me the next lot of rolls to fill. I could tell by the way she was hobbling around that hers were too. Nevertheless, ever the professional, she kept a friendly and competent, if a little hurried manner with the customers and a fixed smile on her face. I too moulded a smile on my face, ignoring the pain of my crushed toes in my oh-so-elegant but oh-so-cramped shoes, and took comfort in the constant ping of the till drawer and the clink of coins as they were dropped into it.

The queues did not seem to be lessening. Joan and I became faster and faster at slapping dollops of tuna mayo and cheese savoury onto opened bread rolls along with handfuls of salad. The floor was littered with stray pieces of lettuce and tomato that had missed their target and whenever she had a chance Lorraine would whip the brush around the floor, hiding the resulting pile of debris out of sight behind the office door.

'We're nearly out of change,' she said as she pushed the brush rapidly round the floor and over my feet. I looked up at the queue and saw Nige squeezing his way to the counter to place a bundle of letters next to the till. Catching my eye he gestured a thumbs-up and winked, nodding his head towards the queues. I smiled and lifted my hand to wave as Lorraine pushed a handful of notes at him and sent him off to get change.

I was crouching down searching in the fridge for a fresh tub of margarine when Lorraine suddenly clutched my arm.

'Disaster!' she said, her face panic stricken, 'The till's broken down!'

'What!' I said, hurrying over to take a look, a bowl of coleslaw still in my hand. I pressed the no-sale button, expecting the drawer to fly open with its reassuring ping but nothing happened. I frantically pressed the other buttons randomly with the same result. Nothing. So much for buying second hand. I groped furiously beneath the counter for a notebook and pen.

'Make a list,' I said flinging them at her. 'Write it all down. Don't forget to itemise each sale and remember you must record vat items separate from non-vat items,' I reminded her.

'Bugger that,' she said, throwing the pen and book back at me. 'I'm just taking the money.' She grabbed a basket from beside the till, emptied it by turning it upside down, and spilling its contents of flapjacks everywhere, and stuffed it beneath the counter to use as a make-shift cash box.

Just then Nige returned with a bag of change that Lorraine asked him to put into the basket as she wildly gave out sandwiches and collected payment. He leaned over the counter, opened the bag and tipped it over the basket, missing it completely, causing the coins to cascade over the floor.

'Holy Polony!' he said. 'Sorry about that,' and he crawled behind the counter beneath Lorraine's feet who had to straddle him as he scrabbled to collect up the scattered coins.

I click-clacked back to the kitchen to finish the sandwich I'd started then turned immediately to go back to the counter as I remembered the dish of coleslaw I'd left balanced on top of the till. Unfortunately, I stepped on a slice of cucumber and the next moment was flat on my back with my sling-backs waving in the air.

'Ooff!' I said, winded and embarrassed. I heard several stifled titters of laughter from the queue as Joan hurried to help me up. I looked up to see Lorraine, Nige on all fours at her feet, with an official looking man holding out an identity card. He looked down at Nige and then at me with distaste.

'Mrs Kenworthy?' he asked.

'Yes?' I said, clambering up and pulling my skirt back into place, aware of a very painful area on my buttock.

'Edward Reeves, Environmental Health.'

CHAPTER FOURTEEN

Mr Reeves preferred to carry out his inspection unaccompanied.

'Carry on with your business as usual, Mrs Kenworthy,' he said sternly as he strode past me and up the stairs and I returned to the backlog of sandwiches that had piled up in my short absence. Joan and I worked as fast as ever to get through them, both of us aware of Mr Reeves poking about in the sink area. I hoped to God we'd left it tidy, but I knew that there were at least two empty tuna tins up there, and I remembered throwing eggshells into the small sink (supposedly reserved for hand washing only) in an earlier panic. I suddenly remembered the pile of sweepings behind the office door and dived for the dustpan and brush, just managing to whisk it into the bin before he marched past me into the office.

'We're almost out of fillings,' Joan said as I returned to cram sandwiches into paper bags. 'And there's still a big queue.' Piles of empty dishes stood on the bench in front of us. We had completely underestimated the amount of sandwich fillings we'd need. I looked to the queue, along the row of waiting customers and I saw Peter coming into the shop and Nige leaving, passing each other in the doorway.

'I'll go and find something,' I said, desperate not to lose customers. I kicked off my shoes, unable to bear the discomfort any longer, past caring that I was treading on breadcrumbs and bits of food in my stockinged feet. As I squeezed past Lorraine at the till and started to jostle my way through the queue she looked up from counting coins into a customers hand and said, 'Nearly sold out of bread rolls, we could slice some of the loaves to make sandwiches.'

'Good idea,' I said. 'I'll find something to put in them.' I padded shoeless to Peter who was standing near the door. He bent to kiss my cheek.

'How's it going?' he asked, looking pleased. 'It looks really busy.'

'It's going brilliantly except that we've run out of sandwich stuff, the till's buggered, there's an Environmental Health Officer inspecting us and I've got a bruise the size of Greenland on me arse.' I said.

'And you've had your shoes nicked,' he said looking at my feet.

'My feet are another sore subject,' I said. 'Very sore.' I remembered that I was supposed to be looking for something to fill sandwiches with.

'Any chance you could serve customers to free Lorraine so that she can help your Mam for a few minutes?' I asked.

'Me?' Peter said looking as though I'd suggested he dance naked on the counter. 'Do I have to?'

During our years at Nutmeg Peter would willingly and happily help with many tasks, building shelves, stock taking, delivering orders, even cleaning, but he hated serving customers. Behind the counter he was a fish out of water, struggling to return to the depths of his safe river.

There are rules to dealing with customers. They are allowed to tell you repeatedly and in great detail, their problems and complaints, but do not wish to listen to yours. You must listen attentively and sympathetically and must never criticise or disagree however ridiculous their opinions. Customers must always be treated with politeness and respect even though they may be rude, patronising and sometimes downright insulting. They must always be greeted with a cheery welcome and must be given the impression that you remember every conversation you've ever had with them and every purchase they've ever made. Peter's character is of a type that is too straightforward and honest for this two-facedness and he does not believe in meaningless small talk. He also has an unrelenting sense of humour and included customers as fair game for the butt of his jokes - of course this is fine behind their backs but not to their faces. He is also under the illusion that everyone to finds them as amusing as he does. We soon learned that he was a bit of a liability when left to serve customers. We often had to deal with the aftermath, such as the irate man who complained he'd been advised to use a cork when he'd asked Peter for a natural remedy for diarrhoea and a woman who'd asked for something for wind and was told 'sorry, we don't stock kites'.

Good product knowledge is also important in order to be able to advise people on the right product for them. There is no point in selling someone something they don't want or need; they will be disillusioned with the service received and will not return. Peter's product knowledge was sparse to say the least, mostly because he was not in the shop when stock was delivered and so did not become familiar with it but also because he did not have a great interest in it. A woman once complained that he'd sold her tamari - a type of soy sauce - instead of tahini - a sesame seed paste. She'd used it to make hummous that she'd served at a dinner party to her unsuspecting guests who had spluttered and choked on tasting it.

Another time during a marketing campaign promoting Japanese foods, he for some reason found the name Umeboshi plums inexplicably hilarious and laughed every time he heard it spoken. I remember watching a woman, who had been examining our carefully displayed selection of Japanese foods, approach him and I cringed waiting for her to mention the 'funny word'. However, she didn't. She said to him: 'What does one do with dried seaweed?' and he replied: 'Hoy it in one's fish tank?'

I had one ear on him now as I ran around the shop manoeuvring people out of the way so that I could scan the shelves for possible sandwich filling ingredients and I cringed as I heard him answer a query about our tuna saying: 'Dolphin friendly, yes. Tuna friendly, no.'
I snatched some tubes of mushroom pate from the shelves and found some packets of soya meat slices in the fridge along with some pots of cottage cheese. Throwing them on the counter I swiftly cleaned the blackboard on the front of the counter with the edge of my apron and seizing a piece of chalk changed the 'Today's Specials' listing to include our new choices.

70

Back in the kitchen I whispered to Joan, 'Where is he?' She nodded towards the office and I looked to see Edward Reeves sitting at the desk writing furiously. My heart sank as I speculated on the content of his report. He gathered his papers, shuffled them together into his briefcase and said: 'You will receive my report in approximately thirty days. I bid you good day.' He gave me a last look of disgust, his eyes moving down to my feet decorated with strands of cress and a shred of lettuce and marched past us pushing his way through the queue.

'Pompous twit!' muttered Lorraine. I was just relieved that he'd gone. At least he hadn't closed us down on the spot. Surely it couldn't be that bad if we had to wait thirty days for his report or he'd have told us straight away, wouldn't he?

Peter made his escape as soon as the Inspector had left, hiding in the office to eat a sandwich I'd quickly thrown together for him. I hadn't a chance to speak to him before he had to leave to return to work.

'See you later,' he said. 'Keep up the good work!'

The pace continued until two o'clock when it stopped as abruptly as it had began. We all collapsed onto stools, exhausted.

'Two solid hours!' Lorraine said. 'Obviously the lunch time rush.'

'I hope it wasn't a one off,' I said. 'If it's like that every day we'll be flying.'

'Or on our knees with fatigue more like,' said Lorraine.

'Talking about being on knees,' Joan said, 'what on earth was the postman doing kneeling at your feet when the Inspector came in?' We laughed and Lorraine explained about the spilled coins.

'And you weren't much better,' she said to me. 'Lying on your back on the floor!'

'Oh don't remind me!' I said cringing at the memory.

We sat chatting about the events of the morning as we drank tea and shared a sandwich made from the last slices of bread. We took turns to get up and serve the now only occasional customer.

'In future we'll make our sandwiches first and put them aside,' I said as I searched about for something else for us to eat and picked up a packet of oat and apple cookies.

'And wear flat shoes,' Lorraine added kicking off her heels and rubbing her foot between her hands.

The events of our first day proved to be typical of the daily pattern. Customers trickled in throughout the morning while we took in deliveries and prepared the fillings and salads. Then, from twelve to two it was all systems go for the lunchtime rush. The afternoons were quieter, enabling us to clear up the kitchen, order new stock and keep on top of the paperwork. We fell into the habit of having a break at eleven forty-five to sustain us through the mayhem until after two when we could at last eat our lunch.

Joan and Lorraine and I worked well as a team, laughing and joking our way through the workload together. They were happy days but I knew they couldn't last. I could not keep taking advantage of Joan's generosity. Our next challenge would be to find a suitable part time assistant.

CHAPTER FIFTEEN

Derek staggered past the shop, loaded down with a great pile of cardboard boxes packed with salad vegetables, as we threw up the shutter and unlocked the door.

'Morning ladies,' he said as he struggled past.

'Morning Derek,' we answered together.

'See you shortly for your daily rations,' he said, grinning as he disappeared into his shop.

Since Nutmeg had opened four weeks ago, we had visited Derek's greengrocery each morning for our salad ingredients. Derek gave us a good discount and had lots of useful information about the local customers. He was also a master of the double-entendre and made every conversation, especially those about his vegetables feel slightly obscene. I had learned to choose my words carefully when speaking to him since on my first visit to his shop to buy a cucumber when I had innocently asked him if he had a big one.

Inside the shop I climbed onto the window ledge to pull up the blinds.

'I'll make the drinks,' yawned Lorraine and picking up the kettle on the way, she climbed up the steps to the sink. As usual we needed a cup of hot strong coffee to get us started, and while she made it, I counted the float into the till and turned the sign from 'closed' to 'open'.

'There you go,' she said and handed me a steaming mug, and we indulged in our first caffeine fix of the day.

'We shouldn't really be drinking this,' I said as the strong hot liquid hit the spot. 'We should really practise what we preach. We have a huge selection of herbal teas and coffee substitutes, I think we should try them.'

'Well you can if you like,' Lorraine said, 'But I need my caffeine.'

After reading and then sniffing several varieties I selected a box of strawberry and vanilla teabags and put them near to the kettle, ready for our next break.

'Morning!' The door burst open and Nadine rushed in. 'Is the bread in yet?' she asked. It wasn't actually the bread delivery that interested Nadine, it was the bread deliverer, Jonathan.

'No you're all right,' Lorraine said. 'You haven't missed him.' With a sigh of relief Nadine deposited her coat and bag in the office and checked her hair in the mirror before coming to join us in the shop front.

Nadine was an old college friend of Lorraine's whom Lorraine had bumped into in town while shopping. Chatting over coffee Lorraine had told Nadine of our new venture and had mentioned that we needed a part time assistant. Nadine had excitedly suggested that she should fill the post as she was presently at a loose end and thought the whole idea sounded a 'right hoot'. I admit that although we were both very fond of her I had reservations when

Lorraine told me that she'd offered her the job. I'd heard many tales of friendships ruined in similar situations; stories of long lasting relationships shattered, of employees or employers taking advantage of the friendship, and of mounting resentments in both parties. However, I need not have worried. Nadine proved to be a tireless worker with great enthusiasm and loyalty for our business and she was also great fun to work with.

She was now placing eggs into a pan of water and setting them to boil, while I reheated the kettle to make her a drink. Lorraine went off to Derek's to buy the day's salad and as she left, Jonathan arrived, well groomed and immaculately dressed as usual, in shirt and tie.

'Morning,' chirruped Nadine and she fluttered towards him helping him to bring in the trays loaded with freshly baked bread, cakes and pastries, all smelling deliciously tempting. I left her to the pleasure of signing his delivery note and hearing the click of the kettle switching off, went to get her drink. I returned just as she was waving him off.

'He's gorgeous,' she sighed as she took the mug from me. 'He's very shy. And I think he's a bit younger than I am. I'd ask him out but I don't want to scare him off. Do you think he's interested in me?' She took a drink from her mug.

'Yewk! What's this?' she asked, pulling a face. I was pleased for the chance to change the subject so that I didn't have to answer her question. Personally I thought that Jonathan was terrified of her, I'd seen her eat bigger men for breakfast and spit them out.

'It's strawberry and vanilla tea,' I said. 'We've decided to go healthy and you're the guinea pig.'

'Here, have a taste,' she said, handing me the mug. I took it and sniffed the hot liquid.

'Smells nice,' I said and took a sip. 'Aw, that's horrible!' I said and I went off to make her a mug of PG. I returned to find that she had checked off the bread delivery and was putting pies and pastries into the display fridge. As usual, most of the bread sold straight from the trays before reaching the bread shelves behind the counter.

Lorraine returned from Derek's with a box of salad and fruit as Nadine and I served the first customers of the day, those who came early for fresh bread, still warm from the oven.

'Better make another cuppa,' she said. 'I've just seen Georgina coming down the bank.'

Georgina had fast become our favourite customer and had visited the shop every day since we opened. She would lean against the counter drinking tea, discussing local gossip and the meaning of life while Lorraine, Nadine and I would scurry about serving customers and preparing sandwich fillings and salads.

She was well into her fifties but looked years younger dressed in her own eclectic style of Oxfam bargains. Her hennaed hair was short and spiky and she had an impressive collection of tattoos and piercings. She breezed in on a cloud of patchouli just as Nadine placed a cup in front of her.

'Mmm,' she said, taking a sip. 'Strawberry and vanilla, lovely.'

'You like it?' I asked. 'Nadine and I thought it was gruesome.'

'That's what I love about this place,' she said. 'The sales pitch.' She took another drink. 'It's an acquired taste,' she said. 'Once you get used to it it's delicious, honest. I'll have a box to take home.' She took a box from the shelf and placed in on the counter as the start of her pile of shopping.

'And how is life with you this morning?' asked Lorraine coming over to join in the conversation.

'It's fantastic actually,' Georgina said with a twinkle in her eye. 'I met a gorgeous bloke at a party last night. He's an artist, up here visiting friends in Newcastle.'

'Sounds like I've arrived just in time,' said Nige, coming in and helping himself to a stool. 'Sounds very interesting.'

'Georgina I don't know how you do it!' Nadine said enviously.

'Come on then,' said Lorraine 'we want all the details, tell all!'

She did tell all, pausing occasionally when customers came within earshot as she described in great detail Marc's muscular frame dressed in tight fitting jeans and linen shirt and his rugged good looks.

'Holy Polony! He sounds gorgeous!' Nige said, drinking the coffee we'd made for him after he'd choked on strawberry and vanilla tea. 'Lucky cow. Are you sure he's straight?'

'I'm aiming to find out this weekend,' Georgina said, causing Nige to splutter and giggle into his coffee. 'He's invited me to Norfolk for the weekend to stay on his house-boat.'

'He sounds like one of those lovely arty bohemian types,' Nige said dreamily.

'Sounds like a right old hippy to me,' Lorraine said.

'And what's wrong with that?' asked Georgina, who had spent the late sixties travelling around Europe with a bunch of artist friends, sleeping rough, selling and bartering paintings.

'I don't find scruffy men attractive,' said Nadine. 'You can't beat a well-groomed man in a nice suit and tie.' Georgina pulled a face.

'No thanks,' she said. 'It would be like shagging your bank manager.'

'My bank manager's quite nice actually,' Nadine said.

'Anyway Marc's not scruffy,' Georgina said. 'Just because he doesn't wear a suit and he's got long hair doesn't mean he's not clean!'

'I know,' said Nadine. 'I just meant I prefer men to look like they've made a bit of an effort.' She suddenly lowered her voice. 'I mean, look at him over there,' she said pointing to a tall man with a baby strapped to his back. His long white legs dangled from the bottom of a pair of Boy Scout type shorts, his large hairy feet encased in a pair of leather sandals. He was picking through bags of lentils examining the labels.

'What a nelly,' she said. 'Fiddling about with lentils!' We all watched as he moved along the shelf and put down his basket to feed raisins to the baby from a paper bag.

'Well, at least he's taking being a parent seriously,' Georgina said, struggling to find something positive to say about him.

'I think he's one of those 'new-men-of-the-nineties', Nige whispered.

'Huh, these 'new-men-of-the-nineties' don't impress me,' Nadine said. 'I don't want a man who's gentle and sensitive and in touch with his feminine side, I want a man who'll drag me upstairs and rip me blouse off.'

'Don't we all dear?' said Nige.

Nadine and Lorraine were both single and constantly assessed our male customers for suitability as partner material. Lorraine was laid back about it, joining in light-heartedly. She enjoyed being single and often stated that her life was fine without the complications that having a man would bring to it. But for Nadine it was a full on manhunt. She had an expert eye and a man could be evaluated and categorised within seconds of entering the shop. Oblivious to the fact that he was part of Nadine's market research, he was rejected or added to her mental list of 'possibilities' as he unsuspectingly surveyed the sandwich menu.

Beneath her bubbly, flirtatious exterior, Nadine was a true romantic at heart and longed to find her soul mate. She knew exactly what she wanted and often thought she had found it only to be disappointed time after time. The image of her ideal man was etched in her mind in such intricate detail that few men came close to fitting her strict criteria.

Believing a slender body to be the key to a man's heart she constantly struggled with various types of diets ranging from the bizarre to the downright ridiculous, totally oblivious of the admiration her curvaceous figure attracted.

Nige departed to finish his round, leaving as usual a pile of packages and letters for us. Georgina left soon after to go to her tie-dye class leaving her basket of shopping behind the counter.

'I'll pick it up later,' she said. I'll be back around twelve.'

Nadine went to finish off in the kitchen and Lorraine and I opened our mail.

'Here's the one we've been waiting for,' Lorraine said, leafing through a sheaf of papers. 'The Environmental Health report from Edward Reeves.'

'What does it say?' I asked. She put it on the counter and we scanned through it. At first glance it seemed to contain a horrendously long list of required changes to our premises and work routines, but on closer inspection, although there were many points – three pages of them – they were mostly minor and easily remedied.

'Replace cracked wall tile above cooker,' I read. 'Renew floor covering to office/storeroom. Fit ramp to front entrance to enable wheelchair access… I'm sure Peter could do most of these for us.' Seizing the opportunity I grabbed a pencil and started a list.

Mr Reeves also advised us to attend a Health and Hygiene course to obtain the certificate that was soon to become compulsory for all food handlers.

'There's a phone number here for Ashington College,' I said. 'The course is run over two evenings and the next one is coming up soon.'

'What's the number?' asked Lorraine, picking up the phone. 'We may as well enrol straight away, then you can tick your list.'

By eleven thirty the details of the required work contained in the letter had been reconstructed into a new series of lists ready for Peter's perusal and we were enrolled on the Health and Hygiene course scheduled for a fortnight's time.

Nadine made mugs of strawberry and vanilla tea; we had made a pact to drink it until the end of the week to see if we would acquire a taste for it as Georgina had suggested we eventually would. As we reluctantly sipped at it, the door burst open causing the bell to jangle furiously and a woman entered, her presence seeming to fill the building as she stomped in, eyes and teeth prominent, giving a bellowing 'Hellooo!' Dressed in the upper class style of very old tweed skirt and shapeless pullover, she carried a huge carpetbag that she placed on the counter before inhaling deeply with a tremendous gasping sound. We looked at her in alarm, not sure whether the gasp was due to some sort of seizure or a prelude to a burst of song. I half expected her to perform excerpts from Mary Poppins whilst producing a hat stand and mirror from her carpetbag. However, after Lorraine had timidly asked, 'Can I help you?' it became apparent that the colossal intake of breath was to enable her to speak without pause at great volume for as long as possible before the next inhalation.

'Hellooo my dears,' she shrieked. 'Just popped in to introduce myself. Dulcie Forbes-Williamson. How do you do? I've heard about you two clever sisters and your little shop on the grapevine. Well done gels, well done I say! I do so admire imaginative enterprise especially in the working classes. I'm all for educating the peasants, har har. What a fascinating little shop, may I say, absolutely divine. Oh, cashew nuts. How lovely. I'll take some of those.' Her breath finally depleted she paused to inhale again giving a gasping 'Wheesh' as she did so. Lorraine, Nadine and I tried to take advantage of the slight pause and attempted to speak, but were drowned out as Mrs Forbes-Williamson set off again.

'Wild rice, super. And Hunza apricots. Oh I'm very partial to Hunza apricots. Delicious with Greek yoghurt and honey. Har har. You wouldn't happen to have a pot of Greek yoghurt? You have? Perfect. And a jar of honey? Oh how wonderful. Simply divine. Wheesh!' She deposited her collection in her carpetbag and continued to stamp around the shelves marvelling loudly at the variety of stock and filling her bag with goods. We obeyed meekly as she ordered us to fetch items and pack her bag, our voices engulfed by her thunderous monologue, which was interrupted only by the occasional 'Wheesh!'

'Well girlies, thank you kindly. I must dash. I'm so very busy at present with my committees. I will certainly recommend you to my Conservative Ladies. I'll settle up with you at the end of the month. See you soon. Pip pip.

Wheesh!' and she was gone, leaving the bell clanging as though it were about to fall off as the door slammed behind her. For a second we were silent.

'She's gone,' said Lorraine, breaking the stunned silence. 'And she hasn't paid. Why didn't you ask her to pay?'

'Well why didn't you?' I retorted.

'I can't believe we all let her do that,' said Nadine. 'She was just so, so...'

'I know,' I said.

'What did she take?' asked Lorraine. 'Yoghurt, honey. What else?' We put our heads together and made a list of the unpaid for items.

'I hope she comes back,' I said. 'There's about twenty-five quid's worth of stuff in that bag of hers.'

There was no chance to discuss the matter further as the lunch time rush was about to start so I quickly made up a sandwich ready for Peter, and placed it in the fridge on a plate. He arrived as the queue was building up and the usual frenzy of sandwich making began. I gabbled the story of Mrs Forbes-Williamson to him over the sandwich bench as I worked.

'So you're telling me that this women walks in, fills her bag with stuff and walks out without paying and the three of you stood there and did nothing because she had a loud voice?' he said.

'We didn't stand there and do nothing,' Lorraine said. 'We helped her choose what she wanted and then packed it in her bag for her.'

'Any chance of being served here?' said a voice from the queue. It was a small bald man Nadine had nicknamed ' Pugnacious Face' who complained daily about the length of time he had to wait for his sandwich to be made.

'Yes of course,' I said, forcing a smile. I saw Georgina enter and come to the counter to collect her basket.

'I'll have that one,' said Pugnacious Face pointing into the fridge at the huge sandwich I'd prepared for Peter.

'Sorry, that one's taken,' I said passing the plate to Peter who took it into the office.

'And what's he got that I haven't?' demanded Pugnacious Face argumentatively. Georgina looked up on her way out.

'He's sleeping with the boss,' she yelled and trotted off up the bank cackling at her own wit.

CHAPTER SIXTEEN

Mrs Forbes-Williamson returned a few days later, although not to settle her bill, while Jim Dixon was visiting us. Jim was a Glaswegian in his late fifties; a dapper little man who worked for Herbfirst, a Swedish based company that produced and marketed organically produced herbal tinctures. We had contacted him after constant requests from customers for herbal remedies and chose Herbfirst because of their reputation for quality products and ethical business practices. Jim had visited us bringing information and samples and we had taken to him instantly. He was a genuine, down to earth man with a quiet unassuming manner, who believed passionately in the products he promoted. An excellent advocate for his company, he glowed with health and we always enjoyed his visits.

Many of the sales reps that visited were smarmy and patronising and as Lorraine and I had a low tolerance threshold for smarmy and patronising people, they usually left the building with a flea in the ear soon after entering. A lot of the male reps seemed to think that because we were female we must be sales assistants working for a male employer and if Peter was around it was assumed that he was our boss.

One of the first to visit in our early days was a condescending orange-tanned youth who swaggered across the shop floor saying to Lorraine, 'Hello darlin', is the Boss in?' Lorraine looked at him with pity and called, 'Someone to see you, Chris,' to where I was cleaning shelves out of view.

'Yes?' I said, wiping my hands on the front of my over-sized apron. 'Can I help?' He looked me up and down and flicked back his hair.

'It's all right love, carry on with your housework,' he said. 'I'm waiting for the boss.' I looked at Lorraine and we smirked at each other realising that he had assumed 'Chris' to be the male version. We left him to wait for the elusive Christopher and carried on as though he was not present. Fifteen minutes later a customer unwittingly enlightened him when observing my diligent shelf scrubbing made a rather obvious joke.

'Working hard there Chris?' he said. 'You can come and clean mine next if you like!' The smugness slipped from the rep's face like wax melting down a candle as he realised his mistake and he stuttered his apologies as Lorraine pointed to the door and I opened it.

However, the award for the most patronising sales rep ever to enter our shop goes to the condom salesman who arrived one afternoon with a box of free samples. We listened politely as he recited his sales pitch, explaining all about the importance of sexual health and reeling off lists of figures and percentages relating to the rapid spread of Aids, but decided that at present it was not a line we wished to stock. In those early days we were still struggling with cash flow and so purchased carefully.

'And why not?' he demanded after we'd declined to place an order. He placed his hands on the counter and leaned towards my face. 'Do you find the subject of sex embarrassing?' I found him intimidating and his manner irritated me but I felt the best way to deal with him was to stay calm and not be goaded into further discussion.

'We don't wish to place an order at present,' I said firmly. 'However, if you'd like to leave your price list we may get back to you in future.'

'Do you realise the damage being caused by the spread of Aids because of people like you?' he said angrily.

'Like me?' I said provoked, forgetting about not being goaded.

'Excuse me!' put in Lorraine. 'We don't have Aids and we're not spreading it, thank you very much!'

'We just don't want to place an order that's all.' I said.

'So, thank you and goodbye,' added Lorraine and she walked off into the kitchen. I began to tidy a pile of leaflets on the counter top.

'People like you make me really angry,' he said. He pointed his finger threateningly. 'So ignorant. You are making Aids a taboo subject. Call yourselves a health shop and yet are too embarrassed to promote a product that could literally save thousands of lives.'

'I am NOT embarrassed,' I shouted. 'We are a health FOOD shop so your product does not fit in with our criteria.'

'Oh I think it does,' he answered. 'Our range of products are produced without undue harm to the environment and are not, unlike some other more mainstream brands, tested on animals.' Tested on animals? The mind boggled.

'For the last time, we are not interested,' I said. 'Now will you please leave?' He looked at me with disgust, anger contorting his face.

'Pathetic,' he said. 'Typical middle-class 'Pretend-It's-Not-Happening' mentality. Probably closet lesbians the pair of you.' Lorraine, who had been crashing dishes around in the kitchen stormed over.

'Right!' she yelled, marching toward him. 'My sister has asked you politely and now I'm telling you straight. GET OUT! Go on. SLING YER HOOK!' She physically pushed him toward the door and he stumbled out shouting his accusations that we were repressed and hung-up.

'BOG OFF!' yelled Lorraine. 'And take your environment-friendly johnnies with you!' she added as she flung his free samples into the street after him to the delight of Georgina who was just arriving for her morning visit. I related the incident to her, although Lorraine was unusually quiet and did not join in. She had obviously taken his insult to heart as we usually saw the funny side of most things.

'Are you OK?' Georgina asked her.

'No.' she said. 'He's really upset me, saying a nasty thing like that.'

'It's not an insult to be called a lesbian,' Georgina told her. 'It just shows how ignorant he is.' Lorraine looked at her, surprised.

'It's not that,' she said. 'It's because he said we had middle class attitude. I'm not middle class, I never will be. I'm working class and proud of it.'

Today Jim had called with information about a Phytotherapy training course initiated by Herbfirst that was highly accredited by the Health Trade. We were keen to enrol believing it vital to be knowledgeable about any medicinal products we stocked and also because it was free of charge. The company was offering to fund the training, which usually cost over a thousand pounds per person, for staff of new businesses, I suppose in the hope of securing a permanent outlet for their products.

Jim explained the main difference between Herbalism and Phytotherapy being that the latter could be explained by science. Many species of herbs and plants have been used successfully medicinally for many years, yet for some of them it is only recently that scientists have been able to explain how they work. Of course this makes absolutely no difference to the healing powers of the plants whether administered in the name of Herbalism or Phytotherapy, however it does provide counter-argument for the many sceptics, including many doctors who still pooh-pooh the whole concept of natural healing as old wives tales and mumbo-jumbo.

We signed the enrolment forms and as Jim filed them away in his briefcase I went to switch on the kettle. We always compiled our order over a hot drink.

'Coffee?' I called to Jim.

'Actually, I've brought some samples of a new product if you'd like to try them?' he said. 'It's a new coffee substitute made from ground acorns and chicory – caffeine free.' It sounded disgusting but I had learned to reserve judgement. I'd thought the same about herbal tea but I was now an enthusiastic convert.

Bringing the tray of drinks to the counter I called to Nadine to come and join us.

'Oh not for me thanks,' she said after sniffing the acorn and chicory drink. 'I'm on a new diet. It's the Pectin-Fibre Plan. You can eat unlimited apples and raisins one day, then carrots and watercress the next, and you alternate for five days and you're supposed to lose half a stone.' She pulled a packet of raisins out of her bag and began to chew on them reluctantly. It didn't sound a very healthy way to lose weight to me but I was used to Nadine's strange weight loss methods and had long since given up trying to talk her into a regular balanced diet.

'Actually this drink is really tasty, a bit like a cross between coffee and Ovaltine,' said Lorraine. I took a sip of mine.

'Mmm, yeah it is. And it's cheaper than coffee. Put a couple of cases on the order and we'll give it a try.'

We checked the shelves for stock needed and Jim filled in his order sheet as we drank. I was signing the bottom of the form when Nadine suddenly said, 'Who is that man? And why does he keep running past the window?' I looked up to see a tall bony man with thinning hair and a pained expression jogging past the window dressed in pinstripe suit and sandals.

'Oh him!' I said. 'I've seen him loads of times running up and down the bank looking really worried.'

'Me too,' added Lorraine. 'We'll have to ask Georgina about him. If anyone knows, she will.' We all moved nearer to the window to peer at the running man. We watched him move at a steady pace past the shops looking around furtively as he ran. He moved in an exaggerated manner, lifting his sandalled feet high so that his knees jutted in points as he ran and his elbows jerked back and forth like a child pretending to be a train.

'Helloooo!' echoed a voice from behind us causing us all to start in fright. Engrossed in witnessing the amusing antics of The Running Man we had failed to hear the entrance of Mrs Forbes-Williamson who was now walking towards the door holding a tub of Ben and Jerry's ice-cream in one hand and a carton of frozen organic raspberries in the other.

'Hello, Mrs Forbes–Williamson,' I began to say, but was cut off by her resonating tones.

'Can't stop,' she boomed. 'In a frightful hurry. Having a dinner party and need something for dessert. Entertaining the Carmody-Browns don't you know? Wheesh. Very big in the finance trade, although you won't know about that of course, coming from an under-privileged background. Har har. Must dash. Pop this on the bill dear, not worth breaking into a twenty-pound note, is it? Har har. Wheesh!'

CHAPTER SEVENTEEN

Georgina did know who the Running Man was.

'That'll be Ernie,' she said, after we'd described him. 'The local nutter. He's quite harmless. He has two hobbies. One is running up and down and the other is asking prices in shops. I'm surprised he hasn't been in here yet.'

'He hasn't,' I said. But he's run past a few thousand times.'

'He'll be in,' she said. 'He'll ask you the price of everything but won't buy anything. Just humour him. As I say, he's quite harmless, poor soul.'

The lunchtime rush was more hectic than ever. We'd started serving toasted sandwiches and though we had a good choice of fillings, it was the baked bean ones that were selling like hot toasties. Very popular and also very profitable due to the present price-cut war between the region's three major supermarket chains. Included in their loss-leaders of cheap everyday staples were tins of baked beans at five pence and standard loaves at sixteen pence, so the toasties cost around three pence to make and were selling at ninety-nine pence a round.

'It's a good mark-up, but do you think it fits in with our 'whole food' principle?' I had asked Lorraine.

'Course it does,' she said. 'Beans on toast, the original healthy fast food. Protein, iron, B vitamins all for ninety-nine pence.'

'Well we've certainly made the big time. Who needs multi-million dollar contracts when you can deal in five pence tins of beans and cheap bread?'

'Don't knock it,' said Lorraine. 'It's a good profit maker. It's our bread and butter. Our bread and beans.'

For the umpteenth time that day I filled the toaster and clipped down the lid. Lorraine and Nadine were side by side at the kitchen bench madly filling rolls so I hurried to the counter to where Peter was tentatively ringing in sales.

'What can I get you?' I asked a burly man whom I guessed to be a builder judging by his plaster-encrusted clothes and regulation bum revealing jeans.

'Could you do me a ploughman's, love?' he asked.

'A ploughman's?'

'Yeah, a ploughman's lunch darlin'.'

'Certainly,' I said and hurried back to the kitchen.

'What's in a ploughman's?' I hissed at Nadine.

'A ploughman's? Like you get down the pub? Cheese and stuff I think,' she said and hurried off to hand over the rolls she had filled. I found a paper plate on the shelves at the back of the kitchen and arranged some wedges of cheese on it. Lorraine was now at the bench watching me with a questioning look.

'I'm making a ploughman's,' I said. 'What else do I need?'

'Er, an apple I think, and a bread roll.' Apple. I ran into the office and began rooting through Nadine's handbag.

'What are you doing?' asked Peter, who was struggling to lift a crate down from the top of a pile of stock.

'Looking for an apple,' I said, locating one in Nadine's bag of diet supplies. 'But what are you doing?' I asked him.

'I'm looking for a case of honey,' he said. 'There's a customer here to collect a case of honey she's ordered.'

'Case of honey?' I repeated. 'We haven't one. There are just the jars on the shelf until the next Karma delivery on Friday. I can't remember anyone ordering a case of honey.' I hurried back to my ploughman's where I sliced the apple and added it to the plate with a buttered bread roll. 'A case of honey?' I thought. I heard Peter ask both Nadine and Lorraine who had taken the order but both knew nothing about it. I looked at the plate. It looked a bit sparse so I threw on some salad and a dollop of chutney. I was covering it with plastic film when it dawned on me about the honey.

'That's for the guy at the front, the builder,' I said to Lorraine, thrusting the plate at her.

'How much?' she asked.

'One ninety-nine?'

'Two fifty.'

'Make it two-ninety-nine,' I said and rushed back to the office. 'Acacia honey, you divvie,' I said to Peter. 'She ordered a jar of Acacia honey. I've put it under the counter for her.'

'But she definitely wanted a case,' he said, still confused. 'She said I've ordered a case of your honey.' I left him to puzzle it out and went to give the customer her honey. Nadine turned towards me.

'Ploughman's,' she said. 'Customer's come back.'

'Not happy?' I said, not really surprised.

'He wants another four for his mates,' she said 'You'll have to do them, I didn't see what you gave him.' I ran off to pinch the rest of her apples and heard Lorraine saying in a very apologetic voice, 'I'm so sorry, I charged you the wrong price before, I should have charged you three ninety-nine. Don't worry about the extra pound for yours,' she said as he paid up without complaint, 'but I'll have to charge you full price for the others.'

'If ploughman's are going on the menu we'll need to get some of those take-away containers with lids,' I said as we sat down to eat lunch at two o'clock.

'And I'll get plenty of apples at Derek's tomorrow so you don't have to nick mine,' said Nadine, affably. She was pulling on her coat to go when she suddenly remembered something.

'Do you fancy going to an eighties disco?' she said. 'There's one on Sunday night at a club in town. I thought we could all go, it'll be a laugh.'

'Oh, great,' said Lorraine enthusiastically. 'I loved the eighties, the music was fantastic. They were great days,' she sighed.

'You're talking as though it was years ago!' I said. 'It's 1992, the eighties were only three years ago!'

'I meant the early eighties. I was at college, we had some great parties and nights out,' she said. 'I'm up for it!'

'Well I'm not,' I said. 'I hated the eighties. The music was so feeble. All that crappy pop stuff that sounded the same from those three old guys, what were they called? Lock, Stock and Barrel or something. And the fashions were awful. Power dressing, remember? Padded shoulders and court shoes. And big hair. I just hated the whole Thatcherite mentality, the materialistic values. The time of the Yuppy. No thanks, not for me. I much prefer the Nineties,' I paused for breath.

'All right, keep your hair on, it's only a disco,' Lorraine said. 'You could give Mrs Forbes-Williamson a run for her money, ranting away like that.'

'I know, I thought you were going to start wheeshing there,' added Nadine. I ignored their goading.

'I just didn't like the greed, the materialism, the grab-it-for-yourself attitudes,' I said.

'I seem to remember you having a bit of that yourself when you fought off crowds for those U2 tickets for you and Peter,' Lorraine said. 'In fact I seem to remember you having a pretty good time of the eighties altogether come to think of it.'

'That's because I make the most of things,' I said.

'You used to like that band who used to sing dead miserable songs didn't you?' Lorraine said.

'I think you mean the Smiths and they weren't miserable. They were reflective and meaningful.'

'Reflective and meaningful!' Lorraine said. 'Mind, you talk a load of shite sometimes.'

'Well at least I wasn't into Fame, going around in leg warmers and ribbons tied in a big bow on the top of my head like some people.' Lorraine ignored this remark.

'And I remember you had a thing about Tony Hadley from Spandeau Ballet,' she said.

'Only because he used to look a bit like Peter,' I said.

'Eeh, yes, he did,' said Nadine. 'Now you come to mention it, I'd never noticed before. Mind you, it was Simon Le Bon who had pride of place on my bedroom wall.'

'I used to fancy Adam Ant,' said Lorraine and I was about to say I did too but Nadine hooted with laughter so I didn't.

'Come with us,' said Lorraine, changing the subject.

'What and make a fool of myself jumping around to naff music dressed in ridiculous clothes?' I said. 'No thanks.'

'Making a fool of yourself jumping around to Led Zeppelin dressed in ridiculous clothes never used to bother you, or your daft hippy mates,' Lorraine said. I ignored this remark.

'No, honestly, you two go,' I said. 'You might meet a couple of men, it would cramp your style having an old married woman along.'

'Sure we can't change your mind?' asked Nadine.

'Positive,' I said.

'Ok, I'll get the tickets this afternoon,' she said to Lorraine as she made for the door. 'Dig out your ra-ra skirt.'

I was listing details of cheques we'd taken in the banking book as a prelude to cashing up when Lorraine called to me, although I didn't catch what she said. I opened the door and listened.

'Quick, he's coming!' she shouted. I put the cheques into the cash box and locked it.

'Who's coming?' I asked walking into the shop and there, in front of the counter, looking a little bewildered was The Running Man. Seeing him close up I realised that he was older than he appeared to be when he was dashing past the window, and also more unkempt. His weathered face was brown and wrinkled like a walnut, his forehead a mass of furrows. His bony wrists extended from the frayed cuffs of his pinstriped suit that was shiny at the lapels and knees. Strands of greasy hair were flattened sparsely over his skull and he rocked from one foot to the other in an agitated manner.

'How much is a loaf?' he asked.

'Well, they vary,' Lorraine said, pointing to the bread shelves behind her. 'Fifty-four pence for an unbleached white or a wholemeal. Granary, sunflower cob and poppyseed plait are sixty-five pence each. Rye loaf and organic multi-seeded loaf seventy pence.'

'Pardon?' said Ernie the Running Man. Lorraine took a breath.

'Fifty-four pence for an unbleached white or a wholemeal,' she said with a reassuring smile and she repeated the answer a little more loudly than before.

'Pardon?' said Ernie. I felt an inappropriate giggle beginning to manifest in the pit of my stomach and I wondered if Lorraine would repeat her list for a third time, so I turned my back and began to tidy the baskets of cereal bars opposite the counter. She decided not to repeat it again.

'Which type of loaf are you interested in?' she asked, patiently.

'None,' said Ernie. There was a pause. 'I just want to know the price.' Another pause.

'Well as you can see the prices are on labels on the shelves beneath each type of loaf.' She was still smiling but I could detect a note of irritation in her voice. Ernie studied the shelves carefully.

'How much is a loaf?' The giggle escaped and I turned it into a spluttering cough. The shop was beginning to fill up and a woman approached me, asking for information about a low cholesterol diet. After a couple of minutes of discussion and showing her products I returned to the counter to serve the queue and heard Ernie say to Lorraine, 'How much was a loaf yesterday?'

'The same as is it today. Fifty-four pence.'

'Pardon?'

'Fifty-four pence.'

'How much will a loaf be tomorrow?'

'Fifty-four pence.'

'Pardon?'

'Fifty-four pence.' Lorraine's voice was growing steadily louder.

'How much is a loaf at the bakers?'

'I have absolutely no idea.'

'Pardon?'

'I said I don't know.'

'The same as here?'

'Couldn't tell you. Look I'm a bit busy so if you don't mind…'

'Pardon?' I caught the eye of the woman I was serving and she laughed knowingly then turned to Ernie.

'The baker is just about to close, Ernie,' she said. 'If you run along you might just catch him.'

'Yes, that's right,' said Lorraine. 'You could ask him how much his loaves are.' Ernie looked around at us, his walnut face wrinkled in a frown then he took off, running out of the door and across the street in the direction of the baker's.

'Thank you,' Lorraine said to the woman. 'I thought he'd never go!'

'No problem,' said the woman. 'You can do the same for me some time. I work part-time in the Post Office and I know what he's like. 'How much is a stamp? Pardon?' Drives me mad!' She laughed as she picked up her shopping and left. The shop was quite busy now and the queue was getting longer so Lorraine picked up a carrier bag and began to pack as I rang in sales. We were both engrossed, heads down over the counter, serving customers when we heard a familiar voice.

'Hellooo! Changed my mind about the starter. The Carmody-Browns have just returned from a cruise so I thought 'Something Greek'. Got some feta and vine leaves and a jar of olives here. Pop it on my bill dear. Toodle-pip. Wheesh!'

CHAPTER EIGHTEEN

'I'm so tired,' yawned Lorraine, as she handed Nadine a colander of rinsed tomatoes. 'My head's banging like it's going to burst.' Her face was ashen and her eyes red rimmed.

'Me too,' said Nadine, rubbing her swollen eyes. She began to wearily cut the tomatoes, dropping the slices into a plastic box. 'I feel terrible,' she said.

'You look terrible, both of you,' I said handing them bottles of mineral water. 'Drink that!' Lorraine took a bottle of milk thistle from the shelf, opened it and swallowed two tablets.

'Take a couple of these,' she said to Nadine. 'They'll help your liver cope with the alcohol.'

'Better give me more than two then,' said Nadine, then held her hand over her eyes as she moaned, 'My eyes hurt when I move them.'

'What a state the pair of you are in,' I said laughing at them. I turned the radio up and sang along loudly and they winced and complained. It is one of the strange quirks of human nature that we take pleasure in other's hangovers and smugly exaggerate how healthy and alert we ourselves are feeling.

'I'll stay on the till this morning,' I said. 'You two need to keep out of sight of customers.' The bell jangled suddenly causing more quivering and head holding.

'Morning,' called Jonathan, and Nadine, looking up in horror, dashed into the office to hide her swollen eyes and white face from him.

'How much did you have?' I asked when Jonathan had left and Nadine had slunk back into the kitchen.

'Well, we're not sure really because they had selected drinks at special eighties prices you see, and after the first few we sort of lost count,' said Nadine.

'Great night though,' said Lorraine, taking a swig of water. 'Loads of people were dressed up and everyone was dancing.'

'Tell her about Adam,' said Nadine smirking. Lorraine's face turned from grey to crimson.

'Adam who?' I asked.

'Adam Ant,' said Nadine. 'Lorraine danced with him all night, you should have seen them strutting around to Tainted Love!'

'And what about you with his mate?' said Lorraine. 'Boy George, ha!'

'You're joking,' I said. 'You never got off with a Boy George look-alike!'

'He was nice!' said Nadine defensively as Lorraine and I laughed.

'Karma Karma Chameleon,' I sang dancing around the kitchen doing a very bad imitation of Boy George.

'Ooh, someone's happy this morning,' said a voice behind me.

'Morning Nige,' I said, turning around. 'These two were at an eighties disco last night and they've found a couple of blokes.'

'Into older men are you?' he said.

'Very funny,' said Nadine. 'It was a nineteen-eighties disco, not a disco for octogenarians.'

'So what are they like?' said Nige settling down to hear the gossip.

'Adam Ant and Boy George,' I said. Nige managed to look amazed, interested and envious all at the same time.

'They were dressed up for the disco,' said Nadine. 'It shows they have a sense of fun.'

'Or it could just show that they're a couple of raving poofs,' I said.

'Excuse me!' said Nige.

'Sorry Nige.' I said. Georgina arrived and was brought up to date.

'Are you going to see them again?' she asked.

'Not sure,' said Nadine. 'I think we gave them a phone number didn't we?'

'I seem to remember you writing something on Boy George's arm with a lipstick that I took to be a phone number,' said Lorraine.

'That's right! I remember now,' Nadine said. 'I must have been well gone. That was my new Clinique lipstick.'

'You should be more careful,' said Georgina. 'It's not a good idea to go giving out your telephone number to strange men.'

'I agree,' said Nige.

'And especially to very strange men in fancy dress,' I said.

'Of course it's ok to drag an artist home from a party for a night a passion, as long as you don't give him your phone number,' Lorraine said to Georgina.

'And you're just jealous,' Nadine said to Nige.

'That was different,' said Georgina. 'I'm older and wiser than you lot.'

'Anyway,' said Nadine. 'I didn't give him my number. I gave him the shop number.'

As the day wore on Nadine and Lorraine began to feel better, though the noise from the gym upstairs did not help. The gym was the bane of our lives. When we'd first viewed the premises and seen the huge sign at the side of the building advertising 'Sam's Gym', we'd naively thought that the two businesses might compliment each other. Customers using our shop might be tempted to join the gym and existing gym customers might be interested in a healthy diet to go with their fitness programme. However, it did not take long to realise that this was not the state-of-the-art type of fitness centre frequented by couples aiming to improve their fitness levels together or singles coming for a lycra-clad workout after a busy day at the office. This was a type of establishment I hadn't believed actually existed outside of 1950's black and white films.

Naively, I'd visited the gym intending to introduce myself to the owners and suggest we help each other out. The gym was accessed up a dark stairwell that opened onto the main exercise area. Naked light bulbs hung from the ceiling giving a murky light that illuminated streams of dust. The stained walls with their spattering of pictures torn from seedy magazines were permeated with nicotine stains and an aroma of cigarette smoke and sweat hung in the air. The proprietors, a couple of muscle bound foul-mouthed thugs who we later named Ug and Pug, were lounging on an old greasy looking sofa at the side of a boxing ring. I think they may have been brothers; they were blessed with the same flat forehead and wide nose with cavernous nostrils, although I believe Pug had slightly more brain cells than Ug. Weight lifting equipment lay scattered around the floor and I stepped over a set of dumbells as I walked in.

'Hello darlin',' Pug said as he saw me. He stood up and leered. 'Come for a workout?'

'No,' I said, already regretting coming. 'I'm from the shop downstairs. I...'

'She looks fit enough to me,' Ug said and they laughed and moved towards me. I felt uncomfortable and edged backwards, catching my ankle on the edge of the weight. I winced and rubbed my foot.

'Want me to kiss it better darlin'?' Pug said and he took another step towards me. I took another step back.

'I've just come to say hello and that I'm from the health food shop downstairs...' I said speaking more quickly as I retreated down the stairs, '...and I thought perhaps you could recommend our shop to your customers and we could perhaps send our customers to you...' My voice and my steps became faster and faster as Ug and Pug followed me down the stairs calling unsavoury suggestions and I jumped the last few steps and fled back to the shop.

The building was very old and not in a very good state of repair. It had in the past been a small department store, now divided into three spaces for separate businesses. The top two floors housed Sam's Sweaty Gym; we rented most of the ground floor except for a small room behind our kitchen presently used as a shoe repair and key-cutting business. The dividing walls had obviously been put in hastily and cheaply and were neither aesthetically pleasing nor soundproof. Sounds travelled through the makeshift partitions, the whirr of the key cutting machine could be heard in the kitchen but the noise from the gym infuriated us. Music thrashing at high volume was our indicator of when Ug, Pug and their posse were in residence. We could hear them clearly, arguing and cursing and dropping weights onto the floor, causing our ceiling to shudder and release showers of dust onto the shelves and on one occasion, a woodlouse onto Nadine's head. Lorraine went to see them and politely explained the problem asking if they could place weights down carefully and perhaps turn the music down, but was sent away with abusive words and gestures. I spoke to Mr Stoker the landlord about them and he often said he would threaten them with eviction but he never did. I think he was afraid of them. I think we were all a little afraid of them, although we never admitted to each other and we certainly did not let it show when they came into the shop. As much as we disliked them, they did spend a fair bit of money with us. Ug and Pug often came to buy lunch for their gang, bringing with them a cardboard box to carry their sandwiches and cartons of soup

.

Today they stomped in asking the usual question.

'What soup ye sellin the day?' shouted Ug. He seemingly had an affliction that made him unable to speak at normal volume.

'Lentil,' I said.

'Has it got lentils in it?' he yelled.

'Yes,' I said. 'That's why it's called lentil soup.'

'Lentils are protein,' he said. 'You've got to eat lots of protein to keep yer muscles like ours,' said Pug.

'Really.'

'Protein gives yer muscles,' said Pug. 'I read it in a body-building magazine,' he said proudly. 'Lentils and beans have loads of protein and nee fat.'

'Ever tried eating fish?' Nadine asked.

'To develop me muscles?' shouted Ug.

'No, to develop your brain.'

'Think yer funny?' said Ug thrusting his square head at Nadine.

'I'm going to cook chilli tomorrow,' I said, trying to diffuse the situation.

'Have you heard of TVP?' Ug and Pug looked at me blankly.

'Is it one of them diseases you get in yer …' Ug started.

'No, no,' I said hastily 'Textured Vegetable Protein. Very high in protein, very low in fat. It tastes like minced beef. I'm going to cook chilli with TVP, peppers, kidney beans…'

'Kidney beans?' bellowed Ug. 'That's a kind of bean. That's good protein. We'll come and get some the morrow.' They took their soup and left.

'I notice you didn't tell them about the side effects,' said Lorraine. 'I had terrible wind after eating some of that TVP, it's put me off using it.'

'Really?' said Nadine. 'I was going to try it seeing as it's low fat but I don't think I'll bother.'

'Do you think it's a good idea feeding it to our customers?' Lorraine said.

'We'll soon find out,' I said.

The following morning I made my chilli using TVP mince along with onions, peppers, kidney beans, tomatoes, garlic and chillies.

'Do you think I'll need to add chilli powder if I've put fresh chillies in?' I asked Nadine and Lorraine. They picked up teaspoons to have a taste.

'Mmm, that's really nice,' said Nadine. 'But I would put a little chilli powder in, it needs to be just a little bit hotter.' Lorraine had a taste and agreed.

'I'm surprised at how nice that is,' she said.

We decided to sell portions in cartons with pitta bread so Lorraine added it to the 'specials' board and to the A-board outside the shop. It sold really well, although everyone who bought it seemed to have a different opinion about how much chilli it should have in it, asking me to use less or to add more next time so I just agreed with them all and left the recipe as it was. By lunchtime we had sold out and when Peter came he was disappointed not to be able to try it.

'You could have kept me some!' he said as I handed him the duster to erase it from the chalkboard outside. I made double the next day and again it sold out. Most of it went upstairs.

'What are they doing with it up there?' I said to Nadine. 'Plastering the walls?'

'I don't know,' said Nadine, 'but I've sold them two lots this morning then I noticed they were back at lunchtime.'

The following day we discovered why it was so popular with them.

'Giz ten pots of that chilli,' said Pug. 'It's great, it makes ye fart like a scud missile.'

'Oh, surely that's not why you're eating it,' said Nadine, repulsed.

'Aye, it is,' shouted Ug. 'We're having a farting competition.'

'Ugh, how disgusting is that?' I said.

'Gross,' said Lorraine. I spooned out the chilli and handed her the cartons and she packed them into his cardboard box.

Pug leaned across the counter and blew a raspberry at Nadine, which caused Ug to laugh hysterically.

'How childish,' Nadine said haughtily. Ug joined his brother in making noises by blowing on his arm to make a rasping sound.

Nadine urgently rang his sale in the till and took the money and they left the shop laughing and making noises, leaving the three of us watching, not amused.

'How disgusting,' said Lorraine. 'I'm sure some of those were real.'

CHAPTER NINETEEN

The next day was one of those glorious sunny days that often occur in May signalling the start of summer. Suddenly shorts and summer dresses appear, the hum of lawn mowers fill the air, and everywhere you look there are people out walking or filling up benches. Everything looked brighter and cleaner as I walked with a spring in my step.

As the shop came into view my good mood evaporated. Ug, Pug and the posse were sitting on the windowsills of the gym, smoking and drinking cans of beer. The huge hinged windows had been opened fully enabling them to sit on the edge with their legs dangling over our shop window. Even this far up the bank I could hear the pulsating music and I could see passers-by crossing the road to avoid walking beneath them, especially as two of the gang were leaning out of the window spitting. I marched down the bank.

'I'm not standing for this!' I yelled up to them.

'Well, sit down then darlin',' Ug yelled back. Quite witty for him. There was an outburst of over-acted laughter and Pug slapped Ug on the back causing him to nearly fall from the sill. He let out a string of swear words and punched out at Pug. Lorraine's car pulled up beside me.

'What's going on here?' she said looking up. The posse jeered and shouted lewd suggestions. Derek came out of his shop and tried to reason with them.

'Come on lads,' he said. 'We all like to have a laugh and a bit of fun but this isn't going to help any of us is it?' Obscenities were shouted at him along with a suggestion as to where he should stuff his vegetables.

'I'm off,' he said cowardly. 'After all they're not really bothering me,' and he scuttled off to the safety of his shop.

'Well he was a lot of help,' Lorraine said.

'Shut those windows now!' I yelled. 'You'll frighten off trade. This is outrageous.' A ginger-haired youth dressed only in a pair of cut-off jeans, his chest sporting a bulldog tattoo, leaned out of the window and mimicked me.

'This is outrageous!' he said in a falsetto voice. He flapped his hands around. 'Get down this instant you naughty, naughty boys!' His mates guffawed with laughter and in rage I picked up a potato from the display outside Derek's shop and hurled it. Amazingly it hit Ginger in the face causing his friends to laugh even harder.

'I'm coming down there to kill you, you stupid …' he yelled. I didn't stay to hear the names he was calling me. I unlocked the shop door and scurried inside, Lorraine at my heels.

They were still there when Nadine arrived.

'I'm going to go and tell them,' she said. 'We'll not sell anything if this continues.'

'I better go and make sure she's all right,' said Lorraine, following her out. I stayed to attend to the few customers who had braved the gauntlet and managed to enter our shop. I pretended not to hear the shouting and swearing from outside as I served customers with a fixed smile on my face. Suddenly, Nadine burst into the shop followed by Lorraine.

'Phone the police!' Nadine yelled hysterically. 'They're off their heads! They've tried to drown me!' She was soaking wet, water dripped from her hair and face onto the floor, forming a puddle at her feet.

'Me hair,' she screeched. 'Look at me hair!' She held up strands of hair like pieces of limp seaweed.

'Calm down,' I said. 'What's happened? What did they do?'

'They threw a bucket of water over her,' Lorraine said and she caught my eye and we laughed.

'It's not funny!' yelled Nadine, which made us laugh more. 'Look at the state of me!'

'Sorry Nadine,' I said. 'Go and get dried off and I'll make you some coffee.'

'Sorry Nadine,' said Lorraine, trying not to smirk. 'I'll get the mop.'

The posse remained at their posts yelling and whistling at passers-by. They harassed Nige as he delivered our mail.

'Are you ok?' Lorraine asked him.

'Don't worry about me, flower,' he said. 'If I had a penny for every time I've been called a big puff I'd have enough to retire to Rio by now.'

Georgina came in red-faced with anger after giving as good as she got.

'What is it about men with muscles?' she said. 'Have you noticed the bigger the muscles, the smaller the brain?' I wasn't sure if this was a general rule but I said, 'Well in their case it is. That ginger haired one stands like he's got invisible footballs in each armpit, he's so blown up he can't put his arms straight.' I told her that I'd hit him in the face with a potato and she said to use a brick next time.

At ten o'clock I was taking a sandwich order on the telephone when a woman entered the shop leading Ernie by the hand. He was soaking wet and was whimpering pathetically. I guessed what had happened. Lorraine thanked the woman for her concern and said we would attend to him. When I put the phone down she had brought him a towel and was helping him to dry off. Nadine handed him a cup of tea.

'There you go darlin',' she said. 'Have yourself a sit down until you get over the shock.' I gave him the stool from behind the counter and he sat shaking looking like a frightened child. I was furious that they could treat him like this; he was such an easy target. It was a cowardly and callous thing to do to someone so vulnerable for the sake of a cheap laugh.

'I'll run him home in the car,' said Lorraine. 'Come on Ernie, I'll make sure you're all right.' I could tell from her face that she was seething. She took his arm and led him out of the door and I heard him say, 'How much is a loaf?'

She returned fifteen minutes later.

94

'I've left him with his Mum,' she said. 'He lives with her, apparently. She was very upset. Says he means no harm to anyone.' She marched into the kitchen.

'Right!' she said. 'Revenge time! Chilli is now off the menu, unless it's for the posse.' She took the lid off my pan of chilli and poured in a full jar of chilli powder.

'Are you sure we should do this?' I said.

'Don't worry,' she said taking a packet of ground senna from the shelves. 'It's all natural ingredients.' The phone rang just then so I didn't get to see exactly what went into the final concoction.

'It's a man asking for Lorraine or Nadine,' I said, holding out the phone to Nadine.

'Oh hi!' she breathed into the receiver. 'I'm fine thanks, how are you? Yes, we had a lovely evening, we really enjoyed it.'

'Sounds like Nadine's fixing you up for a date,' I said to Lorraine. We turned to look at Nadine and heard her say sweetly, 'See you Saturday then, bye!' and she replaced the receiver. 'That was Boy George,' she said excitedly. 'I've arranged for us to meet him and Adam Ant in town, eight o'clock on Saturday.'

'Surely they don't go by those names, do they?' I said.

'Course not!' said Nadine. 'I just didn't think to ask what their names were.' She went over the arrangements with Lorraine.

'Uh, oh, here we go,' I said nodding at the door as our favourite customer arrived.

'Ten pots of yer farty chilli,' said Pug.

'With pleasure,' murmured Lorraine.

'Enjoy yer shower did ye darlin?' he said leering at Nadine. Nadine rose above it and ignored him. He packed the pots of explosive chilli into his cardboard box and paid.

'Enjoy!' called Lorraine as he left the shop.

He came back at about quarter to twelve. He staggered in clutching his abdomen followed by Ug who was doing the same.

'Have you got anything for wind?' he said groaning and bending over. 'I can't stop farting, I'm in agony.'

'Did you win the competition then?' asked Lorraine.

'Eh?' said Pug. 'It's not funny man, me belly's killing me.'

'It's killing us as well,' said Nadine. 'Get them out quick.' I sold them some charcoal tablets and a packet of peppermint capsules.

'You better give us another couple of packets for the lads,' said Pug still doubled up. 'Jonna's worse than us, he canna get off the netty. We must have all caught a bug.'

We didn't get a chance to tell Peter about it as we were rushed off our feet that lunch time. He came in as the three of us were flying around the kitchen.

'Sorry Peter, I haven't had a chance to make you a sandwich yet,' I said.

'No bother,' he said. 'I'm just going to make a phone call in the office then I'll get something myself.'

'Sorry, none left,' I said to a customer asking for chilli. 'I'll make some more tomorrow.'

'We've lost loads of sales from you tampering with that chilli!' I said to Lorraine.

'I know, but it was worth it!' she said. 'They even bought their remedies here!'

Lorraine and Nadine raced around the kitchen filling rolls, making sandwiches and salads and heating up pies and pasties in the microwave. I stayed at the till taking money. The sound of the till drawer was always reassuring, and so were the wads of notes that we systematically transferred to the cash box. During a slight lull in the queue I quickly skimmed the till and took the notes into the office.

'Could you lock these in the cash box…' I started to say to Peter, then realised what he had done.

'That chilli was delicious,' he said. 'Really nice.' I put the notes on the desk and picking up his empty bowl went back into the kitchen.

'What's up?' Lorraine asked. I held up the empty bowl and she threw her head back and laughed.

'You're in for a stormy night!' she said.

CHAPTER TWENTY

During our first few months in business, we embarked upon a steep learning curve. We learned quickly, usually from our mistakes. Sometimes we ordered far too much stock and others too little. Opportunities were missed due to lack of experience and we often used over-complicated routines and methods before realising simpler more effective ones.

Cash flow was erratic, forcing us to take only a minimal salary. Having a fondness for all things luxurious, I sometimes found it difficult keeping to a tight budget. Living without unnecessary treats was challenging but at least we had Peter's salary.

Lorraine was still living with her friend Cheryl and was hoping to find a place of her own. Until we were able to increase our drawings from the business, she took a part time job with an organisation that helped those with learning difficulties to live independently in the community. One of their homes was conveniently situated a few streets away from the shop, and Lorraine worked night shifts there. Three times a week she would leave the shop at five thirty and walk around to Walton House armed with her overnight case. She would spend the evening helping the three residents to cook an evening meal and sort out any problems they might have. She also dispensed their medication. She slept in a small room kept exclusively for staff and so was on hand if needed through the night, which she often was. After organising breakfast, and ensuring the residents were dressed and ready to start the day, she would hand over to the daytime member of staff and walk back to the shop in time to open for the day. As she had little time to get ready or to eat breakfast herself, I would often find her on mornings after her shifts sitting in the office with toast and coffee, applying make-up or doing her hair.

On Monday morning I found her looking worse for wear with a coffee mug in front of her.

'Morning,' I said, taking off my coat and putting my bag in the office. 'How was your shift?'

'Tiring,' she said, rubbing her eyes. 'We'd run out of clean sheets so I had to put some on to wash and then wait for them to tumble dry while I cleaned the rooms. Then after I'd made the beds, Muriel knocked over a vase of flowers and the water soaked her bed so I had to put the sheets back in the machine and start again.' She yawned and rubbed her shoulders.

'What time did you eventually get to bed?' I asked.

'Not sure,' she said. 'It was after midnight. But I was up twice through the night because Bob had nightmares and I had to make him a hot drink and get him back to bed, then Muriel was convinced we had a burglar so I was up checking the place and reassuring her.'

'Don't they drive you mad?' I asked, knowing that the one way to drive Lorraine to distraction is to interrupt her sleep.

'No, not really,' she said. 'I'm really fond of them all. It's like a little family there the way they look after each other.'

Bob and Harry had lived together in Walton House now for two months with Muriel joining them a few days ago. Together they were learning to cope with the everyday stresses of independent living.

Bob was in his fifties and although he found learning difficult and could neither read nor write, he had secured himself a job at the city train station, sweeping up litter and discarded tickets and transporting luggage on a little trolley that he loved to push around. He often called in to the shop to see Lorraine, or if she wasn't there, to chat to us. He would burst into the shop and yell, 'Eeh, you lazy buggers, get some work done. I bet you've been drinking tea all day!' then cackle with laughter. To amuse him we always replied, 'Eeh, you're right there Bob. Lazy buggers us. Been drinking tea all day,' which he thought was a great joke. Sometimes he would grab me saying 'Here's a cuddle for you' and squeeze me tightly, which was embarrassing as he was a short man and his face was just about level with my chest. Whenever I saw him come in, I would dive behind the counter where I knew I was safe as he regarded this area as out-of-bounds. He never did it to Nadine or Lorraine; it was always me he grabbed.

'Just as well he doesn't try it with me,' Nadine would say. 'He'd be suffocated.'

Harry, the youngest at forty-two had no recollection of his childhood or of any family members and had come from a hostel where he'd been sent after being found living on the streets. Seemingly unaffected by the harsh blows life had dealt him, he was a happy character, willing to help wherever he could with great pride in knowing that he now belonged.

Muriel was the newest resident having being recently transferred from a house in the West End. She had lived in various institutions since the age of eighteen months, placed there by her parents when she did not show the signs of development usual for a child of that age. She'd had little formal education, but had absorbed how to cope with life from television, learning from advertisements which products would change her life, from keeping whites clean and having fresh breath to which breakfast cereal would set her up for the day. She learned the jingles by heart and used them as rules to living. The three had forged strong friendships and although sometimes quarrelled, shared their skills determined to prove that they could manage life outside of institutions.

Although these stories were typical of thousands more, it touched my heart to think that there are so many living without people of their own to share their triumphs and tragedies, relying on support given by those paid to care, rather from those who love you because you are part of them. Coming from a close family, I could not imagine what it would be like living without people around you to give unconditional love and to care for you whatever your faults or mistakes. I had always taken it for granted that I had been brought up by loving parents who wanted the best for me.

Lorraine finished her coffee and disappeared into the office to fix her hair and make-up. As I turned the open sign and pulled up the blinds I suddenly remembered something.

'How was your date on Saturday?' I asked. 'I meant to phone you on Sunday to find out, but we went hiking in the Lake District. We left really early and I didn't want to wake you. We spent all day walking in the hills then stopped at a little pub for a meal on the way home. We ended up staying until chucking out time. By the time we drove home it was too late to call you.'

'How far did you walk?' she asked to avoid answering my question.

'How was the date?' I repeated. Lorraine laughed at the fact that I'd not been distracted by her question.

'I'll tell you when Nadine gets here,' she said.

When Nadine arrived they still wouldn't tell me.

'We may as well wait for Georgina and Nige to save us having to tell the tale again,' said Nadine.

Georgina arrived first and drank a cup of camomile tea as she waited patiently for Nige.

'Here he is,' she said spotting him mincing along the pavement and swerving to avoid Ernie who was hurtling down the bank. Nige had his own exciting news to tell.

'Guess what?' he said as he burst through the door. 'Gus has been offered a part in a TV series. It's the big break he's been looking for.'

'That's great news, Nige,' I said.

'What series is it?' Lorraine and Georgina asked together.

'It's a historical romance to be shown in the summer,' said Nige proudly.

'And does he have a big part?' asked Lorraine.

'He's going to play one of the minor characters,' he said, missing a great opportunity for one of his camp jokes. 'It will give him a chance to show what he can do, he's bound to be spotted.'

'I'll put the kettle on to celebrate,' I said and Lorraine took a date and walnut loaf from the display and cut it into slices.

'It's not everyday we have something to celebrate,' she said as she handed it round.

'Do we have anything else to celebrate?' I asked, looking at Lorraine and Nadine.

'Oh yes,' said Nige. 'The big date. How were Adam and George?'

'Maurice and Barry, actually,' said Nadine. Nige chortled.

'Doing the Bee Gees now are they?' he said.

'We may as well tell them, Lorraine, and get it over with,' Nadine said. 'We'll get no peace until we do.' We all settled down ready to listen and Lorraine nominated Nadine to tell the tale.

'We spent ages getting ready,' she said.

'You might have, I didn't,' said Lorraine. Nadine ignored her and continued.

'We decided to get a taxi into town because it was raining and so we were a little early. We stood at the Haymarket watching people going past and trying to see them. We kept nudging each other going 'Is that them? Is that them?' every time we saw a couple of good-looking blokes. After a while we began to feel embarrassed standing there like a couple of old tarts on the look out for men.'

'Speak for yourself!' said Lorraine.

'There were two weird looking blokes standing beside the Metro Station watching us so we decided to wander off, then Lorraine says to me 'They're following us!' I turned around and sure enough, they were, and I was just about to tell them where to get off when one of them says 'Hi Nadine. Hi Lorraine, it is you isn't it? We weren't sure.' Well I tell you, we didn't recognise them either, they looked nothing like we thought they would.'

'Oh no!' said Nige thrilled. 'How bad were they?'

'Absolute stonkers,' said Lorraine. 'Especially Maurice. I mean Adam Ant. With his make up on, his white stripe and everything, he gave the impression that he was really good looking underneath, but without it he was a right minger.'

'A bit like the real Adam Ant then,' Georgina said.

'Well looks aren't everything,' I said.

'Not everything but something,' said Lorraine. 'You can't go out with someone you can't even bear to look at! And it wasn't just that, it was the way they were dressed. Patterned jumpers and slip-on shoes with white socks.' Nige giggled fascinated. 'We thought they'd just dressed in eighties gear for the disco but they wear eighties stuff all the time.'

'Anyway,' continued Nadine, 'they suggested we go to Heroes nightclub but we talked them into going to Fiddler's Bar because no-one we know goes there. We sat at a table and had a conversation. Well, I say a conversation but actually it was more like a competition between Maurice and Barry where you had to out shout your competitor and bore the spectators to death at the same time. Maurice just went on and on about his collection of rare 45's, who recorded them, who produced them, what year they were recorded, blah, blah blah. Barry was under some sort of delusion that he could do impressions of famous people and kept saying 'Who's this? Who's this?' and they all sounded the same.'

'He was rubbish,' said Lorraine, shaking her head. 'He couldn't even do a recognisable Tommy Cooper.'

'We stuck it out for two rounds of drinks,' said Nadine, 'but then they wanted to move on. We were terrified of being seen out with them, so we said we'd just go to the ladies before we went. We were trying to think of a plan when Lorraine noticed that the window above one of the toilets was open.'

'You never climbed out the window!' said Georgina, laughing.

'We did!' said Nadine. 'I gave Lorraine a leg up then she helped to pull me up. We ended up on a roof in a back alley somewhere beside the University. We climbed down the fire escape and legged it to the taxi rank near the hospital.'

'I wish I'd seen you climbing out of the window,' I said. 'I bet it was a right laugh!'

'You should have seen the state of us,' Lorraine said. 'I ripped my skirt climbing down from the window and Nadine laddered her tights and we were both covered in dirty black marks.'

'I wonder how long they waited before they realised you weren't coming back,' I said.

'Eeh, you're a cruel lot you women,' Nige said. 'Probably scarred them for life.'

'Have you heard from them?' I asked.

'No,' said Lorraine. 'And we don't want to either.'

'They've got the shop number,' said Georgina mischievously. 'They'll probably call you today to find out what happened.'

They didn't call. Lorraine and Nadine never heard from them or saw them again, but it was fun to watch them squirm every time the telephone rang that day.

Nige finished his coffee and went off to finish delivering mail in a hurry to get back to Gus. Georgina stood up to leave too, packing her groceries into her basket. Just as she was about to leave, one of our regulars, Josie arrived and spotting Georgina came to hug her.

'How are you?' asked Georgina, obviously pleased to see her. 'You look great, as always!'

Josie shopped with us a couple of times a week and spent a lot on organic produce and expensive herb and vitamin supplements. A glamorous forty-something, she was always beautifully made up with shining well-cut hair. Her stylish clothes were carefully chosen to enhance her colouring and figure, and her shoes and handbags carefully selected to match perfectly. Her jewellery was expensive and tasteful and she had an aura of wealth. She lived in one of the very desirable detached houses at the bottom of the bank, houses that seldom came up for sale. On the rare occasions that one did, it was snapped up for an astronomical price within hours of hitting the market.

'Let me take you for coffee,' Josie was saying to Georgina as she paid for her purchases. 'We can catch up, I want to hear all your news, especially about your new romance,' she said winking at us. They left together, an unlikely looking couple, Josie in her cream suit and pale pink silk scarf and Georgina in Doc Martens and a hand painted boiler suit.

'I didn't realise those two knew each other,' I said surprised, watching as they crossed the road, arm in arm, and headed towards the Saffron café.

'Me neither,' said Lorraine. 'Looks like they're good mates.'

'She's so slim,' sighed Nadine.

'And beautiful,' I said.

'She's so lucky,' said Lorraine. 'The woman with everything.'

'I bet she's got a gorgeous, rich husband,' said Nadine.

'Well he must be loaded,' said Lorraine. 'I've never seen him though.'

'I've seen a picture in her purse, a family group.' I said. 'It's of Josie with an attractive man and two children. Looks like a holiday photo, they all look really happy on it.'

'Lucky bitch,' said Nadine. 'Some people have everything.'

'I know,' I said. 'And she's so lovely we can't even hate her for it!'

'That's true,' said Lorraine. 'She's such a nice person, you can't help but like her.'

Nadine picked up a dish of hardboiled eggs and began slicing them ready to make egg mayonnaise filling and I went to assist a customer who asked for evening primrose capsules. I was reaching up to get a jar from a high shelf when I felt a pair of arms grab me around the waist.

'Eeh you lazy bugger, get some work done!'

'Hello, Bob,' I said, trying to peel him off me.

'Get some work done!' he said squeezing the air out of me.

'Too busy drinking tea, Bob,' I said, 'You know what we're like.' He squeezed me tighter, cackling with laughter and pushing his face into my chest.

'Get him off!' I mouthed to Nadine but she just laughed so I struggled to the till to ring in the evening primrose oil with him clasped to me.

'Come and talk to me, Bob,' said Lorraine pulling his hand and prising him away. 'How is everyone?'

'We're all good,' Bob said.

'And what about Muriel?' Lorraine asked. 'Has she settled in?'

'Aye, and she's me friend,' said Bob. 'I told her about your shop, she's going to come and see you. I said mind, they're lazy buggers in there, drink too much tea.'

'You're right there,' said Nadine on cue. 'Lazy buggers us.' Bob chuckled and headed for the door.

'See you later,' he said. 'Never mind drinking tea, get some work done!'

'She seems to be happy living there,' Lorraine said when he'd gone.

'Who?' I asked.

'The new resident, Muriel. She had trouble of some sort with a resident at the last home she was at in the West End. Actually that reminds me, I need to get some shopping in for Walton House before my shift tonight.'

'Why don't you go now before the lunchtime rush starts?' I suggested.

'Don't you mind?' Lorraine said.

'Course not. It'll save you rushing about later,' I said.

Unfortunately, the lunchtime rush started before she returned, so Nadine and I struggled to cope, bullying Peter onto the till as soon as he arrived. The phone kept ringing; we didn't have an answer machine in those days, and I always stumbled at the dilemma of whether to serve the customers we had and risk missing telephone sales, or to leave the queue to answer it and take the risk that it could just be someone wanting to sell us insurance.

'Go and answer it,' said Nadine standing at the kitchen bench surrounded in dishes. 'I'll cope here, as long as Peter stays on the till.' I hurried to answer it and after taking an order for sandwiches, came back to the till where Peter started telling me about a customer account.

'What do you mean?' I asked, as Nadine and I flung fillings into rolls. 'None of our customers have accounts, we don't do them.'

'Well, this one said she had,' he said, trying to talk to me, ring in sales and take orders simultaneously.

'Which one?'

'The woman who was here just now when you were on the phone and Nadine was in the kitchen,' he said. His multi-tasking attempt suddenly went awry as a customer complained of being over charged and he handed out sandwiches to customers who hadn't ordered them. Nadine took over, expertly apologising to the customer, sorting out the sandwich mix up and taking the next two orders.

'How does she do that?' Peter said.

'Don't worry about it,' I said. 'It's a female thing. Tell me about the woman.'

'She said she had an account that she clears at the end of the month. Big woman, she was. Very loud.'

'Wheesh?' I asked as it dawned on him.

'Mrs Forbes-Williamson?' he asked.

'Yes, you idiot! You've just let her do it again!'

CHAPTER TWENTY-ONE

Just as Peter left to return to work, Lorraine rang to say that her car had broken down and she was stuck on the High Street. I didn't have time to listen to details as the queue was growing by the minute.

'Don't worry, we're coping,' I lied, hanging up the phone and frantically yelling, 'Next please' at the queue. Nadine and I threw sandwiches together, serving as many customers at a time as we could, running past each other from counter to kitchen and back again. By two o'clock we were exhausted.

'I'll put the kettle on before I go,' she said. 'There's something I want to ask you about, if you've time.'

We pulled up two stools behind the counter, relieved to sit down at last, and Nadine pulled a newspaper from her bag.

'I've decided to place an ad in the lonely hearts section of the Daily Echo,' she said. 'I just wondered if you'd help me write it?'

'I'll help if I can,' I said. 'But I've never written anything like that before.'

'I've brought last week's pages so we can get an idea of what sort of things they say,' she said. 'We could pinch bits of ads we think sound good and put it all together to make mine.' We spread the paper over the counter and poured over it.

'What's does WLTM, GSOH and OHAC mean?' I asked.

'*Would Like to Meet, Good Sense of Humour and Own Home and Car*', answered Nadine. 'It's all in code.'

'Oh right,' I said, baffled.

'You see,' she said, 'you have to be very careful what you say because they all have hidden meanings.' She pointed to one of the ads. 'Take this for example. *Cuddly lady, 50's, seeks man to share rest of life with.* That means fat woman desperate for husband.' She pointed to another. '*Male, 37, with lots of love to give right woman after recent separation.* That means man with lots of baggage wants shoulder to cry on about his ex.'

'Some of them don't seem to have hidden meanings,' I said. '*Attractive slim twenty-year-old seeks older man for exciting fun, looks not important, 100% discretion.* There's no hidden meaning in there.'

'That's code for tart seeks clients,' Nadine said. 'That's why I need help, I don't want to give the wrong impression.'

She worked on her ad and I helped between serving customers, and we finally came up with *Blond, fun loving female, 26, seeks genuine, sincere man for lasting relationship.* I wasn't sure about the blond-fun-loving bit, fearing that it could be misinterpreted, but Nadine was happy so she went to find an envelope and a stamp in the office. She came out with her coat on and her bag slung over her shoulder carrying the sweeping brush.

104

'I'll just give the floor a quick sweep before I go,' she said. I let her get on with it. I had long since given up trying to stop her working before and after her shift.

She was sweeping in front of the counter when the door opened and a woman dressed in a thick coat, furry boots and pompom hat came in.

'Hello,' I said. 'Can I help?'

'Have you any Anadin?' the woman asked. 'Because nothing works faster than Anadin.'

'I'm sorry we only stock herbal medicines,' I said. 'You should be able to get some at the chemist up the road.' The woman turned to look at Nadine.

'I'd rather have a bowl of Cocopops,' she said. Nadine stopped sweeping.

'I'm sorry we don't have Cocopops either,' Nadine said. 'We do have some nice types of muesli though.'

'I like Frosties best,' she said. 'They're grrreat.' I laughed politely at the joke but the woman did not laugh so I resumed a serious expression.

'What about a Mars bar?' she said. 'Do you have one of those? Because a Mars a day helps you work, rest and play.' I could see Nadine was trying hard to keep a straight face.

'We don't, but we do have organic chocolate bars and cereal bars if you like those?' I suggested.

'The milk chocolate melts in your mouth not in your hand,' she said.

Right,' I said. We'd had some strange conversations with customers but this one was surreal. Why was she speaking in advertising slogans? Was it a joke? She didn't seem to be laughing although Nadine was.

'You too can have a body like mine,' the woman said to me. 'It's the best a man can get.' I looked past the woman to Nadine who was leaning on her brush sniggering. There was an awkward pause so I said, 'Feel free to have a look around, if you need any help just ask.'

'I'll let my fingers do the walking,' she said and went off to look at the shelves.

'Weird!' Nadine murmured to me as she struggled not to laugh. The woman was looking at our display of handmade soaps and she picked one up and sniffed it.

'You'll be lovelier each day with fabulous pink Camay,' she said to Nadine.

'I certainly will,' Nadine spluttered.

'Nadine!' I said remonstratively. Nadine was obviously enjoying this weird exchange.

'Found anything you like?' she asked the woman.

'Stop encouraging her!' I whispered.

'I like this shop. Its finger lickin' good,' the woman said. Nadine let go of her laughter.

'Hee, hee, that's a good one!' she said

'Is it your shop?' the woman asked. 'It's the real thing.' Again Nadine laughed.

'No its hers,' she said pointing at me. 'She liked it so much she bought the company!' she laughed loudly. I couldn't see what was funny myself. It was bizarre. Nadine was laughing hysterically now.

'Bought the company!' she repeated through her laughter.

'Nadine!' I said again, as she bent over and held her stomach.

'Oh it hurts!' she said, but she was unable to stop.

'Just do it,' the woman said. 'On and On with Ariston.' Nadine laughed even harder.

'Beanz Meanz Heinz!' she spluttered. The woman looked at Nadine, her face expressionless then continued browsing. She seemed to be oblivious to Nadine's laughter.

'Well I must be going,' she said. 'Mums gone to Iceland.' This comment set Nadine off again.

'Bye flower, see you again,' Nadine said, wiping tears from her face.

'Bye,' said the woman. 'Don't leave home without it.'

The woman returned the next day late in the afternoon. I was in the kitchen preparing vegetable lasagne. Lorraine and I sometimes took turns at cooking dinner before we left, so that we just had to heat it up in the oven when we got home.

'That's the slogan woman!' I whispered to Lorraine. Lorraine turned to look.

'Hello Muriel,' she said to the woman. 'It's the new resident from Walton House,' she whispered back to me. Suddenly it all made sense. This was the woman Lorraine had told me about.

'This is my sister, Christine,' Lorraine said.

'Yes,' I said. 'You came yesterday, didn't you? I met you then. How are you settling in?'

'Smashing,' said Muriel. 'For mash get Smash.'

'I'm glad you like it,' Lorraine said, obviously used to these conversations and therefore taking it in her stride. 'They're a nice bunch, I'm sure you'll be happy there.'

'Oh it's much better than the other place,' Muriel said. 'Cantors turn your house into a home. I didn't like the other place. There was a man who used to pester me all the time. Wouldn't leave me alone.'

'Which man?' Lorraine asked, looking concerned.

'The man at the other place, he wouldn't leave me alone.' She picked up a flapjack from the basket on the counter. 'Can you eat this between meals without ruining your appetite?' she asked.

'Muriel, this is important,' Lorraine said. 'Is the man a member of staff or a resident?'

'I'll suck it and see,' she said, unwrapping the flapjack.

'Muriel!' Lorraine said.

'I mean Ned who lives there,' Muriel said. She took a bite of the flapjack. 'Made to make your mouth water, ooh.'

'Muriel!' Lorraine said again. 'This is important, you must tell me.'
Muriel looked at Lorraine as she chewed her flapjack.

'He said he would give me fifty pence if I would go to bed with him,'
she said. Lorraine was shocked and so was I.

'Who's Ned?' I asked Lorraine.

'He's one of the other residents,' Lorraine said to me. Muriel looked
unconcerned.

'Muriel, did you tell anyone? He shouldn't say things like that to you,
it's not right.' I said.

'No, it's not right,' she said. 'It's terrible. Put a tiger in your tank.'

'Listen, Muriel,' Lorraine said. 'You should tell a member of staff if
someone says anything like that to you. You don't have to put up with it.'

'You're right,' she said, 'Because I'm worth it.'

Lorraine put a hand on her arm.

'Do you know how important this is Muriel?' she said to her. 'No-one
is allowed to treat you badly.' Muriel smiled at her.

'Oh it's terrible, I know.' she said.

'Do you understand why it was wrong of him to say that to you?' asked
Lorraine.

'Oh yes. Yes I do,' Muriel answered. 'It's terrible, awful. And I'll tell
you why.' She banged her fist on the counter and said angrily, 'Because to this
day he still hasn't given me that fifty pence.'

CHAPTER TWENTY-TWO

The days, as they are inclined to when you are busy, passed quickly, and soon it was summer. By the end of June we were beginning to feel much more optimistic about the success of our business.

Our stock range had changed enormously since opening. Unpopular lines had been dropped and many more taken up due to customer demand. Products we would never have predicted to be popular sold well; people came from all over town to buy seaweed crisps and we did a roaring trade in liquorice root thanks to the local school children.

We attended the health and hygiene course as requested by Edward Reeves and completed several training courses in herbal remedies and homeopathy and as our knowledge grew so did our range of vitamins and remedies.

We both found the idea working with the body's natural healing systems preferable to the practice of bombarding it with drugs at each sign of minor ailment, preferring to keep the use of strong drugs and medication until absolutely necessary. We devoured as much knowledge as we could, reading medical papers and attending seminars and courses and used the information to compile a self-help guide for customers. We were very careful when we advised people about self-medication and the use of natural remedies and always made it clear that we were not medically trained and advised customers to speak to their GP about any product they were intending to use. We noticed that staff in shops similar to ours often wore white coats but Lorraine was dead set against this idea for us.

'It gives the wrong impression,' she said. 'It makes us look like doctors.' What ever we wore, and even after telling customers we were not medically trained some customers insisted on treating us like doctors, expecting us to have access to their medical files. If a customer had been diagnosed with a specific ailment by a GP then we could suggest remedies and diet changes that may help their condition, but some expected us to examine and diagnose, like the man who came in to ask me about his headaches.

'Mornin',' he said. 'I've been having these terrible headaches. Have you got something for them?'

'What does your GP think is causing them?' I asked.

'Well that's what I'm asking you, what do think's causing them?' he said abruptly.

'Headaches can be caused by many things, you really need to see your doctor first, just to rule out anything serious.'

'What sort of things can cause headaches?' he asked.

'Lots of things,' I said. 'Stress, for example.'

'So you think I'm stressed?'

'Not necessarily, I just meant that stress is a common cause of headaches.'

'Well can you give me something for stress?'

'Yes…no! Well, you need to be sure it is stress first. It may be something else.'

'Like what?'

'Oh I don't know,' I said beginning to get irritated. 'Eyestrain perhaps, or liver problems or migraine. Or it could be something more serious.'

'Well which is it? Am I stressed or is it me eyes or me liver?' he said. Lorraine was filling shelves behind me and I looked at her for help.

'You really need to see your doctor,' she said. 'Headaches are a symptom of many things. When you've had a diagnosis come back and we'll do our best to help.' He looked at Lorraine then at me.

'You're no more help than she is,' he said to Lorraine, nodding his head at me.

'First it was stress then it was me liver, then me eyes, which one is it?' His voice was becoming louder. 'Why don't you just tell me what's wrong with me?' You're thick that's what wrong with you, I thought.

'Your doctor will tell you the cause then you can come back and tell us and we'll advise you the best we can,' said Lorraine in her best patient voice.

'What about taking some blood tests,' he said rolling up his sleeve.

'You need a doctor to do that,' I said. 'We're not doctors.'

'You could be right,' he said and for a moment I thought we'd had a break through. 'I like a bit of a drink, it could be me liver.' Lorraine and I looked at each other in exasperation.

'What will you give me if it's me liver?' he asked.

'We would advise you to avoid fatty foods and alcohol and to take some milk thistle and artichoke,' said Lorraine.

'What if it was migraine?'

'Then I'd suggest feverfew and perhaps a food sensitivity test to see if we could find the triggers.'

'And for stress?' I looked around the room for hidden cameras. Surely this was a wind-up. I often worried about Watchdog coming in and secretly filming us, trying to catch us giving wrong advice to customers. Lorraine was explaining about how stress can deplete the body of B vitamins and about the benefits of avena sativa and valerian supplements for stress symptoms.

I leaned across the counter and placing my hand on his arm looked straight into his eyes. I spoke slowly and clearly.

'Make an appointment with your doctor, just to rule out anything serious,' I said. 'Then come back and tell us what he said and I promise we'll give you as much help as we can.'

'Oh I can't be bothered with all that palaver,' he said. 'Just give us a bottle of each.' We gave in and sold him milk thistle tincture, artichoke tincture, feverfew tablets, B-complex tablets, avena sativa tincture and valerian tablets and he left happy and out of pocket.

Unfortunately, many people came to us because they had lost faith and given up on the medical profession and sadly a few came because the medical profession had given up on them. One of these was Victoria, a young woman with ME.

'Myalgic Encephalomyelitis is believed to be a viral infection,' she told us. 'It stems from the Herpes group of viruses and attacks when the immune system is low. It is very difficult to diagnose and to treat. My doctor has given me test after test but can't pinpoint the cause and so she has come to the conclusion that it is 'all in my head'.'

'Have you thought about seeing another doctor?' asked Lorraine.

'I've already tried that,' said Victoria. 'Unfortunately, ME is not recognised by many doctors.'

'I suppose it's to be expected,' said Lorraine. 'Some of them are still struggling to believe the existence of PMT.' She carried one of our chairs to the front of the counter so that Victoria could sit down. Victoria looked tired, her face was pale and she had dark shadows beneath her eyes.

'I'm being treated by a homeopath, Kara Guilden' continued Victoria, 'and she suggested I speak to you about diet suggestions.' We knew Kara well. She had a good reputation and we often recommended her to customers, and likewise, she sent her clients to see us.

'The main thing we would suggest would be to avoid any foods that will deplete your energy levels or lower your immunity any further,' I said. 'Sugar is believed to reduce the efficiency of the immune system so that's one to avoid. I would also recommend keeping off caffeine and alcohol and any foods that you know affect you negatively. Stick to a good diet, plenty of wholegrains, nuts and seeds, fresh fish and fruit and vegetables and keep off convenience foods and take-aways.'

'Kara suggested I take Echinacea and another herb that I can't remember the name of... astral-something root?'

'Astragalus root,' said Lorraine. 'It has similar properties to Echinacea, boosts the immune system and inhibits viruses, both would be beneficial.' We also recommended Siberian Ginseng to enhance her tolerance to physical stress and Vitamin C and zinc to strengthen her immune system. Lorraine packed the bottles into a cardboard box along with all the food Victoria had bought. Her bill was quite substantial. I felt guilty, as we often did in these situations, making money from people who were ill. I offered her a discount.

'Don't be silly,' she said. 'You need to make a living. I don't mind paying if it makes me feel better.' She leaned against the counter breathing heavily. The simple act of walking a few streets from her flat and having a conversation had tired her out.

'Come on,' said Lorraine, picking up the box. 'I'll give you a lift home.'

Poor woman, I thought when they'd gone. It must be awful to feel so exhausted all the time. But it had given me an idea.

Josie came in before Lorraine returned. She didn't look as radiant as usual. She had lost weight and although as always she was dressed stylishly, her clothes looked slightly too big, giving her a fragile appearance.

'Hi,' she said. 'Just called for a sandwich. Tuna, I think, with salad please.'

'Are you ok Josie?' I asked, as Nadine set about preparing the sandwich.

'Fine,' she said. 'Absolutely fine. Beautiful day isn't it? Looks like summer's arrived at last.' She smiled but the smile did not reach her eyes. She looked strained and pale, her skin almost transparent, her eyes slightly swollen beneath her make up. I smiled back at her. 'Are you sure you're all right?' I asked again.

'Absolutely,' she said picking up her sandwich and dropping coins into my hand. 'I'm off to enjoy this glorious day God has given us. It would be a sin to waste it!' She left, passing Nige in the doorway.

'Morning, Nige,' she said.

'Morning,' replied Nige. 'And how are you this fine day?' but Josie had gone.

'She's in a bit of a hurry,' he said as he put our mail on the counter. 'Mmm, lovely smell of coffee.'

'I don't think she's well.' I said. 'She looked very drawn, like she's lost weight quickly.' Nadine handed Nige his cup of coffee.

'I wish I was that thin,' she said.

'Not that thin,' I said. 'That's too thin. She looks ill.'

'Yeah, but I could eat my way up to a size fourteen,' said Nadine.

'Now, now, some men find fat women attractive,' said Nige. Nadine gave him a look like stink.

'She's not fat Nige,' I said nudging him and realising he'd said the wrong thing he started trying to talk his way out of it.

'I didn't mean that you were fat; I just meant that some men do like bigger women. Although I don't,' he added hastily.

'You don't like thin women either,' said Nadine, offended.

'Why don't you do what I do?' Nige said. 'Go on the seafood diet. I see food and…'

'You eat it,' finished Nadine and I together. 'Nige that's ancient.'

'Sorry,' he said. 'Just trying to cheer you up.'

'Well it's not working,' said Nadine grumpily. 'I'm fed up being overweight. I've tried every diet going.'

'Honestly Nadine,' I said. 'I wish you'd listen. You are not fat, you've got a lovely figure, you're in proportion.'

'In proportion? You mean I'm fat all over,' said Nadine. 'I'm sick of diets, I've been on them for years, I'm twenty-four now.'

'Stone?' asked Nige. Nadine looked like thunder.

'Only joking, pet. Just trying to make you laugh.'

'Well done Nige,' I said as Nadine stormed off to the kitchen and began clattering saucepans.

'I think I'd better go,' said Nige, draining his coffee. 'Honestly some people are so sensitive. See you tomorrow, tara.'

I chatted to Nadine as we worked trying to cheer her, but her replies were monosyllabic and she would not be drawn into conversation. I gave up, suddenly feeling weary, and we sliced tomatoes in silence. I felt drained and tired. When Lorraine came back she sensed the atmosphere immediately.

'What's up?' she asked.

'Oh I don't know,' I said. 'Everyone seems to be fed up at the moment, including me.' I hadn't felt quite right lately, although I couldn't put my finger on what was wrong. 'I'm just tired. I think I've been overdoing it,' I said to Lorraine. 'I've been feeling a bit lethargic and light-headed lately that's all.'

'You do look a bit pale,' she said, concerned. 'Not a good advertisement for a health shop. Perhaps you should see your doctor.'

'Yes, you're right,' I said. 'I'll make an appointment.' And I did intend to. As soon as I had a spare minute.

CHAPTER TWENTY-THREE

'Well, what do you think?' I asked, holding up my poster.

'I think we'll have people taking us for a ride,' said Lorraine. Nadine looked at my artwork.

'*New at Nutmeg*,' she read. '*Free delivery service available. Ask inside.*'

'I thought it would be a good idea for people like Victoria,' I said aware of their lack of enthusiasm. 'If she's having a bad day she can just ring us and we'll nip along with what she needs.'

'You mean I'll nip along,' said Lorraine. 'In my car. Using my petrol.'

'The shop will pay for the petrol,' I said.

'I don't mind doing that for Victoria,' Lorraine said. 'But what about every Tom, Dick and Harry ringing up wanting two bread rolls or a jar of honey?'

'Or a sandwich at lunchtime,' put in Nadine.

'Then we'll have a minimum order,' I said. 'Except for Victoria.'

'And how are we going to deliver sandwiches at our busiest time when it takes the three of us at top speed just to cope with the lunchtime queue?'

'We'll set a time limit. Deliver them late morning before the rush or afterwards in the afternoon,' I said beginning to get irritated at the way they were shooting down my fantastic idea. 'Honestly, the pair of you are so negative, you're just looking for problems.' I snatched my poster back.

'Best to be prepared for the worst,' said Lorraine. 'A problem realised in advance is a problem halved. Forewarned is forearmed.'

'Oh shurrup man,' I said.

The delivery service did bring problems but it also brought a lot of new business. Customers telephoned with their orders before Wednesday and Lorraine delivered on Friday afternoon. Our delivery round grew to around twenty regulars and another twenty 'occasionals'. After lunch on Friday Lorraine and I packed the orders into boxes and carried them to her car ready for delivery. I was curious about the delivery customers, as although I spoke to them on the telephone I had not met them. When Lorraine returned from her delivery round we drank tea and she would fill me in with little snippets of gossip about them.

Mrs Symperton Pyke-Brown phoned in her order sounding like she had a mouthful of marbles. Noting down her order, I always felt as though I should curtsey as I spoke. She ordered *parkets of shoogar* and *wholemeal flah*. We nicknamed her Mrs Symperton Pyke-Very-Posh-Actually-Brown and we mimicked her accent as we put up her order.

'Parse me the flah old gel.'

'I say old bean, could you be a tadge more prudent with the prunes, dahling.'

'Oh do baggar orf you silly arse'

After Lorraine had delivered to her house and reported that she lived in a run down semi with a dilapidated caravan permanently in the drive we changed her name to Mrs Symperton Pyke-Not-Very-Posh-Actually-Brown.

Mrs Bunting called weekly with her order and although I knew she always called at around ten on Wednesday morning, she always took me by surprise with her booming voice vibrating down the telephone.

'Mrs Bunting here,' she would roar. 'B-U-N-T-I-N-G.'

'Good morning Mrs Bunting,' I would say recoiling as I moved the receiver six inches away from my ear. She would proceed to yell her order at me, spelling out words to make sure I understood. Every Friday, as soon as she received her box of groceries from Lorraine, Mrs Bunting would telephone with a complaint.

'My cheese is too cold, C-O-L-D' she complained once.

'Sorry Mrs Bunting,' I said. 'It's because we keep it in the fridge, you know.' To comply with health and safety regulations.

Another time, 'My dried rosemary, R-O-S-E-M-A-R-Y does not seem to be the correct shade of green.'

'Sorry about that, Mrs Bunting. I'll replace it free of charge.' And I'll send you a colour chart next time. And once, 'My bread rolls, are too large, L-A-R-G-E this week.'

'So sorry, Mrs Bunting, I'll make sure they're smaller next week.' By taking a B-I-T-E out of them before I send them.

Week after week I humoured her, refunding money and sending replacements, until she nearly drove me mad.

'I know she's an old goat,' Lorraine said. 'But I really like her. She's such a character.' Apparently, Mrs B-U-N-T-I-N-G was eighty-four and very active and Lorraine always arrived to find her busy with some arduous task, painting her front door, or perched on a stepladder cleaning her gutters and once, pruning roses dressed in only a large straw hat and a swimsuit.

The Derringtons were a lovely middle aged couple who placed an order about once a month. Mr Derrington was a local councillor and was a true gentleman. He was kind and patient and truly cared about the community. Mrs Derrington baked her own bread, bottled her homegrown fruit and made delicious fruit cakes, scones and biscuits. We supplied her with great sacks of flour, dried fruit and sugar and Lorraine always returned with a parcel of her fruitcake and shortbread.

Most of the sandwich orders were from local offices and businesses within walking distance, so Nadine delivered them carrying a large wicker basket. She didn't seem to mind doing this and had a system for counting how many calories she'd burned during each delivery. We discussed getting her a bike with a basket on the front but she wasn't keen on the idea, even though the basket was heavy and she had to return to refill it two or three times. 'You can get lost,' she said. 'I'm not riding about like the Hovis boy.'

Today we were waiting eagerly for her to come back as she had replies from her lonely-hearts ad to show us. Nige and Georgina hung around waiting for her.

Lorraine made us all herbal tea and coffee for Nige and between serving customers we chatted.

'Seen anything of Josie lately?' Georgina asked.

'She was in a couple of days ago,' I said. 'Looked like she'd lost weight.'

'I'm keeping me mouth shut,' muttered Nige.

'He offended Nadine, talking about fat women,' I explained. Georgina narrowed her eyes and said, 'I hope you weren't being sexist Nigel.' She turned to me. 'How was Josie?'

'She looked poorly to me,' I said. 'Tired and pale.' Georgina looked concerned.

'Why are you asking? Is she ill?' Lorraine asked.

'No reason,' said Georgina. 'Just haven't seen her for a few days.'

'It's probably just life in the fast lane catching up with her.' I said. Georgina looked at me.

'She does have a very glamorous lifestyle,' Lorraine said. 'It's bound to tire you out eventually.'

'Yeah, right', said Georgina. She seemed uncomfortable. Perhaps she thought that we were criticising her friend.

'Did I tell you Marc's offered to take me to Paris?' she said, suddenly changing the subject.

'No, when?' asked Lorraine. Nige suddenly became interested in the conversation.

'Ooh la la! I wouldn't mind a few days in Gay Paree with a gorgeous artist,' he said in a really bad French accent.

'He wouldn't be interested in you darlin',' said Georgina. 'Anyway, I can't go.'

'Why not?' we all said.

'I can't leave my cats.' Georgina had a huge collection of stray cats that she took in and fed and cosseted. She was well known locally as a cat-rescuer and often found on her doorstep cardboard boxes containing a litter of new-born kittens or a sick or old, decrepit cat. She never turned any of them away. Although she sometimes struggled to pay bills, she always found money to feed her beloved cats.

'How long would you be away?' I asked.

'A week, ten days maybe.'

'If you leave a key with us we could nip over and feed them,' Lorraine said, voicing what I'd been thinking.

'Yeah,' I said. 'We could do that for you. If you leave your catflap unlocked they can come and go as they please. We just need to put out fresh food and water and give them a little attention. We're here every day. Except Sunday.'

'I can do Sunday,' Nige said.

'I don't know what to say,' said Georgina, genuinely taken aback.

'Just say yes. I wouldn't think twice,' said Nige.

'Right then, I will,' said Georgina. 'Thank you so much.' She hugged Lorraine and I and kissed Nige on the cheek.

'Here, steady on,' he said, looking pleased. 'You'll ruin my reputation.'

Nadine breezed in from her delivery round and put her empty basket on the floor next to the counter. We all looked at her expectantly.

'What?' she asked, looking at our eager faces.

'We're waiting to hear about the millions of men clamouring to get at you,' said Nige.

'What would you lot do without my love life to entertain you?' asked Nadine as she went to retrieve a bundle of envelopes from her bag. 'Don't get your hopes up,' she said. 'They're all crackpots.'

'Oh surely not!' said Nige, disappointed. He had great hopes that Nadine would find the love of her life like he believed he had found in Gus.

'Men are all crackpots in one way or another,' said Georgina. 'You can't let that put you off.'

'Listen to this,' said Nadine, taking a seat and opening a folded sheet of paper.

'*Hi there*,' she read. '*I'm Rob. I'm 32 and run my own successful business. I love nights out at the pub, cinema and animals.*'

'Sounds really nice,' said Nige, hopefully.

'Sounds ok so far,' said Lorraine and we murmured in agreement.

'*I have my own house and car and also my own hair and teeth,*' continued Nadine.

'Own hair and teeth?' repeated Georgina. 'That's a weird thing to say. He obviously hasn't his own hair and teeth or he wouldn't mention it.'

'Exactly what I thought,' agreed Nadine.

'Well not necessarily…' began Nige, feebly but even he had to agree it was one for the reject pile.

'Next one,' said Nadine, shaking open a letter. '*My name's Keith, I'm 35. I'm divorced and have eight children that I look after full-time along with our three Alsatians and two Rottweiler dogs.*' She flung it onto the counter.

'Oh dear,' said Nige whose hopes for a summer romance for Nadine were diminishing rapidly. The rest of us however, were fascinated although trying to appear sympathetic to Nadine.

'This is a good one,' she said. '*My name is Andrew…* blah blah blah…*I am considered to be a good looking chap and indeed pride myself on my striking resemblance to Winston Churchill.*' This was met with great hoots of laughter and Georgina said, 'Sounds gorgeous, Nadine. Go for it girl!' Nadine pulled out the next letter.

'*Hi, I'm Mick,*' she read '*and I'm looking for love after being badly hurt. I enjoy going out although unfortunately I can't do much of this now due to my ex-wife clearing me out. I'm presently living in a flat, my five-bed semi with double garage and sauna having been sold to pay off extortionate costs from my rather bitter divorce. Of course it need not have been as acrimonious as the bitch made it which was very unfair considering she was the guilty party...'*

'Reject!' we shouted in a chorus. Nadine added it to the pile as we laughed.

'This one wants a woman or a man he's not fussy,' she said not even bothering to read it out.

'And I've kept the best until last,' she said. She waited until she had an attentive audience then began, *'Hello, my name is Steven and I am a management consultant. I am 29 and enjoy rugby, travel and walks in the countryside. I am looking for someone special to share days out with, and hopefully a lasting relationship.'*

'Nothing wrong with that one,' said Nige. 'I wouldn't mind him myself. If I didn't have my Gus of course.'

'Wait for it,' said Georgina. 'There's bound to be a sting in the tail.'

'I enclose a photograph of myself and look forward to hearing from you,' finished Nadine. She handed a photograph to Georgina.

'Oh my God!' exclaimed Georgina passing it to me laughing hysterically.

The photograph showed an orange-tanned man reclining, in a way to show his muscles to the best advantage, on a fluffy rug in front of his gas fire and dressed in a minute red leather thong. We laughed hysterically as we passed it around.

'Look at the expression on his face!' said Lorraine, referring to the smug look of conceit as he leered toward the camera.

'But he sounded ok in the letter,' I said, still laughing.

'I wonder who took the photo for him!' said Nige gawping at the picture. 'Perhaps he had one of those timers on his camera and he did it himself,' said Georgina. 'Can't you just imagine him setting the camera then rushing to arrange himself on the shag pile before the flash went off.'

'Can you imagine the ones that he mistimed!' squeaked Nige. 'Ones of his backside as he dived on to the rug and didn't get his pose right in time.'

'I wonder how many of these he's sent out?' sniggered Georgina, holding up the picture. 'How many women in Newcastle have copies of that?'

'Well I'll show you where this one's going!' said Nadine snatching it and holding it up to tear in half.

'Oh no you don't,' said Lorraine grabbing it. 'That's going on the notice board in the office to give us a laugh every morning.' She pinned it amongst the receipts and customer requests and it stayed there until Peter complained that it put him off his lunch when he sat at the desk with his sandwich.

Nadine gave up on the lonely-heart ads after that and decided to concentrate on Jonathan.

'I think he's just a bit shy,' she said. 'He just needs a little encouragement. I'm going to work my charm on him and by Christmas he'll be eating out of my hand.'

'And would you really want a man eating out of your hand?' said Lorraine. 'Like a pet monkey?' I turned to serve a customer as they bantered on and as I moved the room seemed to spin for a second and a wave of nausea passed over me.

'Are you ok?' asked the girl I was serving, looking concerned.

'I'm fine,' I said, but I resolved to make an appointment with my GP as soon as possible. There was something not quite right.

CHAPTER TWENTY-FOUR

If June had been flaming then July was blazing. The newspapers warned of droughts and hose-pipe bans and reported record temperatures.

The Metro station was bustling, swarming with fractious children already wilted by the heat, carrying buckets and spades and inflatable beach toys, their mothers scolding wearily. I left the congested mugginess of the station and made my way through the park. Even at this early hour the intensity of the burning sun was stinging the back of my neck predicting a scorcher of a day. In the park I passed a woman pushing a parasol-covered pushchair. I peeped at the child whose face was partially covered by a pink sun hat and as I caught sight of tiny brown toes wriggling in the sunshine, my stomach flipped.

'Pregnant?' Peter had said in shock when I'd returned from my appointment with Dr McKinley and informed him of his impending fatherhood.

I'd felt shocked too at first, astounded but also thrilled when Dr McKinley had confirmed dates.

'Baby should be due around the end of March,' she said giving me an appointment card for the ante-natal clinic. The initial shock, which lasted about ten seconds, was immediately replaced with a surge of joy.

Peter will be thrilled, I thought, as I left the doctor's room in a daze. Won't he? We both wanted to have children. Some day. We'd talked about it on honeymoon, planned to return to Florida with our children. Some day. Some day when the business was established and I had more time on my hands. But apparently some day had arrived. I left the clinic with my mind in turmoil, a million thoughts racing through it. Excitement at the promise of our very own baby. Wonder at the tiny life that was forming inside me. Realisation of how much our lives were soon to change. Apprehension about the next nine months and, oh my God, giving birth.

Walking down the High Street I passed Mothercare and on impulse slipped inside.

Mothercare. A shop that I'd never entered before, in fact, hardly even noticed but now seemed to beckon like a neon light in the dark. I wandered around the shelves touching tiny socks and vests. Surely babies weren't this small. As a child I'd had a Tiny Tears doll that was bigger than this. I peered into a pram stationed at the end of an aisle and saw a tiny child sleeping peacefully, dark lashes curling over soft cheeks and his perfect little fists tightly clenched. Again I felt a surge of happiness. Would my child look like this? He would be sure to be dark haired and I hoped for Peter's dark soulful eyes. Which characteristics of mine would he inherit and which of Peter's? I placed my hand on my stomach hardly able to believe the precious treasure I was now guarding. As I watched the sleeping child his mother claimed him and smiled as she wheeled him away.

I floated off through the store marvelling at minuscule sleep suits and dresses, soft woollen cardigans and tiny dungarees. I made a mental shopping list, choosing accessories and outfits. I imagined dressing my baby in these tiny clothes and holding him close, soft and warm and smelling of baby powder. I imagined feeling his downy hair brushing my cheek and his soft skin against mine. Turning the corner I walked past bottles and soothers and breast pumps and nipple shields. Breast pumps? Nipple shields? Spell broken, I fled.

Peter was elated. Shocked and terrified but also elated, initially treating me like a delicate, fragile thing; helping me into the bath in fear of me slipping, fetching cups of tea and extra cushions, not allowing me to lift even the lightest parcel. It was very sweet but I hoped it would soon wear off - which it did.

I continued through the park imagining Peter and myself pushing our child on the swing and holding him safe on the seesaw, excited at the wonderful times ahead.

I arrived at the shop and as I came out of the sun into the dark but already swelteringly hot shop, I climbed straight up onto the window ledge to open the blinds and was immediately man-handled down by Nadine and Lorraine.

They had both been thrilled when I told them my news and had shopped for bootees and bibs and baby toys but had treated me like a small child ever since.

'Now, now, Mummy,' Nadine said as I grudgingly stepped down. 'We'll have none of that.'

'You can't go climbing in windows and lifting and carrying,' said Lorraine remonstratively. 'Not in your condition. Sit down and drink your tea like a good girl.'

'I hope the two of you are not going to be like this for nine months or I'll go crazy before I get round to giving birth,' I said.

The heat inside was oppressive. The shop had no back door and there were no windows except the huge plate glass ones at the side and front of the building, which of course did not open, so there was no way to let a breeze of fresh air through the shop. Wedging the front door open did coax in a little air but also noise and traffic fumes from the busy road. We used the extractor fan constantly, hoping that it would move the stagnant air. It whirred relentlessly hour after hour until the motor finally burned out and it dwindled, defeated, to a halt.

The windows magnified the heat of the sun causing us to wilt like delicate blooms in an overheated greenhouse. Pulling down the blinds caused the metal slats to act like over-sized radiators, absorbing the heat from the sun and throwing it back into the shop. Energy drained from us and we became slower and more lethargic as the day wore on.

Although never physically sick, I did suffer from nausea during those first weeks of pregnancy, and the heat and lack of fresh air intensified the biliousness.

'Whoo! It's hot in here!' said a delivery man bringing a parcel.

'Really?' I said irritably, dragging myself from my perch to sign his delivery sheet. 'Can't say I'd noticed.'

'Is that the Tigrette delivery?' Lorraine asked appearing at the office door.

'The what?' I asked 'Tigrette? What's that?'

'It's a new herbal supplement for men with impotence problems. I forgot to tell you, I ordered it last week when you were at the ante-natal clinic.' Lorraine slit open the package and held up a small box depicting a tiger and Chinese lettering and the slogan '*Tigrette. Bring out the tiger in you*'.

'Not very subtle, is it?' I said taking a package.

'Could be worse,' said Lorraine. 'But if you look at the ingredients it's all good stuff.'

'Saw palmetto, ginseng, vitamin E, zinc,' I read. 'We could sell this to help prostate problems too, although the slogan might put people off.'

'That won't put men off!' Lorraine said. '*Bring out the tiger in you*! They'll be queuing to buy it! And I've arranged an ad in the Daily Echo so that should have them coming in droves.' She pulled some posters and point-of-sale materials from the package and handed them to me.

'There you go,' she said. 'Get creative. Make a window display.'

'What with?' I asked. 'What on earth can I use as props?' She did suggest a few things but I decided to go for a more subtle display with the posters and over-sized dummy boxes, and information about the ingredients.

Although we didn't have queues of men arriving to buy boxes of Tigrette as Lorraine had suggested, it was popular, however, the approach of the men varied greatly. Some slunk in shiftily and asked, from the corner of their mouths whilst casually looking at the organic flour display, for 'some of that tiger stuff.' Others wandered about embarrassed until one of us asked 'Is it Tigrette you're after?' where upon they either fled red-faced or gave a muttered 'yes', relieved that the ordeal was over. Lorraine was unlucky enough to encounter a very unembarrassed man who after buying a box, returned to tell her of his success in great detail.

'He was full of himself,' I said emerging from the office where I'd been listening, hiding until he'd left.

'Very cock-sure.' she said.

Sometimes we were more embarrassed than the customers. When Mrs Forbes-Williamson picked up a packet of Tigrette that had been left on the counter and began to read the blurb on the back of the packet I felt my face redden in anticipation of her disapproval.

'I'll take that out of your way, Mrs Forbes-Williamson,' I stuttered, trying to retrieve the packet. 'Must have been left there by a sales rep.'

'Oh I say, '*Bring out the tiger in you*'. Well I must say it's a long time since the tiger in poor old Arthur has shown itself, har har. Ginseng eh? Yes I've heard of that. Very good. Vitamin E. Saw Palmetto. Oh wonderful. I'll take a couple of packets for Arthur. Pop it on my bill. Wheesh.'

I was often surprised at the lack of embarrassment of customers when discussing aspects of their personal health, often in a loud voice in front of other customers. One lady came in for advice about a stomach problem, her symptoms being a bloated abdomen and flatulence. I tried to advise her on diet changes and suggest suitable remedies but she was more interested in describing her symptoms.

'I'm passing wind all the time,' she said. 'It's not a violent release, it's like a constant plop-plop-plop, a bit like when you're trying to light the pilot light on your cooker.'

'Really?' I said, trying not to let my face react. 'Have you considered a food sensitivity test to see if something you're eating is aggravating the symptoms?'

'Actually, it's more of a phut-phut-phut than a plop-plop-plop.' she said.

'Yes. Well I would suggest cutting down a little on your fibre intake and…'

'Sometimes, when it's really bad it can get to a phut-phut-pffssss, phut-phut-pffssss.' I heard a snigger escape from Nadine who was arranging packets of maple and pecan muesli on our 'new product' stand.

'Absolutely,' I said, which was a stupid thing to say but I was struggling with the conversation.

'There! Did you hear that?' she said. 'Phut-phut-pffssss, phut-phut-pffssss.' She looked around at the other customers. 'Did anyone hear that?' Needless to say the conversation deteriorated into a full blown debate as delighted customers joined in with sound effects and suggestions, and a bemused Lorraine returned from the Post Office to a cacophony of whistling, popping and hissing as I struggled to bring the conversation back to a more dignified discussion.

On another occasion, during the lunch time rush, I sold a tube of arnica cream to an elderly lady who said she had fallen and had bruised her buttocks. After paying for the cream, to my horror and to the amusement of the queue, she promptly dropped her drawers, bent over, and asked me to apply it.

Many customers were keen to discuss their mucus, faeces, discharges and personal bodily functions with great expression and without the least embarrassment, which, although we always tried to remain very professional we did sometimes find a little distasteful. Now that I was pregnant the least thing aggravated my nausea and I found these conversations unbearable and would hand over to Lorraine as soon as I felt my stomach beginning to revolt against what I was hearing. Even the smell of the boiled eggs sent me reeling, and although egg mayonnaise had been my favourite, I now couldn't even look at it. Sometimes, when the combination of heat and food smells became overpowering, I would take a walk to the park to escape from the suffocating atmosphere of the shop and would return refreshed and ready to start again until the next bout of nausea.

Today on my walk the air was still and heavy and I noticed dark clouds were gathering. As I entered the shop, huge drops of rain began to fall, hitting the scorching pavements, releasing a hot dusty smell.

'Feel better?' asked Lorraine.

'Yes, much better, thanks,' I said, as the momentum of the rain increased, hitting the windows with force and bringing a coolness to the air. Refreshed by the temperature change I felt recharged and ready to start again. I sat behind the counter and sang along to the radio as I took out the ledger and prepared to tackle a pile of invoices.

'Afternoon darlin.' I looked up to see a burly man standing at the counter.

'Hello,' I said cheerily. 'How can I help?'

'I wondered if you had an ointment for itching,' he said, fiddling with the buckle on his belt. 'I've got a rash on me willy.' I leapt up from my seat as though it was electrified.

'One moment,' I said, as I scuttled into the office. 'Lorraine,' I yelled. 'LORRAINE! Customer for you.'

CHAPTER TWENTY-FIVE

The heat was just as bad, if not worse, the following day.
'I think we'd better take those candles out of the side window,' Nadine said when she arrived. 'Have you seen the state of them?' I leaned into the window and saw what had been my scented-candle display was now a huge blob of molten wax. I attempted to scrape it up with a knife as Lorraine set up the till and Nadine began preparing salads.

Peter carried in four large electric fans we'd bought the previous evening. He positioned them around the shop, laying extension cables everywhere to connect them to the sockets.

'That should help a bit,' he said when they were switched on. 'I'd better get off to work, see you at lunchtime.' The fans did make a slight difference but after a while we realised they were just rotating the hot air and not actually cooling the atmosphere. They also blocked access to the shelves. We spent most of the day moving them around at the request of customers unable to reach the products they wanted.

'I'm absolutely lathered,' complained Nadine as she grated cheese into a dish. 'I'm sweating like a pig.' She turned to see Jonathan placing the bread trays on the counter.

'Oh morning Jonathan, didn't see you there,' she said hastily. 'I was just saying it's so warm in here I'm starting to glow.'

'Phew, it's hot in here,' Jonathan said, ignoring her. 'Isn't it too hot in here for storing food?' Lorraine and I looked at him. It hadn't occurred to us that the food may be affected, we'd been too concerned with how the heat was affecting us personally.

'No, it's fine,' Lorraine said. 'All under control.' As soon as he left the shop I hurried to the kitchen to dig out a thermometer.

'Thirty-one degrees!' I said. 'Do you think it will affect the stock? What shall we do?' We looked around the shelves touching packets to feel how warm they were.

'Oh look at this,' I said picking up some bars of organic chocolate. 'They've melted. We'll have to stuff everything we can into the fridges.' We checked the shelves collecting up things we thought were in danger of being spoiled and piled them onto the counter for Nadine to load into the fridges.

'Nuts and seeds better go in,' I said. 'The oils in them can go rancid with heat.'

'What about dried fruit?' asked Lorraine.

'Don't know,' I said. 'Better not risk it, stick it in.' The upright fridges were soon full so we started filling the counter fridge.

'Better change the temperature setting if we're putting all this stuff in,' I said turning the dial. The fridge gave a loud click and shuddered, whirring into life.

'Holy fishcake, it's hot in here,' said Nige arriving with our mail. 'I've gone all limp. I'd better go and make some coffee.'

124

'What for? To finish us off?' Lorraine said, wiping her face. 'Open a bottle of that chilled mineral water instead. Glasses are in the kitchen.'

Georgina arrived to join us with news that her trip to Paris with Marc was off.

'Oh no!' said Nige. 'Is it all over? The big romance?' He handed her a glass of water. 'Here, you didn't find out he was gay, did you?' he added hopefully.

'No of course not!' said Georgina. 'It's just a change of plan. I'm going to the Lake District for a few days with Josie instead, so I'd still like you to look after my cats if that's ok.' We all looked at her, surprised.

'So what are you and Josie going to do in the Lake District that's more interesting than going to France with Marc?' I asked.

'Nothing. Just relaxing and spending some time together,' said Georgina. 'It's not a big deal.'

'The two of you together?' asked Nige. 'Are you batting for my team now?'

'Don't be silly Nige,' said Georgina, clearly not amused. 'Josie and I are very good friends and we just want to have a bit of time together. End of subject.' There was a serious tone to her voice that prevented us pursuing it further.

'Look at that poor soul,' said Nadine, changing the subject. We all looked to the window where Ernie could be seen running up the bank, dressed in his pinstripe suit and sandals, face purple and dripping with perspiration.

'He's been doing that all morning,' said Georgina. 'It's a wonder he hasn't given himself a heart attack.'

'He's giving me one just watching him,' I said collapsing onto a stool.

By lunchtime, Nadine, Lorraine and I were tetchy and had snapped at each other several times. I checked the thermometer only to find the temperature was rising, aided by the fridges working overtime and blasting out yet more hot air. Customers complained about the heat in the shop and I smiled with gritted teeth and agreed until I finally lost my temper with Pugnacious Face who had complained non-stop from joining the back of the queue to reaching the front. When he complained for the thousandth time I snapped at him saying, 'Shut your face man, you only have to buy a sandwich and then you can leave. We have to work in it all day.' Not the best way to speak to a customer but I was beyond politeness. I was beyond anything except perhaps throwing the salad at the queue and having a good cry. Somehow we coped and when the rush was over, Nadine went up to the sink area to start washing-up.

'Blimey, it's even worse up here!' she said. Usually she whizzed through the job cheerily but today she trudged up the steps apathetically and began the painful process of cleaning up.

Meanwhile, Lorraine and I sniped at each other, becoming crabbier each time a customer complained about the temperature.

'I came for Green and Black's chocolate,' a woman said, 'but you don't seem to have any. Goodness it's hot in here.'

125

'Yes we do, it's here in the fridge,' Lorraine said, handing the woman a misshapen bar of chocolate. The woman put out her hand to take it then noticing that it had obviously melted and re-hardened changed her mind and drew back her hand just as Lorraine let go of the chocolate and it fell to the floor. Lorraine and I simultaneously bent to pick up the chocolate and as our heads collided with a resounding crack, stars floated around my head and I gazed at her with blurred vision. The woman laughed.

'Do you think it's funny?' yelled Lorraine. 'Two people cracking their heads, it's funny is it?' Holding her head with her hand she turned and staggered off into the office and caught her foot in the extension flex causing her to crash to the floor along with one of the fans as the woman fled, unable to control her laughter.

'I've got a bit of a problem up here... what on earth...?' said Nadine as she came down the steps to see Lorraine picking herself up from the floor swearing profusely.

'What sort of a problem?' Lorraine asked irritably, rubbing her knee with one hand and her head with the other.

'The sink seems to be blocked, it's not emptying.'

'Great.'

'I'll nip up to the hardware shop and get a plunger,' I said, glad of an excuse to get out of the place for a while and hoping that the fresh air might cure the headache I could feel starting in my right temple. When I returned, Nadine and Lorraine took turns to attack the plughole with the plunger. I stayed well out of the way. It was unbearably hot up there and filled with steam from the washing-up water. I was serving a customer as a shiny-faced Nadine came down to admit defeat.

'Can't shift it,' said Nadine, pulling at the front of her damp blouse where it had stuck to her skin.

'Phew, it's like a bloody sauna up there,' Lorraine said coming down the steps after Nadine. 'We should put wooden benches in and charge customers to use it.' She wiped away the beads of perspiration from her face.

'We need to unscrew the trap in the u-bend and clear out the blockage,' said Nadine. 'That's what the plumber did when my sink at home was blocked. You have to scrape out all the gunge from the pipe.' My stomach turned at the thought.

'Sounds like a job for Peter,' I said. Actually it sounded like a job for anyone except me. 'Trust it to happen after he's gone back to work.'

'We can't leave it,' said Lorraine. 'The sink is full of dirty water and we need to clear it. Come on let's just get it done.'

'I'd better stay down here and watch the till,' I said.

'We'll do it together,' Lorraine said. The three of us climbed the steps and stood cramped together, too close for comfort in the humid atmosphere. Lorraine unscrewed the trap and as she did she reeled backwards.

'Gawd, what a stink!' she said. 'No wonder the water can't get through, the pipe is blocked solid with grease and stuff.' She started scraping the congealed mess into a plastic bag with a spoon.

126

'Aw, gross!' she said. 'What the hell is it anyway?'

'It's probably all the bits of mayonnaise and tuna and oil and salad stuff that gets washed down the plughole all mixed up and gone off,' said Nadine. That was enough for me. I hurried back down the steps trying to control my nausea.

'Sorry you two, count me out,' I said. 'There's no way I can do that.'

'Get your arse up here now and take a turn,' said Lorraine.

'Sorry, I can't help it. It's my hormones. I'm off for some fresh air. I'll go and get a copy of the Daily Echo to check out our Tigrette ad.' I hurried out of the shop as a spoonful of the rancid gloop whizzed past my ear and splattered on the floor.

When I returned, pipe cleaning and sink unblocking had been accomplished and Lorraine was pouring glasses of chilled mango juice.

'I'll have one of those, thanks,' I said picking up a glass and taking a huge mouthful. The ice-cold juice was delicious. I opened the newspaper and found our advertisement prominently displayed inside.

'Hey this looks good,' I said. 'It catches your eye straight away.' I passed the sheet to Lorraine and Nadine.

'The customers will be pouring in after this,' Lorraine said, pleased. 'What do you think Nadine?' Nadine took a look.

'It's good,' she said. 'But I can see a problem.' Lorraine and I looked at the ad again.

'The phone number. That's not our number.'

'Oh I don't believe this,' said Lorraine. 'We've paid to print a totally useless ad.' I picked up the phone to ring the 'wrong number' and was surprised when Graham from Yogi Health foods answered the call. Graham ran the nearest health food shop to us and we sometimes shared orders and occasionally sent customers to each other if we didn't stock the products they asked for. I explained the situation to him and we laughed, sharing stories of the inadequacies of the Daily Echo.

'So if you could direct any enquiries to us Graham, that would be really helpful' I said.

'Sorry Chris,' he said. 'Free advertising is too good an opportunity to miss.'

'But it's not free,' I said. 'We've paid for it.'

'That's what I mean,' he said. 'It's paid for so I may as well benefit from it. I'll ring the Tigrette rep immediately and get stocked up ready for the rush.'

'You wouldn't do that,' I said. 'It wouldn't fit with your Buddhist ethics!'

'Oh I don't think making the most of opportunities is against Buddha's teachings. Must go, I need to place a Tigrette order straight way.' Lorraine was furious.

'I suppose we can't really blame Graham,' she said. 'And at least he was honest about it. But I'm going to ring Michelle at the Daily Echo and demand a refund. This is the second time she's messed up.'

The following morning was the first time since opening the shop that I just did not want to go in.

'You're not changing your mind about the business are you?' asked Peter, concerned.

'No, it's not the shop, it's the heat. I can't bear it. I feel sick most of the time and the heat drains my energy and addles my brain. I can't think straight. We're all the same, hot and bothered and picking fault with each other.'

By the time I got myself motivated and set off, I was later than usual and arrived to find that Lorraine had already opened up.

'More bad news, I'm afraid,' she said.

'Not the sink again?' I groaned.

'No, the fridge has packed in.'

'Which one?'

'The counter fridge. I think the motor's gone.'

'Is that because we overloaded it?'

'Probably, but also because of the temperature in the shop. It's been working overtime trying to get the temperature down. I rang the company and they're going to exchange it, it's still under warranty.'

'Well that's good news anyway,' I said. 'As long as the same thing doesn't happen again. We need to find a way of cooling the place down. When are they coming to collect it?'

'The guy on the phone said someone would be here at about twelve.'

'Twelve? But that's right on lunchtime. It'll be chaos,' I said. We thought for a moment as Lorraine poured us cold drinks.

'What if we push it outside now so they just need to load it onto their van and won't need to come inside?' said Lorraine

'But what about the big gap it will leave?'

'We could pull the kitchen fridges forward and serve from those,' Lorraine said.

'We'll have to stuff all the food into the small fridges and they're already full up.'

'We'll just have to do our best. We don't really have a choice do we?'

'Ok, let's do it.'

After quickly emptying the counter fridge we unplugged it and began to push it towards the door.

'Be careful,' Lorraine said. 'You're not supposed to lift.'

'I'm not lifting,' I panted. 'I'm pushing and I am supposed to do that, eventually.'

'Well I hope for your sake it won't be like pushing a bloody great fridge through a doorway,' said Lorraine straining to move the fridge. Slowly we inched it along, this way and then the other, gradually walking it towards the door, grunting and sweating as we did.

'It's not going to go through,' I said.

'Yes it is,' said Lorraine. 'It has to. It came in this way.' Unfortunately I was right. We managed to manoeuvre the fridge so that the first few inches of it were in the door way and then it stuck tight.

'It's stuck,' I said, trying not to think of it as another childbirth analogy.

'Shit.'

'We'll have to move it back.' Because we were trapped behind the fridge we had to pull it rather than push, which is a more difficult way to move something and consequently it wouldn't budge. After trying unsuccessfully for a few minutes Lorraine said, 'It's over to plan B then.'

'Which is?'

'You come up with one of your amazing ideas.'

'Right. Might take a while.'

We eventually decided that serving customers over the top of the fridge was the only option. We dragged the kitchen fridges nearer the doorway and set up the till on top of an upturned crate to avoid having to run back and forwards to the counter.

'You do realise we're trapped in here? There's no back door so if there's a fire we're dooooomed,' Lorraine said in her best Private Fraser voice.

'Well there's a cheery thought.'

Nadine arrived with a smile on her face, which soon vanished when we told her she'd have to climb over the fridge to get in.

'Can't I just have the day off?' she asked.

'No. Get your foot on the windowsill and climb up and we'll pull you over,' Lorraine instructed. Nadine was lying over the top of the fridge screeching, with her feet kicking in the air and Lorraine and I pulling an arm each as Jonathan pulled up in his van.

'Give us a hand here,' I called to him as Nadine, suddenly realising he was there, stopped shrieking and smiled serenely as though she were a lady reclining on a day bed.

'Morning Jonathan,' she said, leaving go of my hand to brush back her hair.

'What exactly do you want me to do?' he asked, looking at Nadine's rear end.

'Just give her a shove,' I said and he put his hands on her bottom and pushed as we pulled her arms. Nadine slid over the fridge and crumpled to a heap on the floor.

'Thank you Jonathan,' she said calmly, dusting down her clothes, composed and dignified, only her crimson face betraying her.

'No bother,' he replied, not looking at her. He passed the bread trays over the fridge and left.

'Well thank you very much,' said Nadine as we sniggered. 'I always end up looking a right prat in front of him.'

We spent the morning giving explanations as we handed goods and took money over the huge monstrosity in the doorway. Nige arrived and was put out that he couldn't come in for a coffee.

'You're quite welcome to climb over,' Nadine said. 'But I wouldn't recommend it.'

'No, it's ok,' he said. 'You can pass me a cup over.' He stood outside drinking his coffee and making silly remarks to customers as we ran around the shop to collect their goods.

'It's just like on the continent,' he observed. 'You, know, when they have the fridges out in the street and you buy sandwiches and snacks. Except they have the fridges switched on and full of food. And they're not wedged sideways in a doorway.'

Peter also declined the invitation to climb over the fridge. He struggled to move it for a while, ignoring our comments that he was wasting his time, then gave up, and returned to work taking his sandwich with him.

At one-thirty the men came to collect the fridge and were not happy to see it wedged in the doorway.

'I remember bringing this bugger in,' complained one of the men. 'It only fits through the gap if it's tilted at a certain angle.' After half an hour of struggling the certain angle was located and we all gave a sigh of relief as they carried the fridge to the van. The replacement fridge was carried in and we set to work tidying up. We rearranged the kitchen fridges, returned the till to its rightful place and tidied away strewn carrier bags and discarded wrapping paper.

'Do you think every business is run like this?' asked Lorraine as we loaded the new fridge. 'Or is it just when unprofessional clowns like us try to run a shop?'

'Others probably muddle along too,' I said. 'I'm sure a fly-on-the-wall could tell similar tales about most businesses.' Although I wasn't convinced. Running our business did sometimes have the feel of taking part in a badly acted farce. Over the last six months we had stumbled from one fiasco to the next.

'They say that in business the first six months are always the worst,' I said. 'Things should start getting easier now that our teething problems are behind us. I'm sure nothing else can go wrong. It's onwards and upwards from now.' I should have known not to speak too soon.

CHAPTER TWENTY SIX

Arriving at the shop the following day I was met by our next fiasco. The rubber covering on the floor that formed a walkway through the parquet from the door to the counter had bubbled up into huge blisters giving the sensation of walking across a row of hot water bottles.

'What on earth has happened here?' I asked Lorraine.

'I don't know,' she said. 'It was like that when I came in. The heat must have affected the glue or something.'

'We'll have to sort it quickly,' I said. 'If a customer trips on it we'll be in trouble.'

Nige arrived as we were attempting to remedy the problem.

'That is so weird,' he said pushing down one of the lumps with his foot and watching it bulge out from the sides of his shoe. 'They seem to be full of air.' He tiptoed across the floor from bulge to bulge with his arms held out like a ballet dancer. 'Perhaps they're alien embryos growing underneath until they're ready to burst open like The Invasion of the Body Snatchers.'

'Yes, Nige dear. Keep taking the medication,' Lorraine said. The only thing we could think of was to pierce the swellings with a kitchen knife and squirt glue into the hole to fix the rubber back to the floor. Nige, who had plenty of suggestions but didn't actually offer any practical help, watched intently.

'It reminds me of poor Gus,' he said. 'He once had this huge boil on his buttock and it had to be lanced with a needle and all this pus came out...'

'Too much information thanks Nige,' I said sharply. 'My nausea is bad enough without having to listen to stories about boils on people's backsides.' Lorraine stamped on the last repair attempting to flatten the rubber.

'There, that's it.' The botched repairs seemed to work but left the floor with unsightly marks and spoiled the previously smart look of the flooring.

'Right then, now that's done, coffee time,' said Nige.

'Go on then your turn,' Lorraine said to him and he went, reluctantly, to put the kettle on. With her uncanny ability to arrive whenever coffee was on offer, Georgina entered with Josie.

'Hey everyone,' she said. 'We're back!' Looking suntanned and healthy, she dragged a battered hold-all behind her. Josie followed, wheeling a smart little suitcase and carrying a matching vanity case. She looked more delicate than ever next to the robust Georgina.

'Hi,' said Lorraine. 'Just in time for coffee.' She began to pour two extra coffees but Josie said, 'Not for me thanks, I'm going straight home, I just popped in to say hello.'

'When did you get back?' I asked.

'Just now. We got a taxi from the station,' said Georgina taking her coffee.

'Enjoy yourselves?' Lorraine asked.

'Yes, we had a lovely break. Very relaxing,' said Josie.

'Relaxing?' said Nige. 'I thought you two let loose would be out partying, chasing the men.'

'Sorry to disappoint you Nige, but we just walked and talked and enjoyed the peace and quiet of the countryside,' Josie said. She hugged Georgina and said to her, 'Thanks for everything, I'll ring you later.'

'Sure you won't stay for a coffee?' I said.

'Thanks but no. I'm really tired, I'm going to go home and have a sleep.'

'You do look very tired,' I said concerned. Her face was gaunt making her cheekbones seemed more pronounced. I was sure she'd lost more weight. She smiled wanly and left, refusing Nige's offer of help with her cases.

'Looks like you've tired her out,' said Nige. Georgina sipped her coffee.

'Cats ok?' she asked.

'Yeah, no problems,' Lorraine said.

'What have I missed?' she asked. 'Tell me the gossip.'

'Nothing much,' I said. 'Just a blocked sink, a kaput fridge and a freaky bubbling floor.' We told her of our latest misadventures.

'Where's Nadine? She usually works mornings doesn't she?' Georgina asked.

'She's taking a couple of hours off to get her passport and things sorted. She got a last minute deal so she's off to Salou next week,' I said.

We had decided that we all needed a break and so had arranged a fortnight's holiday each. Nadine had found a bargain holiday so she was going first. When she returned it would be Lorraine's turn then mine. I had called the job-centre to advertise for a temporary assistant to cover our leave and they were sending possible candidates to see us that afternoon.

'Nadine's working a couple of hours this afternoon instead,' I told Georgina. 'She's going to manage the shop floor so that Lorraine and I can interview for the summer job.'

'Need any help on the interview panel?' she asked. 'I'd be great at interviewing. I'd ask some really challenging questions.'

'I bet you would!' I said. 'Thanks for the offer, but no thanks. We don't want to terrify them.'

Lorraine and I discussed how we were going to interview the candidates.

'I think we should keep it very informal,' I said. 'After all it's only a six week vacancy helping in the kitchen and making sandwiches.'

'Yes,' agreed Lorraine. 'Anyone can make sandwiches. We just need someone who is fun to work with and can be trusted with the till.' It sounded so easy.

The first woman we interviewed had a very impressive list of qualifications relating to nutrition, food studies and health. She was much more qualified than we were to run a health business but she had not used a till and did not seem keen to. When we talked about serving customers she said, 'I would find being behind a counter a little demeaning and I certainly wouldn't make sandwiches. I see myself in a more managerial role, analysing the business, improving sales, PR, that kind of stuff.'

'Right,' I said. I was too embarrassed to explain that all we wanted was a sandwich maker and dishwasher so I thanked her and said we would be in touch.

Next was a young girl with a pleasant friendly manner who I took to straight away. This seems more hopeful, I thought. She explained that she had worked in a café so had experience in working with food and in dealing with customers. I judged by the look on Lorraine's face that she thought the same.

'Well that just about covers everything,' she said smiling at the girl. 'Is there anything you'd like to ask us?'

'Yes,' said the girl. 'What is my holiday entitlement?'

'Holiday entitlement?' I repeated. 'There is no holiday entitlement. You do know that the job is temporary? The contract is only for six weeks.'

'So I couldn't have time off for my holiday?' the girl said looking disappointed. 'I have a three week holiday booked for the week after next.' I explained that this would not be possible and she said, 'Oh that's a shame. I really fancied this job.' When she'd left Lorraine said, 'Did she really think she could take a six week job, work three weeks and have three weeks paid holiday?'

'Apparently so,' I said. I was a little disappointed; she'd seemed ideal. 'Never mind,' I said. 'Who's next?'

'It's a man next,' Lorraine said looking at the list of names. 'Twenty-five, presently unemployed.'

He came in announcing loudly that he didn't really want the job but had to attend interviews to avoid having his benefits stopped.

'That must be the shortest interview ever,' Lorraine said after we had swiftly disposed of him before he'd even sat down. We waited for Nadine to bring in the next applicant. Lorraine looked at her watch.

'She's very late,' Lorraine said. 'Not a good start.' Nadine's head appeared around the office door.

'Em, bit of a problem,' she said looking uncomfortable. 'The next lady has asked if you could interview her in the shop.' Puzzled, we got up and followed Nadine back to the shop floor where the reason for the unusual request became apparent. The girl was very large. She'd been unable to fit through the space in the counter. Apparently Nadine had had to come to her assistance when she'd become stuck fast between the fridge and the edge of the counter by pushing her back the way she'd come. Lorraine and I, not wanting to embarrass the girl, carried chairs into the shop, and arranging them away from the counter at the back of the store, spoke to her there.

Unfortunately her embarrassment manifested as aggression. She accused society of discriminating against her and not providing adequately for her needs. Her list of grudges started with our counter arrangement and led onto aeroplane and cinema seats, emaciated catwalk models, small sized clothes in high street stores, and insubstantial lavatory seats.

'Well there's no way she's getting the job,' Lorraine said after we'd pulled her out of her chair and she'd waddled off.

'We can't do that!' I said. 'We can't not give someone a job because they're too fat. It's discrimination. I think it's probably illegal. She could sue us!'

'What ever size she was she wouldn't have got the job,' Lorraine said. 'Can you imagine working with that none-stop whinging and whining about fat people verses thin people?'

'Yes,' I said. 'You're right. And anyway, how could she make sandwiches if she was wedged in a gap in the counter?'

There followed a surreal interview with a woman who spoke in whispers, causing Lorraine and I for some strange reason to whisper too.

'Thank you,' Lorraine whispered to her at the end of the interview.

'We'll be in touch.' The woman touched Lorraine's arm and leaned close. She looked around furtively before whispering, 'Thank you very much,' and swiftly left.

'What was that all about?' Lorraine asked. 'It got more bizarre by the minute.'

'I don't know, you tell me.' I was irritable and tired. Sick of the heat and frustrated by the way the interviews had gone so far. 'I mean she was bad enough, but God knows why you started whispering too.'

'Well so did you!'

'Only because you were whispering.'

'Well you started it'

'No, she started it.'

'But you joined in.'

'Only because you did first.'

'I did not.'

'Yes you did.'

'Didn't.'

'Did.'

'Didn't.'

'Did, did, did.'

'Get lost.'

'Ah, you see that's because you did.'

'Excuse me,' said a voice and we both looked up to see a young girl at the office door. 'I'm here for interview?' I coughed, embarrassed at being caught out indulging in such an infantile conversation. Lorraine shuffled a few papers and composed herself.

'Come in, take a seat,' she said to the girl.

Lorraine always claimed the main reason for giving the girl the job on the spot was because she took us by surprise during our fatuous squabble. I think perhaps this was contributory to the rash decision, other factors being that after

134

the previous interviewees she seemed fairly normal (at the time) and she was the last candidate so we were desperate.

'Well what's she like?' asked Nige the next morning during our coffee gathering. 'Is she as gorgeous as the other three lovely Nutmeg ladies?'

'Thank you Nige,' said Nadine and Lorraine gave him a flapjack saying, 'Flattery gets you everywhere.'

'Sexist twaddle!' muttered Georgina.

'She seems very nice,' I said. 'Her name is Tanya, she's very young and very pretty.' But possibly not very clever, I thought. Although she'd been the best of a bad bunch I had concerns that she had seemed a bit vague at interview. 'I think she'll be great.' I said to Nige. More to convince myself than him.

'Not too great, I hope,' said Nadine. 'I want my job back when I get home!'

'Oh they wouldn't get rid of you, flower,' said Nige. 'Place wouldn't be the same without your smiling face.' Nadine smiled, pleased.

'Mind you're full of the shite today, aren't you?' Georgina said to Nige, but before anyone could reply, Nadine suddenly threw down her plate of flapjacks and began flinging her arms around screaming hysterically.

'What the hell's got into her?' asked Georgina.

'What's the matter darlin'?' Nige asked as Nadine continued to scream and flap about. 'Are your knickers too tight?' Nige, Lorraine and I were used to these mad outbursts from Nadine. It all became clear to Georgina as a wasp flew past Nadine's head and buzzed around her hair.

'Get it OFF!' she screeched galloping around the shop. Her frantic dancing ceased abruptly as she suddenly noticed Jonathan who was watching in open-mouthed fascination, but the cavorting resumed almost immediately as the wasp returned to buzz daringly in her ear. It was all too much and even in the presence of the revered Jonathan she gave in to hysteria and ran out of the door hitting herself on the head with a tea towel. Jonathan put down the trays and eyed us questioningly.

'Mating dance,' Georgina told him. 'As performed by the African Hornbilled Mawonga bird. She was telling us about a documentary she saw last night.' Jonathan gave a forced smile and left.

'I'm never going to get anywhere with him,' Nadine later said sadly. 'But I can't help it. I've always been terrified of wasps. It's a phobia. I just can't bear to be near them.'

I had to admit that wasps were becoming a problem. We did seem to be troubled with more than our fair share of them that summer. They droned around the ceiling dive-bombing unsuspecting customers and congregated in our display fridge, crawling across the glass with intermittent fits of frenzied buzzing. Our solution was to catch them in an old yogurt pot kept especially for the purpose, and throw them out of the front door. Nadine was not happy with this process.

'It's bloody ridiculous,' she said. 'It takes the two of you ten minutes to chase the thing around the fridge, then you run outside to release it and the bugger flies straight back in.' She did have a point. 'Why can't you just use fly spray like normal people do?' she grumbled. She often brought spray cans into the shop which we banned her from using but which I suspect she used when we were not around.

'I've told you why,' I said. 'It's unhygienic to be spraying chemicals around in a food shop.'

'Well what about flypapers? They don't give off chemicals you just hang them up and the insects are drawn to them and stick to the glue.'

'Ugh, how disgusting. I don't even want to think of it.' I said. 'Anyway it's against our principles to kill things.' I said.

'What, even wasps?'

'Yes, even wasps.'

But she was right. We did have a problem.

It all came to a head a couple of days later when I was waiting for a woman to choose a cake from our fridge. The woman bent to peer through the glass then said, 'Did you know there are two flies mating on that apricot slice?' Oh my God, I thought. How gross. I felt my face redden with shame and embarrassment.

'I'm so sorry,' I said, mortified. 'It's the heat you know. We do our best to control it but it's the time of year for insects, isn't it?' Ugh! There was no way I'd ever buy from a shop that had flies crawling on the food. She'd probably inform Environmental Health. We could be fined for this. She contemplated the apricot slice thoughtfully.

'Oh never mind,' she said. 'They weren't on it long. I'll take it.'

CHAPTER TWENTY-SEVEN

Next morning, as I opened the shop door at nine o'clock, three wasps flew in. By the time Nadine arrived there were twelve. Lorraine was flying around after them on the end of a yogurt pot.

'Right,' said Nadine. 'I've had enough. This is how it is. Either the wasps go or I do.' She stood at the door and refused to come in until I'd promised to install an electric insect-zapper.

'I'll order one today,' I told her, 'and by the time you return from your holiday we will be wasp free.'

'We'd better be or I'm not coming back,' she said convincingly.

'There are wasps in Salou, you know,' Lorraine said. 'Giant Spanish ones.' Nadine, who had been about to enter the shop stopped and looked at Lorraine in horror.

'She's just joking,' I said giving Lorraine a shove. 'Come on in and I'll make you a nice cup of tea.' We eventually coaxed her in, but only after Lorraine had used her yogurt pot to dispose of the wasps which returned when the door was next opened.

As though they sensed her fear, the wasps were persistent in their torment of Nadine. Ignoring Lorraine and I they relentlessly victimised her, dive-bombing at her head and buzzing near her ear, causing her to scream and throw down whatever she held in her hands to enable her to wave her arms in the air and slap herself on the head. At eleven o'clock Lorraine and I agreed she had suffered enough. We sent her off to finish preparing for her holiday, repeating our promise to install a zapper while she was away.

I telephoned Edward Reeves at Environmental Health and he advised me on various types of insect killers and gave me details of a couple of suppliers.

'He was very helpful,' I said surprised.

'It's probably one of his hobbies, killing things, the weirdo,' muttered Lorraine. Once Lorraine has decided that she doesn't like someone they are forever deemed devoid of any positive qualities.

I reluctantly ordered a contraption that hung from the ceiling and used ultra-violet light to lure insects to their death. I was promised it would be delivered before four o'clock.

'No assembly necessary,' I was told. 'You just connect it to the mains and it will start electrocuting pests immediately.'

'Thanks,' I said grimly. 'I'll look forward to that.' Lorraine came in to the office as I hung up.

'Our repair work to the flooring hasn't worked,' she said. 'The edges of the cuts we made are curling up. I've just tripped over one of them. We're going to have to replace the whole lot.' I sighed and wondered to myself for the umpteenth time why I was subjecting myself to all this instead of spending my pregnancy relaxing with my feet up or doing a bit of gentle yoga or shopping for designer maternity wear and baby clothes.

'I'll get on to it now.'

I spent the rest of the morning trying to source rubber floor covering at a reasonable price and finally found a supplier who said he could deliver that afternoon. I also ordered a pot of the glue recommended for fixing it to wooden floorboards.

'Will it stick firmly?' I asked. 'I mean will it bubble up or anything if the temperature goes up.' The man assured me that the rubber would stick firmly to the floor.

'But what if it gets really hot in the shop?' I persisted. I wasn't going to pay all that money for the same thing to happen again.

'It would have to reach incredibly high temperatures to affect the glue to that extent,' the man laughed, amused at my stupidity.

When Peter arrived at lunchtime I told him new flooring and an insect killer would be arriving that afternoon.

'An insect killer?' he said with disgust. 'And I suppose it'll be my job to empty all the electrocuted insect bodies from it?' he said.

'Yeah, that would be great,' I said. 'Thanks for offering.' I sat down heavily, and fanned my face with a pile of leaflets. 'I don't think these are ideal conditions for a pregnant woman,' I complained. 'It's a wonder the baby's not like a dehydrated little prune by now.' It was a half-hearted attempt at a joke but Peter looked concerned.

'We need to sort out this problem with the heat once and for all,' he said. 'You can't go on like this.' He marched off to the kitchen and began examining the walls.

'What's he doing?' Lorraine said, watching as he took measurements and made notes.

'Search me,' I said, 'but I wish he'd do it somewhere else.' The shop suddenly filled with a new wave of customers and I slid off my perch and sloped into the kitchen to help Lorraine. We manoeuvred around Peter who seemed to be pencilling marks on the wall and generally getting in our way.

'Can't you do that later when the kitchen isn't busy?' I asked.

'No,' he said jotting down measurements on a scrap of paper.

'What are you doing anyway?' I asked.

'Fixing your temperature problem. I've got an idea,' he said. 'See you later,' and kissing my cheek, he left.

That evening we stayed behind to lay the new flooring and install the zapper.

'Do you need me to stay?' Lorraine asked.

'There's no point in us all being here,' I said. 'Get yourself away home.' She disappeared quickly, presumably before I had a chance to change my mind.

I made some coffee and sandwiches and we ate before starting work. Pulling up a seat at the counter I tackled some of the overdue paperwork as Peter struggled to unroll the floor covering and cut it to size. He muttered under his breath as I toiled with my calculator and piles of invoices. I looked up as I heard him swear with frustration.

'I don't know how you work in this heat,' he complained. 'I'm sweating like a pig here.' Perspiration ran down his face in rivulets and his hair was damp and standing on end from where he'd brushed his hand through it. The closed metal blinds were releasing their heat and as the temperature mounted the smell of the glue became intoxicating. I opened the door trying to cool the air but closed it again as people kept wandering in thinking we were open for business. We worked at our separate tasks in silence, too hot for the effort of conversation.

When the floor was at last finished, Peter attached the zapper to a hook in the ceiling, plugged it in and switched it on. We watched as a fly headed towards the purple glow and both cringed as a loud electrical crackle announced its demise.

'Oh that's horrible!' I said, covering my face with my hands. 'I won't be able to work with that going on.' There was a succession of loud cracks as more insects met their end. 'Turn it off, turn it off!' I said with my hands over my ears and my eyes shut and Peter laughed.

'What are you laughing at? It's not funny,' I said slapping his arm.

'I know, it's barbaric. It's just your reaction to it that's funny.' He flicked off the switch. 'Come on let's go,' he said. 'I've had enough.'

It was almost eight when we left the shop, both of us wilted and drained of energy.

'Straight home or an ice-cold beer first?' Peter asked as we stepped out into the warm evening.

'It'll have to be an ice-cold lemonade for me,' I said, patting my stomach. As Peter pulled down the shutter I breathed deeply to fill my lungs with the fresh cool air of the passing breeze and was suddenly overwhelmed with a yearning to be near to the sea, walking with my feet in cool lapping waves and breathing fresh salty air.

'Let's go for a drink at Cullercoats,' I said. 'Then we can have a walk on the beach afterwards. And a bag of chips.'

'Lemonade and a bag of chips coming up. You're a cheap date,' Peter said, and we got into the car and headed for the coast.

The next day was Saturday which Lorraine and I always worked together. Peter usually spent the day working on the house or the car, going out running or going to the match and so I was surprised to see him when he arrived at the shop at four o'clock. We'd had a busy day and had not been troubled by wasps and flies but had been troubled by the zapper. We both hated it and shuddered every time we heard the deathly crackle.

By late afternoon, the flow of customers began to dry up. Lorraine was in the office bagging up coins to be banked and I was busy in the kitchen chopping vegetables for a vegetable and bean gratin for us to take home for dinner when Peter arrived. I looked up at the sound of the doorbell clanging to see him enter wearing a pair of plastic goggles and carrying a sledge hammer.

'What on earth…?' I said as I watched him walk towards me.

'Hi,' he said as he passed me and began to attack the wall at the back of the kitchen with his hammer.

'Excuse me,' I said. 'Don't mind me standing here in me own shop, minding me own business while somebody comes in with a sledgehammer and starts demolishing me kitchen.' Peter stopped and said patiently, 'I'm solving the heat problem.'

'What, by knocking down the back wall?' I asked.

'What's happening here?' asked Lorraine, who had come out from the office to see what all the noise was.

'It's just Peter knocking down the back wall to give us a draught,' I said. Peter stopped striking the wall and took off his goggles.

'If you look carefully,' he said patiently, 'you will see evidence of a window that has been bricked up. I am going to unblock it to create access for fresh air.'

'And access for wasps and flies,' I said. 'And birds and cats and rodents.'

'And burglars,' added Lorraine.

'As if I'm going to just leave a great hole in the wall!' Peter said. 'You two must think I'm stupid!'

'Well, now you mention it…' I said as he went off to the car to get the next piece of the puzzle. He returned with a mesh screen in a frame that he had designed to be fixed into the hole and a second solid frame that could be fitted over the mesh and bolted into place for security overnight. He assured us it would be strong enough to withstand anyone trying to break in, but we jointly decided there was no need to inform the insurance company of the change in case they disagreed and increased our payments.

Peter had spent the day working on his design, using the measurements he had taken and Lorraine and I had to admit it was ingenious. It took less than an hour to install and was in place before the vegetable gratin had finished cooking.

'Brilliant!' Lorraine said. 'I think it'll make a huge difference.'

And it did. Arriving on Monday morning, we opened our new window, turned on the zapper and by the time our new staff member Tanya arrived at ten we were cool, calm and insect-free.

Tanya looked very nervous. Actually she looked terrified.

'Hi,' she said, 'I'm here,' and gave a nervous giggle. Dressed in a tiny white skirt and pink mesh top, she was wearing a thick mask of make up and had swept up her blond hair into a cascade of curls on the top her head. Her efforts served only to make her look even younger, reminding me of children in those grotesque pageants where little girls are painted to look like women and taught to simper at judges. She stumbled into the kitchen on her silver mules looking like a scared rabbit.

'Don't look so worried,' Lorraine said to her, giving her one of our Nutmeg aprons which she could have wrapped around her tiny body three times. 'If you're not sure about anything just ask. We don't bite.' Tanya gave a high pitched giggle.

'Thanks' she said and giggled again. I hoped the giggle was just a nervous habit and would wear off. Lorraine sent her off to make coffee.

'Have you seen what she's wearing?' I whispered to Lorraine. 'More suitable for clubbing than for making sarnies.'

'Let it go for now,' Lorraine hissed back. 'I'll have a word later when she's settled in.'

Georgina looked distinctly unimpressed as Tanya giggled her hello. Nige arrived blushing and flustered, excited to meet the new member of staff, his movements exaggerated as he minced across to her.

'Pleased to meet you, flower,' he said. Predictably, Tanya looked at him and giggled.

'Eeh darlin', there's nowt to you,' he said. 'You're not the size of tuppence ha'penny. You're like a little sparrow.' Tanya took this a complement and giggled. Nige giggled back. I looked at Georgina and raised my eyes. All this tittering was beginning to fray my nerves.

'I'm sure you'll be very happy here,' Nige said. 'We're like a big happy family aren't we girls?' Lorraine, Georgina and I each forced a smile.

'I've never seen your kind of people before.' Tanya said. 'Only on the telly.'

'What kind of people? Postmen?' asked Nige.

'No. I mean, like, you know.' She stopped, confused then her face cleared as she thought of an explanation. 'You know, them kind of men like Frankie Howard and that.'

'Where did you get this one from?' Georgina muttered to me. 'The Mastermind Championships?' But Nige was grinning like a full moon at being compared with his hero. Unwittingly Tanya had secured his loyalty forever.

'What's that smell?' Lorraine said suddenly and we looked to the hob where our plastic electric kettle was sitting amongst the gas flames slowly melting.

'Bloody hell,' said Lorraine as she grabbed a tea towel and snatched up the deformed kettle. 'You're supposed to plug it in, not put it on the hob,' she said irritably causing Tanya to stutter her apologies.

'Not to worry, no harm done,' said Nige as Tanya's painted eyes filled with tears.

'Yeah, don't worry,' I said afraid she was going to cry. 'Look why don't you go and prepare some salad. You could peel and slice the cucumbers and I'll pop up to the hardware shop, I'm sure they sell electric kettles there.'

'I'll walk up with you,' said Georgina. She paid for her shopping and we left to walk up the bank.

'Where on earth did you get that nelly from?' she said as we walked. 'Giggling and twittering like a half-wit and can't even make a cup of tea!'

'Oh she's not that bad, Georgina,' I said. 'She's just nervous. She'll be fine once she's learned the ropes.' I didn't want to admit to Georgina or to myself the doubts I was already having.

'Not very difficult ropes to learn though are they? I mean, fill kettle, plug in kettle...' said Georgina.

'Let's give her a chance before we start judging. She's only been here two minutes.'

When I returned Nige, who rarely went behind the counter was in the kitchen with his arm around Tanya making comforting noises. Lorraine was holding a bowl of green mush.

'It's much easier if you peel the cucumber first, then slice it,' Lorraine said patiently. Tanya had sliced the cucumbers thinly and then tried to peel each slice with a potato peeler.

'I'm so sorry,' she simpered. 'I'm not doing very well am I?' Again the blue eyes welled with unshed tears.

'There, there,' said Nige. 'Everyone makes mistakes, it's only your first day.' I scraped the cucumber pulp into the bin. Although I was irritated, she looked so young and pitiful it was impossible to be annoyed with her.

'You're doing fine,' I said not wanting her to cry. 'Don't worry, my fault. I should have explained more clearly.' I handed the box containing the new kettle to Lorraine. 'I'll go and get some more cucumbers.'

'Sorry,' said Tanya. 'Sorry.'

'Not to worry, flower,' said Nige. I took some more money from the till.

'Won't be long,' I said. 'Coming Nige?' Lorraine gave him a push.

'See you later, Nige,' she said and reluctantly he followed me out of the shop.

'Don't be too hard on her,' he said. 'She's just nervous. She's very young you know.'

'Look Nige I know you've taken to her but you've got to admit she's been crap so far,' I said.

'Give her time, darlin', that's all she needs.'

'Time? She's only here for six weeks, we haven't got any time.'

'She'll be fine, you'll see. See you later flower, work to do, letters to deliver.'

I returned to the shop with a bag full of cucumbers to find Lorraine on the phone trying to arrange delivery of a new microwave. Tanya had put a metal plate in the old one and killed it.

CHAPTER TWENTY-EIGHT

Looking back, I realise now that Tanya had a hard act to follow. Being used to Nadine's efficiency and speed of work, poor Tanya was never going to impress us with her naivete and bumbling about. I appreciated the fact that Tanya was young and inexperienced and I tried not to be too hard on her, but sometimes it was difficult. Once I discovered her strengths I could put her to work in the areas she was most capable, but I was yet to unearth what she was good at.

Mrs Forbes-Williamson managed to take advantage of being served by Tanya.

'That lady said to put her bill on her account,' Tanya said as I came out of the office in time to see Mrs Forbes-Williamson wheesh out of the door.

'Ok,' I said. 'I'll sort it out.' I was annoyed that Mrs Forbes-Williamson had done it again, but I couldn't really blame Tanya. We'd all let her walk out with unpaid for goods at some point or other. But when Tanya told me she'd given Ug and Pug twenty quid out of the till I was mad.

'They said you owed them twenty pounds and it would be all right to take it out of the till,' she explained.

'Tanya I can't believe that someone could walk into the shop and ask for money out of the till and you think it's ok to hand it over. Didn't it even cross your mind to check with Lorraine or me first?'

'No I thought they must be telling the truth.'

'Why?'

'Because if it wasn't true they'd be telling a lie.' Sometimes I wondered if the girl was for real.

'Tanya, people tell lies. All the time. Especially in shops. They lie about how much change you've given them and they steal things and they try to diddle you.' Tanya looked shocked.

'All of them?' she said looking scared.

'No, no. Of course not. Not all of them. Just some of them. Now and then. But you have to be aware that it does happen and think carefully about what people tell you.'

I tried to explain to her that she needed to be aware of shoplifters and not to leave the shop floor unattended while there were customers in the shop.

'Oh I don't think people would steal things,' she said.

'They will and they have,' I said. 'You need to watch carefully and be aware of anyone trying to distract you whilst their accomplice steals something. You also need to be careful about scams when you're giving change. When a customer gives you a note, make sure you put it in the empty compartment in the till drawer while you count out their change. Then if, for example, they say, that they've given you a ten pound note and you've only given them change from a five, you can check.'

'But what if they have given me a ten pound note?'

'Well then you apologise and give them the correct change.'
Sometimes I wondered if Tanya was just winding me up.

'It's easy to make a mistake when you're busy on the till.' I said.
'That's why I'm asking you to be careful.'

Of course it had to happen while Tanya was alone on the shop floor.
Two women came in, one carrying a very small dog and the other carrying a
very large bag. One distracted Tanya with the very small dog while the other
filled the very large bag.

'But she was so nice to me,' Tanya sobbed afterwards when we'd
found the great void where the contents of a whole shelf had been swept into the
bag. 'And she didn't look like a thief, she had lovely clothes.'

'What have her clothes got to do with it?' I snapped. 'What did you
expect? A stocking on her head and a bag with 'swag' written on it?' Tanya
sobbed even harder and my anger dissolved as she stood in front of me, sniffing
and gulping with her make-up drifting down her face.

'Go and wash your face and get yourself calmed down,' Lorraine said
kindly as she guided her into the office. 'And then put the kettle on and make us
all a cup of tea.'

'And remember to plug the kettle in this time, don't put it on the hob,' I
said sharply.

'She's unbelievable,' I said to Lorraine. 'Do you think she's for real?
Perhaps Graham from Yogi has sent her to secretly infiltrate our business and
sabotage it.'

'No, she's the genuine article.' Lorraine said. 'Class one thickie. I'm
amazed she's survived this long.'

Tanya had difficulties with most things but especially in operating the
till.

'It's very simple,' I told her, not for the first time. 'You just type in the
amounts on the price labels, press subtotal and ask the customer for the amount
shown on the screen. Then you type in the amount of money they give you and
you give them the amount of change shown on the screen. Simple.'

'But how does it know?' she kept asking. 'How does the till know how
much change is due?'

'Because it works it out. It's just like a big calculator,' I said.

'I don't understand.'

'You don't need to understand it. Just do it.'

I found myself hovering around the till every time she took a
transaction ready to correct her mistakes.

'There's not enough money in the till drawer to give this customer his
change,' she said once. 'It's says here he needs ninety-seven pounds and a
penny change.'

'Sorry about this,' I said, smiling at the customer who was waiting in
hope.

'How much was the purchase?' I asked.

'Two ninety-nine.'

'And how much did he give you?'

'A ten pound note.'

'So the customer needs seven pounds and a penny change.' I handed over the money and he left, disappointed.

'But it said ninety-seven…'

'Tanya, think about it. How could someone spend two ninety-nine out of a tenner and get nearly a hundred quid change?'

'But I don't understand. The till said…'

'The till's just a machine. It's just working on the information you put into it.'

'I still don't understand.' she said. I sighed in exasperation. Training a monkey to use the till would have been easier than this.

'You must have keyed in one hundred pounds instead of ten pounds and it's calculated the change from that.'

'Oh. So if that happens you don't give the customer what it says on the screen?'

'Of course not, you adjust it and then do a void on the till. I'll show you how to correct a mistake on the till.' I looked at her. 'Actually, no. I won't show you how to correct a mistake on the till. If you make a mistake, come and get me or Lorraine and we'll sort it out.'

'Sorry. Sorry,' said Tanya as I pulled the cover off the till to read the figures on the paper roll and switched the till into void mode to correct the error. Tanya hovered behind me.

'Go and make another cup of tea. Please,' I said and she sloped off dejected into the kitchen. 'Plug it in,' I called after her.

'She's doing my head in,' I said to Lorraine. Luckily we were vigilant about regularly emptying the till of notes and locking them in the cashbox, otherwise we would have found the takings more than ninety pounds down.

'There's a letter to post I'll send her to the post box.' Lorraine said. 'We're down to our last few stamps, she could get some more at the post office while she's there.' When she had gone we discussed how useless she was.

'She's made such a mess of even the most simple tasks that I'm worried about giving her jobs because of the damage she could do,' Lorraine said. 'She's unbelievably bad.'

'I know, but we can't sack her,' I said. 'Can we?'

'Well I couldn't,' Lorraine said. 'Could you?'

'No. It would be like kicking a kitten. She's so young and pathetic. Maybe we need to build her confidence. You know, to try to help her.' I sighed. 'She's really quite sweet, she just needs a bit of oomph behind her.'

'Like a good kick in the pants you mean?'

'Well not literally,' I said. 'We just need to build her confidence. As Nige keeps saying she's very young. And we were young once.'

'Yeah we were. But we weren't as gormless as that were we?'

'God I hope not. Let's try and help her. We're stuck with her so we may as well try to get something positive out of it.'

'Ok, I'll go along with that,' Lorraine said. 'We'll really work hard to boost her self-esteem and improve her skills and by the end of the six weeks she'll be ready to move on and get her career started.'

'Or maybe we'll even keep her on permanently.'

'Yeah.' Pause. 'No.'

'No,' I agreed. 'Maybe not.'

Tanya returned from the post-office and we began our campaign immediately.

'I was just saying to Chris how well you're doing,' Lorraine said smiling at her.

'Really?' said Tanya. I felt a pang of guilt at the look of pleasure and amazement on her face and I resolved to work harder at building her self-esteem.

'I thought I wasn't doing very well,' she said.

'Course you are,' I lied. 'Don't worry about a few little mistakes. Everyone makes mistakes. You should hear about some of the daft things me and Lorraine have done in our time.'

'Oh like what sorts of things?' asked Tanya.

'Well like the time Lorraine forgot to…'

'Yes, well we haven't really got time to tell you now,' interrupted Lorraine.

'Some other time perhaps,' she said giving me a warning look. 'Now Tanya,' she said. 'If you give me the stamps you bought I'll show you where we keep the postage book.'

'Stamps?' asked Tanya looking puzzled.

'Yes,' said Lorraine gently. 'Remember, I asked you to buy thirty first class stamps and post my letter?'

'Yes, that's right. I did buy thirty stamps and I put them on your letter before I posted it.'

'What all of them?' Lorraine barked.

'Yes, it took me ages to fit them all on. I had to put some on top of each other.' She stopped and looked at Lorraine, her bottom lip quivering. 'Have I made another mistake?' Lorraine took a breath.

'No, no,' she said. 'Not at all. You used your initiative and that was, er, good. Wasn't it Chris?'

'It was,' I said. 'Great. Good idea. The letter will get there really fast. Won't it?'

'It will. Like really, really fast.'

'Yeah. Like maybe it'll even get there yesterday, ha ha.'

'Oh good,' said Tanya. She gave a nervous giggle. 'I was worried for a minute there. I thought I'd done something wrong again.'

CHAPTER TWENTY-NINE

On Wednesday Nige came scurrying in excited to tell us his news that Gus's TV debut was soon to be screened.

'Tomorrow at six-thirty,' he said. 'I'm so excited. He's so talented, I just know he's going to be really, really big someday.'

'Are the two of you going to celebrate?' asked Georgina. Nige's face fell.

'No. Unfortunately Gus has to go and watch it with some of his colleagues and his actor friends.'

'He has to?' asked Georgina scathingly. 'Why can't he watch it with you? Or take you along to meet his friends?'

'Oh well, you know how it is,' said Nige. 'Gus has to be seen with the right people, you know. It's for the good of his career. I don't mind watching at home. Anyway I think he's embarrassed about me watching it.' For a couple of seconds none of us spoke, then Georgina said, 'Why don't we all watch it at my place? We'll have our own little party. I'll order pizza and cheesecake and we can watch it together.'

'Really?' said Nige looking pleased. 'That would be great. I'll bring the wine and we'll make a night of it.'

'Why don't we make it about five-thirty so that you can come over as soon as you lock up here?' Georgina suggested.

'Sounds great,' I said. 'I'll look forward to it. Now, who wants coffee?'

'Not for me thanks,' Georgina said. 'I'm going to call in on Josie.'

'How is she? We haven't seen her for a while.'

'She's fine. Just a bit under the weather.'

'Well it's a hard life, being rich,' Lorraine joked. 'Must take it out of you.' Georgina smiled and lifted her hand in a wave as she left.

I made drinks for the rest of us and as I carried the tray through to the shop I watched as a customer filled a basket with goods. This is going to be a good sale, I thought. I watched as the woman put the basket, piled high with shopping, onto the counter and Tanya began keying the prices into the till. I was itching to take over and lingered beside the counter. The customer asked for vitamin C pills and royal jelly tablets and as I instinctively moved forwards to reach for them from the shelves behind the counter Lorraine leaned over and grabbed my sleeve.

'Let her do it herself,' she hissed. 'Show her we have confidence in her.' I moved away reluctantly and kept watch from the kitchen as I drank my tea.

'Stop watching!' chided Lorraine and I moved from the bench and began to open a carton that had been left by the kitchen shelves.

'She looks like she's buying a lot of stuff and I don't want to miss any add-on sales,' I hissed.

'Just let her do it!' Lorraine said. 'She'll be fine.'

'Ok, ok,' I said. I bent down and opened the big cardboard carton and lifted out cans of tuna. Lorraine's right, I thought. Tanya will never have confidence in herself if we don't show that we have faith in her. I stacked the tins of tuna on the kitchen shelf.

'That looked like a good a sale,' I said to Tanya as her customer left with four carrier bags of shopping. 'She must have spent a fortune!'

'No, not really,' Tanya said. 'It only came to four pounds ninety-eight.'

'Four ninety-eight?' I repeated. 'It couldn't have. Those royal jelly tablets cost six ninety-nine alone without the other stuff.'

'Oh, I don't know,' Tanya said confused. I wrenched the cover off the till roll and began reading the figures.

'You've only rang in two items,' I said. 'But she bought loads.'

'No, no, honest,' said Tanya. 'I rang all the prices in, honest I did.'

'Well where are they then?' I said pointing at the till roll.

'Why don't you let me deal with this?' Lorraine said calmly. 'You go and telephone Karma and give them our order and I'll sort this out with Tanya.' I stomped off into the office. Four pounds ninety-eight. She'd let the woman walk out with at least forty quid's worth of stuff. Build her confidence in six weeks? We'd have no business left in six weeks.

By the time I'd phoned in our order I was a little calmer and Lorraine brought me a cup of herb tea.

'Chamomile,' she said. 'To sooth your nerves. Tanya has gone.'

'Forever?' I asked hopefully.

'No. For the day. It's after two o'clock.'

'Did you sort out the mess she'd made?'

'We worked out what she'd done. She'd rang in the amounts but hadn't pressed the enter key. Unfortunately the woman wasn't a regular customer so we might not see her again.'

'Oh,' I groaned. 'Tanya is such an idiot. What are we going to do with her?'

'Take pity on her and try to help her.' Lorraine said virtuously. 'She thinks she's upset you.'

'Well she's right she has' I said.

'I told her it was just your hormones and that you would apologise to her tomorrow.'

'Well thanks a bunch.'

'Surely she can't do anything else wrong,' Lorraine said.

'I wouldn't hold your breath.'

The following morning was grey and wet and I arrived at the shop to find Lorraine cooking something in our huge stockpot.

'Huh, August!' I grumbled shaking the water from my umbrella.

'I know, it's bloody freezing,' Lorraine said as she stirred.

'Mmm, smells good,' I said. 'What is it?'

'Mushroom soup,' Lorraine said. 'We seem to do lentil and vegetable just about every day now, I thought we should try a few different varieties so I came in early to make a start.'

'Good idea. Can I have some, I'm starving.'

'I think it's an elephant not a baby you're carrying, the amount of food you're guzzling,' Lorraine said, ladling some soup into a bowl for me. I moved two boxes of mushrooms and sat down to eat.

'You've got rather a lot of mushrooms there, haven't you?' I commented. 'How much soup are you making?'

Lorraine looked at me.

'Ok, I'll come clean,' she said. 'But don't get mad. Tanya messed up the veg order. Yesterday I asked her to order a twenty-pound bag of potatoes and a pound of mushrooms and to ask Derek to drop them off as usual. He arrived first thing this morning with a pound of potatoes and…'

'…twenty pounds of mushrooms,' I finished. 'Wouldn't he take them back when you told him the mistake?'

'No. I tried. He said he'd ordered them especially from the market and he wouldn't be able to get his money back.'

'Awkward so-and-so. He could have sold them in his shop.'

'He said he'd already bought enough for his shop,' said Lorraine.

'It won't take too long to use those,' I said looking at the two cartons piled with mushrooms. 'We could do mushrooms with the vegeburgers too, that'll soon use them up.' Lorraine pointed to a stack of mushroom cartons on the back shelves that I hadn't noticed.

'Bugger.' I said. 'I thought it was just these.' I grabbed a pan. 'Fancy trying a mushroom burger now?' I asked.

Nige arrived, giggling in anticipation at watching Gus on TV that evening.

'There's not mushroom in there,' he said.

'Oh shut up Nige,' groaned Lorraine.

'I can't help it I'm such a fun guy. Hey you're not laughing. Fun guy, fungi, geddit?'

'Yes we get it, it's just that it's not funny.' said Lorraine grumpily. But nothing could sour Nige's mood today. He picked up a mushroom from one of the cartons on the counter and flung it at Lorraine.

'Oh get with the beat Baggy,' he said, bursting into a rendition of The Bear Necessities. As he danced around the shop, Ernie ran in the door and said to Lorraine, 'How much is…?' He stopped mid sentence to turn and look at Nige who was shimmying across the floor holding imaginary coconuts. Ernie looked back at Lorraine in horror then turned on his heels and fled.

'This place gets more like Cold Comfort farm every day,' Lorraine grumbled. 'Here! Baloo!' she yelled at Nige who was shaking two packets of brazil nuts above his head like a pair of maracas as he wobbled about. 'Get this down you,' she said handing him a fried mushroom sandwich. 'We've got another eighteen pounds of the things to get through.'

149

When Tanya arrived we set her to work cleaning shelves. Surely she couldn't do any damage cleaning shelves. She declined a mushroom sandwich and donned the apron and rubber gloves I had ready for her. I decided to give her step by step instructions to avoid any possible mishaps. She watched as I cleared an area of the shelf then washed and dried it.

'Next give it a good polish with the wax,' I said rubbing the shelf vigorously. 'Then dust the packages before replacing them.'

'Right,' she said. 'I'm sure I can do that.' I left her to it.

Fortunately (for us), the day remained cold and damp and so our soup was a popular choice at lunchtime. Peter was served with two bowls of mushroom soup followed by a mushroom vegeburger with extra mushrooms.

'Don't ask, just eat,' I told him as I piled more fried mushrooms on his plate.

'They're not magic mushrooms or something are they?' he asked suspiciously. 'Did you get them off Georgina?'

'No, they're Another-Tanya-Mistake-Mushrooms,' Lorraine said. I reminded him that we were going to Georgina's that evening as he left with a thermos of mushroom soup for his workmates.

'Right, what kind of pizza would you like?' Georgina asked.

'Anything but mushroom,' I said. We were gathered in her tiny sitting room, Nige pacing around the floor.

'Sit down Nige, you're getting on my nerves,' Lorraine said as Georgina went off to phone the pizza shop.

'I can't,' said Nige. 'I'm too excited. Just wait till you see my Gus. He's such a fine figure of a man.'

'Sit down,' I said, pushing him into an armchair. Georgina returned with an opened bottle of wine and some glasses. She handed a glass to Nige.

'Drink that and calm down,' she said. 'You've got another half an hour to wait yet. The news is on first.' She handed a glass of wine to Lorraine and gave me a glass of orange juice. I looked longingly at the wine.

'Do you want a small one? Half a glass won't hurt,' Georgina said.

'No. Better not. I'll stick to my juice,' I said.

'Never mind, darlin',' said Nige. 'I'm sure you'll make up for it after the baby's born. Speaking of babies, how's my little friend Tanya doing?'

'She wasn't too bad today actually,' I said. 'She managed to clean the shelves without any mishaps.'

'No she didn't,' Lorraine said. 'She dropped a bag of flour in the bucket of water and she put everything back on the shelves in the wrong place.'

'Well without any major mishaps then,' I said.

Peter arrived at the same time as the pizzas and I went to the kitchen with Georgina to cut them into slices leaving the others to watch the news.

'What's that they're watching?' Georgina asked.

'Something on the news about the Duchess of York,' I said.

'That's what I thought,' Georgina said. 'I could have sworn he said something about a man sucking her toes.' I laughed and she did too.

'You must have misheard,' I said. We arranged the pizza and coleslaw on trays and carried them to the coffee table where Peter was kneeling in front of the television setting the video recorder.

'So what role does Gus play?' Peter asked, pressing buttons as he pointed the remote at the TV.

'I'm not sure,' said Nige. 'You know, I think he's a little bit embarrassed about being so talented. When I ask about it he changes the subject. He's very secretive about the whole thing. He said he was meeting his actor friends but he didn't mention the show. I told him I was coming here tonight but I didn't say we were going to watch, and he seemed relieved. I don't think he wants me to see it, he's so self-conscious, poor lamb.'

Video set, pizza distributed and wine flowing we settled down to watch. As the news programme ended, we cheered at the announcement that '*The Tide will Turn, a tale of passion, intrigue and suspense*' was about to start.

Twenty minutes later Gus had still not appeared amongst the collection of stereotypical characters delivering their cliché lines. The heroine acted her way through a progression of disasters, through gloomily lit scenes and dreary music, which swelled to a crescendo to emphasis each tragedy. The plot was so depressing it was almost funny. Georgina poured more wine.

'I wonder when he'll come on,' Nige said looking worried.

'Don't worry, Nige. It's only just started,' Lorraine told him. 'There's another forty minutes to go yet.'

'But it's very good isn't it?' Nige said. Desperation showed in his face. For a second none of us answered then we mumbled our agreement.

'It is, Nige. It is'

'Yes, yes, excellent.'

The drama rattled on. And on. We watched as undernourished, overworked children perished in the workhouse, crops failed, fire destroyed homes and families were wiped out by cholera.

'This is crap,' Peter muttered in my ear and I nudged him to keep quiet. I was having difficulty in staying awake. My eyes were fighting to close and I struggled against them, wriggling in my seat and stretching my face trying to shake off sleep. The urge to drop my head on Peter's shoulder and escape from this excruciating boredom by descending into sleep was intense, but somehow I resisted. I had long lost the thread of the plot, and I shuffled toward Peter trying to glimpse the time on his watch.

A few minutes before the end of the drama, there must have been some sort of miraculous occurrence, as I suddenly noticed that the music had changed from dismal to a more sentimental ambiance and a happy ending appeared to be materialising. Our hapless heroine, dressed now in brocades and pearls, hair swept up with jewelled combs, seemed to be travelling in a coach with a handsome young duke. But where was Gus? Had I missed him during one of my

151

descents into sleep? I'd have to pretend I'd seen him or Nige would never forgive me.

'There he is!' yelled Nige suddenly, 'That's him, that's my Gus!' Like shop dummies suddenly coming to life we simultaneously rose and leaned towards the television in time to see the back of a footman dressed in tights and a powdered wig as he opened a carriage door for our happy couple to descend. We watched, tense with expectation, waiting for the camera to turn back to the footman, but after a shot of the simpering couple it retreated to a sweeping panorama of a stately house as the credits began to roll.

Nige stared at the screen for a moment, silent in his disillusionment. We too sat in silence, none of us quite knowing what to say. Nige looked at each of us in turn, his face flushed, then swallowing his disappointment said, 'He was good though wasn't he? My Gus? And he looked good in his costume?'

'He did Nige,' said Georgina. 'You're right there. He's a fine figure of a man.'

CHAPTER THIRTY

September arrived, changing green to red and yellow and bringing cool but golden days that reminded me of my wedding day, almost a year ago.

The all-day morning sickness that had been my constant companion vanished overnight. I awoke waiting for the usual feeling of nausea to sweep over me and when it didn't, I rose and dressed cautiously, waiting for it to strike. But it had gone. The tiredness and nausea that had become part of my everyday life disappeared leaving me revitalised and with more energy than I'd had for a long time. Now that the first weeks of discomfort had gone, I had more energy than I'd had for a long time and found that pregnancy suited me.

Lorraine flew off to Malta and Nadine returned to work. I was so glad to see her back. I welcomed her with a hug and told her how much she'd been missed.

'I'll put the kettle on and you can tell me all the news as we work,' she said, obviously pleased at how delighted I was to see her. She noticed the new flooring and she admired the insect-zapper and the new window. As we prepared the salads I told her about our evening at Georgina's and about Gus's television appearance. But when I told her about the exploits of Tanya, she laughed so much she lay down her knife and held her sides.

'You're making it up,' she said wiping her eyes.

'I'm not, it's all true, honest. Just wait till you meet her, she'll be here any minute.'

Nadine found Tanya's incompetence sweet and amusing at first, but amusement soon turned to irritation as Tanya's slow and disordered methods of working interfered with Nadine's routines.

'Do we really need her?' Nadine asked me when Tanya had gone to post another letter. 'I think the two of us could manage without her.'

'You're probably right,' I said. 'But she's staying. Never mind. She's only here for another four weeks.'

The week passed uneventfully, with Nadine and I conspiring to keep Tanya out of the kitchen but also away from the till.

'What else can I give her to do?' I asked Nadine. 'I need to give her chores on the shop floor away from harm.'

'What about shelf cleaning?' Nadine said.

'She did it last week.'

'Ask her to do it again.'

'I could but it would be a bit mean, making her wash the same shelves for four weeks.'

'How about paying her to not come in?' I ignored that suggestion and said, 'I think I'll ask her to compile a file of all the products we stock. That would keep her busy for ages.'

'Are you sure you can trust her to do it properly?' Nadine asked.

'Doesn't matter. I don't need another list, I can throw it away when she's gone.'

'You can't do that!' said Nadine. 'You'd be paying her for nothing.'

'Why not? I'm paying her for nothing now. I have to pay her anyway and this way she can't do any damage and she'll feel that she's being really useful. Then we're all happy.'

Our take-away food was increasingly popular. We regularly added to the menu trying new recipes. Our home-made soup sold especially well and we cooked a different variety each day, lentil and vegetable, carrot and coriander, cream of asparagus, leek and potato and sweetcorn chowder.

Nige appointed himself as soup-taster and each morning declared the day's recipe to be superior to the previous. It amused him greatly to ask for 'a soupcon of soup' and then after tasting it, exclaim 'souper'.

With our menu of sandwiches, toasties, burgers, soup and baked potatoes, lunchtimes were busier than ever and with Tanya out of the way, happily compiling her lists, Nadine and I worked like a well-oiled machine, taking orders, preparing and wrapping food, determined not to lose a single customer.

During the second week that Lorraine was away, I held an Italian week with the intention of making themed weeks a regular occurrence if it was a success. I had negotiated some deals with Karma, so that we could give our customers lots of special offers. When the delivery arrived, I assembled a window display with pasta, sun dried tomatoes, olives, capers, cannellini beans, borlotti beans, cep mushrooms and pine kernels along with an Italian flag and models of the Leaning Tower of Pisa and a gondola that I'd borrowed. Amazingly, it didn't look as tacky as it sounds and after faffing around for two and a half hours, I was pleased with the effect.

Strings of Italian flags festooned around the place and surfaces draped with red, white and green cloths to display our special offers finished the look. Nadine brought a cassette of Pavarotti that we played constantly. It was popular with the customers and did add to the theme but also became very irritating after the first fifty playings.

'What about giving our take-away menu an Italian feel too?' Nadine asked.

'Good idea,' I said. 'What did you have in mind?'

'An Italian soup? And perhaps cooked pasta with a sauce in a box to take away?'

We discussed ideas as we worked and decided on minestrone soup, penne with Mediterranean vegetables, and panini with red pepper, mozzarella and pesto. I also cooked some Italian inspired dishes using some of the ingredients we had on sale and assembled a table to offer samples to customers with free recipe sheets.

'Gawd, that tastes like an old man's sock,' Georgina said when she tried my gnocchi with Gorgonzola sauce.

'Do you mind!' I said to her as she pretended to spit it out, grimacing and making disgusting noises. Two women who had asked for a sample now changed their minds.

'Actually I'll not bother. I've just had my lunch,' one of them said. The other nodded in agreement and they left.

'Thanks a lot Georgina, I'm trying to run a business here,' I said.

'Sorry, but I'm just being honest.'

'Honest? So you're saying you've eaten an old man's sock before?'

'Well if I did I'm sure that's what it would taste like.'

'Well that's just your opinion. And I'll thank you to keep it to yourself,' I said. I wasn't happy about losing two potential customers or about the slur on my cooking skills. 'Gorgonzola is an acquired taste and you obviously haven't acquired it,' I said, peevishly. A group of people entered the shop and I gave her a warning look.

'Here, give me one of your aprons,' she said taking one from the hook in the kitchen. She stood beside the tasting table and after removing the dish of gnocchi said brightly, 'Good morning ladies. May I offer you a sample of our delicious Italian fare? We have baked polenta with walnut sauce, vegetable and chick pea soup, or how about our delicious mushroom and almond risotto?' The women tasted the dishes eagerly, asking questions and looking at the displays of ingredients.

'Why not take one of our free recipe sheets,' Georgina suggested. 'Ingredients are available here for you to produce these delicious meals at home.' The women piled their baskets with packages and Georgina gave me a smug look.

She stayed for a couple of hours, chatting to customers and giving out samples and I replenished her table several times with fresh dishes of hot food. I had to admit she was good. As the piles of ingredients disappeared rapidly she would call to Nadine and I to fill up the displays.

At two o'clock custom tailed off and she came and put her head on my shoulder.

'Have I redeemed myself?' she asked. 'Am I forgiven?'

'Yes, I suppose so,' I said, laughing. 'Actually, you were great, we sold loads of stuff.'

'So how about a free lunch then?' she asked. ' I'm starving after giving out food to other people all morning.'

'Yes, of course,' I said. 'You've earned it. You can finish off that Gorgonzola gnocchi.'

Derek thought the Italian week was a great idea. He called in on Monday just before we closed to tell us how he'd benefited from it.

'I've had loads of women in after me plum tomatoes,' he said. 'They're all bringing your recipes and asking for the ingredients. I've sold loads of courgettes and aubergines and I've sold as many peppers today as I usually sell in a week.'

155

'That's good,' I said. 'Why don't you take some of my recipe sheets for your customers, then you could send them to us to buy the rest of the ingredients?'

'That would be great,' he said. 'I thought I might do some special offers on some of me veg. That's if you don't mind me joining in.'

'Course not,' I said. 'If we work together it will help us both.' I gave him some recipe sheets and a spare string of flags and he went off to decorate his shop.

Our special offers were successful and sold well, especially the range of organic frozen pizzas, although I did have one customer who wasn't impressed.

'I'm looking for a three-cheese pizza,' she said after rummaging through the freezer and disarranging the piles of boxes.

'I'm sorry, there isn't a three-cheese variety in that range,' I said.

'You haven't got a three-cheese pizza?' she said. 'But it says there, Twenty-five percent off all varieties of Great-Living Organic Pizzas.' She pointed at the sign above the freezer.

'Yes, but they don't have a three-cheese in the range,' I said.

'Well why does it say all varieties then?'

'Well it means all the varieties that they do,' I said.

'Well that's just stupid,' she said.

'How about a different variety?' I asked, looking through the glass lid of the freezer.

'I wanted three-cheese.'

'They don't do a three-cheese.'

'Well it says there all varieties.'

'But like I said they don't do a three-cheese variety.'

'Well I think it should say Twenty-five percent off all varieties of Great-Living Organic Pizzas except Three-Cheese.'

'Yes, ok, I'll change it,' I said. The customer is always right. I forced a smile. 'They do six varieties,' I said. 'Cheese and tomato, sweetcorn and pineapple, wild mushroom, roasted red pepper, spinach and ricotta and courgette and basil.'

'Oh all right then,' she grumbled. 'I'll have cheese and tomato.' I lifted the glass lid and searched through the pile of boxes. Unfortunately I couldn't find a cheese and tomato pizza amongst them.

'Actually, I'm very sorry, we don't seem to have a cheese and tomato, they must have sold out,' I said. 'We've got spinach and ricotta or…'

'But I wanted cheese and tomato. Actually I wanted three-cheese but…'

'…they don't do them,' I finished.

'Don't they do cheese and tomato either then?'

'Yes, they do them it's just we haven't any left.'

'So it should really say Twenty-five percent off all varieties of Great-Living Organic Pizzas except Three-Cheese and Cheese and Tomato.'

'Right,' I said. 'Spinach and Ricotta is very nice. How about one of those?'

'Oh just give me the red pepper one then,' she said. 'I can't stand spinach.' I found a roasted red pepper pizza and took it to the counter to put it in a bag.

'One ninety-nine please,' I said.

'One ninety-nine? What about my twenty-five percent off?'

'That's with the twenty-five percent off.'

'How much are they without the discount like?'

'Er, about...' I couldn't remember and I tried in vain to work it out. 'If they're one ninety-nine with twenty-five percent off they must have been two pounds eighty...no...two pounds...oh I don't know, but they're definitely one ninety-nine.'

'That's scandalous. You can get pizzas for ninety-nine pence in SuperSavers.'

'Well why don't you get one there then?' I said now coming to the end of my tether.

'Because they haven't got any in.'

'Oh, well that's different,' I said sarcastically. 'Ours are only fifty-pence when we haven't got them in.'

'Fifty pence?' she said. 'That's cheap. I'll come back.'

CHAPTER THIRTY-ONE

'Well?' I said to Peter. 'Come on then. Get it over with.' I'd just returned from the hairdresser with a new hairstyle.

I'd decided on a perm. I'd visualised myself with sexy tumbling curls, like a Pre-Raphaelite model. The hairdresser had advised me to have it done about a week before I went on holiday, 'to give it time to soften.' So here I stood looking like an electric shock survivor.

'Well, it's different,' Peter said.

'Different to what?' I said. 'Normal hair?' I looked in the mirror and pulled at the tight curls. 'Oh look at it, it's horrible!'

'I thought you liked poodles.'

'Very funny,' I said. I stared in the mirror. It was awful. I looked like the fat one out of Little and Large. 'It feels all hard like wire wool,' I said touching it.

'It'll come in handy for scrubbing the pans,' Peter said. I looked at him and scowled.

'Your jokes are so unfunny,' I said. 'It's just pure jealousy.' I patted the wiry curls. 'You're just jealous because you don't have hair like this.'

'Actually I do have hair like that,' Peter said. 'It's just not on my head.'

'Don't worry, it'll soften,' Nadine said when she saw it. 'After a couple of washes it'll be lovely.'

'Gus's friend has a wig a bit like that,' Nige said.

'There, you see,' said Nadine. 'It must be a nice hairstyle if Gus's friend wears a wig to look the same as you. I bet she looks lovely doesn't she?' she said to Nige.

'It's a he,' Nige said. 'And yes he looks great in it. He's an entertainer. He wears it on stage.'

'Oh great,' I said. 'So what you're telling me is that I look like a transvestite.'

When Georgina arrived she didn't say a word about my hair. I wondered if Nadine had warned her not to.

'Can't stay,' she said. 'I'm off to see Josie. She's ill. I just want a sandwich and some fruit juice to take for her.'

'She's been ill for some time hasn't she?' I said. Georgina nodded.

'Some of these flu bugs are really hard to shake off,' Nige said. 'When Gus had flu last year he was ill for weeks, I had to do everything for him. I mean he managed to get himself along the road for a couple of drinks with his mates, poor boy, but he was exhausted when he got back.'

'Here, take this for her,' I said, ladling hot vegetable soup into an insulated carton. 'Tell her we're thinking of her.'

The day wore on slowly, as days do when it's your last working day before a holiday. I checked the clock regularly as the hands crawled across the afternoon. Eventually, the end of the day approached and I went into the office to start the cashing up process.

'Chris!' Nadine hissed through the door. Her face was red with excitement. 'Come out here quick. You'll never guess who's just walked in.' I hurried out to see a well-known Geordie actor who'd starred in a comedy series and who'd had a couple of singles in the charts. I'd read that he was currently filming a gritty drama series set in the centre of Newcastle. Nadine was pulling ingredients out of the fridge to make him a sandwich.

'Sandwiches are finished,' I whispered to her. 'We've cleaned the kitchen.'

'I know, I know,' she said. 'But he's a celebrity. We could put a poster in the window saying he eats our sandwiches.' I went to the till to serve a customer who was watching intently.

'Have you seen who it is?' she mouthed. I nodded trying to look blasé and give the impression that a famous person visiting the shop was not an unusual occurrence. 'I'm trying not to look too star-struck,' she said, staring at him with her mouth open.

Our 'celebrity' strutted around the shop looking at his watch impatiently. Nadine wrapped his sandwich and took it over to him. By now there were four people in the queue, all trying to act as though they'd not noticed him.

'I'll just be a minute,' Nadine said in her best posh voice. 'There's a bit of a queue.' She smiled at him.

'Never mind the bliddy queue,' he said. 'Just ring the bugger in.' Nadine's look of total admiration was immediately replaced by one of great offence.

'I'm sorry but there's a queue, you'll have to wait,' she said, dropping the posh accent.

'Just give us the sodden sandwich man, am in a hurry,' he said throwing a ten-pound note at Nadine. Nadine's indignation burst into life.

'Don't throw money at me!' she snapped at him. 'You can wait your turn like everybody else.'

'Do ye knaa whee ah am?' he yelled at her. Nadine put her hands on her hips.

'Yes I do know who you are,' she shouted. 'YOU'RE THAT BIG GEORDIE GONK OFF THE TELLY AND YOU CAN BUGGER OFF. NOBODY TALKS TO ME LIKE THAT YOU BIG IGNORANT GALOOT. GO ON, GET OUT!' He snatched up his sandwich and left without waiting for his change as Nadine yelled after him: 'AYE, GO ON GET OUT,' and her parting shot, 'AUF WIEDERSEIN PET!'

He never returned, and we didn't use the poster idea.

'That's it, everything's in,' Peter said as he lugged the last suitcase into the back of the car and closed the tailgate. We were going off to a cottage in the Lake District for a couple of weeks of rest and relaxation.

'I need to call at the shop on the way,' I told Peter.

'You're joking,' he said. 'You're on holiday. Surely you can forget the place for a couple of weeks.'

'I need to update Lorraine on what's been happening,' I said. Lorraine had returned from Malta the previous evening and although I'd spoken to her on the phone, I needed to run through a few things with her in the shop.

'I'll drop you off while I go for petrol and check the tyres and stuff,' Peter said. 'But I want to be away by ten at the latest.'

'Ok, ok,' I said. There was no way I could forget about the shop while I was on holiday. I was already planning to telephone each evening to see how things were going but I thought it best not to mention it to Peter at present.

Nadine was in the kitchen preparing salads when I entered the shop. Lorraine looked sun-tanned and refreshed as she spoke to someone on the phone. She finished the call and came to greet me with a hug. Tanya wandered about obviously at a loss for something to do.

'If you've nothing to do you could unload those packs of tuna onto the kitchen shelves please Tanya,' Lorraine said to her then turned to me. 'Coffee?' she said.

'No, I better not,' I said. 'Peter's coming back for me in about half an hour so we'd better get down to business.'

We went through the figures for the past two weeks and I updated her on stock orders, new products and the customer order book.

Before leaving I began to pack a box with groceries to take to the cottage. As I chose a couple of bars of organic chocolate, Jonathan arrived carrying his pile of bread trays. Suddenly there was a loud bang from the kitchen followed by a scream from Nadine.

'It exploded!' she screeched. 'It's all over me face!' I hurried to the kitchen to see what had happened. Nadine continued to scream. She was pebble-dashed with tuna. Her hair was dotted with it, there were bits on her face and a chunk was stuck in her right eyebrow. Brine dripped down her cheeks and she blinked and spluttered groping for a towel, tin opener still in her hand.

'What on earth...?' I started, as Jonathan tutted, put down his trays and left.

'Sorry Nadine,' Tanya stuttered. 'I think that was my fault. I put the tin of tuna on the gas ring by mistake and when I realised I put it back on the shelf and hoped you wouldn't notice. I didn't want to get wrong. Sorry.'

'I thought it felt a bit warm when I stuck the tin-opener in it,' barked Nadine. 'Look at the state of me!' She brushed bits of tuna from her clothes. 'God, I stink!'

A car horn sounded and I looked to see Peter waiting in the car outside. Laughing to myself, I took my box of goodies and left them - Nadine shouting loudly about incompetent people, Lorraine trying to pacify her and clean her up with a tea towel, and Tanya sniffling and mumbling her apologies.

CHAPTER THIRTY-TWO

I thought about the shop less and less as the beauty of the Lake District enveloped me. Day by day I felt myself slowly relaxing and the stresses and worries of the business seemed far away and unimportant.

Each day we packed food and waterproofs and set off towards the hills. Those days spent walking in some of the most beautiful unspoilt areas of our country were amongst my happiest ever.

I have always loved mountains; their vastness and energy invigorate me. Walking beneath their towering height I felt overawed by the enormity of the untamed power of nature. Even days of rain did not spoil it. The black heavy clouds and rolling mists added greater rawness and drama to the wildness of the mountains and I revelled in it. We walked every day, talking about the baby and making plans for our future. Peter, concerned about my pregnant condition, carried my things in his rucksack and urged me to slow down as I hiked over stony pathways and climbed over boulders. He made sure of many rests at tearooms and country inns, but I was restless to keeping walking. I had never felt so energised.

Lorraine was ecstatic to see me back at work. Two weeks with Tanya had taken its toll.

'Never again,' she said to me when Tanya was out of earshot. 'She's cost us a fortune and we've had to work harder to compensate for her being here. Next time we'll just manage by ourselves.'

We bought Tanya a leaving present and took her out to dinner, where the cost of a table of glasses she'd managed to knock over was added to our bill, so all in all employing her turned out to be quite an expensive affair. However, we did boost her confidence a little while she was with us and she did manage to get a job in a café in town with the help of our very carefully worded references.

After a couple of days, Lorraine, Nadine and I were back to our old routines and our holidays seemed like distant memories.

October arrived and we started to make plans for Christmas. We stocked up on cake and pudding ingredients and devised a Christmas cake recipe using as many of our ingredients as possible. I baked one as a sample. I cut it into slices and displayed it beneath a dome-lidded glass dish on the counter.

'Ooh lovely,' Nige said, helping himself to a slice. 'It's a bit early isn't it? Not even November yet.' He took another slice and I smacked his hand.

'Gerroff,' I said, 'it's for the customers. I'll make one for you and Gus later if you like but keep off this one. You've already eaten nearly half of it.' Nige stuffed the cake into his mouth.

'Mmm, delicious,' he said. 'Just one more, last one, honest.'

'Last one,' I repeated as he took another. 'And no it's not too early. This is the best time to make it so it has time to mature before Christmas.' I had printed copies of the recipe to give away to encourage people to buy the ingredients.

'Lovely,' a woman said, tasting it.

'Would you like a recipe?' I asked. 'We stock all the ingredients you'll need.'

'Oh heavens, no,' she said. 'I'm the worst cake-maker ever. But I'll pay you to bake one for me.' I took her telephone number and promised to ring her with a price. I told Lorraine about the idea of baking Christmas cakes to order.

'We could do Christmas puddings and mince pies too,' I said.

'And what about wheat-free and sugar-free stuff for customers with special dietary needs?' Lorraine suggested. 'And perhaps nearer the time we could think about doing nut roasts too.'

We spent the evenings perfecting and costing our recipes and by the end of the week we had a price list of home-made Christmas goodies available to order. We sent recipe sheets to our delivery customers, which prompted them to order their Christmas cooking ingredients. Mrs Derrington bought flour by the sackful along with kilos of currants, sultanas, raisins, dates, apricots, and cherries.

'She's baking for the church Autumn Fayre,' Lorraine explained when she returned from the delivery round. 'They're raising money for African orphans.'

'Then we should really offer a discount as our contribution to the charity,' I said. 'We'll have to sort something out.' The insect zapper suddenly crackled loudly causing Lorraine and I to jump.

'I thought we'd finished with all that, now that summer's gone,' Lorraine said. 'I didn't think we'd get any more flies now.'

'It was probably a wasp,' I said. 'It was too loud for a fly. Although I thought they'd all have died off by now.' There were a couple more loud cracks from the machine during the morning so at lunchtime I asked Peter to empty it.

'It seems to be full of moths,' he said tipping the contents of the tray into the bin. 'Poor things.'

'Yuk,' I said, turning my eyes away from them. I don't like moths.

The machine was quiet for the rest of the afternoon, as was trade.

'Let's sit down for five,' I said. 'I'll put the kettle on.' Lorraine and I sat on stools behind the counter but as usual Nadine drank her coffee as she worked.

'I may as well dust these shelves while its quiet,' she said.

'Come and sit down for five minutes,' I said. 'Have a break.'

'I can have a break while I work,' she said illogically.

'Actually it's after two, you've finished your shift,' Lorraine said.

'I know,' Nadine said. 'I just want to give these shelves a quick going over before I leave.'

'Shouldn't we be doing something too?' yawned Lorraine as I poured us another cup of tea. 'We should really use this quiet time to catch up with paperwork and stuff.'

'Yeah I suppose we should,' I said lazily.

'Saved by the bell,' Lorraine said as the telephone burst into life and she got up to answer it. I gathered the empty cups and was rinsing them when Lorraine returned.

'That was Julie Bradley,' Lorraine said.

'Who?' I asked. Lorraine hurried to the bookstand and began searching through the titles.

'Julie Bradley from the Daily Echo. She published that article about us when we opened.'

'How could I forget?' I said drolly. 'What did she want?'

'She's bringing her photographer to take some shots of us,' Lorraine said as she frantically spun the bookstand searching for something.

'Me as well?' Nadine said excitedly.

'Oh you're joking,' I said. 'Not again. Why? When's she coming?'

'Tomorrow. She's writing an article about using natural ingredients to make beauty treatments. She wants us to whip up some recipes and apply them so she can take photos.'

'Can I be in them?' asked Nadine'

'You can be in them all if you like Nadine,' I said 'but you'll have to model the beauty products.'

'Oh wow!' Nadine said. 'I'm going to be a model!'

'Ah, here it is. The Book of Natural Beauty' Lorraine said. She pulled out a book and started leafing through it. 'There's loads of stuff in here we can use. Facemasks, hair treatments…help me find what we need.'

'I will in a minute,' I said running into the office.

'Where're you going? Come back,' Lorraine called after me.

'To ring the hairdresser,' I called back. 'I need a new style now that my perm is growing out. I don't want another disastrous photo like the last one.'

Nadine left in a state of excitement about the following day's photo shoot.

'I probably won't sleep,' she said. 'I can't wait! See you tomorrow!'

Lorraine and I spent the rest of the afternoon picking out recipes that we thought would be suitable for Julie's article. We changed them a little, substituting ingredients here and there so that we weren't blatantly stealing the author's recipes but also to include ingredients we had at hand. At half past four I put on my coat to go to my hair appointment.

'Leaving a bit early aren't you?' Lorraine said.

'It was the only time she could fit me in,' I said.

'Are you sure you want to go?' Lorraine asked. 'You know you're never happy with the result.'

'Yes, it'll be fine,' I said. I was always optimistic before I went. One day I was going to leave a hair salon with a fantastic cut and this could be the day.

'Just be careful what you ask for,' Lorraine warned.

'I'm just getting a straightforward bob and perhaps a colour,' I said. 'Can't go wrong with that.'

The bob was ok I'll give you that. But the colour was a disaster. And this time I couldn't even blame the stylist.

'I think you should go lighter,' she said. 'I could do you some nice plum highlights?'

'No, I want to go darker,' I said quickly. The word plum conjured up a vision of me with a bright purple head.

'It's a shame your hair is so dark,' the stylist said. 'Unfortunately it's too dark to go blond but I could lighten it quite a bit.'

'Yes I know my hair is very dark, but I want it darker,' I said irritated. What was wrong with dark hair? I'd always quite liked the colour of my hair. What's so good about being blond anyway? I thought, looking at the stylist's ash blond hair set off by her tanned face. In comparison my dark locks and pale complexion made me look like Morticia.

'What about auburn, or a nice mousey brown?' she suggested. Mousey? That did it. I wasn't swapping my lovely dark brown colour to be mousey.

'I'd like it dark please and I'm in a hurry, if you don't mind. Thankyou.'

'It's very dark,' Peter said.

'I want it dark,' I said huffily. I wasn't going to admit to him that I hated my new jet-black barnet. 'The style's ok though isn't it?'

'Uh-huh-huh,' Peter replied.

'I mean it's a bit short, but it'll grow.'

'Uh-huh-huh.'

'And it's better than the perm.'

'Uh-huh-huh,' he said and I suddenly noticed he was speaking with his lip curled and his collar turned up.

'Get lost,' I said slapping him and I heard him say, 'Ladies and jennelmen, Elvis has left the building,' as I left the room.

The following morning Lorraine and I arrived at the shop early to mix up the recipes for the natural beauty article.

'This smells delicious,' I said as I mixed a bowl of crushed strawberries with natural yogurt. I stuck my finger in the bowl and licked it. 'Mmm, I'd rather eat this than cover my face in it.'

'What's it for?' Lorraine asked.

'It's a cleansing facemask. Apparently the strawberries cleanse and tone and the yoghurt soothes.'

'Have a try of this one,' Lorraine said, so stupidly I did.

'Uhh! That's horrible,' I said. 'What is it?'

'Honey, seasalt and tumeric face scrub. The seasalt exfoliates, the tumeric clears impurities and the honey nourishes.'

'Do you think we've got enough here?' I asked Lorraine looking at our dishes of concoctions.

'Yeah, I think so,' said Lorraine. 'I reckon that should be enough.'

'Morning,' Nadine called as she came in excitedly. 'I'm all ready for my modelling assignment. When's the photo shoot?'

Lorraine and I looked at her perfectly applied make-up and freshly blow-dried hair.

'Nadine you look gorgeous,' I said. 'But you do know we're going to cover you in squashed strawberries and yoghurt?'

'And there's an olive oil and egg hair treatment for you to try too,' Lorraine added.

'Ha, ha, very funny,' Nadine said.

Julie Bradley arrived with Michelle, the photographer who'd taken the hideous photo of us the last time. Julie interviewed us about our natural beauty tips. We were prepared this time and gave careful and well-rehearsed answers to her questions. I was quite impressed with the way we spoke so confidently and knowledgeably about a subject we hadn't known anything about yesterday. Julie took lots of notes and seemed pleased with the information we'd given her. The insect-zapper crackled intermittently as we spoke and I made a mental note to ask Peter to check it again. Nadine prowled around the shop waiting for her big moment. Michelle set up her camera equipment and fiddled about with light meters and lenses.

'Right, just the photos to do,' Julie said, packing her notes into a file in her briefcase. We went through to the shop front to find Nadine draped on a chair in front of the counter.

'How do you want me?' she asked smiling.

'With this on your clock,' said Lorraine slapping a handful of mashed cucumber on her face.' Nadine was less than pleased.

'That's freezing!' she said. 'What is it?'

'It's just cucumber,' I said. 'Very nourishing for the skin,' I added in my role as natural beauty expert.

'What about my make-up?' Nadine complained. 'Your covering it up!'

'Nadine that looks great,' I said, adding a bit to her nose.

'It's horrible,' she said, 'Don't take a photo of me like this, I'll look like a gargoyle. Ew! It's dripping off my chin!'

'Wait till we get the olive oil on her hair,' Lorraine whispered to me. 'She'll go mental!'

Michelle snapped away as we applied the mask. Julie seemed interested in the recipes, picking up bowls and sniffing the contents and smearing some on her wrist. Michelle stopped snapping and fiddled with her light meters.

'Bit of a problem here,' she said. 'The cucumber mask is almost transparent so it's not showing up on the shots. It just looks like part of her skin, like she's got a lumpy deformed face.'

Nadine looked horrified and began rubbing off the mashed cucumber.

'Try something else,' I said. 'Try the yogurt.' I slapped a spoonful onto Nadine's face. But Michelle had the same problem with that.

'It's too white,' she said. 'These are black and white shots, it's not showing up, she just looks like she has very pale make-up on. You need something with a little more colour and preferably more texture.' We looked at the contents of the bowls. They were all similar in colour and texture.

'What about that?' Julie suggested, pointing to a dish in the fridge.

'That's pease pudding,' I said. 'It's for the sandwiches.'

'Would that do?' Julie said to Michelle, holding up the dish.

'Yeah, that looks better, try it,' Michelle said, re-positioning her camera and looking through the viewfinder.

'I'm not having pease pudding...' started Nadine as Lorraine and I slapped it on with glee.

'Sorry darlin' I'm a bit late this morning,' Nige said as he breezed in then looked at Nadine struggling as she tried to resist having her face covered in pease pudding.

'Hello, what's going on here?' he said, breaking into an exaggerated smile and putting one hand on his hip as he saw Michelle with her camera.

'Don't ask,' I told him. 'Not unless you want to stay and be a model.'

'What is it?' he asked, looking in the bowl that Lorraine held as we put the finishing touches to Nadine's mask. 'It looks like...'

'Pease pudding,' finished Nadine. 'Pease pudding. Yes, I'm sitting in the middle of a shop, having pease pudding put on me face, and you'll never guess? It's going to make me look beautiful! And then just incase anyone misses it, I'm going to have me picture in the paper looking like a right prat.' She was not happy. Nige looked at her, speechless for once.

'Looking good,' said Michelle clicking furiously.

'One moment,' Lorraine said. 'What about this for a finishing touch?' and she stuffed a strawberry in Nadine's mouth.

'I'll have to go, I'm late,' Nige said reluctantly. 'Eeh this shop gets worse every day. I've always said it should be called the Nut Shop.'

'Perfect,' said Michelle. 'All done.' Lorraine helped Nadine clean off the pease pudding in our tiny washroom. I stayed on the shop floor serving customers as Julie and Michelle packed up.

'Bye,' Julie said. 'I'll send you a free copy as usual,' and she left with Michelle and her boxes of equipment.

Unfortunately Nadine had some sort of allergic reaction to the pease pudding and after washing found it had left her with an angry red rash.

'What ever you do don't laugh when you see her,' Lorraine warned me, which of course made me laugh in anticipation before I'd even seen her.

'Sorry Nadine. We wouldn't have used it if we'd known,' I said to her, but she could tell I was trying not to laugh. Her face was red and inflamed and I knew it wasn't funny in the least, but like a naughty child I couldn't seem to stop my face from smirking.

'It's not that bad,' I said to her.

'Yes it is,' she snapped. 'It was supposed to be a beauty treatment. I look like a monkey's arse.' Her remark finished Lorraine and I off and we laughed hysterically.

When our free copy of the evening Echo arrived, we opened it with more than a little trepidation.

'Hey, it looks really good,' Lorraine said and Nadine and I pushed her out of the way to see it. There was a photo of Lorraine and I applying the mask to Nadine's face, and next to it a huge close up of Nadine, her face covered in pease pudding and a strawberry in her mouth. She's going to freak any minute, I thought. Nadine hated to be seen looking silly and everyone in Newcastle read the Daily Echo. Everyone we knew would have seen it.

'I look like a right nelly,' Nadine said, laughing. I was relieved that she was taking it so well and was treating it as a joke.

'I'm glad you're not upset by it,' I said to her. 'I know you were hoping for a more glamorous shot.'

'I'm not bothered about looking stupid,' she said. 'No-one will recognise me with all that on my face.' She looked at me and smirked. 'And anyway, they've made a mistake and printed your name under the photo.'

CHAPTER THIRTY-THREE

The mysterious moths continued to throw themselves at our zapper. Every evening Peter emptied the tray of their dead bodies.

'Where on earth are they coming from?' we asked each other, baffled. It was a complete mystery to us. We started to notice the occasional one flying around the shop during the day. Loath to kill them, Lorraine would catch them in a paper bag and release them outside. Nige found this very entertaining.

'Eeh, I've never seen anything like it,' he giggled as Lorraine swooped on her prey with a gaping paper bag. 'You could set yourself up as a pest control expert. You'd need a bigger paper bag for rats though.'

'Well it's better than killing them,' Lorraine said as she ran outside to release her latest captive. 'We need to find out where they're coming from,' she said. 'They just seem to materialise and throw themselves at the zapper.'

We did find out. Later that day a customer who'd earlier bought a basket full of Christmas cake ingredients returned with a bag of dates.

'I bought these earlier,' she said, 'and there seems to be a fly inside the packet.' I took the sealed cellophane packet from her and saw an insect crawling over the dried fruit inside. It was a moth. I involuntarily dropped the packet and shuddered. I apologised to the customer profusely, which seemed to disarm her as she realised my disgust was genuine.

'Not to worry, these things happen, but I'd like another packet if you don't mind,' she said.

'Of course,' I said and I walked to the shelf to get one. Picking up a pack and turning it over to check it, I saw that it too contained a moth. I dropped it in horror and quickly picked up another two packs, one in each hand, turning them over and discovered that not only did they contain moths but also grubs. Oh my God, I thought. We're infested! In a panic I quickly pushed the whole stack of date packets to the back of the shelf where they fell down behind the displayed dried fruit.

'I'm sorry,' I said to the customer, who was choosing a pack of flapjacks from the counter display. 'We don't seem to have any. I'll give you a refund instead, if that's all right.' I also gave her the flapjacks free of charge and she left happily. As soon as she'd gone I bolted the door. Calling for Lorraine to come through from the office I hurried to retrieve the infested packets.

'These dates are crawling with moths and maggoty things,' I said throwing the packets on the counter.

'Oh my God!' Lorraine said when she saw them. 'This must be where they've been coming from. There must have been eggs on the dates and they've hatched in the packets.'

What followed was one of the worst afternoons we experienced during our time running the shop. I closed the blinds and the two of us systematically scanned the shelves checking packages for signs of the insects. Our horror grew with each discovery of infestation.

'They're in the apricots,' I said. 'But I don't understand how they got in there. The packets are sealed.'

'I don't understand it either,' Lorraine said. 'But they're in the figs too. And the raisins and sultanas.'

We threw the packets into a heap on the floor.

'What shall we do with them?' I asked. 'We can't leave them in the shop, I'm worried about them spreading to other foods.'

'I think it could be too late for that,' Lorraine said grimly. 'All these nuts and seeds are infested too.'

When Peter arrived we explained what was happening and he examined some of the packets.

'Look,' he said. 'The affected packets have tiny holes in the cellophane. They must be able to eat their way into the packets to feed and to lay eggs on the fruit.'

'Euwch!' I said. 'How disgusting.' I often opened packets of dried apricots to nibble on as an afternoon snack. 'Oh my God,' I said clutching my stomach. 'I've eaten moths' eggs. They're probably developing into maggots inside me alongside the baby. They'll come flying out when I give birth.' I felt faint at the thought.

'Get a grip,' Lorraine said. 'Even if you have eaten moths' eggs it won't do you any harm.'

I found some black bin bags to load the packets into and Lorraine helped me fill them with stock to be destroyed.

'Look at it all. What a waste,' I said as the bin bags were filled.

'I'll put them outside the door,' Lorraine said. 'We have to get them out of here before we lose everything.' I felt as though we already had. This could finish us off. All the weeks of hard work, developing our product lines, getting to know our customers and becoming part of the local community could all now have been in vain. We worked together, silent except when the discovery of another range of contaminated foods made us curse with frustration.

'What about the flour?' I asked. 'Do you think that will be safe?'

'I don't think we can risk it,' Peter said. 'Anything in a packet will have to go. Glass jars and tins are the only packaging that we can be sure have not been pierced by the insects.'

'But that's most of our stock,' I said, unable to hold back my tears. I threw the bag of flour I'd picked up back on to the shelf, and as its weight hit the shelf, two moths flew out from behind it. We watched them as lured by the blue light they flew to their deaths. This time, none of us flinched at the crackle.

'We've been so naive,' I said. 'It didn't occur to me that they would be living and breeding in the food. I thought they were coming in from outside. We should have done something sooner.'

'Hindsight's always a wonderful thing,' Peter said. He dropped a pile of contaminated packets into one of the bin bags.

169

Peter worked quietly without cracking a single joke, making me realise just how serious the problem was. If even Peter couldn't find humour in this, then I knew it was bad.

'I'll start taking this stuff to the tip,' he said. 'You need to get on the phone and call Rentokill and get them in as soon as possible.'

'Rentokill?' Lorraine said, horrified.

'You'll have to. If we want the business to survive, we need to make sure this contamination is dealt with thoroughly and quickly. If word gets out about this, the shop will be finished.'

'How much do you think this will cost us in lost stock?' I asked Lorraine. She looked at the empty shelves.

'A few grand at least,' she said. 'Four or five maybe.' My heart sank. This was the end of Nutmeg. We hadn't even survived a year.

The pest-control man arrived at eight o'clock. I was glad it was dark when he came, the fewer people who saw him arrive, the better. He swept into the shop as though he was auditioning for a part in Ghostbusters dressed in a white zip up all-in-one suit with hood and face mask and holding what looked suspiciously like a vacuum cleaner hose attached to two cylinders strapped to his back. We watched as he sprayed the shelves, floors and walls.

'What is it you're using?' we asked.

'It's a chemical insecticide,' he said through his facemask. 'Don't worry, it's good stuff. It starts working immediately. It'll get rid of the little bastards no bother.'

'But what about the food?' I asked. 'It'll contaminate our stock.'

'Perfectly safe,' he said cheerfully. 'Otherwise it wouldn't be allowed in food shops.' I looked at Lorraine. Neither of us were happy about it. Here we were selling natural and organic foods without artificial additives or chemicals and our shop was drenched in insecticide. It ran down the shelves and walls, dripping onto the floor and leaving streaks of powdery residue as it dried.

'I'll get some hot water and a cloth to clean that off,' I said.

'No, you can't do that,' the man said, laughing at my stupidity. 'It needs to be left like that, what's the point of washing it all off?'

'But you said it would work immediately,' I said.

'Well it will. But you need to leave it on to make sure it gets them all.'

'For how long? It looks manky.'

'Until you're sure the insects are gone. Personally I would leave at least a month to get any new hatchers.' A month! I thought. No way! I'll have it washed off before that. I watched as the solution was sprayed over our white painted walls, droplets splashing onto the floor.

'He's happy in his work isn't he?' Lorraine said to me as we watched him spray the counter. He whistled and sang as he worked, stopping occasionally to relate distasteful tales of infestations of bed bugs, cockroaches and rodents he had dealt with. I wish he'd just get on with it, I thought. I felt tired and tearful and just wanted him to finish so I could go home. I gave a sigh of relief when he'd worked his way around to where he'd started.

'I'll just refill and go around again to make sure,' he said unhooking the canisters from his back and I went into the office as I felt a tear escape.

'Come on we'll get through this,' Peter said hugging me.

'I know,' I said. 'I'm just a bit tired.' It must be my hormones, I thought. I seem to cry at anything these days.

When he left, we checked the shelves and found them littered with dead moths. Peter swept them into one of the rubbish bags.

'What about tomorrow?' I asked. 'How can we open with most of the stock gone?'

'We'll have to open,' Lorraine said. 'We can't afford not to. We need to make as much money as possible if we're going to get through this.'

'What if we've already sold some of the contaminated stuff?' I said.

'I think that's a certainty judging by the amount of stuff we've found,' Lorraine said. 'We'll just have to apologise and give refunds if we get customers returning stock.'

'They might not come back,' I said gloomily. 'I wouldn't return to a shop that had sold me food crawling with maggots and moths.' We looked around at the empty shelves.

'You need to get a story together about why the stock has gone,' Peter said.

'Why?' Lorraine and I said together.

'Because you don't want this getting out. You know how news like this spreads and gets exaggerated.'

'Well we can tell Nadine and Nige and Georgina can't we?' I said.

'No,' Peter said. 'Don't tell any one. If this leaks out it could be the end for you. Just say you had a huge order from a catering company or you're re-merchandising the shelves or something. Think of something that sounds feasible.' I felt a bit uncomfortable about lying about it but I knew he was right. I looked at Lorraine.

'We've come too far to throw it all away now,' I said. 'We have to get through this.'

'But surely we can tell Nadine,' Lorraine said.

'Yes,' I said. 'I can't lie to Nadine. And she's a part of the team. I think we should tell her.'

'Well just Nadine but no-one else,' said Peter. 'And make sure she knows how important it is to keep it quiet.'

'I can't leave the shelves like this,' I said. 'They look filthy, and so do the walls.' A film of grey powdery residue covered practically all the shop's surfaces. 'I'm going to wash it off.'

'Don't you think we should leave it like he said?' Peter said. 'It'll just take a couple of adult moths to survive to start off a whole new infestation.'

'Well we could at least clean it off the walls and fronts of the shelving,' I said. 'We could leave it at the backs of the shelves and anywhere where there are crevices or cracks where there could be moths or grubs.'

'I'll do it,' Lorraine said. 'You look dead on your feet. Get yourself home to bed. You have to look after that nephew of mine.' She patted my bump.

'Or niece,' I said. 'Are you sure? I don't like leaving you here on your own.'

'Course I'm sure,' Lorraine said. 'It's only ten past nine. It won't take me long. I'll be tucked up in bed by ten o'clock. Off you go.' I didn't argue. I felt exhausted, drained. I collected my things and Peter and I left.

CHAPTER THIRTY-FOUR

The next morning we explained the situation to Nadine.

'It's so unfair,' she said, close to tears. 'We've all worked so hard for it to come to this.'

Nige noticed the empty shelves as soon as he arrived.

'What's going on here?' he asked. 'Had a busy day?'

'Just having a change around,' I said. I hated lying to him but Peter was right. Nige thrived on gossip and even if he tried he would be unable to help himself from blurting it out to the next person he encountered. Luckily he was too excited about the fact that Gus had secured a part in a pantomime to take an interest in the contents of our shelves. Being cast as Baron Hardup in the local production of Cinderella had given Nige plenty of fodder for his camp jokes. We laughed half-heartedly at his predictable jokes and he left unaware that we were facing imminent closure.

We worked in an atmosphere of false optimism, trying to keep a positive attitude, but each time we turned away a customer our spirits sank to further depths. Occasionally a moth would flutter out from the back of a shelf and immediately Nadine would kill it.

'I know you don't like it,' she said. 'But they have to go.'

I was just glad they were small moths and not those big brown hairy ones that sometimes came in our bathroom window and terrorised me in my shower.

'You're worse than I was about the wasps,' Nadine said, as I dived across the shop to avoid one that had fluttered out from the back of the shelves.

'You're even too scared to kill them!'

'I don't want to kill them,' I said. 'You can't kill things just because you're scared of them.' Actually the thought of squashing a moth's pulpy body made me feel sick.

'Sorry,' she said as she whacked the moth with a rolled up price catalogue. 'But we have no choice. Either we wipe them out or they wipe us out.' Lorraine was still reluctant to kill them and continued with her paper bag method. There were fewer flying about now, although dead ones appeared frequently on the shelves.

'They must be down the back of the shelves between the pine-cladding.' Nadine said as she swept them up. 'They must be crawling out to die as the insecticide does it's stuff.'

'I think I'll go out for a walk, get some fresh air,' I said.

'Are you ok?' Lorraine asked.

'Yeah, I just need to get away from this for a while if you don't mind.'

I walked up the High Street looking in shop windows envious of the normality of it all. Customers browsing and buying, assistants serving and taking money. My heart sank as I thought over the morning's trading. Although the lunchtime sandwich trade had been as busy as ever, overall our takings were well down.

I thought back over the months we'd been trading. We had overcome so many problems and now it seemed inevitable that we were going to close. Is it all worth it? I wondered, not for the first time. In a few months I was going to have a new baby. Did I really want to keep struggling on? The thought of throwing my hand in and giving up sounded an attractive option. I could stay at home with the baby. Why put myself through all this? Perhaps I should talk to Lorraine and suggest we cut our losses and get out before things get any worse. I couldn't see things getting any better; I didn't know how to make things any better. I'd tried but I couldn't think of anything else to do. I'd checked with our insurance company to see if we could claim the cost of lost stock but it was a no go. I'd also contacted Karma to explain that they'd supplied us with contaminated goods but their Stock Control Manager was adamant that the source of the problem lay elsewhere.

'If we had contaminated stock we'd know about it,' he told me. 'There's no evidence of contamination in our warehouse, believe me, we'd know if there was an infestation, and we've had no reports of contamination from other customers.' He was very convincing. I began to doubt whether the moths had come from Karma after all. Perhaps they'd been dormant somewhere in the building and the intense heat of the summer had caused incubation. Maybe they'd simply come in from the field behind the shop and finding a food source had stayed.

I turned off the High Street intending to walk through the park and back to the shop. As I passed the library I had a sudden thought and hesitating, turned in and walked up the steps.

After being directed to the Natural History section, I hunted through the shelves. This is what I need, I thought as I lifted down a huge volume entitled 'Moths and Butterflies of the World' and carried it to a table. Bravely I scanned the pages looking at the illustrations, searching for one that resembled our moths. Unable to help myself, I grimaced and squirmed, grunting noises of disgust to myself as I turned the pages. I have always had an abhorrence of moths. Something about their furry bodies and antennae, and the way they sit with wings folded in a dark mottled lump makes me shudder.

An old man at the opposite end of the table stopped reading his newspaper to watch me as I pulled faces and cringed. Each page held in full colour the magnified image of yet another juicy-bodied moth, showing in detail each spindly hair on its body. I turned the pages of the book squirming and muttering to myself as I flicked through the pages. The pictures went on and on. How many moths were living on our planet for goodness sake? I began to think that the world was over-run by moths. Who knew where they were lurking?

The chapter on tropical moths almost sent me into nervous breakdown and to the amusement of the old man I slammed the book shut feeling the prickle of perspiration on my forehead. I knew he was watching me although he turned away hurriedly as I looked up, like someone avoiding eye contact with the loony on the bus. I took a few moments to compose myself, took a few deep breaths and resumed my search.

Many of the moths looked similar to ours and I listed a few as possible suspects. However, when I found the Indian meal moth I knew I'd found my man. The picture was identical to the creatures we'd emptied from the zapper tray.

White caterpillars, two centimetres long, adult moth, one centimetre long, I read. I scanned through the paragraphs looking for relevant information. *Indian meal moth larvae feed on any grain or grain product, including flour, seeds, nuts, dried beans, dried fruit and chocolate.* That's just about everything we stock! I thought. *The larvae may be found in unlikely places because of their tendency to leave food sources to wander in search of a place to spin their cocoons. Larvae can penetrate unopened packages therefore all potentially infested foodstuffs should be destroyed.* And then perhaps the most useful piece of information found within the last paragraph. *Although not native to Britain may be imported with contaminated foods.*

After scribbling down the facts on a scrap of paper, I hurried back to the shop to tell Lorraine what I had found. I was sure now that the moths had been brought in on contaminated foods and as most of our stock came from Karma they were the most likely source.

'I've found some information about the moths,' I said to Lorraine as I rushed in. Lorraine looked up from something she was reading.

'So have I, come and look at this,' she said. 'The new Karma catalogue has just arrived. Read this.' She pushed the catalogue across the counter toward me. It was open at the first page, the information page that held company news and details of new products. She pointed to a short piece at the bottom of the page.

'Unfortunately, due to a problem with insect contamination, hazelnuts are currently out of stock. We are hoping to find an alternative supply and will inform you as soon as we have available stock. We apologise for any inconvenience this causes.'

'I'm sure that's the source of our problem.' Lorraine said. 'Although it doesn't specify moths, that must be what they mean by 'insect contamination.' And thinking about it, the hazelnuts were heavily contaminated weren't they? It should make it easier to prove.'

'I think I may have the other part of the solution here,' I told her. 'I've identified the moths and using that evidence along with this,' I pointed to the paragraph in the catalogue, 'I don't think they have a leg to stand on.'

We were right. After presenting our evidence, Karma quickly backed down and agreed to pay us compensation for the lost stock. Luckily, Lorraine and I had listed all the stock we had destroyed and it was agreed that we would settle for a replacement of goods lost. The delivery arrived the following Friday and once again family and friends stepped in to help us repackage and sort the goods.

The kitchen was usually busy during lunchtime with Nadine, Lorraine and I running about at full steam, but with the addition of my Mam and Joan weighing and packing dried goods it was chaotic. Dishes of sandwich fillings and salad jostled for space on the benches along with newly packaged bags of dried fruit, nuts and seeds waiting for labels. We constantly got in each other's way, bumping into each other and pushing each other aside to make space to work. Our usual method of working together in such a tight space had been tightly honed over the weeks to resemble a well-rehearsed dance routine as we glided past each other passing dishes back and forth. With the addition of two extra bodies in the kitchen we stumbled into each other, tripping over sacks of flour and each other's feet and dropping things on the floor.

Irritating as it was I would not have dared to complain. Weighing, packing and labelling was a lengthy and monotonous job and we were grateful for the help.

The work continued non-stop over the weekend as we worked in shifts and Nutmeg opened on Monday morning, re-stocked.

'Here we go, another day at the Nut Shop,' Lorraine said as she filled the till and I went to switch on the kettle. We were tired but glad to be still trading.

We saw few moths now; occasionally one would flutter out from the depths of some crevice only to be dealt with quickly, either by a deathblow from Nadine or a paper bag by Lorraine.

'There's one!' Nadine suddenly said as we chopped salad. I looked to see a moth fluttering weakly behind Lorraine who was talking to a customer about the benefits of Echinacea.

'I'll get it,' Nadine said, tearing a piece of card from the top of a carton holding cans of tuna. 'It looks half dead all ready.'

'Not in front of a customer,' I hissed at her and I grabbed at her arm as she rolled the card into a weapon. We watched as the moth circled round and round daringly close to Lorraine's head. Lorraine suddenly spotted it, as did the customer and all eyes followed its meandering path as Lorraine continued her lecture.

'Echinacea supports the body's immune system by stimulating the production of white blood cells...' Lorraine told the woman, her eyes rolling as she followed the insect. She paused for breath and Nadine, the woman and I watched in fascinated horror as she breathed in, sucking in not only a lung full of air but also the moth. The three of us watched, our hands involuntarily moving to cover our mouths as Lorraine gulped, the disgust of realising what she'd just swallowed showing on her face as she said in a tight voice,

'...enabling the body to fight off infection. Excuse me.' Slamming the bottle of Echinacea onto the counter she hurried into the office and up the stairs to the washroom coughing and retching as she went. Nadine and I, not knowing what to say or do stepped forward to the counter.

'Six ninety-nine please,' I said to the woman and Nadine put the bottle into a paper bag. The woman, still with a look of disgust on her face, paid up without speaking and left. I heard the toilet flush and Lorraine staggered down the stairs still looking a little green.

'Right,' she said grabbing Nadine's rolled up card. 'This means war. No more piddling about with paper bags. The next one I see is mincemeat.'

We hadn't seen Georgina for a couple of days, so when she arrived just before closing I was pleased to see her.

'Hi stranger,' I said as she approached the counter and I noticed she looked as tired as we did. She must have been ill, I thought.

'Are you all right?' she asked. 'It's so sad isn't it? And so unfair.'

'You've heard?' I said surprised. I wondered who had told her about the moths. Honestly. You couldn't keep anything quiet around here. 'How did you find out?' I asked.

'I've known about it for a while' she said.

'But how? How could you know if even we didn't know?'

'She told me all about it from the start,' Georgina said.

'Who did? Lorraine?'

'No, Josie.'

'But how on earth did Josie know about it?' I said. Georgina hesitated.

'Well they told her, she asked them to tell her the truth.'

'The truth?' I said. 'Georgina what are you on about?' Georgina looked at me.

'What exactly are you talking about? she asked.

'Moths,' I said. 'Aren't you?'

'Moths? No I'm not talking about moths!'

'Sorry,' I said. 'I think we're talking about different things. What were you talking about?' Georgina walked around the counter and put her hand on my arm.

'Sorry,' she said. 'I thought you'd heard. Josie died this morning.'

CHAPTER THIRTY-FIVE

Josie? Dead? Feeling as though I'd been hit in the stomach, I walked to the door, turned the closed sign and locked the door.

'I'll make us some tea,' Georgina said as Lorraine and I tried to take in the news. I felt the shock in the pit of my stomach and although I was not aware that I was crying I could feel hot tears on my face. Lorraine did not cry. At first she was stunned by the shock and kept saying 'No, no,' as though she could not bring herself to believe it. Georgina returned with a tray of hot drinks that she placed on the counter.

'Josie had cancer,' Georgina said. 'Very few people knew; she wanted to beat it. She wanted to fight for her life and she felt she could do that best if she was treated normally by everyone. She needed to confide in someone so she told me – we'd been friends for a long time.'

'How long had you known her?' Lorraine asked.

'Since we were children.' Georgina said. 'We were very different, but we were great friends. I loved her like she was my sister.' Her voice faltered and she sobbed, wiping away tears with her hand. Lorraine was sobbing too now, but I now felt strangely calm, as though the truth was slowly seeping through me, numbing me with its pain.

'So that's why you went away on holiday together?' I said.

'Yes. She knew then that she was nearing the end. She wanted to go back to Windermere one more time. She'd had happy times there with her husband and children.'

'Her husband,' Lorraine said suddenly. 'How is he? And you say she has children? How are they all coping?

'She was a widow,' Georgina said. 'And her children are dead too.'

I looked at her. None of this seemed to making sense. 'Josie had a very unhappy life,' Georgina said. 'She was dealt more than her fair share of life's cruel blows.'

'But she was always so positive and so cheerful,' I said.

'We envied her,' Lorraine added. 'Her money, her lifestyle. I thought she was happy.'

'That's one of the reasons I loved her,' Georgina said. 'She was so strong, so thoughtful of others. Even when she was suffering inside she put on a brave face to the world.' She put down her cup and took out a tissue to blow her nose.

'Josie's family lived a few doors up the street from us. Her father was an alcoholic. He was quite an unnoticeable little man until he'd been drinking and then he became aggressive and violent. Josie was terrified of him. My mother often put her up on the sofa when she had fled from him in fear. She spent more time with my family than with her own. Yet she was very resilient. She always stayed positive.

'At university when the rest of us were skipping lectures and hanging about smoking pot, Josie was working hard. She was determined to make something of her life. She worked in London for a while in an art gallery – a very prestigious one – and did well for herself. It was while she was back in Newcastle visiting me that she met Alan. He was a local artist. He had work exhibited at the Laing and she met him at a viewing.' Georgina's voice was low and flat, her gaze focussed beyond Lorraine and I, as though she was seeing into the past as she reminisced. 'They fell for each other straight way. We could all see they were perfect for each other. They married and settled here in Newcastle and had two children. They were so happy.'

'I saw a photograph once in her purse,' I said, remembering. 'It was a shot of her with her husband and a little boy and girl.' Georgina nodded.

'Ben and Katie,' she said. 'And of course her husband, Alan. They only had six years together. Christmas Eve 1971, Alan took the children to a pantomime. Josie had bought the tickets for a treat but had been ill with flu so decided not to go. Alan and the children were killed in a car crash on the way home. Hit by a drunken driver. Ben was five and Katie three.' Lorraine and I were sobbing uncontrollably now.

'Josie blamed herself. Firstly because she'd bought the tickets and secondly because she believed she should have been killed with them. She was quite ill for a while, in and out of hospital with depression and such. But as she got stronger she vowed to use the rest of her life helping others. And she did. I'm not saying she was an angel or anything, she had her faults like the rest of us. But she was a good soul and she did a lot for others over the years.'

'But we didn't know,' Lorraine said. 'We thought she was just a rich woman spending her days enjoying herself.'

'Well she was and she did,' Georgina said smiling through her tears. 'But she had a lot of heartache too.'

I learned valuable lessons from the shock of Josie's death. I'd made so many assumptions about her life, putting together vague impressions and bits of information to build a picture of a perfect existence, ignorant of the suffering and loneliness she'd endured. I determined not to be so quick to take others at face value, forming quick opinions and arrogantly believing that I had them sussed out without really knowing and understanding them. It was so easy to judge people and to get caught up in pointless gossip, criticising and making assumptions about them and enjoying putting them down. I had done my fair share of it over the years and yet always felt so hurt when I'd discovered that others had done it to me. Now I realised that although I was unaware of what others were coping with, and saw only the outward symptoms, I was quick to judge them and to take offence at what I had decided were their motives for their behaviour.

I realised now that we all experience life differently, and our individual experiences and circumstances mould us and cause us to behave as we do. We are essentially all the same, struggling to make sense of the world, learning how to cope with life and searching for love and happiness.

We all have to deal with personal tragedy and loss. We all experience times when we are struggling to cope with what life has thrown at us, battling with our demons and suffering behind brave faces. And yet when we are free from pain and life is good, we often stubbornly refuse to cherish and take joy in the good things we have, preferring to grumble and complain about some petty injustice, or the weather, or last night's TV programmes.

Of course, human nature being as it is, I have slipped back into old ways many, many times. But whenever I think of Josie, I renew my determination to change.

CHAPTER THIRTY-SIX

Lorraine and I decided that one of us should attend Josie's funeral and the other open the shop for business as usual. After a lot of deliberation, I stayed at the shop and Lorraine attended the funeral with Nige and Georgina. When they returned I made coffee and we drank it as they related details of the service and talked about Josie.

'I'm thinking of organising a sponsored walk,' Georgina said. 'To raise money for the cancer department at the hospital where Josie was treated. Fancy joining in?'

'Yeah, let's all do it,' said Nige. 'What about it girls?'

'Yes, I'll do it,' Lorraine said. 'How far is it?'

'I haven't worked out the finer details yet but I was thinking of a route of around six miles along the coast,' said Georgina. 'I was going to arrange it for after Christmas, probably the end of January.'

'Put us down for it. I'll walk and Chris can waddle,' Lorraine said patting my bump.

'And put Peter's name on the list too,' I said. 'He can waddle with me.'

The next morning I arrived at the shop later than usual having been to the antenatal clinic.

'Everything ok?' Lorraine asked.

'Yes, fine,' I said taking off my coat. 'Just a routine check-up.' The phone rang as I put my bag in the office and I answered it.

'Hello, I want to talk to one of them sisters,' a woman's voice said loudly.

'This is Christine speaking,' I said. 'How can I help?'

'Are you one of them sisters what owns it?' I sighed and sat down on the office chair. I had a feeling that this was going to be a long conversation.

'Yes, I'm Christine, one of the sisters.'

'Are you the old one or the fat one?' As I've already mentioned, customers seem to have a right to insult those who work behind a counter, shop workers being lesser human beings. I suppose technically I was the old one – although Lorraine could hardly be described as fat – though with my bump I could qualify for both. I chose not to answer.

'Can I help?' I said sharply.

'Yes. You can tell me why Supersavers are selling vitamin C for ninety-nine pence.' Ninety-nine pence? Surely not. That was miles cheaper than ours.

'I've really no idea,' I said. 'You'd have to ask someone at Supersavers.'

'I came in yesterday and bought some vitamin C off one of the sisters, the fat one, and she charged me three-ninety nine. And now I've just been to Supersavers and they've got vitamin C for ninety-nine pence.' Now I remembered her. I'd sold her the vitamin C and she'd been difficult then. I was peeved that she was calling me 'the fat one' especially as I remembered her as being at least four stones heavier than I was.

'I can't comment without seeing the product,' I said snottily.

'I want me money back.'

'Certainly,' I said, trying to speak calmly. 'If it's unopened you can return it and I'll exchange or refund.'

'What about me bus fare? Will you pay that?'

'No I won't,' I said. 'Actually I don't even have to give you a refund if there's nothing wrong with the product, I'm doing it as a courtesy.'

'Well there is something wrong with the product.'

'And what is that?'

'It's too dear.'

'That is not a fault. However, as I've said, if you wish to return it I will give you a full refund.'

'Even if I've opened it?'

'No, not if you've opened it.'

'Why not? I only got it yesterday, I've only taken one.' Realisation that there was no way this woman was going to be reasonable made me decide to cut my losses and end the conversation.

'Right, ok. Just bring it back and I'll give you a refund. Goodbye.' I replaced the receiver with a clash and went to switch on the kettle.

'Who was that?' Lorraine asked.

'Just some stupid woman wanting a refund for some vitamin C I sold her yesterday,' I said, forgetting again that I was now non-judgmental and accepting of others. 'Silly old bat said she could get it in Supersavers for ninety-nine pence. She wanted to know which sister I was, the old one or the fat one.'

'What a cheek, so I'm the fat one?'

'No, apparently I'm the fat one, you must be the old one.'

'I wish I'd answered the phone,' Lorraine said. 'I've seen the Supersaver vitamin C. The reason it's only ninety-nine pence is because there are only thirty tablets in a box and they're only ten milligrams each.'

'Ten milligrams?' I said. 'Are they worth taking? Ours are ninety tablets at five hundred milligrams each. When she comes in for her refund I'll tell her she'd be better off eating an orange.'

'I'll do better than that, I'll throw her out if she starts with me.'

Georgina called later to show us her new tattoo.

'It's in memory of Josie,' she said. 'Want to see it?'

'Yes,' I said without asking where it was and beginning to regret saying yes as she started to take down her jeans.

'What do you think?' she asked.

'What is it?' Lorraine asked, turning her head and squinting at the swollen black blob on Georgina's behind.

'It's a dragon,' she said proudly. 'Good isn't it?' To me it just looked like a very painful bruise, oozing pinpricks of blood.

'It looks a bit, er, tender,' I said.

'Well I've just had it done half an hour ago,' Georgina said. 'It takes a while to settle down.'

'It's great,' Lorraine said. 'Isn't it?'

'Yeah,' I said. 'Great.' Personally I'm not sure that I would take it as a compliment if someone had a dragon tattooed on their arse as a tribute to me, but there you go, each to their own.

'I can see you're both busy so I won't stop to pay,' Mrs Forbes-Williamson said as she suddenly swooped in, grabbing handfuls of packages from the freezer and stuffing them in her carpet bag. Lorraine swiftly grabbed a carrier bag that she used to cover Georgina's naked buttock, although she seemed perfectly at ease standing in the middle of the shop with her dragon on view.

'…just a few bits for the Operatic Ladies lunch. In a hurry as always, har har. Put it on my bill dears, cheerio, wheesh.'

Later, as we cashed up I felt really low. Josie was on my mind a lot and I was fed up with complaints and pettiness from customers and especially with Mrs Forbes-Williamson who now owed us a small fortune. Lorraine sighed as she counted coins into moneybags.

'Fancy a bit of retail therapy?' she said. 'I need cheering up. Let's go to Barratt's Garden Centre and buy a Christmas tree and some decorations for the shop.

'What tonight?' I said.

'Yes, why not? It's November next week, we need to get the place decorated soon. Most shops are already full of decorations.' I looked through the window across the road to the shop fronts filled with tinsel and fairy lights.

'Ok then,' I said, 'Let's lock up and go. It'll cheer us up.' Lorraine finished cashing up as I rang Peter to tell him not to come and pick me up, as we were going shopping.

'I might be late,' I said. 'We're thinking of having something to eat while we're out.'

'Ok, enjoy,' he said. 'Don't spend too much.'

As usual the garden centre had an impressive Christmas display. A huge section of the store had been given over to decorations and the whole area was filled with fairy lights and twinkling decorations. Many of the ornaments were musical and their tinkling tunes competed with Bing Crosby as he crooned from hidden loudspeakers.

'Oh wow, I love it!' I said as we wandered amongst the displays oohing and ahhing at the various decorations.

'Oh look, he's so cute,' Lorraine said pointing to a dancing, singing snowman but I preferred the huge lit snow-globe complete with Father Christmas gliding through the sky over snow-covered roofs through a snowstorm. We walked through displays of tinsel and baubles, Christmas stockings, candles, wreaths of holly and sprigs of mistletoe, garlands of gold and silver, velvet ribbons, glittered pinecones and Christmas themed cuddly toys.

There were baubles and tree decorations in every colour and style imaginable; Victorian toys, animals, birds of paradise, wooden soldiers, spheres, spirals, candy canes, glass angels and stars, all beautifully displayed in a sparkling rainbow of colour.

'Oh look at these,' Lorraine said suddenly, stopping at a display of baubles with hand-painted messages. She picked one up and handed it to me.

'Look,' she said. 'Baby's First Christmas. Let me buy you one of these.'

'But it's not his first Christmas until next year,' I said. 'Or hers.'

'I know, but I just want to buy it for my nephew.'

'Or niece,' I added. Lorraine held up two baubles.

'Silver or gold?'

'Oh gold, definitely,' I said. 'Thank you. I'll tell him his Auntie Lorraine bought it before he was born.'

'Or she,' said Lorraine.

At the end of every display area was a Christmas tree, each decorated in a different style and colour scheme, each more impressive than the last.

'Let's have this one, it's beautiful,' we said about each, until we saw the next. We finally decided on a traditional red, gold and green theme and chose a tree to place in our window with huge shiny baubles in cherry red and dark green and lengths of gold tinsel to drape around it.

'Lights, we have to have lights,' Lorraine said, so we added four boxes of coloured fairy lights to our trolley.

'What about one of these to drape around the counter?' I suggested. We chose two lengths of garland made from imitation boughs of holly and ivy, decorated with glittered pinecones, holly berries and red velvet bows.

'And what about a matching wreath for the door?' Lorraine said putting one in the trolley without waiting for an answer.

'Is that it? Are we done?' I asked.

'Better have more lights just to be on the safe side,' Lorraine said, so we grabbed another four boxes.

We passed the restaurant on the way to the checkouts and the delicious smell of hot food drifting out made us realise how hungry we were.

'Fancy something to eat?' I said, looking at the menu. 'They have quite a few veggie choices. Mmm! Vegetable lasagne with chips and salad. Or three bean chilli with rice and garlic bread. Lorraine squeezed past the trolley to have a look.

'Mushroom quiche with baked potato and salad,' she said. 'That sounds good.' We decided to pay for our stuff and stash it in the car before heading back to the restaurant. I ordered the lasagne and Lorraine chose the quiche and we tucked in.

'I was thinking about Christmas in the shop,' I said. 'I notice a lot of shops in town have late shopping nights, I thought perhaps we could have one too.'

'What do you mean?' Lorraine asked. 'Do you mean like staying open late one night a week?'

'No,' I said. 'I was thinking of a one-off Christmas shopping evening where we could have music and perhaps mulled wine and nibbles and people could shop, but it would also be a bit of a social event too.'

'Do you think it would work?'

'Well we've nothing to lose by trying it,' I said. 'And a lot to gain. Apart from extra sales it would be good for customer relations.'

'Yeah, why not?' Lorraine said. 'We could make up some of our made-to-order Christmas goodies and offer samples. We may get more orders.'

'We could stock up on Christmas goodies, mincepies, cranberry sauce, and stuff,' I said. 'And also non-food stuff that people might buy for gifts such as candles and books and make some Christmas displays.'

'What about hampers? We could get some baskets and make up our own hampers,' Lorraine said.

'Or we could let customers fill their own baskets and we could wrap them,' I said.

'Let's start organising it tomorrow,' Lorraine said excitedly.

'Got a pen?' I asked as I rummaged through my bag for a scrap of paper. 'I need to make a list.'

It was nearly ten when Lorraine dropped me at home.

'I may as well leave the stuff in the boot and bring it in tomorrow morning,' Lorraine said.

'Strange,' I said. 'The car's not here. Peter must have gone out. He didn't mention he was going anywhere.'

'Do you want me to come in with you?' Lorraine asked.

'No, course not,' I said. 'The match is on he's probably gone to the pub to watch it or something.'

'Ok then,' Lorraine said. 'I'll see you tomorrow. I can't wait to get started organising our Christmas Shopping Extravaganza!'

'Me too,' I said. 'See you tomorrow.' I closed the door behind me and after throwing my coat over the banister, went into the kitchen to put the kettle on. As I put a teabag into a mug my eye caught a note on the table.

Gone to the shop. Ring me. Peter x.

Why would he have gone to the shop at this time of night? I knew he was keen to get the last of the jobs done that Edward Reeves had stipulated on his report, but I couldn't imagine him wanting to do them late at night especially when the Newcastle match was on television. I picked up the phone and rang the shop number.

CHAPTER THIRTY-SEVEN

'Hello.' Peter answered the phone.

'It's me,' I said. 'What's happening?'

'I had a call from the police,' Peter said. 'There's been an incident.'

'What kind of incident?' I asked, beginning to panic. 'Are you all right?'

'Yes, I'm fine, don't worry. They called to tell us that some one has smashed one of the shop windows so I came straight here. I'm waiting for the repairmen to finish boarding it up.'

'Oh my God! Is there much damage?' I said, my heart sinking.

'Well there's glass everywhere but nothing's been taken. The police think it was just a drunk on his way home from the pub. For some reason he decided to throw a deck chair through the side window.'

'A deck chair?'

'Yes, you know, those old fashioned ones with the wooden frames and the canvas seats that were really difficult to put up. My Mam had some when we were kids and none of us could ever put them up without...'

'Yes, yes, I know what a deck chair is, but why? Why take a deck chair to the pub and throw it through our window on the way home?'

'We think he took it from a skip in the back lane,' Peter said. 'But the good news is, there were witnesses and the police know who he is.'

'Who is he, do we know him?'

'Just some local drunk from those semi-derelict flats at the back of Church Road.'

'Have they arrested him?' I said. 'Is he going to pay for the damage?'

'I don't know,' Peter said. 'Look I'll have to go, Mr Stoker's just arrived.'

'Who?' I said, forgetting for a moment.

'Mr Stoker, the landlord. I'd better go. After I've spoken to him I'm just going to make sure the building's secure and then I'll come home. We can sort out the mess in the morning.'

As soon as he'd hung up I rang Lorraine. She must still have been on her way home, as I had to try a couple of times before I got her. I told her the news.

'For God's sake, what else is going to happen?' she said. 'It's just one bloody thing after another. I'm beginning to feel like the whole thing's not worth it.'

'I know,' I said. 'I've felt like that a few times over the past couple of weeks. But we can't give up yet.'

'I know,' she said. 'I'm just so tired. I can't believe our bad luck at the moment. Do you think I should drive over there?'

'No, Peter said he'd be leaving as soon as the window was secure. We'll sort it out in the morning.'

The damage wasn't as bad as I'd anticipated. Peter had swept up most of the glass from the floor, Lorraine swept up a few bits he'd missed and went outside to sweep up the pieces that were scattered across the pavement.

'I've found glass in the big fridge,' I told Lorraine when she returned. 'We'll have to throw out all this food.' The large counter fridge, which was glass fronted but open at the back held loads of stock; quiches, pastries, cheese, coleslaw, salads and huge dishes of olives. We couldn't take the risk of missing a shard of glass in some of the food so we threw it all away.

'What the hell's happened now' Nadine said when she saw the side window boarded up with huge sheets of chipboard.

'A drunk smashed it last night,' I told her. 'Threw a deck chair through it. We're having to bin all this food from the fridge in case it has glass in it.'

'The shop looks awful from outside,' she said.

'It looks awful from inside,' Lorraine said. I looked at it and thought for a moment.

'You know, I think it would be a good idea to have it bricked up. We could shelve it, it would give us loads more room for displaying stock.' Lorraine looked at it thoughtfully.

'I think you're right, she said. 'And it would probably help with the heat problem too.'

'Only thing is, our insurance covers contents only. Buildings are Mr Stoker's responsibility. He'll probably just replace the glass.'

'Let's hope he has adequate insurance,' Lorraine said.

Nadine returned from Derek's with the day's salad and we started our usual routine of making the fillings. As we worked a policeman arrived to update us with news of our deck chair thrower.

'Good news,' he said. 'We've got your man. He's admitted throwing the chair through the window, says he didn't know what he was doing, he was drunk.'

'That's good, I'm glad you caught him,' I said. 'So what happens next?'

'It's up to you,' he said. 'You can prosecute, take it to court, but as it's his first offence I would recommend that you agree to settle things between you.'

'How do we do that?' I asked.

'Tell him you'll drop all charges if he pays for the damage.'

'So we get him to pay to replace the food we've had to throw out?' Lorraine asked.

'And the window repair,' he said.

'The window is the responsibility of the landlord, he would need to pay him for that,' I said.

'Well that's up to you to sort out. But don't forget, you need to add on something for being disturbed at night, petrol costs for having to drive here, something for the inconvenience, something for the stress you suffered... If you're in agreement I can arrange for him to come in and sort it out.' I looked at Lorraine and she nodded.

'Yeah, ok,' I said. 'He's not a big bloke though is he?' The policeman smiled.

'No, he isn't. You don't have to worry about him causing trouble. He's very shame-faced, it's the first time he's done anything like this and I think he's had a shock. Hopefully it'll be his first and last offence.'

Later we sat with Nige and Georgina talking about what had happened. Unable to sit still and talk without working, Nadine polished the counter as we chatted.

'So you had an intruder?' Nige said. 'Did he come intruder window?' We all groaned.

'He didn't actually come inside,' Lorraine said. 'He just smashed the window with the deck chair.'

'I bet you'd like to deck him,' he giggled. 'Do you get it? Deck him? Deck chair?'

'Shut up and drink your coffee,' I said. Georgina pulled out a bag of knitting.

'I'm knitting squares for blankets for orphans,' she said holding up a misshapen knitted piece.

'That's a square, is it?' Nige asked, giggling. 'Didn't they teach you at school that a square has four sides of equal length?'

'It's supposed to be a square,' Georgina said, pulling at the corners. 'It's for one of the charities that Josie supported, I thought it would be nice to help them. I've finished ten so far.' She pulled out more lumpy pieces of knitting and spread them on the counter to show us.

'It's very kind of you to help them,' Lorraine said as we looked at the collection of badly knitted squares.

'They're going to Rumania,' Georgina said.

'They certainly will, the state of those!' laughed Nige. 'They're going to remain here! Hee hee, do you get it?'

'What's the matter with you today?' Lorraine asked him. 'Have you been watching kid's TV or something?'

'I'm just trying to cheer you all up,' he said. 'I thought it would be nice to have a laugh.'

'That's really thoughtful of you Nige,' Georgina said. 'But it would help if your jokes were funny.'

'I'm sorry, I'm just excited,' he said. 'I'm going to a Guy Fawkes party next week with Gus. All his actor friends are going from the pantomime, I'm going to meet them all.'

'That's nice, Nige,' I said. 'I hope you enjoy it.' I was glad that Gus was involving him in his life, he usually kept his life with Nige and his acting separate.

'Mind I hate fireworks,' Nadine said. 'I think they should be banned.'

'So do I,' Lorraine said. 'Every year it's the same story, animals and children maimed or even killed.'

'They are pretty though,' Georgina said. 'I think they're really effective if they're used properly.'

'But they're not though, are they?' Lorraine said. 'Kids have been setting them off for days now around our way. There's over a week to go yet.'

The discussion was interrupted by the arrival of Mr Stoker. Nige and Georgina got up to leave and Nadine went to tidy the kitchen as Lorraine and I spoke to him.

'I hear the culprit has been caught,' Mr Stoker said.

'Yes,' I said, 'the police were here earlier.'

'Let's hope they lock him in a dungeon and throw away the key,' he said which I thought was a bit extreme but I smiled politely.

'I've had an estimate for replacing the glass in the window and it's going to be astronomical,' he said. 'The glass that was broken was the original window, put in when the place was built and regulations about glass are different now. For a window of that size, strengthened glass has to be used and it's very expensive.'

'But your insurance company will pay for that won't it?' Lorraine asked.

'Well, ahem, there are a few complications,' he said, revealing the fact that he didn't have adequate cover. 'What it boils down to is that it will be cheaper to have the wall bricked up.'

'Oh right,' I said, pleased.

'I know you'd rather have the window replaced but it will help me out if you'd agree to go for the wall.' I looked towards the boarded window. Great, I thought. That's what we wanted. I opened my mouth to say so but Lorraine beat me to it saying, 'But it looks awful like that.'

'Oh it won't look like that when it's done properly,' Mr Stoker said. 'I'll have it properly plastered and painted.' Lorraine and I hesitated.

'And of course I'll pay for shelving to be put up, it will give you lots more display space.'

'I suppose it means we could use the outside wall for a huge sign advertising the shop,' Lorraine said.

'Good idea,' said Mr Stoker. 'It would catch the eye as people drove down the bank. Probably bring you new customers.'

'Expensive though,' Lorraine said.

'Well I suppose I could pay for that as well,' Mr Stoker said reluctantly. 'As long as you don't go over the top. Keep it reasonable.'

'Ok, you've persuaded us,' Lorraine said, and Mr Stoker went away to start making arrangements, happy that he'd saved money.

Later in the afternoon I went to serve a customer who waited at the counter.

'Hi,' I said to man who looked vaguely familiar. 'Can I help?' The man shuffled from one foot to the other, his face red. I remembered who he was. The complaining customer Lorraine had named Pugnacious Face. I waited, ready to ward off one of his complaints but he seemed unable to speak, or to look me in the eye.

'Yes?' I prompted.

'I'm very sorry,' the words rushed out. 'I've come to pay for the damage I did. To your window. With the deck chair.'

'It was you?' I asked surprised. He nodded, his face reddening further. He was very shame-faced and I thought it would be best to take the cheque graciously and put him out of his misery. I gave him the figure we'd calculated that included a small sum for the inconvenience we'd been caused, as we'd been advised. Lorraine however, was not going to let him off so lightly.

'Well, well,' she said. 'I'm very surprised at you. Coming in here every day, assuming the role of a respected member of the community, tut, tut, tut.'

'Yes, yes,' he mumbled. 'I'm very sorry…don't know what got into me.'

'Alcohol perhaps?' she said. He looked down at his feet squirming.

'I can assure you it was completely out of character,' he said. 'It will never happen again.'

'I hope it won't,' Lorraine said. 'Disgraceful behaviour. You do realise we've saved you from a very embarrassing predicament?'

'Yes, yes…thank you.'

'And I hope we can rely on your custom each lunchtime in future to make up for the distress you've caused?'

'Of course,' he said meekly. 'If I'm not barred.' Lorraine looked at him as though she was considering this.

'No,' she said. 'We'll still serve you. But on the understanding that there'll be no more complaining about how long you have to wait in the queue.'

'Of course…thank you,' he said. He tore the cheque from his chequebook and handed it to me before making his escape.

'You enjoyed that, you cruel bugger,' I said to Lorraine as he scuttled out of the door.

'I certainly did,' she said.

CHAPTER THIRTY-EIGHT

We were all looking forward to our first Christmas at Nutmeg. Lorraine, Peter and I stayed late to decorate the shop. I worked on the window display while Lorraine decorated the counter area and Peter sorted out the hundreds of strings of fairy lights we'd bought. It felt too early to be doing this being only just November, but as the tinsel and baubles gradually transformed the shop, Christmas spirit slowly took over us. Lorraine put on a CD of Christmas songs and although initially we groaned to hear the same old cheesy tunes, we were soon singing along.

We'd bought far too many fairy lights. Peter hung string after string across the walls and along the windows. He draped them over shelves and above the counter; they were everywhere. When we'd finished, Peter turned off the overhead lights and for a few seconds we waited in total darkness for him to switch them on. The shop suddenly came to life, shining with hundreds of twinkling lights, their reflections dancing amongst the garlands of golden tinsel. The counter was swathed in greenery, and adorned with red berries and velvet ribbons. The tree stood proudly in the window, red and gold shining from its branches. I felt as though I was glowing myself as that magical childhood Christmas feeling of awe and excitement flowed through me.

We decided to hold our Christmas evening on the first of December, which gave us a month to prepare. I designed leaflets giving details of the evening which my Mam and Dad offered to deliver. Orders for our home-made cakes, puddings and nutroasts were still coming in thick and fast and we pencilled a couple of evenings in the diary intending to come in and prepare them all in bulk.
Boxes of Christmas stock, specially ordered for the evening, were stacked at the rear of the office and each day more were delivered and added to the pile.
Scented candles, fancy glass bottles containing essential-oil foam bath and body lotions, hand-pressed soaps and cruelty-free cosmetics. Boxes of organic chocolates, beautifully packaged bags of dried fruits and nuts, organic Christmas cakes and puddings, stollen, marzipan sweetmeats, jars of luxury mincemeat, preserves, cranberry sauce, and candied fruits in handmade boxes. Packs of organic hand fried crisps, Bombay mix, Japanese rice crackers, and bottles of Christmas cordial, cloudy lemonade and gingerbeer.

Lorraine spent a morning contacting local artists and craft stall owners with an offer to sell their crafts on a sale or return basis. Without exception they jumped at the chance to make extra sales and arrived swiftly with boxes and crates of goodies. Lorraine and I excitedly unpacked the boxes as they arrived and examined contents, finding ceramic nativity scene figures, hand-printed cards and gift tags, home-made crackers, hand-dipped candles, carved wooden bowls and figures, hand-thrown pots and plates, wooden toys, hand-stitched Christmas stockings and tree decorations.

We bought a job lot of baskets in various sizes for customers to make up their own Christmas hampers but decided to use some of them to assemble gift packs and hampers using some of the artists' items and also stock from our shelves.

'I wouldn't mind this one myself,' Lorraine said as she wrapped cellophane around a basket containing a hand made coffee pot and cups, organic coffee beans and chocolate mints.

'That looks great,' I said. 'I would make up a few of those, I think they'll be popular.' I arranged an oil burner with bottles of essential oils and tea lights in a basket and wrapped it, decorating it with swirls of gold ribbon.

'What about doing some gold, frankincense and myrrh packs?' Lorraine suggested.

'I've got frankincense and myrrh oils here,' I said picking two bottles from my selection of essential oils, 'but what can I use to represent gold?'

'You could use some of the handmade soaps, the ones wrapped in gold paper?' Lorraine suggested. I went off to get them and was busy trying different ways of packaging them when the phone rang. Lorraine answered it and I heard her arranging an appointment and giving directions.

'Who was that?' I asked.

'A salesman. He's coming to see us at three today.'

'With what?'

'Aloe vera juice.'

'But we already stock it. We get it from Karma.'

'Yes I know, but he sounded gorgeous. I'll have to take it off the shelves before he arrives and I'll just order one case.' I looked at her and shrugged.

'What's the point in that?' I asked.

'Well we sell loads of it, it won't come in wrong,' she said.

'But it's wasting his time and ours, when we can get it from Karma with our weekly delivery. Why bother?'

'Because he had one of those lovely soft Scottish accents.' She smiled dreamily.

'You've got a thing about Scottish men haven't you?'

'Yeah, it's the accent. It's so sexy. He sounded like Marti Pellow.'

'I don't think Marti Pellow will be around here selling aloe vera.'

'But he might look like him. Anyway he sounds gorgeous,' she said. She nudged me and said 'I hope he's wearing a kilt.' I wasn't amused. We were too busy to waste time with sales reps however nice they sounded on the phone.

'Well you can see to him,' I said. 'We've got enough to do without wasting time talking to salesmen especially when we don't need their products.'

'Oh don't worry,' Lorraine said. 'I'll deal with the sexy Scotsman. Just leave him to me.'

The day past fairly uneventfully except for an old lady asking for some of our 'orgasmic bread'.

'It's nice bread but it's not that good darlin',' Nige told her as I wrapped an organic loaf for her. Later in the afternoon I went up to the post office with the mail and to pay some bills.

When I returned I was aware that Lorraine was speaking to someone who was standing out of sight, behind the shelving. Lorraine turned to look at me and as she did her face flushed and she gave me a warning look. I walked towards the counter puzzled by her expression and as I moved past the shelves the mystery person came into view. He was about five foot four tall and the same in width and was wearing a pair of stained corduroy trousers with a grubby tee shirt. The little hair he had was greasy and had been carefully combed across his head to cover as much of his scalp as possible. For some reason – nerves? – he was perspiring heavily and as I looked a drop of sweat fell from his nose to the floor.

'This is Christine, my business partner and sister,' Lorraine said without looking at me and in a flash I realised that this was the sexy Scotsman. An involuntary snigger escaped as I managed to mumble 'hello' before squeezing past Lorraine and hurrying into the office where I collapsed into a heap of silent mirth. I hung on to the back of the office chair and tried to control myself but I was at that stage of hilarity where it is impossible to stop. Tears ran down my face as I desperately tried to calm down. I did not want the poor man to hear me laughing at him, although the joke was really at Lorraine and not him. I took a few deep breaths and composed myself. After wiping my eyes with a tissue, I took another deep breath and sauntered back into the shop trying to keep a fixed expression on my face.

Sexpot had his back to me. The back of his head and his neck were shining with perspiration. He was busy unpacking bottles of aloe vera from a box. I risked a quick look at Lorraine and she mouthed something at me. I couldn't make out what it was. It looked like she was saying 'flies'.

'Here we are,' the man said placing bottles on the counter. 'Have a wee look and see what ye think.' I looked at the bottles on the counter and my eyes moved beyond them to his worn trousers. His flies were undone.

'Excuse me,' I spluttered and hurried back to the office where I collapsed on the office chair and laughed until I was nearly sick. I didn't – I couldn't – return to the shop floor until he'd gone, and I spent the rest of the day taking the mick out of Lorraine. I sniggered and giggled all afternoon; every time I thought of it, it set me off again. At first Lorraine laughed with me, albeit a little sheepishly but she eventually became irritated with my inability to let it drop and told me in no uncertain terms to be quiet.

I got years of mileage from that sales rep. I still tease Lorraine today about her sexy Scottish salesman.

CHAPTER THIRTY-NINE

I woke with the delicious realisation that it was Sunday and snuggled into my duvet intending to drift back to sleep. A repeated tapping noise began to penetrate my mind, drilling into my consciousness and I pulled the duvet further around my ears. The irregular tapping continued until a particularly loud crack made Peter and I start up.

'What the hell's that?' he asked as another crack came from the direction of the window. He leapt out of bed and pulled back the curtain.

'It's Lorraine,' he said, grabbing his jeans and pulling them on. 'Throwing stones at the window. What time is it for God's sake?'

'Six-thirty,' I said, pulling on my slippers and padding downstairs to let her in.

'About bloody time,' she said as I unlocked the collection of bolts on the front door and opened it. 'Didn't you hear the doorbell?'

'Well good morning to you too,' I said. 'What's going on?' She looked tired and there were black smudges on her face and clothes.

'I've been ringing you all night,' she said. 'I couldn't get an answer.' At the time we only had one telephone, which was in the sitting room. We kept meaning to get an extension to the bedroom but hadn't yet done so.

'I've been at the shop all night,' Lorraine said as we walked through to the kitchen.

'Why, what's going on?' I said. Peter came into the kitchen pulling a sweatshirt over his head.

'What's happened?' he asked.

'There's been a fire at the shop,' Lorraine said.

'Oh no!' I said. 'How bad?'

'Well it's still standing,' she said, 'but there's a lot of damage.' Peter filled the kettle and switched it on as Lorraine spoke.

'I had a call from the police last night at about quarter past two to say that the Fire Brigade were dealing with a blaze at the shop. They'd tried to ring you but couldn't get an answer and I'm on the list as the next keyholder. They tried Mr Stoker too but apparently he was away for the night. I was in such a panic I drove straight over there but the firemen wouldn't let me in until they had assessed the damage. I had to wait ages outside and it was freezing.' A fire? At the shop? I couldn't believe this latest bit of bad luck. I suddenly thought of our festoons of fairy lights and my heart sank.

'How did it start' I asked.

'They don't know yet, the Fire Brigade is still investigating the cause, but...' Lorraine's eyes filled with tears and she sobbed as she said 'I think it was me, I think I left the fairy lights on.' She had voiced the fear that was causing my stomach to churn.

'If it was the fairy lights then it was both of us,' I said. 'We left together.'

'But I was last out. I locked the door.'

194

'But I should have noticed them too, it's not your fault.'

'It may not have been the lights,' Peter said. 'And even if it was, it was an accident.' He handed us a cup of tea each but I couldn't drink mine. My stomach was churning. I couldn't believe we'd ruined our livelihood because of a stupid mistake.

'I think we should wait until the cause is confirmed,' Peter said. 'It could have been started by something entirely different, the lights may have nothing to do with it.' We sat in silence for a few seconds. I think we were all thinking the same. We knew in our hearts it had been caused by the fairy lights.

'How bad is the damage?' Peter asked.

'The kitchen's pretty much taken out,' Lorraine said. 'The back wall is burned through to the gym. You can see the gym stairs, or I should say the remains of the stairs. Most of them are gone.' She took a drink of tea and Peter and I waited in silence, there was not really anything we could say.

'Apart from the kitchen the rest of the shop isn't too badly burned. But it's the smoke damage that's the problem. Everything is covered in black greasy soot. And there's water damage from the hoses.'

'Can it be fixed?' I asked. 'Or is this the end?'

'I think it's the end,' she said. Peter and I looked at her in stunned silence. 'Oh I don't know, Chris, I'm just so tired and fed up I can't think straight at the moment. As I say I've been there since about half two, I came straight over here because you weren't answering the phone and I was ringing your doorbell for ages. Honestly you must have been out cold, the two of you, I was banging on the door and ringing the bell for ages before I starting throwing stones at your window.' Our bedroom was right at the back of the house.

'We can't hear the door bell or the phone from our room,' I said. 'We need to get a phone put in the bedroom.' I looked at Peter who had been promising to sort it for months but hadn't got round to it.

'Yes, I know,' he said. 'It's on the list.' He put down his mug.

'We'd better get over there and see the damage ourselves,' he said, going off to get ready.

'The water is on but the electricity has been switched off until the fire-safety officers have checked the exterior cables', Lorraine said. 'You'll have to heat water on the gas hob like I did last night.'

'As long as we have hot water for cleaning and for making tea we'll be ok,' I said, trying to sound cheerful.

'Cleaning up won't be easy,' Lorraine said. 'Be warned, you'll be shocked when you see the state of it.'

'You need to go and get some sleep,' I said to Lorraine. She looked awful; tired and dirty and so crestfallen. 'We'll do what we can, you can join us later when you've had some rest,' I said.

'I'll have a shower and try to sleep a bit then I'll be over to help,' she said.' Be careful. Don't over do it. Think of the baby. He's more important.'

'She,' I said.

I could smell the sour odour of the fire as soon as I got out of the car, and when Peter opened the shop door I could taste it too. As I walked in, the acrid atmosphere stung my eyes and nose and made me cough. All I could see was black. The smoke had penetrated everything, covering every surface, every shelf, every package, bottle and jar, with a cloudy residue, leaving nothing in its path of destruction. The kitchen wall was partially gone; the edges of the remaining section were charred and black, revealing the destroyed stairs beyond. The kitchen floor was flooded; unrecognisable melted shapes lay amongst the murky water with the charred remains of the benches. The insides of the windows were smeared with an oily residue and the boarded window, still waiting to be bricked up and now covered in a film of dirt, added to the look of devastation. I looked around in shock and burst into tears.

'Come here,' Peter said, putting his arms around me. 'We'll sort it out. We've survived worse than this.'

'No we haven't,' I sobbed. 'Not as bad as this. There are too many things against us. I think something's trying to tell me to give up.'

'And are you going to?' he asked. I sobbed uncontrollably into his chest. I'd had enough. I just couldn't face this.

'Yes,' I said, raising my head and wiping my face with my hand. He looked down into my eyes and raised an eyebrow, waiting.

I looked around at our creation, our pride and joy, black and rank, totally destroyed and I cried some more. We had worked hard to create this place, overcome so many obstacles, and we'd been so proud of it. We'd only been here a matter of months but in that short time Lorraine, Nadine, Peter and I had grown to love it, working and laughing our way through the days, making new friends and watching the business grow. I looked at the remains of the kitchen benches where Nadine, Lorraine and I spent lunchtimes flying around making sandwiches. I thought about our plans for the Christmas shopping evening and saw the boxes of stock, black and soot covered. I noticed the remains of our Christmas garlands, melted and drooping and our beautiful Christmas tree, ash covered and filthy, lurking in the corner of the window like a huge black spider. I looked at the charred counter, where Georgina and Nige had shared so many coffee breaks with us, laughing and chatting and putting the world to rights and I knew I didn't want it all to end. I thought about Josie, fighting her cancer alone and I felt ashamed of my tears.

'No,' I said. 'I'm not giving up. They can throw anything they like at us. They can sod off, we're not going.' Peter smiled and hugged me and I could almost feel the relief flooding through his body.

'That's more like the cantankerous old boot I know and love,' he said. 'Right, where do we start?'

CHAPTER FORTY

I was overwhelmed by the task ahead. I didn't have a clue where to start so I put some water on to boil. We couldn't start cleaning until we'd cleared out the debris but it made me feel as though I'd made a start. Peter nipped down the bank to Patel's Convenience Stores to buy rubbish bags.

'Gupta didn't charge me for them,' he said when he returned. 'And he said he'll be down to help as soon as Karisha arrives to take over. Dave from the printers was in there and he said he and Jean will be down after lunch to help out.'

'That's really kind of them,' I said feeling tears welling up again. There was a strong sense of camaraderie amongst the traders on the bank. We'd been welcomed into the local community since our first day. Our neighbours had befriended and supported us and now that we were in trouble they came gallantly to our aid.

Rick from the tool hire centre brought scaffold and equipment and helped with clearing up. Derek used his van to cart off bags of spoiled foodstuff to the tip.

'Do you ever get that déjà vu feeling?' Peter asked as he carried the bags to the van. It was heartbreaking to have to once again dump thousands of pounds worth of damaged stock. Some things just needed a good clean; most of our Christmas craft stock had been well-wrapped and was retrievable but foodstuff and anything made from fabric or paper was stained and impregnated with the smell of smoke and had to go. I kept careful lists of what was removed. I didn't know how on earth we were going to replace it all but felt it was best to keep a record.

Family and friends arrived and I filled bucket after bucket with hot soapy water as we scrubbed the shop from top to bottom. Peter, helped by my Dad, stripped the damaged wood from the kitchen, taking measurements and making a list of materials needed for repair work.

Nadine arrived and burst into tears when she saw the damage.

'Lorraine rang me earlier,' she said. 'I couldn't believe it when she told me what had happened.'

'I know,' I said hugging her. 'I was the same when I saw it. But we're going to get through this, we've got that Christmas shopping evening to sort, remember?'

'Yes,' she said drying her tears. 'Sorry, I just got such a shock.' She went off to find a scrubbing brush and set to work.

Georgina who'd been told about the fire by a neighbour came to help bringing Nige. He wasn't much help with the physical work but he kept the tea and coffee flowing and amused us with his joking and chatting. Although he was suffering from a hangover, he was on a high about the fireworks party.

'It was great,' he said. 'Gus introduced me to all his friends as his soul mate. It was like he was really proud of me and wanted everyone to meet me.'

'Well it's about time!' Georgina said, as she and I knelt side by side scrubbing the kitchen floor. 'He's been treating you like muck for years.'

'He doesn't mean it,' Nige said. 'It's his artistic temperament.'

'Whatever you say Nige,' she said.

'Anyway, it was a great night,' Nige said 'but I'm suffering for it now. I've got one hell of a headache and my eyes feel all swollen.' He looked at his reflection in the blackened window. 'Does my face look puffy?' he asked. Georgina and I looked at each other and resisted.

'Go and make some more coffee,' Georgina said.

By the time Lorraine arrived at two, I was feeling much more optimistic. Lorraine too seemed more optimistic after her rest. She was amazed by the progress and, like me, was moved to tears by the generosity and kindness of family, friends and neighbours. She joined in the work amazed at how many people had turned up to help. Everywhere there were people working busily, cleaning, scrubbing, removing rubbish, joking and chatting.

At half past two a fireman called to let us know that the electricity supply had been re-connected and a huge cheer went up as lights and music were switched on.

'Thought you'd like to know,' he said. 'We've been able to confirm that the fire was started by a firework put through the letterbox of the gym. Seems someone had a vendetta against the owners.'

'Well that could have been anyone,' Georgina said. 'They're not exactly popular around here.' Lorraine and I looked at each other and gave a joint sigh of relief. Thank God it wasn't our fault. The sense of relief was enormous. And now we might even be able to claim on our insurance.

'Are you all right darlin'?' the fireman said to Lorraine putting his arm around her, much to the envy of Nadine and Nige. 'You got a bit of a shock last night didn't you?'

'Yeah, I'm fine,' she said. 'Thanks for everything you did last night.'

'No problem,' he said. 'I'll leave you to it. Take care.'

'And just what did he do last night?' Nadine asked suggestively. 'He's gorgeous!'

'He put the fire out, you tart,' said Lorraine. 'Him and the other seven. I made them all a cup of tea.'

'The other seven!' Nadine exclaimed. 'You mean you had eight firemen to yourself at two o'clock in the morning?'

'And you made them tea?' added Nige.

'Yeah,' Lorraine laughed. 'I was a right state. I had my jarmies on under my coat and no make-up on and my hair was all over the place.' Nadine looked horrified. I laughed to myself. I knew it would be Nadine's nightmare to be seen by eight firemen with a hair out of place, never mind no make-up.

'We were all coughing and choking with the smoke and they asked if I could make them a drink. The water and electricity were off so I opened a couple of bottles of mineral water and boiled it in a pan on the gas ring. The only teabags useable were the organic darjeeling because they're sealed in a foil bag and so weren't smoke damaged. And I used organic milk. They all said it was the best cup of tea they'd ever had.'

'So it should be,' I said. 'Mineral water, organic darjeeling and organic milk!'

'But did you get us a date?' Nadine asked.

'I had other things on my mind at the time,' Lorraine said.

'I wish I'd been there,' Nadine said, and she continued her cleaning task, off in a fantasy.

Throughout the day our neighbours provided us with a steady supply of food. Martha from the butcher's brought trays of bacon sandwiches, which were greatly appreciated by the helpers. Bags of hot chips, cartons of soup, sandwiches, cakes and even a whole Indian banquet from the take-away arrived, all gratefully received.

Mr Stoker came to assess the damage, reluctantly acknowledging that he would have to foot the bill for repairing the damage to the gym and to our kitchen wall. He promised to ring me when he'd arranged a date with the builders to repair the kitchen wall and also to brick up the side window. He'd been unable to contact Ug and Pug. They seemed to have disappeared from the face of the earth. They never returned and the gym was later re-let. We never saw them again and we did not miss them. It was worth the trauma of the fire to be rid of them. (Years later Lorraine swore she'd seen a photo-fit picture of one of them on crime-watch.)

The cost of repairing and replacing our kitchen fittings and equipment and all the stock would fall to us. I put my list-making talents to good use and compiled lists of everything damaged. I intended to ring the insurance company first thing Monday morning.

We worked until eight and our friends left with hugs and sincere thanks for everything they had done. We were enormously grateful. Already the kitchen looked better. The burnt wood had been removed and the floor mopped and cleaned. There was still a gaping hole in the wall, which we would have to leave for the attention of the builders. The shop shelves and counter had been scrubbed back to their original condition. The walls had been cleaned too but it was evident that they'd need a couple of coats of white paint. Luckily, the parquet floor had not been damaged. After a good scrub and a coating of wax polish it looked as good as new. The materials for replacing the kitchen shelves and worktops were stacked in the office ready for Peter and my Dad to fit them.

Now all we had to do was re-stock. Again.

CHAPTER FORTY-ONE

Surprisingly, making a claim from our insurance company proved to be much more straightforward than I'd anticipated. After sending a representative to inspect the premises and complete several documents in triplicate, it was confirmed that we would receive a cheque within a few days. I rang Karma who agreed to send out replacement stock on the understanding that as soon as the cheque arrived and cleared we would send payment.

Mr Stoker was as good as his word and builders arrived to repair the fire damage to our kitchen wall and the gym and also to brick up and shelve the side wall where the window had been. While we waited for the new stock to arrive, Peter re-built our kitchen shelving and benches and Lorraine and I gave the shop interior two coats of white paint. The Karma delivery arrived as promised and again the shop floor was filled with stock waiting to be sorted and placed. Once again the troops came to the rescue and we worked together to get everything ready for the re-opening.

The cheque duly arrived enabling us to pay Karma and use the remaining money to replace other things we'd lost.

Gradually the shop returned to its former glory, everything was repaired or replaced, painted or cleaned and the shelves restocked and new Christmas decorations hung.

I was concerned that during the period we were closed our regulars would find somewhere else to shop and would not return. I need not have worried. As the news of the fire spread, helped along by a short news report on the local radio and a paragraph in the Daily Echo, cards and good will messages came flooding in from customers and from colleagues in the health trade.

Three weeks after the fire we were ready to re-open.

'We did it!' Lorraine said as we unlocked the shop. 'Can you believe it!'

'We couldn't have done it without the help of our friends and family.' I said. 'We owe them a huge debt.'

'I know,' Lorraine said. 'They've been great.' I opened the blinds and Lorraine went to put the kettle on. It felt so good to be back in the old routine.

'I didn't realise how much I'd miss this,' I said. 'I'm so glad to be back.'

'Me too,' agreed Lorraine. 'I'm glad we didn't give up.'

Nadine arrived, her face beaming.

'It's great to be back,' she said, hugging us. 'You know, I really only meant this job to be temporary but the fire has made me realise how much I love it here.'

'That's what we've just been saying,' Lorraine said. 'Coming so close to losing everything made us realise just what we've got.'

Although we were all exhausted we worked cheerfully, greeting our regular customers as they returned and welcoming new ones. We had only two days until our Christmas evening so between making fillings and serving customers we made preparations for the big night. We were planning to close at the usual time then re-open at seven, so we'd have a couple of hours to transform the shop. We spent any free moments gathering everything we needed and making sure that all the stock was priced and ready to be displayed.

Those two days were very busy. It was as if everyone who had ever visited the shop called in to see us and to commiserate about the fire. To be honest we became bored with it, but we knew they meant well so we listened politely and repeated the same answers to the same questions, then changed the subject and gave invitations to our Christmas evening.

One woman came to look because she'd heard the radio report and was curious to see what we stocked.

'I didn't know you were here until I heard the report about the fire on the radio,' she said. 'Although I must say, I got the impression they were talking about a much bigger concern.' She walked about the shop looking at the shelves in a very disdainful manner. Perhaps it was unintentional, possibly just the way she held her head as she looked down her nose at our stock but it seemed to me that she was not impressed. The way she kept muttering 'oh dear' added to the condescending attitude.

'Can I help you with anything?' I asked.

'I doubt that very much,' she said and continued to look with scorn at the shelves. Peter, who had just finished his sandwich and was eyeing up the cakes, made a face like a horse behind her back.

'To tell the truth I'm a bit disappointed. I thought finding you would mean I'd be able to shop here instead of having to travel into Newcastle,' she said.

'What do you usually buy in Newcastle?' I asked. 'We probably stock it too. If we don't I could order it for you.'

'Oh don't worry dear. I've had a look at your shelves and the selection here is far inferior to my usual shop in town.' Peter did his horse face again and I discreetly slapped him. I knew what that face meant. It is very rare that Peter takes a dislike to anyone, but snobbery is one thing he really can't stand.

'Don't you stock Heatherington's olive pate?' the woman asked.

'No, but we do have the Karma one. It's very good,' I said.

'Oh no, no, no. I only use Heatherington's. It's far better. I see you have Wild Country herbal teas. My usual shop only stocks Pure Leaf teas. They are so much more preferable. You know, they only use herbs that have been organically grown on a mountainside in Switzerland and are hand picked.' Peter's horse face was getting longer. The woman sighed. 'Well I may as well buy something seeing as I've travelled all this way, but I can't seem to find anything.'

'We've got plenty of oats for your nosebag,' Peter muttered, and I slapped him again.

'I do need some honey but you don't seem to have the type I use,' she said. 'My usual shop only sells honey produced by monks.'

'We only sell honey produced by bees,' Peter said. The telephone rang and I hesitated before going to answer it. Lorraine was out and I wasn't sure leaving Peter on his own with the woman was a good idea. It was just a matter of time before he insulted her. I could see it coming.

The phone call was someone trying to sell us advertising space in a publication I'd never heard of so I quickly ended the conversation and hurried back.

'Haven't you any organic kidney beans?' I heard the woman say to Peter. 'I only ever use organic beans. I feel they are far superior, don't you agree?' Unfortunately I was just too late to intervene and I cringed as he answered, 'Oh absolutely. I find I always get a much better quality fart with an organic bean, don't you?'

CHAPTER FORTY-TWO

Lorraine turned the sign to 'closed' and locked the door.

'Right,' she said. 'Let's get started.' I was jumping up and down with excitement. I'd waited ages for this.

'Ooh, I can't wait for everyone to get here,' I said.

'Me too,' Lorraine said, and we ran to get the first boxes of stock.

'Eeh, you're like a couple of bairns going to see Fenwick's window,' Nadine said, laughing.

'Come and help me with these,' I said carrying the boxes of stock into the shop. Nadine and I unpacked them as Lorraine assembled the folding tables we'd borrowed and placed them around the shop. There wasn't much space between them.

'There's not going to be enough space,' she said. 'If I leave them here there'll be no room for customers.'

'We'll have to think of something else then,' I said. 'We'll need plenty of room. There's going to be loads of people coming.'

'How many do you think will turn up?' Lorraine said.

'Oh loads,' I said. 'We've invited everybody and their granny.'

'What if we push the centre shelves back?' Lorraine suggested. 'Then we can use the space in the centre of the floor.'

Peter arrived as we were struggling to move the huge shelving units that stood in the middle of the shop floor. He took over and moved them for us although he wasn't very pleased.

'Who's stupid idea was this?' he panted as he struggled with the first one.

'Hers,' Nadine and I said pointing at Lorraine.

'Actually I think it's a good idea,' Lorraine said.

'You're just going to have to put them back again at the end of the night,' he said.

'No, you are,' Lorraine said. 'We can't move them.'

'Don't you think they would be easier to move if we emptied them first?' I said. I was a bit concerned about the purple hue of Peter's face as he heaved and pushed.

'Haven't got time,' Lorraine said joining in with the pushing. I moved forward to help but Peter wouldn't let me.

'No lifting heavy boxes either,' he said.

Once the shelves were back against the walls we had much more space to work in. The small tables were set up and covered with gold and red cloths ready for the stock. Lorraine made a lovely display of all the edible goodies: jars of preserves, cranberry sauce, tinned chestnuts, olives, pates, Christmas cakes and puddings, stollen, chocolates and marzipan fruits. Nearby on a smaller table we placed a selection of baskets for people to make up their own hampers and gift baskets. We had cellophane wrapping and ribbons ready behind the counter to finish them off.

I covered the counter with a red cloth and put out dishes of food samples including our homemade nutroasts, Christmas cakes and puddings. I had borrowed a huge punch bowl with matching glass cups from the pub at the foot of the bank, and Nadine went to make non-alcoholic punch using bottles of Christmas cordial, spices and sliced fruit. Trays of canapés lined the kitchen benches, ready to pop into the oven and we arranged dishes of nibbles along the counter.

The ceramic nativity figures and hand-thrown bowls looked very effective arranged on gold fabric, as did the handmade Christmas cards and decorations. We added gold ribbons and holly to the displays and Lorraine arranged vanilla and cranberry scented candles around the counter and tables. When lit, they smelled delicious and their soft light along with the twinkling of the fairy lights gave a lovely warm ambience.

'I think we're ready,' I said. 'We just need music.' Peter arranged the speakers on the top of the pushed-back shelves, carefully draping the cables out of sight. He switched on the CD player and Silent Night floated softly into the air.

'Oh it's gorgeous!' Nadine said tearfully. 'To think what it was like only a few weeks ago.'

'It's beautiful,' I said emotionally. Lorraine too was in tears.

'I can't believe how wonderful it looks,' she said and we looked around, wiping tears from our eyes.

'Daft buggers,' Peter said scoffing a piece of Christmas cake.

'Gerroff!' I said slapping his hand. 'You could at least wait until everyone's here.'

Georgina and Nige arrived at seven o'clock on the dot. Georgina brought a picnic hamper full of homemade mince pies.

'I know you said you hadn't time to cook everything you'd wanted to for tonight because of clearing up after the fire. So I thought I'd help out. These were made with ingredients from Nutmeg so if people want to order some, I'll help you bake them.'

'Oh Georgina that's really kind of you,' I said hugging her. Lorraine fetched a glass plate and we arranged some of the pies on it. 'I'll pay you for the ingredients,' I said.

'Don't be silly,' she said. 'I don't want the money. I did it to help you out.'

'And this is my contribution,' Nige said holding out a CD. Peter took it and read the cover.

'Tijuana Christmas?' he said.

'Oh great!' I laughed. 'We used to have that at home when we were kids, remember Lorraine?'

'Yeah,' she laughed. 'Can't wait to hear that, Chris and me used to love it when we were little. We'll put it on later when everyone's here. Thanks Nige.'

'What is it?' Nadine asked.

'It's sort of like a Mexican brass band playing Christmas carols,' Lorraine told her. 'They play them all jazzy and dancey.'

'Right,' she said obviously none the wiser.

Lorraine poured us each a glass of punch and we tried some of Georgina's mince pies. We sat and chatted about our plans for Christmas and Georgina told us that she was going to Norfolk to stay with Marc and meet his family. Nige told us all about Gus's part in the pantomime and how well the rehearsals were going. We chatted about past Christmases and had another glass of punch. I sneaked a look at the clock. Quarter to eight and still no one else had arrived. We had more mince-pies and talked about the events of the past year. Nadine poured more punch and we toasted Josie's memory. The CD had been set on repeat and as Silent Night started again for the third time I glanced at Lorraine. She looked back and smiled grimly.

'It's still early, there's time yet,' she said out of earshot of the others.

'Come and have a look at our stock,' I said to Georgina and Nige leading them to the table of crafts.

'Oh, oh. Starting the hard sell now are you, now you've softened us up with punch and mince-pies?' Nige said.

'These are lovely,' Georgina said. 'I'll definitely have one of these little angels. Can I take it now or will it spoil the look of the display before other people have seen it?'

'No, just take it now,' I said. I had a horrible feeling it might be our only sale of the night. I think Nige saw my worried expression because he suddenly said, 'And I'll have one of these carved bowls for Gus, he likes things like that,' and in all the time we'd known Nige it was the first time he'd ever bought anything from us.

'Just ring it in the till yourself,' I said to Georgina, too embarrassed to take her money when she'd been so generous with the mince-pies. It was Peter who eventually said what we'd all been thinking but had not wanted to mention.

'Do you think anyone's going to turn up?' he asked, looking at his watch. 'It's twenty-five past eight.' There was an awkward silence in which I debated whether to continue pretending I was ok with the fact that no-one had turned up, or come clean and admit defeat. I opened my mouth to speak but was cut off by the door bursting open as someone entered bellowing 'hellooo!' It was Mrs Forbes-Williamson.

CHAPTER FORTY-THREE

'Oh how terribly marvellous! This looks wonderful!' Mrs Forbes-Williamson said. 'So seasonal! Now before I begin there's the small matter of my account. By my reckoning I owe you six hundred and twenty-eight pounds and fifty-two pence so I've rounded it up to seven hundred pounds to include a little Christmas tip. Thank you so much my dears, wheesh!' She held out a cheque to a stunned Lorraine, who took it as we both stammered our thanks, but Mrs Forbes-Williamson was already engrossed in filling her carpet bag, exclaiming loudly at the loveliness of everything. Georgina went to get her a glass of punch, and as she did, the door opened again as more people arrived. Lorraine greeted the new arrivals as Nadine handed around mince-pies. Georgina was pouring more drinks.

'Do you want me to stay on drinks duty?' she asked. 'You're going to need to make up some more punch soon.'

'That would be a great help,' I said as I slipped two trays of canapés into the oven. I could feel myself beginning to relax now that a respectable amount of people had arrived.

My parents arrived, as did Peter's family. Familiar faces were everywhere. Mr and Mrs Derrington were filling a basket to make a hamper and Dave and Jean from the printers were sampling the Christmas cake. Gupta and Karisha were drinking punch and laughing with Georgina and I could see Ernie who was contentedly running on the spot in the corner. Everyone seemed to be happily browsing and chatting. We'd sold loads of stuff already and the samples, especially the mince pies were going well.

People kept arriving and I saw Peter go to turn up the volume of the music as laugher and chatter filled the shop. Lorraine was busy on the till, Georgina was pouring punch and Nadine handing it out so I grabbed two trays of mince pies and moved into the crowd.

'More punch please,' I called to Georgina as a new wave of people arrived. I went to greet them but was suddenly stopped in my tracks by a pair of arms around my waist and a face snuggling into my chest. I held the mince pies above my head as Bob said, 'There's a cuddle for you.'

'Hello Bob, have a mince pie,' I said, trying to disentangle myself.

'I've brought Muriel,' he said, and I noticed she was standing beside him, dressed as always in her bobble hat, zip up coat and boots.

'Hello Muriel,' I said. 'How are you?'

'I'm fine,' she said. 'I'm only here for the beer.' They took a mince pie each and Bob told everyone in earshot that we were lazy buggers.

Victoria arrived by taxi, looking more robust than usual. She said she felt she had reached a turning point and was getting stronger every day although she still tired easily. I brought her a chair and she sat happily chatting and drinking punch.

'Jonathan's here,' Nadine told me excitedly as she checked her reflection in a nearby Christmas bauble and went off to corner him.

Peter had changed the CD to the cheesy one and the noise level rose. I saw Bob pull Muriel to a space on the floor to dance and as others laughed and clapped, I was amazed to see Mrs Bunting, who was dressed in a remarkable ensemble of flapper dress, feather boa and dancing shoes take to the floor energetically.

'Always loved to dance,' she said as she strutted her stuff to Slade. 'Won lots of awards as a young gel don't you know, at the Regency Ballroom. I say, love to D-A-N-C-E.'

Peter was chatting to Derek who had brought a box of mistletoe. I saw Nige take a sprig from the box and as his eyes went to Peter I snatched it from him.

'Don't even think about it,' I said menacingly.

Karen and Margy arrived and I hurried to greet them then hurried straight off to put the next lot of canapés in the oven. I noticed a cluster of people holding out notes near the till as Lorraine frantically wrapped goods and gave out change. I went to help her, wrapping goods and taking money and I was pleased to see that the till was bulging with money. Mrs Forbes-Williamson was quickly re-building her debt as she collected items in her carpetbag and ordered our home-cooked Christmas fare.

'These mince pies are delicious dear, put me down for a dozen,' she said. Her face was flushed and her eyes looked slightly glazed.

'I'll put you down for two dozen,' Lorraine said. 'A dozen to eat and a dozen for the freezer.'

'She looks drunk,' I said to Lorraine as we watched her demolish another mince pie. She wandered off and I heard her explaining to Georgina about a garden shed she was thinking of buying for her husband for Christmas.

'Gus is here,' Nige said excitedly as he squeezed past me to reach the glasses of punch. 'He's brought tickets for us all to go and see his pantomime next week!'

'That's really kind of him,' I said as Nige hurried back to Gus with two glasses of punch.

'Where is he?' Lorraine said and we looked through the crowd to get a glimpse of Gus but couldn't see past the dancers. Someone had put on the Tijuana Christmas CD and the floor was crowded. I could see Nadine dancing with Jonathan and noticed she had hopefully tucked a sprig of mistletoe in her hair.

'I hope Gus's pantomime is better than the TV drama,' Peter said to me. 'I couldn't sit through that again.'

'Hey Peter,' I said to him. 'Do you think Mrs Forbes-Williamson looks a bit drunk?' We looked to where she was talking to Georgina and eating a mince pie at the same time.

'I'm sure Arthur would love a garden shed,' she was saying. 'You know how men love to potter about doing nothing and of course when I've had enough of him I can just send him off down the garden to waste time doing whatever men actually do in their sheds. The problem is, I can't decide whether to have it delivered in pieces or have it erected. I've been looking at prices, you see, it's three hundred pounds for the shed just on it's own, or if you get the man to come and erect it, it's three hundred and seventy pounds for the shed and the erection, wheesh.'

'And how much is it just for the man with the erection,' Georgina said. Mrs Forbes-Williamson paused for a second as she absorbed Georgina's comment then she spluttered, spraying pastry crumbs as she guffawed with laughter.

'Man with the erection!' she repeated laughing hysterically.

'She does seem a bit squiffy,' Peter said as we watched her reach for another mince pie, spilling her punch as she did.

'I'll kill her!' I said suddenly.

'Who? Mrs Forbes-Williamson?' Peter said.

'No. Georgina. It's the mince pies. She must have put something in them. I thought everyone was a bit merry. I remember her telling me about how she once made a cannabis cake and her mother's friends unwittingly ate it and they all went to the Church bingo night stoned.' I edged my way over to Georgina.

'A quick word please Georgina,' I said, smiling at Mrs Forbes-Williamson as I took hold of Georgina's arm and forced her to the kitchen.

'You've spiked the mince pies haven't you?' I said. 'You put cannabis in them.'

'What?' said Georgina. 'Don't be silly, of course not.'

'Georgina, I'm not stupid. Look around. This isn't a shopping evening. This is a wild party.'

'How could you think I'd do something so irresponsible?' Georgina said. 'I'm very hurt.' She sounded very convincing and I believed her.

'Sorry, Georgina,' I said, 'it's just...well look at them.' I nodded to the shop floor where a congo of dancers, led by Mrs Bunting was winding across the floor.

'This modern music isn't a patch on the music of my day,' she was shouting to Nige, who was behind her.

'I know Mrs Bunting, it's S-H-I-T-E, isn't it?' Nige shouted back as he shimmied along draped in gold tinsel. Mrs Forbes-Williamson was telling everyone about the man with the erection, Nadine and Jonathan were dancing frantically, Lorraine and Victoria were laughing hysterically about something and Derek was trying his luck with his mistletoe.

'You've got to admit they give the impression they've all been on something,' I said.

'Well, yes,' Georgina admitted. 'That'll probably be the vodka in the punch.'

'The what? Vodka? You put vodka in the punch? It's supposed to be non-alcoholic,' I said. 'Georgina I'm six month's pregnant for God sake. I've been drinking that!'

'Keep your hair on. I made sure yours didn't have vodka in it, I'm not that daft.'

'Georgina!'

'Well look at them! They're having a great time and you've made a mint out of them.' That was true. I'd emptied the till three times and they were still spending.

'Chris,' Lorraine called to me. 'Who's that bloke dancing with the Christmas tree?' Georgina took the opportunity to make her escape, disappearing amongst the animated bodies.

'I don't know but he's lovely,' I said. 'I think it must be Gus.'

'No wonder Nige puts up with so much crap from him,' Lorraine said. 'He's gorgeous!'

'You might like to know,' I said to her quietly. 'There's vodka in the punch.'

'Vodka? I thought I felt a bit happy. How…who…?'

'Georgina,' we said together. Suddenly the music stopped and a cheer went up.

'What's happening now?' I said trying to see. Gus had climbed onto the counter.

'Do Tom Jones,' Nige yelled to him, and Gus gyrated his hips and sang 'It's not Unusual' as the crowd cheered and whistled.

'Shall I tell him to get down?' Lorraine asked. We watched Gus dancing and I saw Nige's face beaming as he looked up at him.

'No, leave him,' I said. 'Look at the pride on Nige's face. And anyway he's quite good.' I took another tray of canapés from the oven and replenished the dishes with our samples of food. I looked up to see Julie Bradley with Michelle behind her.

'Hi Julie, Michelle,' I said. I was surprised to see them. Perhaps Lorraine had invited them. 'Nice to see you both. Can I get you a drink and a mince pie?'

'Lovely thanks,' Julie said as Michelle fiddled with her camera. 'We heard about tonight and thought we'd take a few shots and do a bit of a write up for the Echo. It'll make a nice little story about how you've bounced back after the fire. Good publicity for you.'

'Great,' I said looking around. God knows what she'll write about this, I thought. Gus noticed the camera immediately and turned to sing directly at Michelle who clicked away as he danced furiously.

Georgina came to collect more glasses of punch.

'Am I forgiven?' she asked as she filled the glasses.

'Course you are,' I said. 'It's been a great success hasn't it?' She hugged me and kissed my cheek.

'Best thing that ever happened to this street, this shop,' she said drunkenly. 'Happy Christmas darlin'.'

I looked around at everyone enjoying themselves, family, neighbours, new friends and old. Most of these people I didn't even know this time last year, I thought. I caught Peter's eye and smiled at him and he pushed his way towards me through the crowd.

'All right?' he asked putting his arm around me and we moved into the doorway of the office.

'Yes,' I said. 'Turned into a great night hasn't it?' Clapping and cheering erupted as Gus finished a song, then silence fell as he began to sing again.

'Have yourself a merry little Christmas…' he sang softly and the fairy lights blurred as tears of happiness filled my eyes. I looked up at Peter. I am so lucky, I thought. A gorgeous husband, a thriving business, a new baby on its way…

'This time next year,' I said to Peter, 'we'll be preparing for our baby's first Christmas. Buying toys and filling a little stocking.' Peter smiled and patted my bump.

'Wow!' he said. 'He just patted me back.'

'She,' I said and I laughed as the baby kicked against his hand.

'Hello in there,' he said. 'Daddy here,' and we laughed together. Peter put his head against mine.

'Love you,' he said.

'Love you too,' I said. Could life get any more perfect? Peter bent his head to kiss me and his nose bumped mine as we suddenly pulled apart, startled by a grunting sound.

'What was that?' I said, and we turned and looked into the darkness of the office. Flat out on a pile of dismantled cardboard boxes and snoring drunkenly, was Mrs Forbes-Williamson.

Printed in Poland
by Amazon Fulfillment
Poland Sp. z o.o., Wrocław